RABBLE'S CURSE

RABBLE'S CURSE

CATHERINE ANN FOUGHT

NEW AMERICAN LIBRARY

TIMES MIRROR

NAL BOOKS TRADEMARK REG. U.S. PAT. OFF. AND FOREIGN COUNTRIES
REGISTERED TRADEMARK—MARCA REGISTRADA
HECHO EN CRAWFORDSVILLE, INDIANA, U.S.A.

SIGNET, SIGNET CLASSICS, MENTOR, PLUME, MERIDIAN and NAL BOOKS
are published by The New American Library, Inc.,
1633 Broadway, New York, New York 10019.

Designed by Jo Anne Bonnell

First Printing, May, 1980

1 2 3 4 5 6 7 8 9

PRINTED IN THE UNITED STATES OF AMERICA

Library of Congress Cataloging in Publication Data

Fought, Catherine Ann.
Rabble's curse.

I. Title.
PZ4.F78Rab   [PS3556.078]   813'.54   79-27305
ISBN 0-453-00381-8

FOR:
JEAN, SUE, CAROL, AND PEG

... that our daughters may be as
cornerstones, polished after the
similitude of a palace.

Psalms, 144:12

And to be baited with the rabble's curse. . . .

Macbeth, V, viii

PART
1

1

I'd barely returned home that Thursday night to my apartment, walking those last six blocks from the courthouse through a drenching rainstorm after emerging from the eerie glitter of the Boston subway, when I heard my telephone. Now I knew right off it was Aunt Chloe before I'd even picked up the receiver; it was uncanny how I could tell when she was going to call. There always seemed a periodicity about it. I mean, a little time would go by, then somehow something would begin to slowly tighten like a rope reeling quietly taut, and before long that telephone in my apartment would jangle. I'd even been tempted on occasion to pick up the receiver and say, "Hi, Aunt Chloe," but then I'd thought: What if it's really one of my clients? Why, that client would be sure to think I'd gone bonkers and wonder what in hell I was doing trying to provide his defense in court!

Well, it *was* Aunt Chloe. She and Uncle Simon and my fourteen-year-old brother, Tim, live in Vermont, in a little town called Rowe. Rowe was the last name of one of the men who founded the place a couple centuries ago; I haven't the foggiest idea why they named the whole town after him. Some of those towns were named for people who had merely stopped overnight (Thoreauton), cut a tree (Bruce's Cutting), planted a tree (Higgin's Grove), operated a sawmill (Simpson's Mill) or a ferry (Pinkerton's Crossing). Rowe wasn't much of a town when you came right down to it: There were 2,127 people, 14 dogs, and 37 cats, give or take a few dogs and cats; there was barely any fluctuation among the people. It was an eddy in the civilized world, but there were a lot of Vermont towns that way still, isolated but integral.

3

Vermont was founded on separateness, not conformity, and was united by it. Rowe seemed like a product of the rough-hewn, granite soul of its countryside: fiercely independent, dedicated to its invincible isolation, determined in its inviolable unity. What was more, Rowe still hadn't put in dial telephones, and Tremont to the north had had them for years. Why would they *need* dial phones they wondered; it would only put Minnie Stouffer, who'd managed the telephone lines in her parlor for twenty years, out of a job. Besides, anyone could holler across the common to find the neighbor he wished to reach. I'd thought they all liked to feel that for a while longer they'd resisted "progress," that archenemy they nonetheless coveted, because occasionally Aunt Chloe and Uncle Simon, as well as some of the other folks in Rowe, ventured out to the new shopping center in Tremont for a look at the world. Rowe was an anachronism which sometimes made me want to laugh.

So Aunt Chloe called me. Yes, everything was fine. Tim was still doing well in school, even passing his Latin. Pause. Yes, he still had that job at the store helping Pops Rampsie with the groceries three times a week. Pause. Yes, we're all fine, fine.

I could see Rowe as Aunt Chloe was talking. Most of the people in town worked at the mill, making blankets, yard goods, shawls. The mill was a big dark building with blackened bricks situated in a hollow two blocks from the big central common. Around that common were grouped old houses dating from before the turn of the century. New England towns all had commons; that was half the charm of the old places. They used to be the center of life. People could graze their cattle on them. One could look out his window, a hundred years back, and see what his goat was up to. They provided central areas where the inhabitants could gather to mount an attack against the Indians, protected by that ring of houses. They led to the church, the store, the undertaker. What else was there?

When I visited Rowe, I could feel the lull in life's throbbing, as though my heart had just skipped a few beats. There was a hiatus in time, an absurd interval in the pace of things. It sure was a far cry from the flow of life in Boston, where I was a legal counselor, a woman lawyer, or a "la-dee law-ya," as some of my male adversaries liked to say. But they didn't say that when I was on their side; then it was "Lisa Sanderson" or even "Attorney Sanderson." On occasion they even pulled out my chair at the defense table. I knew very well that Tremont wasn't the center of the world and that Rowe wasn't that far off the beaten path, at least anymore. But it was a good deal the center of my life in most ways. Aunt Chloe, Uncle Simon, and Timmy were my only living relatives, and that made Rowe pretty special to me. In fact, sometimes it was more significant to me than Boston, so you could see how my universe was constructed. It wasn't the density of the population that was important; it was the weight it claimed in your soul. That tilted everything toward Rowe.

So Aunt Chloe called. Tim was fine, pause, he was working with Pops Rampsie at the store, pause. Was Aunt Chloe breathing hard? Had she had a stroke? Couldn't she think what else to say? That wasn't Aunt Chloe; she could talk an arm off without half trying.

"Everything all right, Aunt Chloe? Uncle Simon's OK?"

"Of course," she answered. Too quickly. "You have any plans to come up here sometime soon?"

"Tell you the truth, I've been thinking about it," I said, erasing before my eyes the stack of briefs sitting on my desk. OK, I'd take them to Vermont. The reek of drying plaster in my office where the ceiling had partly fallen in wasn't conducive to coherent thought anyway, and I couldn't perch indefinitely in the court building while repairs were completed. I might retreat to my apartment, a small two-room jumbled hole (I wasn't a neat housekeeper). But as I talked to Aunt Chloe, I thought: it's May; what am I doing in this place with the world out there? To hell with plasterers, the courtroom, the judge's red velvet chambers!

"I'm coming, Aunt Chloe!" I almost shouted into the phone. "How about this weekend?"

Aunt Chloe's voice relaxed; the tension dissolved until she sounded almost a little teary. "That will be wonderful, wonderful, dear. You'll be coming Saturday morning?"

"Absolutely," I answered. I could remember looking into a mirror just that morning at my pasty complexion, dulled by a winter of riding that tube to work and back every day, rarely popping up into the fresh air. My blond hair, which usually curled (so much that I'd sometimes considered getting it straightened until Afros became popular), now hung limply. My blue eyes looked vaguely moldy, as if I were peering out onto the world through dirty windows. Why, you're a thirty-two-year-old workaholic, I'd thought, sticking my tongue out at my image.

I couldn't wait to get there. "By the way, I'll be flying my plane, Aunt Chloe. Don't wait around for me. I'll get a lift into town."

Her voice was firm. "We'll be there, Lisa, don't you worry."

I hadn't been worrying, but now something began to tick at me. "You're sure everything's all right up there, Aunt Chloe?" I asked for the sixth time.

"Of course, dear. What could be wrong?"

That's exactly what I was beginning to wonder.

My office is a pretty small cave on Tremont Street, for which I pay an arm and a leg rent every month. It boasts an unpolished, rapidly tarnishing plaque on the door, LISA SANDERSON, ATTORNEY-AT-LAW. Very impressive. I fixed up the place with zingy plaid couches and a bomb-burst rug, as if someone had poured orange paint over an eviscerated grizzly bear, but the place *still* looked kind of washed out. Last Tuesday, when part of the ceiling fell in, the landlord mobilized plasterers and repair people, who'd been swarming all over the place since. I finally told them, "As long as you're fixing the ceiling, rip out the interior of the place, and put in something that looks good; I'm sick and tired of cracks and stains and hunks of ceiling falling on my head, like Chicken Licken." Only to me it *did* feel as if the world were collapsing.

The plasterer said, "OK, lady, it's gonna take awhile. Where you gonna go while we do this job?" and I answered, "Don't you worry yourself. I've got resources you wouldn't believe," so I set up shop in a tired little anteroom in the court building. I had to be in court most of the next week anyway, adoption case, and in chambers with the judge, so where I set up shop was immaterial as long as I had a roof.

You see, I'm in the scrambled eggs trade, mixing up poverty law, some divorce stuff, and cases involving life-style problems like drug abuse with kids. Nonvictim offenses. A lot of kids I represent can't pay. They simply have no money. So I take them on anyway, and those kids have me when they can. I'm always finding envelopes full of nickles and dimes beneath my door.

Some of my kids get picked up by the cops because they didn't go to school—truancy cases. Then they get picked up because they talked back to the cops. Resisting arrest is an offense, and it is usually posited in those terms. A kid is out on the street. We have a curfew. The kid is violating the curfew, so the policeman walks up and asks for an ID. Maybe he does it in an accusing voice, and the kid says something rude back. Simple rudeness isn't an offense, but a cop could easily convert it into one; he might decide the kid was

6

creating a disturbance, or speeding, or causing some petty violation. Those kids call me.

Late Friday afternoon I had to reverse an adoption proceeding; the two-year-old girl with the golden hair a couple had adopted had turned out to be autistic. Apparently she was incapable of learning. Last week a psychiatrist had come into the judge's chambers, where we were all sitting, and described autism, a form of childhood schizophrenia. The parents didn't want anything more to do with the kid. The psychiatrist was a big man who danced around like a ballet dancer, explaining his findings. The parents had begun to look more and more alarmed, while the judge sat there listening to this man with his fingertips touching delicately before him.

I felt a tug at my skirt and looked down at the little girl. She was one of the prettiest little kids I ever saw. I reached down and picked her up. She sat on my lap, playing with a button on my blouse, while we completed the legal requirements, filled out the forms in triplicate, with the judge's signature on the bottom in purple ink. Fine, we'd sundered a relationship; I handed the baby back to the parents, who would return the child to the adoption center in the morning. Case dismissed!

The judge turned back to me after they'd gone. He'd put on his coat; he actually wore a homburg.

"You looked very nice with that child in your lap," he said. "What's a girl like you doing in this shitty business?"

I'd heard variations on this theme before, but then I looked at his eyes. I saw the fatigue and the birds' feet and the bags. He'd been up late like me, reading briefs, court decisions, and legal precedents.

"Thanks, Your Honor. But I wouldn't take that from anyone but you." He walked me to the door and put his arm around my shoulders, fatherlike. He was a nice old guy. "It's a shitty business," he repeated, then opened a big umbrella and disappeared into the rainy night, making a big black blob against the streetlights. It was night by this time, and he probably had a wife and dinner waiting for him. I was in no hurry; there was only me. I picked up a grinder at Andy's Pizza Palace and washed it down with cold beer.

When I got home, I cleared off the bed, transferred the stack of briefs from the kitchen counter to the bedside table, made a cup of tea, piled into bed, and read half the night. By 2:30 A.M. I'd cleared up most of the documents and unceremoniously dumped them on the floor; the judge'd have a fit if he knew what I'd done with those venerable sheets

7

of paper that one of his assistants had prepared so laboriously. Once I'd flushed a particularly obnoxious argument down the john, in pieces. It stuffed up the plumbing for three days.

At 3:00 A.M. I turned off the light and started off to slumberland, listening to the faint buzz of rain against the windows of my room. But I was restless and tossed fitfully until dawn. What could be the trouble with Aunt Chloe and Uncle Simon and Tim? I asked myself. Perhaps nothing, and I was simply in need of some time off. Sure, that was undoubtedly it.

Toward morning I fell into a tortured sleep. At least in a few hours I'd be a long ways from lawcourts, plaintiffs, and defense attorneys.

The next morning I cracked an eye, and the sunlight practically blew me from my bed. Beams here and there like stabs of pure gold. I couldn't wait to get into my airplane, feel the controls in my hands, start burning up the runway before takeoff. I was like one possessed! I threw on some old slacks, a sweat shirt, slammed doors, downed some orange juice, then began throwing things into a valise, tiptoeing over all those briefs; they made dandy footing. I scarcely needed a rug on my bedroom floor with all that paper underfoot. I locked the door but felt an amiability toward a burglar: Let him have anything he wanted. If he went to that much trouble, he could take anything he (or she, I wasn't a sexist) could physically carry away.

My plane was out there on the flight line, preening itself, stretching in the sunlight.

One day a year ago I put together all those nickles and dimes and bought myself part of a small Cessna along with ten other people. I could probably claim an eighth of a propeller and two spark plugs. At any rate, the plane was mine for the entire weekend. Flying was my one luxury; it made up for that crummy office and my blitzed-out apartment.

Nobody fooled around with that airplane. There wasn't a speck of dust on it. It smelled of Simonize and new varnish. It gleamed in the sunshine like a polished red bird. It cleared away the smell of juvenile court. On some days all that fresh ozone at 5,000 feet even cleared away the smell of criminal court. But nothing wiped away the odor of prison. For one miserable year after law school I worked as assistant prosecutor for a DA in Boston; I thought life as a prosecuting attorney sounded terribly exciting, where the action was. The first kid I sent up for grand theft changed my mind. I took one look at the prison, vomited discreetly behind the gate, resigned my job, and turned to defense law. I also bought a piece of the Cessna.

I picked up the cowling, examined the maze of wires, checked the carburetor just as I had been taught in flight training school (I attended two nights a week all last year), examined the undercarriage, then climbed in. I tested the controls, just to make sure nobody'd crossed anything in a sudden fit of mechanical zeal, taxied to the end of the one paved runway, and took off. God, glory. The ground shrank away. Far below, there was a toy earth covered with rows of mechanical houses and deviant roads, seemingly purposeless.

An hour and I was over the Vermont border. Fifteen minutes later I saw Rowe with Tremont to the north. Tiniest town I ever saw, Rowe. Whatever inspired someone to choose that particular piece of real estate for a town? What did he ever see in it? Of course, the river. Tiny river, though, but that was where the power came from for the mill. I hovered a few minutes above the town, circling over the common, a small oval at the center of Rowe, looking almost like a racecourse with the road edging the green core. I could just make out the roof of Uncle Simon's house: black slate with a small chimney protruding to one side. In ten minutes I'd reached Tremont. I taxied up to the small air service building, climbed out of the plane, told the attendant to refuel it and park it on the flight line, that I'd give him further instructions later on. When I looked over, there were Aunt Chloe, Uncle Simon, and Timmy. They must have been waiting for me since dawn. I waved energetically at them.

Tim must have grown two feet. He'd been afflicted with the same curly head of hair as mine; both of us were green-eyed, string-bean types. Only now I had to look up at him because he was almost as tall as Uncle Simon. Once Mom thought he was going to be short, so she sent to Florida for crates of fresh oranges. Tim devoured them as if they were strawberries, one after the other. All those vitamins, Mom kept saying, they must do something good. Well, they had. My kid brother was almost a man. I hugged him, and he didn't even look embarrassed.

"Aunt Chloe," I yelled. "You look terrific!" I squeezed her, feeling the rolls of fat beneath her neat dress. She'd always been plump, Uncle Simon tall and straight. They reminded me of a picture I saw once of the Trylon and Perisphere of the New York World's Fair: one straight, the other small, angled, squat, but complementary, as if they belonged together, a pair.

You'd think they were dressed up for church, just to meet me at the airport. I'd forgotten how old-fashioned they were, kind of formal. Respectable types. Then Uncle Simon threw his arms around me, and I remembered the good feeling it always gave me. He was my father's brother and had always looked like him with that rather ascetic face, high cheekbones, head of steel-gray hair. For just a moment, when I glanced at him sideways, he looked like Dad. It gave me a momentary shock, seeing at that minute so much of my dad in Uncle Simon, and I had to gulp and swallow hard.

We strolled, the four of us, arms about each other, to Uncle Simon's old Buick. He'd owned it for as long as I could remember: dark moss green with a hood ornament depicting the Winged Victory above a stainless grille. He didn't drive very much, living right in the town where he worked. Saturday mornings he always polished up the car. It had 30,000 miles on it in fifteen years of driving. He said awhile back that he intended to keep it until it became eligible for antique auto plates. That shouldn't be far off. Uncle Simon was a bookkeeper at the Rowe mill and walked the two blocks to that brick building every morning, rain or shine, sometimes crooking an umbrella over his arm when it looked showery.

"It's so good to see you," I found myself exclaiming over and over. I roughed up Timmy's mat of curls playfully, then looked from his face to Aunt Chloe's, Uncle Simon's, and back again. "You all look great. Have things been going all right?" There was the question again. At that moment I could see something guarded in their faces, an imperceptible pause. I was sure of it now.

Aunt Chloe changed the subject ever so gently. "Look," she said, "there's a really nice new restaurant on the edge of Tremont. Let's go there for lunch. We can drive around a bit first. Uncle Simon planned it; he wants to take us out, sort of special."

I knew that Uncle Simon didn't make all that much money, that going out to eat was rare. When Mother and Dad died and they took Timmy six years ago, money became pretty thin. I also knew that Dad had an insurance policy which took care of Timmy mostly, but still, it was expensive, raising a kid. Aunt Chloe and Uncle Simon had never had children of their own, and I knew they felt we belonged to them now. I felt the same way.

"I'd love it," I told Aunt Chloe. She had her heart set on it, and although I ate out about six nights a week at hamburger joints, I wasn't about to let her know.

"You still playing baseball?" I asked Tim. There were only a few weeks of school left, and Tim played third base on the JV team. He'd had to try out for that position against boys older than he, and I knew how proud he was of it. Rowe had no high school of its own, so Tim rode the bus to the regional school, just this side of Tremont. That bus traveled twelve miles daily, but Tim didn't seem to mind.

He looked away from me a little too carelessly, I thought. He'd grown up with me, and although I'd gone to college and law school, I still knew him pretty well. Didn't I? Had I lost touch somehow?

We jostled in Uncle Simon's old Buick over the bumpy dirt road which led from the airport to the main drag toward town. Airports didn't seem to be overwhelmingly big business in this part of the world. I saw five other planes on the entire flight line, one an old Stinson that looked as if it might fall into a shower of bolts and rusted plates if anything touched it.

"Too far to go," said Tim. "Too late." He was still looking away, his hands on the knees of his dungarees, but now he turned back to me. He flushed a little. "I mean it's pretty late when I get home after practice. So I quit."

I contemplated him curiously. "Wasn't it before? I mean, it didn't bother you then, did it? What's so different now?"

Aunt Chloe was studying the scenery, an old gravel pit blasting a scar across the countryside, with elaborate attention.

Uncle Simon's head loomed so tall that he constantly grazed the ceiling of the Buick. Now I realized why he'd probably kept the old car all these years; most cars wouldn't seat him comfortably. He turned partway in the seat. "Things change, Lisa. We're getting old. Things aren't the way they used to be. Even in a town like Rowe, things keep changing."

I stared at the back of his head; then I glanced at Timmy. He'd already tanned and was developing into a well-built kid, kind of sinewy, with that growing look about him where he was a few pounds ahead of his last pair of pants, with a torso so long and lean that it hadn't a chance to settle into any kind of final shape yet.

So what was so different? As I surveyed the countryside, I couldn't see a blade of grass that was out of place from the last time I'd come up here.

"The mill, Uncle Simon? You say there's no strike? I recall last time I talked to you, you were worried. Has that all gone by?"

He began to nod in affirmation, then stopped. "Nobody knows yet, Lisa. All these years, no union. Never even thought about it much. Now there's a lot of talk. Got a textile union from Fitchburg trying to stir things up. Union man's been up here a couple times this week, people coming and going. Lots of speech making."

"How do you feel about it?" I asked him, leaning forward.

Aunt Chloe had been gazing out the window, listening. Now she turned back toward Simon, twisting to face me. "Worried, that's what Simon is. Me, too. All that talk, talk, talk. Speechifying! Why, if they paid you for listening to all those words, we'd all be millionaires."

Most of the people in Rowe weren't well-off, but they weren't exactly poor either. I sent money along regularly to help out with Timmy—I knew that a growing boy put a dent in Uncle Simon's income, not that he'd ever complain about it. But they lived well, considering; this part of Vermont wasn't exactly cosmopolitan, and there was little to do that required a lot of money.

"Are people going to join in?" I asked. "Any of your friends?" I was thinking of the neighbors around that central common. "The Ritchies or the Callaghans?"

I could see Mr. Callaghan now, a florid-faced Irishman who'd been Uncle Simon's friend for years. He went hunting with Uncle Simon in the fall, and the two couples played cards together almost every week.

"Don't know yet. Have to see."

So that wasn't it. I turned back to Timmy. "How's Buzz? Is he still doing well in that special class?"

Tim nodded and swallowed; then suddenly he exploded. "He's doin' shitty, Sis, he's doin' shitty, and—" I thought Tim was going to choke.

I couldn't believe my ears. "He's . . . what?"

"Some guys got hold of him last week and beat him up!"

I grasped Tim's arm hard. "Why . . . in hell . . . would they beat Buzz up?"

I simply couldn't imagine anything so inconceivable, so downright ridiculous. Buzz Sardoe was Tim's next-door neighbor. I knew him to be retarded, but not so badly he couldn't get himself dressed or eat. He even progressed through school at his own pace, even if it was pretty slow. Mrs. Sardoe had reared the boy by herself. She did sewing for people and made cakes and cookies on order. Mrs. Sardoe wasn't all that swift mentally, either, but she worked hard, and she loved her son.

"Who beat him up?" I asked. "Who'd do a thing like that?"

"Some guys," answered Tim, concentrating on Uncle Simon's neck.

Uncle Simon had turned into the parking lot of a small restaurant. Through a big picture window I could see the red-checked tablecloths. "I'll tell you about it when we get inside," said Uncle Simon. We slid into a parking space, and I grabbed Timmy's arm in the back of the car. "I want to know," I said to him quietly. "Tell me, Tim. What the hell's going on?"

He shrugged off my hand, guiltily, then looked at me. His eyes were brimming. "I'll tell you, Sis. Later."

A waitress with a fanny wiggle led us to our table. Bless her heart, Aunt Chloe had made reservations for us, for lunch yet. There were ten other people in the entire restaurant. This was a big deal.

"Once a month Simon brings me here," said Aunt Chloe, shrugging off her faded blue coat. "It's real nice German cooking."

I looked at Uncle Simon. He'd barely had a chance to hang up his coat, but I could stand it no longer. "Now tell me."

Uncle Simon pulled his chair into the table and began to speak in a low voice. I didn't like the way he was looking around, first at the table next to us, then at the waitress. Whenever anyone came too close to our table, he stopped talking.

"We've got some people come into Rowe lately," he said. "They got run out of town by the cops in Tremont."

"What kind of people?"

"Young hood types."

"What do you mean by that?"

He looked over at me and said again, "I mean hood types." I was trying to figure out if Uncle Simon realized what he was saying, especially when the only law violations I ever heard about in Rowe were mill hands who drank too much beer on Saturday nights, causing an occasional minor disturbance.

"What have they done, Uncle Simon? Besides Buzz."

Uncle Simon was shaking his head. "Not so much I can tell you. But they're . . . mean." Uncle Simon's voice had dropped away again, as though he'd been caught tattling in school. He was feeling guilty about telling me!

Aunt Chloe picked up the story. "They raise cain," she said. "Saturday nights they raise cain, right on the common. They're nothing but rabble, rabble. Believe me. Sometimes we can't even sleep."

"Then why don't you get Clyde Oldham?" I asked. "Isn't he still chief of police?"

Uncle Simon shrugged. "By the time Clyde pries himself out of bed, pulls off his long johns, and gets himself down to the common either they're gone, or they pipe down. Last weekend Clyde showed up when they were carrying on; only he'd been laid up with bronchitis and could hardly talk, kept barking away with his throat clogged. Those guys in the common just sat and stared at Clyde, didn't even bat an eye, just kept fixing on him. Finally, the one they look up to, Aversa Rampsie's boy Bob, the one whose younger brother, Jaimie, is Tim's age, says to old Clyde, 'Look who's making a noise, the police chief yet, disturbing the peace.' Just then Clyde had an awful fit of coughing. So Bob picks up one of those chains you use on tires in the snow and throws it over his shoulder, sort of casually, and walks up to Clyde. 'Ain't that right, big old police chief?' this guy says to Clyde, and you know what? Clyde began to back away, an inch at a time perhaps, but he was backing just the same. So another guy, they call him Hunk Hudman, got the idea, and they both started advancing. Pretty quick another one, Bingo something or other, he's from Tremont, joined in. Luckily Clyde'd left his car parked on the edge of the common, and he dove right in, head over heels."

"Would they have hit Clyde with the chain?" I asked Uncle Simon.

He shrugged. "Dunno. I wouldn't have waited around to find out, would you?"

"How many people does Clyde have working for him now?"

"Two, same as always. Ed Rhymer and Paul White. Both only part time, though. We never needed any more."

"Where do those guys come from?" I asked. "Are they all from Rowe except Bingo?"

Aunt Chloe broke in. "Aside from the Rampsie boys and maybe one other, they're all from Tremont."

"How many are there?" I was beginning to feel like a prosecuting attorney examining a witness.

Tim had been keeping his own counsel, listening to us, slowly devouring a cheeseburger and chips. His legs were thrust out on either side of his chair. "Seven or eight," he said, wiping his mouth with the cloth napkin. "It varies. Sometimes only three or four. I heard that the cops up in Tremont kept hassling 'em, pulling them off the streets for vagrancy, that kind of thing. So they came down here."

It was a familiar technique. I'd worked with a lot of police. Some of them I liked, and some were impossible. I'd known cops to lie sometimes. When things got tight in their jurisdiction, they were apt to

15

run offenders out of town, harass them so they'd go elsewhere. Police could make life pretty hot for a young punk. So they'd pried them loose in Tremont, sent them packing to Rowe. Didn't sound exactly like judicial progress to me.

"Have they been here for long?" I asked Timmy.

He held up a couple of pretty grimy fingers. "Two weeks, maybe. Maybe more. Seems like a long time."

We finished lunch and walked out into the sunshine. The trees were fringed with yellow-green as new leaves began to pop along the tired old winter stems. Back in the woods there was still snow, Uncle Simon was telling me, but you'd never know it here except for a spring dampness in the air and a spasm of frost hidden in the warmth of the sun. How could anything be wrong anywhere? I was thinking, and I stretched my limbs like a cat enjoying the first heat from a wood fire.

We drove back to Rowe; the car engine hummed as if it had been honed by Rolls-Royce. Uncle Simon pampered it like a colicky child. As a result, that collection of bolts and valves responded with enthusiasm and even respect to his touch. He sailed down the road as if at the helm of a particularly seaworthy craft, with no qualms as to wind and weather.

I'd driven this road easily a hundred times. Just before Rowe it widened briefly over a bridge, turned a corner beside Rampsie's store, and there before us was the Rowe common. Around were grouped those old houses: Uncle Simon's white clapboard, the Sardoes' frame, the Brittons' bungalow, Rampsie's store with its sagging front porch, the Callaghans' garrison colonial, and a dozen or so others. Each seemed sedate and just a little smug, claiming its just share of the long plot of green as a front yard. Above all, to the south, I could see riding high against a cloudless sky the smokestack of the Rowe mill.

"Thank God they're not there yet," breathed Aunt Chloe. I looked at her quickly—there was open relief in her face. But Aunt Chloe had always been concerned with noise and dirt—she protested when cars without proper mufflers circled the common and sent explosive echoes bounding back and forth against the broad façades of those old homes. Still, Aunt Chloe wasn't a complainer, although I knew for a fact that she regarded the common as partly hers. What concerned me was that Timmy and Uncle Simon also looked quickly at the common, then away again, and I could see the set to Uncle Simon's face in that brief moment.

"When do they come?" I asked. *"Every* night?"

"No," answered Uncle Simon, easing the car into the driveway next to the house as carefully as you'd place an egg in a rack. "Don't get so excited, Chloe. For all you know, they'll never come again. Relax on it a bit." But I watched Uncle Simon, in spite of his words, steal another furtive glance at the common when he emerged from the car.

The old house looked wonderful: Uncle Simon said he'd painted it in the fall, and the clematis was budding over the white fence beside Aunt Chloe's garden. Ivy had already popped on the old brick chimney, almost hiding it. I could see a couple of bold phoebes disappearing under the eaves at the corners of the roof, setting up shop for the summer.

My room had been carefully tended; Aunt Chloe'd even placed flowers in a large vase on the dresser. My bed appeared somehow old-fashioned and terribly chaste; the coverlet had been made by my grandmother, Uncle Simon and my dad's mother, and was treasured in the household. It was a narrow, fluffy bed, which I'd slept on as a child when I came to visit. I unpacked my suitcase, then went downstairs. Uncle Simon had already disappeared out into the garage and was doing something to the car, and I could hear Aunt Chloe moving around in the kitchen. I caught sight of Timmy standing beside the front door.

I tapped him on the shoulder. "Let's go for a walk." He nodded slowly, his face drawn. We strolled out onto the sidewalk around the common, two of my steps to his one. Suddenly I glimpsed Buzz Sardoe heading toward a hole in the privet hedge before his house, like a small animal seeking its burrow. There was no mistaking Buzz; he walked slightly stooped, his oversize head a bit to one side as if it weighed too much, his overlong arms hanging loosely at his sides. He and Tim had been friends since they were infants. He exhibited the ingenuously happy nature of a kind I'd seen in deficient children before.

"Buzz!" I yelled. We'd now crossed the street and were standing not fifteen feet from him. He was partway through the shrubbery when I put my fingers to my teeth and whistled at him, a couple of good long blasts I knew he'd recognize.

He stopped abruptly, freezing for an instant, then threw himself into that hole made by years of comings and goings until the privet had finally given up growing in that place.

I turned to Tim. "What in blazes is wrong with Buzz? You'd think he'd never seen me before. Didn't he know me?" I began to think that

18

perhaps his condition was deteriorating so that he couldn't recognize old friends, and a sudden shock of alarm ran through me.

Tim looked away. "Oh, he knew you all right."

"Then why didn't he say hello? Didn't he know I wanted to see him?" I still peered disconcertedly through the dark aperture in the shrubbery.

"He's scared," answered Timmy.

"Of me? Come on, Tim."

"Not of you, Sis. Christ's sake."

Tim and I were obviously not on the same wavelength.

"Then what's he afraid of? Those guys? Has that done it to him?"

Tim nodded. "They hurt him." He began to say more, then stopped abruptly.

"Hurt him? How?"

Tim didn't answer. I could feel something on my scalp, like prickles.

"Tell me," I demanded again.

Tim's cheeks flooded with tears, and my kid brother was crying. The sobs filled his chest.

"Do Aunt Chloe and Uncle Simon know?" I asked him gently. "I mean, what happened?" I was beginning to understand slowly that something had gone wrong he couldn't even tell them about.

Timmy's voice was clogged, choked. "That old barn behind the Macys' house," he finally blurted out, "the one up in the woods nobody uses? That's where they took him. Bingo Keaton, Bob Rampsie, a couple of their friends. About five of them. Buzz is a trusting sort of kid, never thought they'd hurt him at all; he went with them like they were taking him to a picnic." Tim had to stop again to find his voice. He coughed a couple of times and finally continued. "Buzz even thought it was some kind of game. And th—they were teasing him along, you know, like saying they'd give him something."

I was starting to hurt.

"They started pushing him around, back and forth between them, until he was dizzy. He kept telling them to stop. They wouldn't stop. They started bumping him off the wall of the barn. You go up and see, a couple panels got pushed out right where he hit."

I was biting my lip so hard I could feel the blood.

He shook his head while the sobs racked his chest. He could barely talk again, and his body was squirming. "They undressed him, see"—I'd put my arms around Timmy, my face on his back, in the hollow between his shoulder blades; he sounded as if he were

19

strangling—"and they took . . . his . . . dong . . . and tied a rope around it." Suddenly Tim could talk, and I could listen; it was anger taking over. Tim even turned around and faced me. "They took turns pulling on that rope until he was so bloody the rope wouldn't hold anymore. Then they left him there, on the floor of the Macys' barn, until I heard him cryin' out a couple hours later when I was passing by." Tim coughed again, his cheeks paled, and he moved away from me as if he needed air.

"Will he talk. . .?" I started to ask, but couldn't finish the sentence; I was breathing too hard.

"He talks to me, nobody else. He couldn't . . . you know . . . go to the bathroom until yesterday. Wouldn't let his mom or me take him to the doc."

"Can't we take him to the hospital in Tremont?" I asked Timmy. "Would he go if you asked him?"

Tim shook his head. "He'll hardly talk to me, Sis. If he thought you knew, he'd die. He seems to be all right, healing OK." He kicked the ground beneath our feet. "But I hate them shitty guys, I hate them. Bastards!" He spit the words, and I glanced at his face. I'd never seen that look on my brother's face before, on it were disillusion and hatred. It broke my heart to see it. The kid wasn't fifteen yet, and his face was full of venom.

We turned back toward the house. Aunt Chloe was preparing dinner. "Have a nice walk?" she asked me.

I nodded absently, then realized she was looking intently at me. "Oh, yes, lovely, Aunt Chloe. Tim and I just took a little stroll."

"Growing up to be a nice boy, Lisa, don't you think?"

"Sure is. Wish Mom and Dad could see him now."

I began to busy myself making a pie, something I hadn't done in months, maybe even years, and it was fun. Besides, it helped to be doing something. Uncle Simon was out sweeping the garage; I could hear the swish of his broom. It seemed like all the Saturdays I could remember in this house. No one was going anywhere in any kind of hurry; the world was as solid as these walls and warmed by that sunshine. For a while I almost stopped thinking about Buzz.

Aunt Chloe turned to me abruptly. "Something's going on with Buzz that no one's talking about," she said. "Are you ready to tell me about it?"

I looked at her, astonished. "I wish I could, Aunt Chloe. I gave my word. Buzz is all right—that's the important part."

20

Aunt Chloe threw up her hands. "I can't understand what's happening in this town. There's no sense to it."

I could hear Timmy upstairs plinking his guitar, slowly and sadly. The guitar used to be mine, but when I didn't have time for it anymore, I gave it to him, and he taught himself to play. The familiar stroking of the strings moved through me with melancholy but with familiarity in this house, like the old days.

"When will you hear more about the strike?" I asked Aunt Chloe. "Who decides on it? The workers?"

She nodded, pushing a strand of hair from her eyes, leaving a spot of white flour on her temple. She, too, was rolling pie dough.

"This week," she answered, her head bent. "At least I've been told so. Depends on the vote, how many people the union organizers can persuade. Some people want it; some don't. Some like the change, don't mind the disruption; others want to continue the same way as always. I've got no complaints, nor does Simon. But some young ones are all for busting the old ways and maybe a few heads in the process. Never heard folks around here that excited before. All for a few pennies in the paycheck every month."

"Couldn't you use it?" I asked her. "I'd think you'd welcome it."

Her jaw was firm. "I'd not complain. Please don't misunderstand me. Ordinarily we'd probably welcome the strike, and we'd vote for the change, too. But right now we're scared what it might cost to get it, considering. . . . "

It was the old story of a union entering a mill town. I was amazed to think there wasn't one already. It must have considered this a backwater, too.

"Maybe it'll work out all right, Aunt Chloe." I really couldn't see what she was worrying about, but I watched her frown, rolling the pie dough.

"I'm too old," she answered simply.

Before dinner Uncle Simon returned from the garage and carefully washed the grease from his hands. I knew he'd been fooling around in the innards of that old Buick. He had a special grease soap to take all that junk off. Tim opened the back door so quietly I didn't even hear him come; when I turned around, there he was. He'd come from the direction of the Sardoe house. I smiled at him, touching his shoulder.

"Buzz says to say hi," he told me. "He said he'd see you around."

"He doesn't know you told me . . . about the barn?"

"I'll tell him sometime, but he's still too shook."

I understood then that Tim had made an act of trust, informing me. There were still a few minutes until dinner, so I walked out into the backyard with Tim. The late afternoons were light now that daylight savings had come, and I enjoyed the stolen hour. A month ago night had settled by this time, and down in Boston I'd have emerged from my office or the courthouse to a world immersed in darkness except for the measured wattage of streetlights. Today I felt as if I'd wrestled the gods for their precious daylight and won.

We'd just about finished with the blessing before dinner, a custom my relatives had hung onto through the years as fervently as they walked to church every Sunday morning. I was offhandedly listening to Uncle Simon's musical baritone invoking the Lord's grace when I heard a backfire out in the street.

Aunt Chloe stiffened as if she'd been shot. Timmy didn't move a muscle. I jumped from my chair to look out the window, but Uncle Simon grabbed my arm.

"We'll eat dinner, like always," he said firmly. "What goes on out there is none of our concern until we finish in here."

I didn't want to argue with him, but I'd begun to seethe again about Buzz, and I wanted to get a look at those apes. Already I could feel that anger within me, just about shoulder height and rising, and I ached to stare at the objects of my mounting frustration.

But we sat quietly and finished our meal. Soon I could hear the sound of more engines out on the common, and more backfires; through it all we sat as quietly as if nothing was happening. We even carried on sedate conversation; Aunt Chloe was saying that the Callaghans were coming over to play bridge tonight, its being Saturday, just as they always did, and Uncle Simon was making small talk about the old Buick engine. It was so damn eerie I couldn't stand it, so I finally turned to Uncle Simon, red in the face, and said with as much control as I could muster, "I'm sorry, Uncle Simon, this is absolutely driving me nuts," and rushed to the window to look out. In a second they were staring out the window right behind me, chins jutted forward, eyes masked behind the curtain.

Out on the common were four cars and six or seven guys ranging from about twenty to twenty-five years, talking and laughing. Two others were leaning against their cars. They didn't look like anything special to me, just a gang of guys hanging around on Saturday, the kind you see anywhere. Trouble was, this was an awfully small town, and nobody'd hung around here before.

22

"Which one's Rampsie?" I asked Timmy.

"The tall one." He pointed to a thin, gangly guy throwing peanuts into the air and catching them in his mouth.

"And his brother, Jaimie?"

Tim leveled a finger toward a shorter boy perched on a car hood.

"Was he in the barn with Buzz?" I asked Timmy in a low voice.

"I don't know, but I doubt it. Jaimie's not all that bad. He's younger. Works at Rampsie's grocery on the nights I'm not there. Pops Rampsie is Bob and Jaimie's uncle."

"Was Jaimie in trouble in Tremont, too? I mean, did the police try to get rid of him the way they did the others?"

Tim shrugged. "Don't see how they could. He's been in school all the time. Takin' manual training in that new technical wing up there. Besides, he's worked at that store off and on for a long time, vacations and like."

I looked out the window again. "Who's the big one in the middle?"

"Hunk Hudman, and that other guy, the one with the red hat, that's Bingo Keaton." Keaton was wearing a big sombrero, the brim curled up, and it had a cord with a wooden slider on it to hold it under the chin. While we were watching, Keaton removed his hat, smoothed his black hair straight back on his angular head, then replaced the hat, rocking it back and forth to settle it over his fleshy ears.

We left the window and thoughtfully cleared the table. Aunt Chloe insisted we taste her pie. She'd just begun to cut it when we heard shouts again. I stole another glance out the window to discover there was a fight going on out there. A man was lying on the ground. I didn't know who he was, but that fat, blubbery type, Hudman, was kneeling on his arms, straddling his head, while two other guys held his legs, pulling on them as if they intended to remove them from his body. The guy getting stretched was understandably protesting at the top of his lungs, but those men kept hauling on him as if this were the great tractor pull at the fair.

Then I saw a tall, baggy man, casually smoking a cigarette, slowly saunter over as if to hear the complaints from the guy on the ground a little more clearly, even solicitously lean over him, remove the cigarette from his mouth a little nonchalantly, and then lower it onto the imprisoned man's face!

I couldn't believe this was happening. "My God!" I kept repeating the words. "My God! My God! Aunt Chloe, did you see that?"

By now the man on the ground was writhing violently, fighting to get

23

loose, but those men had him, all right, and they weren't about to let go.

I was so frantic I began to wrench open the front door, but I found Uncle Simon holding it, restraining me with his hand on my shoulder. "No," he said. "Lisa, no." I didn't even know what I had in mind, except that I realized I was intending to yell at them because I was clearing my throat and making funny noises in it. Suddenly the guys out there picked up that man from the ground, clapped him on the back, and walked with him over to one of the cars parked nearby. Then they all climbed casually into their machines and took off as if they were having fun and games.

I couldn't believe it. "Did you see *that*?" I asked, turning to Uncle Simon. "What they were doing to that man? My God!"

Uncle Simon's face was full of fury, the same look I'd seen on Timmy's. "I told you," he said. "They're animals. They have no principles, no conscience. I mean it. . . . "

Aunt Chloe nodded. "Animals, Lisa. They're a curse of some kind, you mark my words, a curse. I swear it."

"Rabble's curse," said Uncle Simon. He listened to the sound of the words, then repeated them, almost in a whisper: "Rabble's curse!"

Whatever you called them, they were bad medicine, I thought. "You think they'll come back?" I asked, still incredulous.

Aunt Chloe's lips were tight. "They seem to, every day or two. Once you think you've got rid of them, back they come like a herd of locusts."

I didn't bother to tell her that locusts come in swarms, not herds, but I knew for sure what she meant.

After we'd managed to get through dessert, I heard a gentle tapping on the back door. Aunt Chloe started to get up.

"That'll be Buzz," said Tim. "I'll go."

"What*ever* is wrong with that boy?" snapped Aunt Chloe. "He and Tim tiptoe around outside like a couple of thieves. I think he's lost the few brains he's got."

Uncle Simon dropped his fork on his plate. "Chloe! That's no way to talk about the boy. He can't help it, what he's got."

Aunt Chloe nodded, chastened. "All right, Simon. I'm sorry, really I am. But he could at least come to see us, like always. Lord knows, *we* never harmed a hair of his head."

"Give him time, Aunt Chloe," I said, leaning toward her. "Leave Tim with him right now. It may be the best thing."

24

I could see Uncle Simon contemplating me, his chin resting on one hand. I knew right off that he understood I knew something he didn't. "Do what Lisa says," he answered slowly. "We'll just give him time."

In a few minutes Timmy returned. I was helping Aunt Chloe clear the table. "Buzz says he wants to see you," he said to me quietly. "He sent you this." It was a large pure orb of glass, with fractured bright blue lights deep inside.

I smiled. "What did he send me his marble for?"

Timmy smiled, too. "He said it was a gift."

The night was too warm for a coat. I told Aunt Chloe I'd be back, then walked down the steps with Tim. "Don't even mention his bruises," admonished Tim. "He's still scared."

Ahead of us, Buzz furtively edged from the bushes, his head to one side, arms swinging loosely. Tim needn't have worried.

"Hi, Buzz," I said, draping my arm casually over his shoulder. "Gee, but it's nice to see you. Been a lot of weeks." Since Christmas, I was thinking, when there was still snow on the ground, and Buzz was wearing an old stocking cap his mother had knitted for him and a windbreaker. "That's a really terrific marble."

Buzz suddenly broke into a grin, his crooked, self-conscious smile. For a moment at least he'd forgotten the other night.

"'Lo, Lize," he said. "Long time, no see." Then his smile flattened out again. "Real long time. You stay some?"

"A long weekend. Maybe I could squeak out a couple of extra days."

I knew immediately he had something on his mind from the way he kept peering at me from beneath those long lashes. "How you come?" he asked. "Not with your car?"

Now I understood. "Nope. I came in the airplane. I don't suppose I could persuade you to come for a ride with me, could I?"

Back came the grin. "Sure," he said. "That would be just lov—sure. I go ask my mom."

I laughed. "We're not going right now, Buzz. Wait until tomorrow. Let's try for tomorrow morning."

Then I caught sight of the bandage at the back of his head and the purple welts on his arms.

"Glad you here, Lize." he said. He stood one foot on top of the other, socks falling down around his bony ankles, looking up at me as if I were eight feet tall. "Glad you here, Lize," he said again.

"Me, too, Buzz. Don't forget tomorrow. We've got a date, you and Timmy and me."

"I'll go to bed and—" He pantomimed with his head on both hands, folded beneath his cheek.

"—Dream." I laughed. "Sometimes I dream about airplanes, too. Tonight I'll dream about taking you in my airplane. You can be in *my* dream."

He blushed, and I laughed again. Tim was grinning, too. "See you tomorrow, then," I said, and returned to the house.

"Good kid," I told Aunt Chloe.

"When he's not being a pest, which is mostly." Then she looked at me. "But I think sometimes that all those who have the brains maybe got shortchanged for understanding, so maybe it works out even. Buzz isn't lacking for understanding in most ways that count." She was wearing her apron, and I helped her wipe dishes. I almost liked the chore because I could talk to Aunt Chloe. She was as broad and as firm as the sink and moved the dishes around without thinking about them, as if they were part of her unconscious self, leaving her free to talk. She chattered even with the soapsuds sliding over her hands, wafting tiny bubbles of soap about in the air. Aunt Chloe always was an animated talker when she got going. Today she began to tell me about the Rampsie boys, and I listened and wiped and stacked the dishes.

"You never knew Aversa Rampsie, did you?" she was saying, rattling the dishes in the sink. "Well, she was a good woman, I can tell you that, and I can even remember when those two boys were born. Both of them, Bob and Jaimie. Jaimie was so sickly they didn't know if he'd pull through. Used to have a farm, back up in the woods somewhere, and about the time Jaimie was born, they moved to town. You know where their house is now, that old wreck of a place a block off the common, next to Water Street?"

I knew. It looked vaguely like the Before pictures I'd seen in magazines, followed by gloriously retouched and revamped After. Only this Before was authentic dump. There was a large front porch which had lost its supports and sagged on one end. Boards had sprung all along the length of its peeling, pitted surface. They'd never been repaired. A couple of shutters hung loose. Several windowpanes had been broken last time I'd driven by, and I could remember that cardboard, newspaper, or something had been used to plug up the holes. It hadn't been painted in recent history.

"Aversa Rampsie isn't living now, is she?" I asked Aunt Chloe. "I

26

seem to remember something about her, I think, in the Tremont paper."

Aunt Chloe shook her head. "She died. She just died. Nobody rightly knows why. I don't think anybody really knows, either Hadrian, her husband, or any of their kin, or the doctor who pronounced her dead. Maybe she just gave out."

"There wasn't any foul play?"

The thought stopped Aunt Chloe. "I'd never thought about it, Lisa. I suppose"—she was lost in thought for a moment—"it's a possibility."

"There was no autopsy?"

"No."

"Hadrian's still alive then?" I'd almost stopped wiping, listening to Aunt Chloe.

"If you want to call it living. He's drunk ninety percent of the time. Sometimes I don't think he knows night from day. And mean! Lord, is that man mean! Minnie Callaghan saw him throw the oldest boy, that's Bob, right off the end of the porch one day when she was driving by a few years back. Hadrian had him over his head, like he was a block of wood, and smashed him right to the ground. Minnie almost drove off the road, she was so frantic, then started to yell out the window at the man. But Bob, when he hit the ground, rolled right under the lip of the porch. But as he was rolling, he reached up an arm for his father's leg and caught the man off guard. Minnie said Hadrian fell forward off the edge of the porch head first with a terrible wrench and landed face first in a mud puddle. Minnie said if there'd been anything solid on that ground, Hadrian woulda been killed."

Aunt Chloe paused a moment and looked at me, her face set in lines of disbelief and outrage. "You know what happened then? That boy rolled out from under the edge of the porch, jumped to his feet, and held Hadrian's face in the mud until he almost drowned. Don't that beat all?" Aunt Chloe shook her head, looking as if she didn't know whether to laugh or cry. "Not that the old man didn't deserve it. But did you ever hear of such goings-on in a family?"

In my business, I'd come in contact with a lot of kids like Bob Rampsie, and some of them didn't have brutal fathers; they thought up their nastiness all by themselves. Still, you wouldn't expect Bob to turn to charitable acts after a beginning like that.

"How about Jaimie?" I asked Aunt Chloe. "Tim doesn't think he's the same way."

Aunt Chloe shook her head and began to clean the sink. "He doesn't

27

have that inside like flint, always drawing sparks. Some people are always like that, drawing sparks. Not Jaimie so much. Pops Rampsie, over at the store where Tim works? He's Hadrian's brother, you know, but the two men never could stand each other. Pops is a loner like the others, but he doesn't have the meanness of the devil in him.

They were a strange lot, I agreed; by now I'd seen just enough of them to believe practically anything Aunt Chloe told me about their backgrounds.

We'd chatted so long over dishes that I'd almost forgotten the Callaghans were coming at eight—in fifteen minutes. Their house was just beyond Rampsie's store; all they had to do to get there was walk around the common. They must have done it a thousand times, back and forth around that common; Simon and Chloe, too. All four had been born and brought up in Rowe, gone to school together when it was a one-story shingled building. The school had long since been demolished. It had stood one block from the common, on School Street. In this town, *nothing* was far from the common. Beyond School Street were the woods and, of course, the mill. One could just see the northernmost brick wall of the mill from an upstairs bedroom window at Aunt Chloe's. But you always knew it was there, even if you couldn't see it, because usually you could smell the chemical it used in tanning or in the dyes. And you were perpetually aware of that big chimney which prodded a hundred feet into the sky as if testing the atmosphere or accusing the gods. That chimney seemed to me some kind of miracle of construction to remain standing through New England winters and nor'easters, both of which frequently lifted shingles from houses. It swayed in fierce winds, but whoever had made that thing had known what he was about. The shadows of the day revolved about it like a sun dial, and at noon in summer the long line of the chimney cast its likeness across the green of the common, neatly dividing it in two.

Aunt Chloe was changing her dress. She stuck her head in the door.

"Will you take a hand tonight," she asked, "when I'm getting dessert?"

"Aunt Chloe, if you only knew how long it's been since I've played bridge. Since the last time I was here, all those months."

"It makes no difference," she said firmly. "You always were a tricky bridge player."

My devious legal mind, I guess. I loved to play bridge and outfox my opponents. Uncle Simon was the shrewd one, bidding outrageously on negligible count and making it!

Minnie and Stu Callaghan had been married over forty years, had three daughters, all of whom had married local men and moved to other parts of the country with their families. Minnie and Stu had played bridge with Simon and Chloe almost every Saturday night of those forty years. The funny thing was that they looked a lot like Aunt Chloe and Uncle Simon. Both Minnie and Chloe were short, although Aunt Chloe was plumper; Stu was tall like Uncle Simon, but with a heavier frame. Stu still claimed a hint of ruddy hair like soapsuds above the ears. I doubted that Uncle Simon had lost a hair of that thick and wavy mat over the years, although it had turned steel gray.

I changed into a jump suit and then I went downstairs to see Minnie and Stu. I could tell that they were already playing cards from Stu's grunts, the long pauses, and Uncle Simon's intermittent exclamations of "All right, now," and "Thataway, Chloe."

Minnie jumped up when she saw me to throw her arms around my neck. "Hi, Minnie," I said, embracing her, meanwhile shaking hands with Stu behind her back. "You both look marvelous. How nice to see you!" In a few minutes everyone sat down again. Minnie picked up her cards once more, then glanced up at me.

"Have you taken a look yet at the types sitting around our common?"

Stu fanned his cards, calculating while he talked. "They're doing more than sit, Minnie. Unfortunately. You heard what they did to Buzz Sardoe? Beat him up."

I nodded. "I heard, Stu. What I can't figure is, what do they hang around here for?"

Stu shrugged. "Rampsie's store, for one thing. They get plenty of free handouts. Nothing much else around here, 'cept the police let 'em alone."

Minnie looked indignant. "Well, there's plenty else around here if you look for it. What do you mean, there's nothing here?"

"Pipe down, Minnie," answered Stu. "It isn't the Great White Way if that's what you're thinking."

Still ruffled, Minnie picked up her cards.

Stu was still looking at me. "I think they've got wind that there's trouble at the plant, all this strike business. They're hanging around waiting, like vultures. I saw a bunch of them listening to the speeches yesterday in front of the mill, taking it all in." Stu was a shop foreman, overseeing one of the carding operations.

"You mean *that's* exciting?" asked Minnie. "Seems dull as sawdust to me."

"Depends on what you're looking for," answered Uncle Simon. "Like Lisa said, there's not all that much exciting around here. Maybe they intend to liven things up a little. Seems they already have. And I guess folks up in Tremont didn't appreciate their games, so they've come down here to entertain us."

I nodded. Those men weren't kids any longer; Bob Rampsie appeared closer to my age, old enough to have matured for better or worse.

I didn't have too long to sit around speculating about them. At a quarter to eleven, just when I was contemplating Aunt Chloe's hand while she warmed the pie. I could hear the backfires once more. They instantly shattered our bridge game along with the peace of the neighborhood.

4

"We'd better get home," said Minnie, clutching Stu's arm. "But how?" She suddenly looked frightened.

"Spend the night here," said Aunt Chloe. "We've got extra room."

"We can't," moaned Minnie. "We've got Chancey locked in the kitchen, and he'd tear the house apart." Chancellor, their Irish setter, probably didn't have enough teeth left by now to tear anything apart, but I knew they'd never leave him alone. He was like an adopted child of their older years.

Tim banged the back door; he'd been over at Buzz's. "They're back," he gasped. "Buzz hid under the covers, shaking. I lit out for home."

We pulled back the curtains and stared out into the common. Car lights glared for a minute as other vehicles arrived, then were quickly extinguished. We could hear voices and shouts.

"Where do they get the booze?" I asked Tim.

"Rampsie's selling beer now. He just got a liquor license last week."

"Who got it for him?"

"Mr. Trumbull, the Rampsies' lawyer."

I remembered Trumbull. He'd been through the Harvard Law School, but a long time ago. We could almost see his house from here, even spotting one of the many tall columns before it when we stood on the front steps.

"When does Rampsie close his store?" I asked Tim. "Doesn't he have to close at five o'clock on Saturdays?"

Tim shook his head. "Not anymore. Now he can stay open until nine

31

on Saturday nights, on Sunday until five. But he can't sell beer on Sunday until noon."

Uncle Simon grasped Stu's arm, having reached a decision. "We can head through back lots, behind the Sardoes' and the Macys'," he said. "But then, we'll have to come out on the street by the Brittons'. Why don't we drive? Wouldn't it be simpler?"

Minnie shook her head, suddenly resolved. "Drive? Just to our house? Why, we must be acting like a bunch of hens. This is Rowe, remember? What could happen to us in Rowe? We belong here as much as they do. Back lots! I'd feel like a Halloween prankster."

"Just the same," said Uncle Simon, "we'll do what we have to do, prankster or not."

"Well, I'm going home," said Minnie firmly. "I don't care about the rest of you." With that she stalked to our closet and began to pull out her coat. "Back lots!" she exclaimed again in disgust. "Just like common thieves."

Stu crammed his pipe into his pocket in frustration. "Come on, Minnie. There are better times than this to get your back up."

"But it's our town," she moaned plaintively. "You're going to give in to those . . . hoodlums?"

"I'll walk over with you," said Uncle Simon quietly to Stu.

"Oh, no, you won't," Aunt Chloe retorted, overhearing. "Then you'd have to walk back alone. I'm going, too."

"So are Tim and I." I'd already slipped on my sweater, glacing at Tim. "The more of us, the better."

Nevertheless, when we left the house, without having made a conscious decision, we immediately set out the back way. Now I *did* feel like a thief. We stole out the rear of the house, quietly opened the gate to the Sardoes' yard, skirting the trees and crossing their driveway. Next we followed along a path across the Brittons' yard. Both houses were dark and a little eerie as we tiptoed like second-story men through their property. The crowd on the common had grown to twelve or thirteen. I could see them through the spaces between the houses; somebody'd turned on a radio at full volume so I could feel the beat way back there in the shrubbery. It even seemed as if the ground were moving ever so slightly.

Tim was leading. "Feels like we're playing cops and robbers," he whispered. "This is where we hide when we're playin'."

I could believe it. There were clumps of bushes back here, sheds, the barn behind us where Buzz had been beaten up, trees, fences. We had to pick our way slowly because the ground was uneven. But Tim knew the way so well that he could have directed us blindfolded. We continued across lots until we came to Rampsie's store. When we emerged from the dark into the lights of the store, the crowd on the common wasn't paying the faintest attention to us, and I began to feel a little foolish. The men out there were smoking, and some of the noise had died down. They looked pretty peaceful, sitting out there in a group: relaxing on the back of a big flatbed truck, lying on it while they smoked, or sitting lazily with their legs hanging down over the edge. We saw Minnie and Stu to their door and began to retrace our steps.

We'd returned about as far as the other side of Rampsie's store and were debating whether to go behind the houses once again or to walk up the sidewalk when someone called out to us.

"Hey, back there," the voice yelled, lazily, with a kind of slow drawl, almost a southern accent, but without the flat vowels. "What ya hangin' around in the shadows fer?"

We swung around as if we'd been struck or had been caught doing something sly and dishonorable. I stared out into the common; at first I couldn't make out a thing because all the car lights had been flashed on again, all together, as if it had been planned and they'd seen us all along. The cars were pointing toward us, and I felt as if I were on a stage, looking out over the footlights.

"Jesus!" exclaimed Timmy. "Jesus." His voice was a little quavery, but he stood firm and immobile like a rock.

We kept coming in the headlights. Aunt Chloe was crying to herself, very softly so you could hardly tell, and I could hear Uncle Simon repeating over and over again, "It's all right, Chloe, just keep coming, just keep coming, that-a-girl, pretend you don't see them."

We looked away and doggedly marched down that sidewalk, listening to the sound of Uncle Simon's voice. I could see every crack in the pavement, all the damage inflicted by frosts, all the little pockmarks and irregularities when the cement was cast.

Someone called again. This time there were shadows as figures interposed before the headlights. The shadows were long and thin, and they climbed the walls of the houses, then mixed with others, finally disappearing into a black sky. "Ain't you gonna talk to us?" asked a voice beyond the lights. There was a laugh, loose and guttural, and as I turned away, I knew those shadows were moving, but I didn't want to see.

33

"You want to take to the woods?" asked Tim in a whisper, not looking at me.

"No! We're in better shape if we keep out on the sidewalk."

We were now in front of the Brittons house again; for a second I thought I saw a light inside. Maybe they'd already called Clyde Oldham.

We kept walking. Suddenly, in front of me materialized a figure, tall and lean. For a moment I thought him merely another shadow, expecting it to wheel away like all the others.

"Dahlin', where you been?" the man said to me, reaching out a hand to touch me. I shrank back so fast I rammed into Timmy. Aunt Chloe stood there, frozen.

"Leave her alone," hissed Uncle Simon. "Don't touch her."

The man recoiled. He took a step toward Uncle Simon. Then he laughed. "What could you do about it, old crow? If I touch her, I mean? You're pretty snitty for an old buzzard."

I was holding Timmy's arm. "Let us go by," I pleaded, conciliatingly. I tried to act neither hostile nor friendly.

Now there were other men about us. Their shadows spun against the light.

"What'll you give me," the man asked, "to let you go?"

Now I could see him better. He was a tall, very thin, light-boned man with long dark hair hanging somewhat in his eyes. His skin was dark, like an Indian's, even in this glaring light, and he had an Indian's high cheekbones. I could see the hardness in his eyes and the brittle-hard look of contempt in his expression. His body appeared tense, as if a spring were coiled inside it, and in a moment that lithe power might unexpectedly snap one way or another.

"Where'd you come from?" he asked again, standing in my way.

I didn't dare antagonize him. "Just visiting. We're tired. Let us go home, will you?"

His voice was so quiet that I could barely hear him. I felt an icy chill on my back, and I inadvertently shivered. He reached out to take my arm. "Let's you and me go off and talk someplace, quietlike."

Uncle Simon reached forward and grabbed his arm. "I told you to get your hands off her," he said.

Suddenly Uncle Simon spun around, and with a shock I realized that the man had hit him. Aunt Chloe sent up a shriek into the night air.

For some reason the man in our path backed off. I grabbed Timmy by one arm, Aunt Chloe by the other, and pushed them forcibly

34

toward the sidewalk leading into our house, a short distance away. I realized that Uncle Simon had been hurt, but this was no place to examine our wounds. We ran past the Sardoes' and tore up into our walk. I didn't know why those men weren't following, why they'd seemed to have turned back; they were pretty drunk, but maybe they'd also felt remorseful at hurting Uncle Simon. At any rate, when their leader stood aside, they all faltered. It took us barely a minute to reach our front door, but I could feel the blood hammering in my ears and Aunt Chloe's plump body wobbling with every step.

We waited while Uncle Simon fumbled in his pocket for the keys. I'd never known him to lock the door before, it was an entirely unaccustomed occurrence, and he had to search a minute. I prayed the door would open, clenching my teeth together in despair; there were no lights around this side of the house since we'd gone out the back way into the night. But the old lock tumbled with a dull and creaky thud.

I was the last one in, pushing the others. I turned around for one brief second and saw the men still out there under a streetlight. They might have been a crowd of kids coming home from a basketball game, standing there, except that I could still see the guy, the tall one, looking back at us. The light was shining off his teeth.

He raised his can of beer toward me, took a swig, and threw the can into the street. I could hear the hollow metal of the can bouncing, echoing off the hard surface. "Bye, dahlin' " the man was calling as he stood beneath the streetlight. "Hey, dahlin'."

Aunt Chloe was hysterical. She stood in the middle of the room, quivering, unable to take off her coat. Her trembling was uncontrollable, her whole body shaking.

Uncle Simon needed help to take off his jacket; his arm was entirely limp at his side.

"What'd he hit you with?" I asked Uncle Simon, looking at the bruised skin as he rolled up his shirt.

"He had something in his hand. Heavy. Never saw it."

"The beer can?" But it wouldn't have been heavy enough, even full.

"A rock, most likely. I could feel the shock clear up to my shoulder."

Aunt Chloe was slowly recovering from her terror. Her eyes were hollow, and her cheeks flushed. She touched Uncle Simon's arm gently. The hysteria had gone from her voice now that she realized Uncle Simon was hurt. "I'll get some cold water for the swelling. Then we'll have to call Dr. Almquist."

"This time of night?" asked Uncle Simon. "I'll wait until morning."

I glanced at the tall clock in the corner near the stairs. Almost midnight.

"We'll call him now," said Aunt Chloe. "It won't wait."

"Chloe, he won't come," persisted Uncle Simon. "He'll have to buck that mob, too."

"How about Clyde Oldham?" I asked. "Won't he give him an escort? That's what this town hires a police chief for, isn't it?" I looked out the window as I was talking and could see the lights out there. The music from the common seeped beneath the doors and through the window cracks. My head was on fire from it. "I'm going to call him, ask him to get the doctor—what's his name—Almquist?" I didn't even know there was a doctor in Rowe.

I leafed through the dog-eared telephone directory. The police chief was listed in bold-faced letters. His house was located a block back from the common, so perhaps he hadn't heard all the noise, although that possibility was inconceivable to me tonight.

The phone rang at least ten times, with no answer. I held on, almost afraid to sever the possibility of help between the police chief's house and ours. Finally, a sleepy voice croaked feebly into the receiver. "Hullo. Police chief."

"Chief Oldham, this is Lisa Sanderson, remember me? I'm Chloe and Simon's niece. Well, I'm here for a while, and we're having trouble on the common. Some people out there are carrying on, and we were accosted in the street just now. We need a doctor for Uncle Simon, but somebody'll have to escort him over here."

Oldham didn't sound too impressed. "Nothing to worry about, Miss Sanderson," he answered in a laconic, sleepy voice. "These kids come and go all the time." He was obviously suppressing a yawn. "Give 'em a few more days, and they'll clear out; you can bet on it."

I couldn't believe my ears. "Chief, have you heard what's going on out there? Just stick your head out the window and listen. And I'm not kidding you, we need a doctor over here. He's not about to come by himself, with those men on the loose."

There was a long pause. "Chief?" I finally asked, thinking there was something faulty with our connection.

"All right. I'll see what I can do." His voice sounded very doubtful. I could hear the phone click.

I relayed this negligible information to Simon and Chloe. Uncle

Simon's arm was swelling more and turning purple. There was a very large welt on one side.

We sat down to wait. I made a cup of tea for Aunt Chloe and me and gave Uncle Simon a drink of brandy. The pain was beginning to get to him, and all I could find in the house was aspirin.

I sent Timmy to bed; he'd been pretty busy fetching stuff for Uncle Simon: cold water, ice, the ice pack at the back of the bathroom closet. I went upstairs with Tim to say good-night, after double-checking the doors to make sure they were locked.

Tim and I sat on his stiff bedroom chairs and peered out his dormer window. "Who was the tall guy?" I asked him. "The one who stopped us?"

"Bob Rampsie. He's the one I told you about."

I'd seen him earlier, but at long range. Close-up, drunk, with his lascivious features, I didn't recognize him. He was the same man who'd extinguished his cigarette on his friend's face.

"Do you know the others, Tim?"

"I think his brother, Jaimie, was out in the street, behind us."

"Dandy. Who else?"

"Hunk Hudman. He comes into Pops's for beer all the time. Bingo Keaton, too, the guy with that hat. Only they don't pay for the beer they swipe it. Don't even bother to put it under their shirts or anything."

I stared at Timmy. "Doesn't Rampsie mind? I mean, he *likes* to have his beer ripped off?"

Tim shrugged. "I don't think he sees. If he does, he turns his back. Maybe he doesn't want to cross them. Besides, Bob and Jaimie's his nephews."

Even Pops was too scared of them to make waves!

"I can understand that he's afraid of Bob, Tim, but doesn't he care that Jaimie's mixed up with that crowd?"

"I don't know what he thinks, Sis. He's not a very open guy, kind of gruff."

We watched awhile longer, and then, in the distance, I could see car lights skirting the far side of the common. I held my breath as the two lights approached, riding up and down gently over the swells and hollows of the street. The car came to a stop outside our house. On the side was painted the round gold insignia of the chief of police.

Suddenly I was aware of the crowd out in the common; they must have seen the chief's car, too. Lights dimmed, and the music that had been thumping out into the night lessened its throbbing. The chief emerged from the car, and with him was another man, carrying a black medical bag. I raced quickly down the stairs with Tim behind me.

We let the two inside. The chief, to my surprise, was wearing his uniform. The doctor was a broad-shouldered man of medium height with curling sideburns and thick bronze-colored hair. He was dressed in faded Levi's and an open-necked checked shirt, and he carried a battered medical bag. He was a very good-looking man, and I found myself inadvertently staring at him. Something drew me to him immediately. He totally surprised me. I'd begun to think of everyone in this town as over fifty years old; Dr. Almquist must have been in his late thirties. The lower edge of those rebellious sideburns were faintly gray, but he had a vigorous, athletic stride. He glanced at me as if he too were faintly surprised, shook his head by way of saying hello, and turned expectantly toward Aunt Chloe. I wondered what he was doing here in this small town. Aunt Chloe led him immediately to Uncle Simon, who was sitting in a living-room chair, his arm propped on a pillow, with an ice bag placed over the swelling.

The police chief was standing beside the door, holding his hat by the visor; he appeared to be in rehearsal for a play. His dumpy figure seemed encased in clothing made for someone else. His stocky legs bulged in the thighs, and his stomach protruded above the stiff black belt. He was a big man who must have gained weight over the years. I could see him as a high school football player whose muscles had grown soft and lost their elasticity.

"Miss Sanderson? Are you the one who called?"

I nodded at him. "Chief, those people out there have been making a public disturbance all night. I can testify to it myself, make a sworn affidavit if necessary. Not only that, one of them grabbed my arm and struck Uncle Simon. That's simple assault in any criminal code, and I'll be glad to sign the complaint and bring charges."

The chief peered at me uneasily. "You some kind of lawyer or something?"

"I practice down in Boston. I've come up for a few days to see my relatives."

He scrutinized me pretty carefully, then motioned out the window. "You know these guys can get a little rough sometimes."

"So I've heard. I don't see any reason to let them get away with it, do you?"

He shook his head barely perceptibly, his eyes on my face.

38

"You knew they roughed up Buzz Sardoe?" I asked.

"But that was kid stuff. You know how kids are." He put on his hat and suddenly appeared much taller.

"No, how are they, Chief?"

"There's been a lot of pranks. Kids do it all the time."

I swallowed hard. "Have you happened to notice how old those *kids* out there are? They were kids a long time ago. And what they did to Uncle Simon was no prank. When Bob Rampsie put his hand on me, that was against the law, too. You aren't allowed to touch, molest, or seize—"

"You're sure it was Bob Rampsie?"

"That's what Timmy says, and he knows him."

"But wasn't it dark?"

It felt as if I were being grilled by the prosecution. "I don't understand, Chief Oldham. You don't think those men should get away with this?"

He shifted his feet uneasily. "I just want to be fair, Miss Sanderson, that's all. It won't do for a responsible police officer to go rounding up innocent people. I guess that's all I'm saying."

I felt distressed enough about Uncle Simon to be persistent. "But didn't you hear all the noise out there tonight? The neighbors will tell you. It was really a public nuisance."

Chief Oldham turned and looked out the window beside Uncle Simon's door. "I'd really have to say, in all fairness, that when I arrived tonight, things were pretty quiet out there. A few kids, yes. But it's Saturday night, and the local bucks ain't got that much to do down here, come Saturday night. If they want to make a little noise, and I stop 'em, they're going to get into worse trouble."

It was a point almost well taken except for the singular fact of Uncle Simon's arm. Suddenly I heard Dr. Almquist's voice behind me.

"But it was more than a little noise, Clyde, and that man in there has at least a chip out of the bone in his radius. That's not just a little fun."

I turned quickly to Dr. Almquist. He was leaning casually against the doorjamb, taking in our conversation. "Is there anything I can do to help Uncle Simon?"

Dr. Almquist shook his head. "I just told Mrs. Sanderson to put him to bed. I gave him something to kill the pain and to sleep. But he'll need an X ray first thing in the morning." He turned back to the chief. "Come on now, Clyde. My patients have been telling me about the noise on the common. It's been going on for a while now."

39

"You've heard it?" the chief asked.

"No. I live too far off the common. But I've been told—"

The chief thrust out his jaw. "Then that's just secondhand knowledge, Dr. Almquist. Nobody would pay you any heed for that."

"Is that true?" Dr. Almquist asked, abruptly turning to me. He had a quizzical look in his eye. I nodded slowly at him.

"Hey, listen," he said, suddenly reaching out to shake my hand. "I'm sorry. Name's George. Pleased to meet you."

He seemed a really nice guy, with crinkly gray-blue eyes. I could feel a gentle pressure in his hand, and for some reason I wanted to hold onto it for a moment. This had been a kind of insane night, and his hand was steady and warm, welcome. I'd have liked to rub my fingertips against his; instead, I reluctantly withdrew my hand.

"I'm Lisa. Thanks for helping my uncle. Sorry to get you out so late."

"Forget it. I'm a nighthawk. I was up reading. Your uncle's arm's going to be pretty darned sore for a while."

Something resolved in me with his words. Despite Oldham's growing impatience to be off, I turned to him. "Where do you have lawyers, Chief Oldham? In Tremont?"

Oldham's hand rested on the doorknob. "Sure, Miss Sanderson. If you've got a complaint, why don't you ask them to help you?" I recognized the edge of sarcasm to his voice, but mostly I knew he wanted to get back into his bed. "There's even a judge up there."

As we moved outdoors through Uncle Simon's big front door, the common was silent. Again, no one was around. The place appeared dark, empty; above us a sedate moon rode in a cloudless sky.

"See," said Oldham, "I told you. Once they've had their fun, they'll move on. Just a little pranking, come Saturday night."

I switched on the bright outside lights illuminating the front walk. In the light I could see the haggard lines on the chief's face and detect a pale expression of distress on it. He didn't look well to me.

"Holy Jesus!" George exclaimed suddenly. When I wheeled to look at him, he was staring down the walk out onto the street. I sucked in my breath and turned to look where he was pointing.

Oldham made a bolt for the front steps, then raced down the walk as fast as he could go in his tight uniform.

There, blocking the street, was the police cruiser, tipped over on its side as incongruously as an abandoned child's toy. In his frustration,

40

the police chief was trying to push against it, hammering with his hands, to right it again.

George followed him, gently pulling him away. "Come on, Clyde," he said. "You're not going to do a damn thing that way. You'll just have to wait until morning for help."

Oldham stood looking up at George blankly, except for one emotion, which I recognized immediately. Oldham's eyes were wide and glazed, and his lips trembled ever so slightly. Now I understood something I hadn't known before. I could even sympathize with Clyde Oldham: He was scared to death of those men out there in the common.

I borrowed Uncle Simon's keys and drove the chief and George home. The common was deserted. Beneath the streetlights I could see the shine of beer cans. In places the grass was damp with dew, indented by the tires of the cars parked on it. The vehicles and men had vanished into the night, leaving behind Uncle Simon's broken arm and a solitary car on its side.

We were silent as we circled the common. Each of us seemed to be anticipating that cars would suddenly roar out at us from one of those silent side streets which extended from the common like spokes from a wheel. But the night was still and alone to us. The chief was obviously embarrassed and chastened, trailing his fingers through his thinning hair.

George was still talking gently to him. "Someone will help you move the cruiser in the morning, Clyde," he said. "But people driving through town may have difficulty getting around it in the morning because it's blocking the road on that side of the common."

"I'll figure out something," Clyde was muttering. "Come morning, I'll get my deputies, and together we'll—"

"How many deputies do you have now?" I could remember asking Aunt Chloe the same question.

"Two, part time, same as always. Never had cause for more. Peaceful town, Rowe. Never had any cause. . . ." He lapsed into silence.

George was thoughtful, his words slower. "Listen, Clyde, for what it's worth—you'll have to try to do something about this situation in

42

Rowe. You and your deputies, I mean. Things aren't going to get better; they'll maybe even get worse if you don't make an effort. I think you can stop a lot of it if you clamp down. All that drinking and noise at night, for instance. We all know that today it got a little out of hand."

Oldham became a little testy. "What do you want me to do, arrest the whole lot of 'em? It wouldn't get us anyplace. Besides, they'd just come back."

We were pulling up before Oldham's house. It was a small frame building, low among the trees. Directly behind it was the chain-link fence at the edge of the mill property.

"You're going to have to take charge, just the same," said George thoughtfully. "Perhaps we can help." He opened the car door and steadied the chief, but Oldham had recovered now, piqued perhaps by George's remark about holding the intruders on the common within bounds. When he walked to his front door, it was with a smooth step and an erect stature.

I turned the car in his driveway, holding my lights on the chief's front door until the house lights came on.

"Is he all right?" I asked George. "He's frightened. And he doesn't look well either."

"Just hitting the booze too much. Always had a drinking problem, but all this is too much for him."

I groaned. "And he's our sole law officer? No wonder the men aren't responsive to him. They weren't even intimidated."

"It's not entirely his fault. Clyde has a frail little wife who tries to make ends meet on a police chief's salary. No one else wanted the job. Clyde took a couple of courses at some police academy, but he's never had many problems here. Once someone dumped a hot car by the side of the road; another time a bad check bounced at Rampsie's store—for something like twenty bucks. Never any rough stuff."

I reluctantly drove George to his house, a couple of blocks away. I liked talking to him, listening to his voice telling me about Clyde Oldham in this dark car, and I didn't want it to end.

"Have you lived in Rowe long?" I asked him. "I thought the nearest doctor was in Tremont."

I could see his smile in the semidarkness of the car. "Eight months. I'm in Rowe only four days a week because I have an affiliation with a clinic in Boston. Down there I spend two days a week at the clinic, another at Mass General. Associate staff. Most of the hospitals require a large number of part-time doctors."

George pointed out his house, a large, sprawling Victorian structure with elaborate lacework on the edge of the roof. There was a light shining outside his door, another from deep inside the house.

"Do you live here all by yourself?" I could just make out the third story barely visible against a dark sky.

"No. I have a daughter, Clarissa. She's nine. And there's a housekeeper who takes care of her while I'm away."

I looked at him hesitantly, not wanting to pry. In my silence George helped me. "I'm divorced, you see. My wife didn't want Clarissa. I did. And there was no doctor this side of Tremont. Now the townspeople don't have to travel so far for medical care. Worked out really well. Until now."

I could see the dark shape of George's head in the car. Rowe's lucky to get him, I was thinking. A million small towns urgently needed good doctors, advertising constantly for them in the professional journals.

"I'm glad you're here," I told him. "Maybe we're going to need all the people we can get together. By the way, do you know anything about Trumbull, the lawyer? I think I met him once a long time ago."

George nodded. "He's the one who represents the mill when it needs legal advice. I understand he gave legal assistance to one of the Rampsies up in Tremont: car theft or something like that. Trumbull keeps pretty much to himself, doesn't mix with anyone. Once asked me over for a drink after the mill had an open house when the new wing was completed. Trumbull and I were trailing the crowd that day, I had Clarissa with me; they were giving out cider and doughnuts to the kids. Trumbull came over and introduced himself. Withdrawn type in some ways, stiff little mustache, smokes a long, curved meerschaum. The man's bright enough, believes in law and order; at least he tells you about it all the time. But he's worried that justice won't be served, he says, that the lone criminal before the bar might have his rights unwittingly violated. I told him once that the majority needs its rights supported, too."

I was sitting facing George in the car, feeling a warmth from his presence and perhaps even an excitement, and I could smell the tweed of his coat and a faint odor of tobacco.

I knew what George was talking about. "He finds a challenge in getting someone off," I said. "There's lots more intensity about it. He convinces himself he's serving justice, the minority, the oppressed. He

44

comes off clean, even altruistic." I shook my head. I'd seen many lawyers like Trumbull. Lord help the poor majority. "And I imagine he's independently wealthy enough with the mill account," I conjectured, "so he can indulge himself in that interpretation of justice."

"Exactly," answered George. "He's a marvelous dilettante lawyer. This is his territory, and he wouldn't want to be pushed out of it. He'd be tough, I think, if he were challenged, especially by a woman. Yet I can't say exactly why."

I turned it over in my mind, the necessity, if it were ever to arise, of facing Trumbull.

"Oh, I'm just an attorney like he is," I replied somewhat cavalierly. "Forget I'm a woman."

"That'd be tough," answered George with a grin. He held out his hand. "Say, I hope you'll be around for a while. I've really liked meeting you."

I could feel the warmth of his palm against mine and the strength in his long fingers. "It's . . . so nice meeting you, too, George. Really nice. I'll be here awhile. And thanks for your kindness to Uncle Simon." I met his smile in the dark and felt suddenly better than any time since I'd returned to Rowe.

Returning home, I skirted the overturned car and slid into Uncle Simon's driveway. I was humming a little tune, still feeling mellow, looking forward to seeing George again, already anticipating it. But as I looked up at the lights inside the house, I could feel my mood shift because I knew it was going to be a hard night for my aunt and uncle, nursing along that injured arm. They weren't complainers, never had been, and we'd get through it somehow. But I knew I wasn't going to be able to sleep. I could feel it rebelling in me already. This was going to be my night to pace.

Aunt Chloe and Uncle Simon had already gone to bed; I could hear the slow whisper of voices in their bedroom. The pills George had left on the telephone stand were gone. In a few minutes I could even hear Aunt Chloe snoring, soft as a teakettle bubbling on the stove. Timmy had returned to the back upstairs bedroom, and all was quiet. After a half hour of tearing my bed to ribbons, with the sheets inextricably mixed up with my pillow, I got up, threw on my robe, and came downstairs. I crammed my hands in the bathrobe pockets and started walking, back and forth, around and around.

One thing had become abundantly clear: I certainly couldn't go back to Boston to practice as if nothing'd happened. I simply couldn't leave Uncle Simon, Aunt Chloe, and Timmy now. Maybe I could get someone to cover for a while down there. I'd have to wring that someone's arm; poverty law and all those nickles and dimes under the door weren't going to lure anyone to handle my exclusive clientele. But I'd had a hell of a lot of challenge going in my practice, and what was more, I had some good friends who were as involved as I in my little outpost of the law. So I'd call them tomorrow. And I'd have to return the airplane if I were going to take an extended sojourn at this end of the world.

I looked out our front window, past the overturned car, to the common, bathed in the lights from lampposts, around the circle to the far side of the giant oval. Up there, barely visible to me, were the large old houses at the far side, those columns belonging to Trumbull's house, the road to George Almquist's, the tower on the mill smokestack, winking with a tiny red light required by law for aircraft warning. It looked like a small red star, an impostor in the diadem, trying to ingratiate itself with the sovereign pinpoints up there.

I turned back and heard a step. "It's only me, Sis," Tim said almost apologetically. I appreciated his solicitude, but it dawned on me what a sorry state it is when you're scared by who might be behind you in your own house, in a town of two thousand people.

"What's the trouble?" I asked him. "Can't you sleep either?"

He shook his head.

I sat down on the couch; there was no point in wearing a hole in Aunt Chloe's carpet.

"Listen, Tim. Maybe I'll stay here for a while, take a little vacation. Rowe looks pretty good to me."

He looked at me kind of sideways as if I'd lost my brain cells. "You wanna vacation in Rowe?"

"Sure. Why not? I haven't seen all of you in quite a while."

"You're crazy, Sis. What do you want to hang around here for? Especially now, with what's happened. . . ."

"Listen, Tim, I said I need a vacation, OK? Where and when I want it are my business."

When he looked up quickly at me again, he smiled momentarily, then glanced away. "I almost asked," he said. "But I didn't think you could probably swing it."

I playfully tousled his hair. "Listen, I'll take you and Buzz for a ride in the plane tomorrow, like I promised. Then I'm going to deliver it

46

back to Boston and stay for a couple of days, get things wound up down here. Maybe George can bring me back."

"Dr. Almquist?"

"He's down there several days every week."

I could see him figuring carefully. "Uncle Simon isn't going to be able to drive, right? And Aunt Chloe never learned. So you can use their car if you need to get around."

"Uncle Simon already asked me. Now why don't you go back to bed?"

"All right. Thanks, Sis."

"For what?"

"For staying."

I put my hand on his shoulder, then impetuously gave him a hug. "Good night, Tim."

Dad's face was right before me every time I looked at Tim; it always startled me how much alike they looked. Dad was a controller in one of the terminals at Logan Airport in Boston when we were growing up. He used to wear a little curved microphone around his head and spoke into it in a clear, firm voice. I loved to hear Dad talk; he was so used to speaking carefully that even at home, when you were halfway across the room, you could understand every word he said. His voice radiated confidence and calm, even when he was upset; it was vital to pilots that they understand him and sense his competence. Sometimes Dad would take me up into the tower and let me sit quietly at his desk while he spoke out across the airwaves to the lumbering planes just landing on the long, flat runways. Later, when Timmy was old enough, Dad would take him along, too. I was eighteen years older than Tim, so I had been around for quite a while before they had him. At that time we lived not far from here because Dad wanted us to live in the country, and Mom could be near Chloe and Simon while he was on duty at the airport; controllers, like pilots, had odd schedules—on a few days, off a few days—not like the working schedules of other people.

Sometimes Mom would go to Boston by bus to meet Dad, especially when she wanted to shop, and ride back with him. She used to love the trips back; they'd go out to eat and drive through the night, watching the lights of the towns they passed. It was an intimate time for them, after three or four days apart, with the prospect of a long weekend together. They'd drive slowly and talk, and sometimes she'd fall asleep on his shoulder. When they'd come into the drive, often I'd be up, and

Dad would be rousing Mother out in the car; then she'd come in, laughing, her eyes squinting in the light. Once he picked her up and carried her into the house; she was a short, slight woman, a feather in his arms. I could hear her now, laughing and protesting, telling him to put her down. But he carried her anyway, as if she were a bride, and dumped her unceremoniously on the couch. She'd been wearing a hat, which fell off to the floor, and she looked all askew, but she loved it and talked about it afterward.

Six years ago this month she went down on the bus to meet Dad, stopped to shop at the downtown Boston stores, then took a cab to the airport. Mother and Dad had dinner outside the city, then drove slowly home, clinging to the outside lane of the highway as they talked. Ahead of them a tractor-trailer in their path went out of control, veered across the highway, spewing a trail of gasoline and rammed a string of guardrails. There was nowhere for them to go. The gasoline on the highway ignited, and before they could react, their car exploded.

Afterward the truck driver was brought into court on a drunk driving charge, but it was before the days when breatholator tests were given routinely by police, and the charge didn't stick. I read lawbooks for weeks afterward, trying to find some way to bring that truck driver to court, but it was no use. I knew I'd never succeed in avenging my feelings on the man, but at the time it helped to try. In the process I became fascinated with the legal profession, the way lawyers can help clients, and the reasons they fail. The money Dad left me put me through law school.

At law school I went around in a vacuum at first; the first six months I almost died of self-doubt partly because I was a woman. In my section were 120 men and 7 women. Three times a day I was asked what I was doing in law school when I could be home married to some nice guy. The man who asked it usually put it in a kindly tone, as if he had my welfare at heart.

After my first week in class I lost my stagefright. The faculty was hard on girls, but it toughened me. That first week a professor, whom I later grew to admire, called on me. That day I hated him. It was my first class in contracts. He began by asking me whether marriage was a bilateral or unilateral contract. I said that it was a bilateral contract, of course, but I didn't sit down for one hour until I'd tried to explain it in social and halting legal language. I was panicked and sick, but I did it. Later that year I entered the moot

48

court competitions, which were mock appellate arguments, and won a scholarship. Then I didn't need as much money from Dad's estate, and there'd be more for Timmy later. Somehow all that seemed an awfully long time ago now, though.

When I awoke the next morning, I looked out on a bright and golden morning, a lovely New England spring day. There was a trace of moisture in the air and a faint hover of fleeting mist over the grass of the common. Tim was already up, peering out the front window; he appeared smothered in pajamas and a large bathrobe with a football insignia on the back.

A wrecking crew had already righted the police car. Chief Oldham out there was giving directions and anxiously examining the scratches on the bright gilt paint of his cruiser.

"They've been out there for a half hour," said Tim. "Chief's frantic, yelling at the guys. You'd think that car was made outta glass."

Tim and I had breakfast, and when we looked again, the car was gone. There wasn't even any dust on the road to indicate where it had been overturned.

"Find Buzz," I told Tim, "and let's get going. Don't you have to work at Rampsie's later?"

In his haste, he almost ran into Uncle Simon, whose arm hung in a sling made from an old sheet which Aunt Chloe had knotted behind his neck.

"How does it feel?" I asked him.

"Look," said Aunt Chloe. With a firm movement of her hand she flipped back the cuff of his sleeve. Beneath it, Uncle Simon's arm was terribly swollen and colored purple, green, and yellow.

I examined it thoughtfully. "You could press charges against Rampsie for assaulting you on the street. I think that you should. It would even be in the public interest."

Aunt Chloe served Uncle Simon the same kind of mealy cereal he'd been eating every morning I could remember. She looked at me doubtfully. "Lisa, we're getting too old for a thing like that. Why, we'd have to fill out a million sheets of paper, go tell all kinds of people what happened. Like when someone sideswiped Virginia Macy's car, she had to spend two days running back and forth to Tremont."

"I'll do it for you. If it'd get rid of those people in the common, wouldn't it be worth it?"

Uncle Simon answered for her, his eyes narrowed. "It *would* be worth it," he said, barely breathing the words. He took a spoonful of the cereal, thinking, then looked at me again. "How would we go about it?"

"I think we should talk to Chief Oldham again, remind him about your arm, even show it to him. Then persuade him to take George Almquist's testimony in a sworn affidavit. That's all you'd really need."

"Would I have to go up to Tremont like Virginia Macy?"

I shook my head. "Doesn't the district judge sit down here when he's needed? I mean, on mill business sometimes?"

Aunt Chloe reflected, her head to one side. "Now and then. A couple of times, like last fall when a couple of mill hands got into a fight and one was hurt badly, and once when someone burglarized Mudge's garage."

"That would be it. Misdemeanors. They'd be tried locally. Felonies would be handled in Tremont, most likely. Where did the judge have his chambers?"

"Town hall," answered Aunt Chloe. "Where else?"

"You mean there's really a town hall in Rowe?"

"Sure. It's only a little room connected to the firehouse. But Sarah Wellington sits there, keeps the birth records, deeds, things like that. Then, when we have a town meeting, they move the fire engine out into the street, and we've got all kinds of room."

I shook my head wonderingly. Rowe never ceased to amaze me.

"All right. I'll call Oldham."

I picked up the phone. This time Oldham answered promptly, and I explained about Uncle Simon's arm and of our intention to press charges. I also impressed on him that we really needed his help because he was the only law officer in Rowe. I was hoping that even if he wasn't determined enough to use legal action last night when he had first seen Uncle Simon's arm, perhaps the mistreatment of his cruiser might have changed his mind.

"Uncle Simon's complaint might take some of the wind from their sails, Chief. It could help. Will you call the district judge?"

A distinct silence fell over Oldham's end of the line. I shook the phone, thinking there was something wrong with it. I'd had better connections to Los Angeles than to the other side of Rowe.

"Dr. Almquist says there's real injury to Simon's arm?" Oldham asked. "I'm sorry to hear it. Tell Simon I feel bad about it."

"So you'll call the district judge, Chief Oldham?"

Another silence. "Miss Sanderson, I don't think you know this town. It just doesn't help to be so hasty, to get riled up so fast. Matter of fact, ask Simon. He'll tell you that every now and then the kids around here get to acting up. Couple of months ago some of them climbed over the mill fence, began running around in those storage sheds. Then we got a few locks, and all that stopped as fast as it started."

"But surely you know that was different, Mr. Oldham. Those kids didn't cause any damage. Yesterday we were accosted, and Uncle Simon was hurt. And previously Buzz Sardoe was attacked."

Another silence. "But like I said, that was after dark, Miss Sanderson. How can you really be sure who did it?"

"It was Bob Rampsie; Tim knows him. And we saw him clearly under the streetlights." I hesitated. "I don't understand, Chief. Why are you so reluctant?"

"Reluctant? Who's reluctant?" As soon as I heard the word slide off his tongue, I understood. It was only eight-thirty in the morning, and Oldham had already been drinking. I remembered with discouragement what George had told me last night.

I was about to hang up, to forget the whole thing, when Oldham surprised me. "Miss Sanderson, we could always get the boys together, peaceablelike. I'd go along with that. A peaceful powwow, right out in the common."

I suddenly felt a bitterness twisting my tongue. "Would it help your cruiser, Chief? Your powwow, I mean?"

"My police cruiser! Why?"

"Are you willing to discuss that peacefully? It really doesn't bother you that they turned it over?"

He was suddenly embarrassed. "It's all right. I ain't complaining."

I couldn't stop. "How good of you, Chief Oldham. You're the soul of restraint. Nero liked to fiddle; you like meetings." I took a deep breath. "I'll talk to Uncle Simon and see how he feels about it."

52

Uncle Simon was drinking his coffee, his swollen arm on the table before him. He'd heard everything I said. "He doesn't want to do anything, does he?" asked Uncle Simon. "I knew that Clyde wasn't exactly a ball of fire, but I never realized he'd be a regular old lady."

I sat down beside Uncle Simon, equally discouraged. Because I saw Uncle Simon's dejection, I ransacked my brain to find something positive about Oldham's procrastination. "Perhaps it isn't all that bad," I began lamely. "Maybe it'll even get us somewhere. The great god of arbitration, Uncle Simon. There's a lot to be said for it."

"I'll believe it when I see it," he answered glumly.

Tim poked his head through the door excitedly. "Buzz and me are ready, Sis. Buzz is running around, pretending he's an airplane. We'll wait in the car."

Uncle Simon tossed me the keys. "It's all yours, Lisa. Guess we're going to have to depend on you from here on."

That old car of Uncle Simon's even boasted a floor shift, but he'd kept it in mint condition; the shifting mechanism felt as if it were immersed in liquid mercury, so smooth were the controls.

The three of us sat in the front seat. Buzz, next to the window, bounced up and down, rocking from side to side. "Err-plane, err-plane," he was chanting. "Lize, can I steer, just like last time?"

"Don't see why not, Buzz. Now sit still until we get there."

My plane was parked on the flight line, bright in the morning sunshine. While Tim helped me walk around it for inspection, Buzz touched the metal skin.

"Nice," he said, rubbing his fingers across the slick surface. Then he rubbed it affectionately. "Ni-ce." While I opened the cowling, Tim pointed out the parts of the plane to Buzz; Tim had been my copilot off and on for so long that I was sure he could fly it without me.

I strapped the kids in, and we rolled down the runway; the plane sucked itself off the asphalt and purred into the blue sky. The great dark eyes in Buzz's misshapen head clouded in fright as we left the earth behind, but in a moment they were as active as two beans. "Look," he said, drooling slightly, pointing far below. Tim, in the back seat—the sophisticate—was pointing out the fairgrounds with its large, circular track, the river, lumberyard, then the school which the kids attended. You could see the black roof with its finlike ventilator on top.

We followed along the road to Rowe, and even before we got there, we saw the mill smokestack; only nothing was coming out of it today because the mill was quiet. We flew over the tiny town below; from here we saw clearly the long oval of green in the middle and the roofs of the houses about it. The roofs were all different shapes: L or T or H. Buzz squealed and pointed toward his house, and I dipped a wing over Uncle Simon's. There wasn't a soul on the streets; if there were, we could have seen him from up here.

That really surprised me. It was Sunday morning, and almost everyone in town attended church. I turned to Buzz. "Doesn't your mother go to church?" I pointed downward. "Why isn't anyone on the street?"

Buzz looked at me from the corner of his eyes. "They's scared, Lize, Mama say that. Mama say she never go to church again." Then Buzz retreated into the corner of his seat, scrunching down.

"Because of the men down there? Is she afraid of them?"

"Of course, Lize. Naturally." He strung out the syllables. "Na-tur-ally. Same with evy-body."

I turned to Tim. "Then they know what happened to us last night? When we came back from the Callaghans'?"

"Of course. Everyone always knows what happens right off." I didn't doubt it; people in small towns seem sometimes to have a second sense about their neighbors.

I turned back to Tim. "We're going to talk to Bob Rampsie: Oldham, Uncle Simon, Dr. Almquist and I. You think that's a good idea?"

Buzz watched me with wide eyes. Tim and I conversed above the vibration of the propeller and the roar of the engine.

"Don't talk, Lize," said Buzz, drawing back again. "No good, Lize, no good." He reached to cover his ears with trembling hands.

Tim leaned over the seat toward Buzz. "You gotta try, Buzz. Don't you see? Sitting and talking to them, man to man, that's a good thing."

"No good," said Buzz, shaking his head. "No good."

Near the airport I relinquished the control wheel and let Tim and Buzz fly. I'd brought along a cushion for that purpose. Buzz perched on top of it, his legs dangling, while I directed him how to turn to right and left. He wore a silly grin on his face and licked his lips as he turned. Then he began to drool again. For Tim's turn, they exchanged places over the low seat. Tim tried a stall, and Buzz screamed, holding his stomach, as the plane dropped away. Finally, we landed and took the slow drive back to Rowe, buying a softy cone on the way.

We'd just rounded the corner into Rowe when, right before us at the head of the common, we saw a car parked on the road, almost blocking it. A man sat on the hood reading the Sunday papers.

"Here we go again," I muttered, and Buzz ducked down under the dashboard.

On second sight the car wasn't a car, but a truck, the one that I'd seen on the common last night. On the front of the cab, leaping forward into space from the front point of the hood, was a large silver bulldog, snarling directly at my face.

I stopped the car. The common was quiet and warm, gathering the golden light of the day. The only movement out there belonged to some pigeons, pecking out errant grass seeds they'd overlooked last fall.

"Can you move that truck?" I called to the man sitting on the hood. "Who is he, do you know?" I whispered to Tim.

Tim shook his head. "He's a new one." The man was short, dressed in nondescript jeans and an old, ragged shirt. Most of him was hidden by his newspapers. "Rampsie's got a lot of friends."

"Go around, lady," the man called laconically. "Can't you see we're parked here?"

"You're right in the way," I called back. "This is a public thoroughfare."

The man waved carelessly to the other side of the common. "I tol' you, lady, you can go around."

"And you can move it."

"Maybe I will later," he retorted, elaborately turning the page of the paper. "And then again, maybe I won't."

I sat there a minute longer. "Right now you're guilty of an offense. You want to try for a misdemeanor?"

Suddenly a head poked up behind him in the cab of the truck. This time I recognized him; it was Bob Rampsie. He took a look, then jumped down from the cab, stretching like a tawny cat, and ambled slowly toward me with hands in his pockets and eyes on the ground. Finally, he looked up.

He wasn't flirtatious or insinuating like last night or sarcastic or armed with that sly smile. He looked as if he felt rotten, perhaps suffering a hangover.

"You're raising hell," he said to me. "A guy can't even sleep."

"Tough," I answered. Somehow I couldn't help smiling because the situation was so ridiculous. "But how about getting that truck out of the road? Can't you pull it over so someone can get by?"

He draped his hand over the side mirror projecting from my car. "It just ran out of gas there, lady, so that's where it's going to have to stay."

"Too bad," I retorted. "The gas station's two blocks away. It would take three minutes to walk over there. I'll give you ten. After that, I call Chief Oldham."

He let go of my mirror and looked in at me. "My, my, you're a regular hothead, aren't you now? Last night you threatened me, and here you go again. What are you trying to do, stir things up?"

The guy left me breathless. He was bright. Most thugs I'd known in court were dumb.

"Listen, Bob," I said, spinning my tactics, "is there any way we could persuade you to get out of here, to leave everyone alone? This is a small town. What do you get out of hanging around here; there are lots of other places. Move on, OK? Give somebody else a treat."

Now it was his turn to be amused. "But, dahlin'," he said, backing off slightly to look at me, "I *like* it here. So does Charlie. Don't you Charlie?" The man, still sitting on the hood but listening to us, grunted and returned to his paper. "You see, Charlie says he likes it here, too."

I was beginning to flood with frustration and anger. "Bob, please get that truck out of the road, or I *will* call Oldham. I mean it."

Rampsie looked at me and began to laugh. "Call him! Go ahead! See what Chiefy will say. You see what happened to his car last night? Real high wind. You want a high wind to blow your car over, too?"

I thought of this car, which Uncle Simon had owned for so long and entrusted to me, and of the many months it would take for him to replace it.

"Listen," I said, "let's get together, you and your friends and a couple of us, to talk awhile. All right? This afternoon, right out here in the common?"

It took Rampsie by surprise. I could see him turning over the idea in his mind. Finally, he stepped back, clicked his heels together, and bowed slightly. "Ma'am, I'm always game to talk. One thing I sure like to do is talk. Isn't that right, Charlie? Talk, talk, talk." He laughed. "But don't hurry yourself none, lady. I'm not going anyplace. Spending the day right here in this old sunshine."

I looked into the flecks of his eyes while I shifted the car to back up. Suddenly he moved forward to wrench with an abrupt and savage gesture the side mirror off Uncle Simon's car, and he handed the torn aluminum, screws still dangling, through the window to me. "Don't

56

forget this thing," he said, his lips in a grimace. "Wouldn't want ya to get into any accident, just 'cause you couldn't see behind. I'm worrying about you, lady, can't you tell?" Then he stepped aside with another dramatic sweep of his hand.

I could feel something snap inside me. I backed up as if to leave, then gave the old car all the power it could muster at short range. I raced up around the truck, tearing into the green common grass, veered alongside the vehicle, and regained the road on the other side. My wheels threw up mud from the soft ground, spattering the side of the truck and spewing over Charlie, still sitting on the hood. It made a mucky mess of the common. But I arrived intact around the truck and drove into Uncle Simon's driveway a little muddy but triumphant. Through the rearview mirror, I'd glimpsed a momentary flash of Rampsie's furious and incredulous face.

Aunt Chloe had been watching the whole thing from the front window. She led Tim and Buzz, who were both somewhat shaken, into the house protectively while I got on the phone to Oldham.

The chief didn't seem particularly eager for his meeting now; he announced that he'd been digging up his garden.

"But you suggested it, Chief, and I've already invited our mutual friend, Bob Rampsie. I said in an hour."

Finally, he agreed. I called George.

"Sure, I'll be over," he said. His voice was full and resonant on the telephone, and I found myself smiling. "By the way," he was saying, "tell Simon he's got a good-sized bone chip and a hairline crack in that arm. The cast will have to stay on for six weeks."

I glanced over at Uncle Simon; he was peering out the front window again, our favorite indoor sport. Beneath his loose shirt sleeve I glimpsed the gleaming white edge of a new plaster cast.

"I'll tell him, George. It's a shame."

I relayed the message about the fracture to Uncle Simon. "Can you work all right with it?" I asked him. Uncle Simon was a bookkeeper at the mill.

Uncle Simon rubbed his head dejectedly. "Have to change things around some. I'd need two hands for the files, can't type. But Minott can help with that." I dimly remembered Minott Swett, the other bookkeeper.

"You could bring some home so I could help," Aunt Chloe said.

A half hour later George rang the bell. He looked very serious, glancing frequently out onto the common. He was wearing a shirt open at the neck, from which I could see just a tiny curl of dark hair. To my astonishment, I had a sudden wild desire to touch it and had to restrain myself. Why, you're an absolute adolescent, I told myself, almost blushing. Then I remembered the law student I'd cared for not so long ago, and I realized with a shock that he'd looked a lot like George. Dark, curly-haired men with character in their faces like George always did a number on me. Well, the law student had gone back to his high school girlfriend, leaving me to suffer for a while, but I'd got over it. Here was another guy I felt like touching, the first in a long while, and I was already worrying whether I'd get hurt this time, too.

It was a little cool out, and I found myself shivering, so I retrieved my sweater from the closet.

"Group's gathering," said George, pointing. He was wearing a blue cardigan over his open shirt, and I tried hard as I could to ignore the fact that the blue just matched his eyes.

I could make out three men standing together out there; one was Rampsie's tall, hollow-chested form. Near the curb was parked a large maroon Imperial.

"Who in blazes is that?" I asked George. We both squinted into the sun. His sweater was a loose-weave basket stitch; I'd made one just like it for my classmate that time.

"Oldham . . . and"—he hesitated—"I'll be damned. Trumbull."

We strolled out to meet them. Oldham was dressed in the same uniform he'd had on last night; by now it was pretty wrinkled and a little soiled. Suddenly it was receiving a lot of wear.

Trumbull was a large man, squarely and solidly built, dressed in a well-fitting suit. He'd probably been to church even if no one else could get there. Somehow he didn't look as if much bothered him, and I got the feeling that not much stood in his way either. There was an aura of confidence about him. Across his waist stretched a gold watch with a tiny Phi Beta Kappa key dangling from it.

"James," said George, moving toward Trumbull, "this is Lisa Sanderson." I could feel George's palm touching the small of my back as he made the introduction, friendly and open. Trumbull and I shook hands; his skin was smooth as a woman's, nicely groomed with even nails, and I could feel the heavy gold metal of his signet ring.

Rampsie wore a supercilious smile on his face as if he were enjoying the proceedings hugely, and he looked almost agreeable for once. His hair was even combed.

58

"Have you met Bob Rampsie?" Trumbull asked, and was about to introduce us.

"We've met," I said, trying to keep the edge out of my voice. "A couple of times."

Chief Oldham was trying to act as master of ceremonies. "By consent of all parties," he began, "we've decided to meet out here and see if we can't agree. . . ." It sounded very correct, taken from the Rules of Procedure, but odd out in this place.

Trumbull ignored him completely. I'd recognized the insignia of the Harvard Law School on his ring.

"Harvard Law isn't what it used to be," he began telling me. I heard you went to Brooklyn Law School." He chuckled. "They still make the girls sit on one side of the room?"

I could feel my hackles rise. "Last I heard. Sure hope they never change."

"Could we get on with it?" Clyde Oldham asked impatiently. Bob Rampsie was lounging with elaborate disregard against a tree. Suddenly I saw someone behind him, shorter and even thinner than Bob.

"Who's your friend?" I asked Bob.

"Oh, did I forget?" Oldham asked. "Meet Jaimie Rampsie, Bob's brother." The boy appeared almost undernourished, with a rush of acne across his face. He didn't move when he was introduced, but his face contorted in an embarrassed grimace.

"We want to know if there's any way to clear out the common," I told Trumbull. It was obvious that he was here as attorney for the Rampsies, that this wasn't a casual stroll, and that the maroon job parked at the edge of the common belonged to him. "There's been a lot of running around in the night, scaring people, and the music goes on till morning sometimes."

"Such as when?" Trumbull asked.

So I told him about last night and Uncle Simon's arm. "Bob Rampsie, here, struck him, and the arm's going to be in a cast for six weeks."

"That's true," George said. "I took the X rays this morning. There's a nasty hematoma—"

"You're sure it was Bob?" Trumbull persisted. "It's very dark out here at night."

I pointed to the streetlights.

"Well, it could have been an accident," Trumbull said. "Those things happen. Maybe you were blocking the sidewalk, and he fell against you, trying to get around."

The man was slippery as an eel. "We weren't blocking the sidewalk, James. We'd been walking the Callaghans home. There'd been so much going on out there that we didn't want them to go home alone. That's a pretty sorry state—"

"You've seen all of this, what she's referring to, George?" Trumbull fingered his paisley tie, making sure it was still tucked neatly inside his vest.

"Not directly. But my patients have been telling me about it. Been going on for two, three weeks now."

Oldham had been standing quietly, listening to the exchange.

"Tell him about your car, Chief." I pointed to Rampsie. "They turned it over right in front of our house when the chief came over to investigate the noise. I had to drive him home."

"*Who* turned it over, Clyde? Did you get a good look at them?"

Oldham shrugged. "Didn't see them do it exactly. But those boys were making lots of noise like Miss Sanderson says."

I didn't think Oldham had it in him!

Trumbull glared at Oldham. "Then you're going to back Miss Sanderson's charges?"

The chief shook his head slowly. "Yes and no. There's damage to the cruiser, that's a fact. It's a mess on one side, with a big dent. I don't like that." He scratched his head for a moment, then spoke in a conciliatory tone to Trumbull. "You know as well as me, James, that boys will be boys, and this here is a pretty small burg. So I says, 'Live and let live.' That's what I been telling Miss Sanderson. There's room for everybody, long as they behave. Rowe isn't one of those high-type suburbs you read about with a fleet of policemen. We gotta do as best we can." He gestured toward Bob Rampsie. Now Jaimie, looking pale, stood beside his brother. "These kids grew up here, and I don't think we should turn our backs on them."

I was getting heady on all that altruism; it was blowing across the common from Oldham in gale force. "We aren't," I snapped. "Nobody's turning his back on anyone."

George spoke up angrily. "You've got a man with a broken arm, Chief. Can you explain that away just as easily?"

The chief looked at George and shrugged again. "All I'm saying, Doc, is for God's sake, let's give the kids a chance." He turned to Bob. "You'll behave yourself, Bob? You don't want to upset folks like this. Rowe's a law-abiding community."

"Was," I corrected him.

60

"You've seen too much of the big city," Trumbull said to me. "Up here things aren't so high-pressure. We do things differently. High-pressure law isn't for us." I almost laughed. He obviously didn't know my law practice, the legal consultations I have with kids on the front steps of the courthouse or even in the back alleys behind the jail.

"Bob will keep his nose clean, I'm sure," continued Trumbull good-naturedly, as if he were addressing a public gathering in this empty common. "He's got our confidence."

Well, he didn't have mine, but I was willing to try anything. "All right, James. I don't know why, but I'll stick my neck out if you will. There's a sucker born every minute."

I meant me. Apparently Bob Rampsie thought I meant him, for he started to protest.

Trumbull placed his hand on Rampsie's arm. "Don't get upset, Bob. She doesn't mean it. It just takes awhile to get used to our ways."

"Cut it out, James," said George. "She's almost as much of a native around here as you are. She doesn't need that."

Trumbull turned over his neat hands before him, studying the nails. "No offense. Let's call the meeting adjourned and start all over again, clean slate. Chief, you keep the peace, and Bob will help you. No more problems."

Suddenly I felt as if I'd been disturbing the citizens of Rowe. With his insidious persistence, Trumbull was trying to do a number on all of us. I felt for a moment as if I'd been conned by a master. In that moment I wanted to protest, swear, shout. Instead, I laughed to myself, turned to George, and asked him if he'd like to come home with me for a cup of coffee. When we turned silently away, walking slowly without turning back, I wondered what they were thinking. Did they really think we were vanquished? Then I heard Trumbull laugh, and then Rampsie, and I knew exactly what they thought.

7

"Could you give me a lift back from Boston?" I asked George. We sat behind the house, looking toward Uncle Simon's barn. The swallows building nests under the eaves of the old structure flashed over our heads.

George leaned back casually, his hands behind his head. He looked so relaxed that I wanted to smile and, again, touch him; instead I laid my hand on the arm of his chair.

"Sure. I was coming back on Wednesday, but I'll delay if you'd like. How can I get in touch with you?"

I jotted down my phone number on a scrap of paper. Then I could contain it no longer. I told George what Tim had related to me about Buzz's torture at the hands of the Rampsie crowd. I'd thought that someone responsible should know, particularly a doctor; that horrendous knowledge had been prodding my conscience like a thorn.

George was stunned, as I knew he'd be. I could see his jaw muscles clench as he listened.

"Buzz may need some help," I said. "Tim told me today. He isn't healing properly. Could you get to him?"

George had begun to pace around the little patio. "I examine the kids at school once a year, with the help of a Tremont doctor. I could easily do it early. The man up there would understand, and I'd make sure to get Buzz in my group."

George drove me to the airport; his daughter accompanied him. She had George's dark bronze-blond hair and almond-shaped eyes. She was a quiet, well-behaved child, but subdued.

"Do you know my brother, Tim?" I asked her.

She nodded shyly.

"You'll have to come over to our house soon," I told her.

I showed them the plane, paid the attendant for parking space, made a walk-around inspection, and took off. As I flew over George and Clarissa, I dipped a wing and jazzed the power in response to their waves.

Strong tailwinds carried me back to Boston rapidly. I peered down on crowded freeways, thronged with people; up here I could see two other planes, both transatlantic jets circling for landing at Logan. As I looked down on Boston, I wondered: Was this the real world, or was it in Rowe? Did anyone really care what was happening in a town of two thousand people? When I landed, I picked up the Boston *Globe*; six people had been shot in Boston yesterday, and an old lady had been garroted in her apartment.

So where was Rowe? Well, you see, it's this small town in Vermont where some guys are making a lot of noise at night; they mistreated a kid, made obscene gestures, and blocked the road.

Really? Pardon me while I yawn. Wait until I tell you what happened to my aunt Minnie or Jody or Hester down in New York!

So where was the real world? Why get stirred up about a handful of people in that town, where did you say it was, in Vermont?

Because they're my relatives, you see, and they live in the only place I can call home and because I love them, understand?

Sure. I come from somewhere I call home, too.

In the next two days I made some order of my apartment and called Helen Roentsch, a good friend of mine, and one of those fortunates who had sat on one side of the room with me at the Brooklyn Law School. She understood my kind of law, saw some of the same kids that I did, and we invariably followed each other through the same courtrooms and before the same judges.

"Can you cover me for a while?" I asked her. "I need to spend some time in Vermont."

"Vacation?" she asked me.

"Not exactly. Unless I'm very much mistaken."

I heaved a sigh of relief when she said she'd see my clients; I'd do the same for her sometime.

Then I began cleaning up the stuff on my desk. I'd been representing a small local homeowner against an insurance company. While a man

63

was turning his car around in my client's driveway, he inadvertently ran over some berry bushes planted at the edge of my client's property. This insurance company was one of the big ones, the kind that liked to send up skyscrapers into the blue to tickle the Lord up there. The insurance man was on the phone, asking me what my client thought his bushes were worth.

Well, I hadn't the vaguest idea, and neither did my client. Just then a colleague stepped into my office over a bond case, so I turned to him and said, "Tom, what would you say a berry bush is worth? Just off the top of your head?"

He pondered a moment. "Well, I'm not exactly sure, but somewhere around six dollars."

I reported to the insurance company's man on the phone, saying: "Our expert says the going rate for berry bushes is six dollars a bush. Your client destroyed eight bushes. That's forty-eight dollars." I was looking over at Tom while I was talking, smiling at him in a self-satisfied way.

The insurance man said, "Oh, where did your expert get that figure?"

Well, I was trapped; I was also in a hurry, Tom was waiting, and I was worried about another client, so I said, "That's from the National Berry Gardener's Price-Gougers' Handbook"—or something like that.

I hung up the phone and had to look Tom in the eye. *That* wasn't easy. "Forget you heard that," I told him. I was really ashamed, squirming underneath, and thinking to myself: You idiot, aren't you supposed to be an honest defender, exemplar of the law, and here you are, perjuring yourself. Not only that, but you've got a witness, and he'll never talk to you again.

But Tom was a lot older and wiser than I: he'd been around the world a bit, so he said, "All right, forget it. So maybe you lied to them when you shouldn't have, but one of these days you'll learn that they're lying to you, too."

So Tom and I continued to work on the bond case, we had paper spread all over the desk, when the phone rang. It was the insurance man about the berry bushes.

"I've got that book right in front of me now," he said to me, without even a hint of duplicity. "You remember, that book you were mentioning? Well, it's been supplemented. The cost of a berry bush is now four dollars and fifty cents. So we owe your client only thirty-six bucks, not forty-eight."

I hung up the phone and had hysterics right on Tom's shoulder. "Come on," he said, "I'll buy you a drink." Of course, that shot the next two hours, but I needed it. I figured the guy had earned his twelve bucks. I saw no reason why that company shouldn't build another skyscraper right next to the first, and line it with solid gold. It could be a monument to all the suckers, and I could have my name in gold-leaf near the door along with a million others: *Lisa Sanderson, Who Helped Make This Building Possible*. I could come each day and touch the plate just for kicks.

On Tuesday night I called George at Mass General to see if he was still leaving the next morning or if I had to catch the bus. For a moment I found myself listening to his voice again, and I had to shake myself to hear what he was saying.

"I was just about to call you," he said. "There's something going on up there, and I think we'd better leave tonight."

The delight of the ride north with George assuaged my anxiety about my relatives for a moment, and I almost didn't hear the tension in his voice.

"Why, what's going on, George?" Then I felt the cold grip of something on my heart, and my thoughts raced instantly to Tim and Chloe and Simon.

"Apparently the strike is about to start, and pickets are mobbing the place. At least that's what my housekeeper says. She reports that most of the people up there marching around aren't even from town; she's never seen them before."

"I'll be ready," I told George. "Give me a half hour."

He was down in front of the apartment ringing the bell in twenty-five minutes. By then I'd been waiting for five minutes. I'd never dreamed I had so few belongings when it came to moving out fast. I could live in a closet, I was thinking, so why did I bother to rent an entire apartment? A goodly portion of my earthly belongings were stuffed into a valise. When I looked up, there was George standing in the light of the lobby; I took in a sharp breath of air when I saw him, just in the relief and pleasure of it. He looked worried.

"When did your housekeeper call?" I asked.

"About noon. But I was making rounds and couldn't get back to her until a couple hours later. She's apt to panic a bit, but I thought I'd better see what was going on for myself." He picked up my valise as if it were filled with feathers and placed it on the back seat of his car while I slid in front.

65

It was dark by now, and the traffic appeared as ribbons of light streaming by. George moved the car out of the city deftly and carefully, driving beside the dark mass of the Charles River, beneath the lights of the towers.

A long way up the road, when our eyes had become blurry from watching out for traffic, we stopped for a cup of coffee and a hamburger. I looked at the clock in the diner: ten o'clock. Another hour to go.

As we drove I found myself longing to place my head on George's shoulder and to press myself against him, but I resisted successfully; instead, I laid my hand on the cloth of his coat on the seat beside me. Watch it, old girl, I told myself. Let's not run over; you got hurt once, remember? Watch it.

But I smiled at him and said, "I really appreciate the lift, George."

"Glad to do it," he answered. "Besides, it's nice to have company. It's a long drive."

Am I special at all? I wondered. Am I special company? Does it make any difference that it's *me?* I rubbed my fingers over the tweed of his coat.

"Where do you come from?" I asked him, looking away into the night. "Boston?"

He shook his head. "The Midwest, a little town in Wisconsin. Tell you the truth, it looks something like Rowe."

"You've still got relatives back there?"

"No. Both my mother and father died when I was a kid. My grandmother raised me, even helped me through medical school. Grandfather was a doctor, the old kind you hear about who went out in buggies or sleds to see patients. He used to let me go along with him sometimes."

So I told George about my parents, killed on this very road we were traveling. I felt pretty close to him, telling him about my parents.

"They were really good people," I said, "and sometimes I miss them like crazy. There's just no substitute. . . . " When my voice fell off, George reached over in sympathy and pressed my hand. It felt warm and strong and comforting. "But Aunt Chloe and Uncle Simon are wonderful, and I love them . . . " I said, and my throat began to ache.

I found my voice again. "What made *you* settle in Rowe in particular? There are lots of other little towns in this radius from Boston."

"Because some of my wife's relatives used to live in Tremont. We'd come through Rowe to visit them, and I thought it an awfully pretty town. That common—with the snow on it—made me think of Wisconsin."

The sky had become overcast, the stars snuffed out by encroaching clouds; by the time we reached the road to Rowe a light rain was falling, and George had to keep the windshield wipers going.

We knew that something was going on before we rounded that last curve; there was a glow over the trees and the heavy smell of burning in the air. As we turned into the common, before us was a huge bonfire with sparks from its incandescent cone shooting into the night sky in a giant pillar of fire and charred ash. At least fifty people were running, or shuffling, or dancing about it as if in some kind of pagan orgy. In that firelighted arena, everyone appeared to be wearing a blood-red mask. I looked anxiously toward Uncle Simon's to see only blackness. Nor could I make out any lights in any of the other houses around the common.

"I'll walk you in," said George, taking my arm in Uncle Simon's driveway. I could see the anxiety in George's face; he was worried about Clarissa.

We didn't need lights; the roaring flames lit our way to the back door of the house. At first there was no answer when I knocked, and I could feel alarm surge through my body like an electric shock. Where had everyone gone? But I'd forgotten to tell Aunt Chloe I'd be back tonight. I knocked with a kind of syncopated beat, thinking that maybe she'd look out, and thank God, suddenly her face appeared above me at the window. In a moment a small light flashed on, and the door opened with a rush.

George said good-night hastily and returned to his car. I watched his lights move slowly up the circle around the common in the opposite direction from the fire. Then I turned to Aunt Chloe. "What in heaven's name's going on out there?"

"Come inside," she said. "Quickly, quickly." Tim was sitting beside the front door with Uncle Simon, peering out those two front windows. They didn't even comment on my return; they were staring as if their lives depended on what they saw.

"What is it?" I asked again. "Strike rally?"

Uncle Simon grimaced. "It's out of hand. At first only speeches. Now they're whooping it up, supplying free beer."

About midnight, explosions began to erupt from the fire. "Gunpowder," said Uncle Simon. "Someone's throwing it into the fire." Even here inside the house we could smell it burning, hear the reports, and see the flashes. It felt as if we'd just been invaded by an unnamed enemy which had encamped out there in the midst of our houses.

There was absolutely no chance of our sleeping, even if we tried.

"Is all that beer coming from Rampsie's?" I asked Tim.

Tim pointed to the lights at Rampsie's store. "Pops brought in a big load today. Truck backed right up to the door. Half the store is filled with beer cases." Good old Pops Rampsie sure knew how to turn a profit!

"Where are his nephews? Are they missing out on all this excitement?"

"I saw 'em," answered Tim, his voice a little hushed as if they might overhear. "They had that truck earlier, cruising around. They're out there somewhere. . . . "

Uncle Simon and Aunt Chloe suddenly determined that they were going to ignore the hubbub and prepare for bed. Well, if they could, I could despite the fact that I felt a little jumpy and startled every time I heard another explosion. I walked into Tim's room under the pretext of saying good-night to him, but I needed to keep on talking and to feel another presence. We visited idly for ten minutes, trying to pretend that those sounds didn't exist. Then I went resolutely to bed, cramming a pillow over my head to muffle the explosions.

I was all right until three in the morning. Then I heard a thump on the front door and the sound of laughter.

Oh, God, I thought, looking out my window. The fire on the common had waned into a mound of red-hot embers, and by now the dancing furies had mostly gone home, but downstairs, outside the front door, were a few half-stoned rowdies.

Aunt Chloe was already up, and so was Uncle Simon; I could hear their slippered feet in the hall outside my room. Timmy was knocking on my door and whispering through the crack. I was out of bed in two seconds. Down below were four men; I could make them out in the light from the upstairs window. One was Bob Rampsie, another was Keaton, but the other two I'd not seen before.

"What are they doing?" I whispered to Aunt Chloe.

She shook her head nervously. "They were over hammering on the Sardoes' door a few minutes ago," she whispered back. "I think they're looking for more liquor."

"Are the doors all locked?"

Uncle Simon nodded. "Don't worry, I double-checked it twice before I went to bed."

Downstairs there was a banging on the door. We were huddled in the upstairs hall, with the dark stairwell before us. "We know you're in there," somebody was calling. "We know you're in there, so open the door." They all sounded pretty drunk, and now they'd started clubbing at the door with something. I could see it glowing in the dark and smoking. A brand from the fire!

"What are they going to do?" asked Aunt Chloe in a frightened voice.

"Be quiet, don't say anything," warned Uncle Simon softly.

"I know who's up there," called a voice, haltingly, drunkenly. I knew very well it was Rampsie: I couldn't miss the inflection, even though he was slurring his words. "Come on out, baby," said the voice, singsong and mocking.

"Come on out," called another voice, echoing the first. "We wouldn't hurt you. Don't you want to play?"

"Pussy, pussy," called Rampsie. "Pretty pussy wants to play."

Suddenly there was a tinkle of breaking glass, and Aunt Chloe jumped. "What is it?" she begged Uncle Simon tearfully.

"They've broken the front window," he answered, sucking in his breath.

"Can they get in?" I asked Uncle Simon quietly.

"They can do anything they want to. But that window's pretty narrow, and it's a few feet off the ground, so it might not be too easy."

I knew that the front door was constructed of heavy oak and that they'd have trouble breaking it in. Then I smelled smoke, and I realized that it wasn't left over from the fireworks.

"The curtains!" Aunt Chloe moaned, leaning out from the upstairs windows. "They're setting fire to the house." She'd begun to wring her hands and cry.

I ran around the upstairs, looking for something to drop on them, anything, and then I saw the big old thunder pot Aunt Chloe kept in the back bedroom to soak clothes in. I grabbed it, tore into the bathroom, and started to fill it with hot water from the tap. Uncle Simon was right behind me. He was handicapped by that injured arm, although he discovered he could steady it while I adjusted the water. In a few minutes it was full, and together we carried it to the window, staggering slightly under its weight. The steam seeped from it in clouds, and it was so hot we had to use bathroom towels to keep from singeing our hands.

Uncle Simon slowly eased open the window; luckily it glided

soundlessly, while I rested the heavy pot on the sill. Then, working together with an unspoken effort, we tipped the hot contents of the pot onto the men below us.

For one moment there was a stunned silence; then shrieks. Rampsie'd found his voice with a vengeance, and all four of them were screeching obscenities up at us in the dark night. Someone was kicking at the front door as if to break it in, but it was holding. It sounded as if all the demons of hell had come to plague us.

"You want more?" Uncle Simon asked, and I nodded quickly. We filled the pot again and lugged it back to the window. Cascading through my anguished head was a picture of those castellans of the Middle Ages protecting their domains from the invader. If I'd had boiling oil, I'd have chucked that out on them, too. I could feel one part of me reverting to infuriated animal, another viewing the transformation with alarm, the third saying, "I don't give a damn." My legal, dispassionate mind had just gone out the window with the water.

There was a heavy smell of fire from downstairs now. One of the men outside turned and hurled up at us the burning torch he'd used to set fire to Aunt Chloe's draperies. It hit the house right next to the window where we were watching but dropped harmlessly to the ground below.

"We've got to get to the fire downstairs," gasped Uncle Simon, but Tim was already partway down the stairs.

The drapes were made of some kind of fabric that melted but didn't burn, and the gloppy stuff had dripped all over Aunt Chloe's couch and a crocheted afghan she'd taken two years to make. All the time we were running back and forth to the kitchen for towels and water, she was crying. I didn't blame her when I peered around at the damage: the window, couch, afghan, draperies.

But, I wondered, what would have happened if those men had broken into the house; what fate would have befallen all of us? I shuddered at the thought because I'd just about come around to Aunt Chloe's way of thinking: Those men hadn't a speck of conscience among them. I'd seen that plainly in Bob Rampsie's face just before we'd cascaded that scalding water on him, the bestial set to the man's features. He wasn't like men I'd known before. Why, he had a kind of permanent snarl to his face, and a distinct hunted look, yet he was the hunter.

The next morning the common was a disaster scene. Litter, smoking ruins from the fire, even uprooted trees disfigured the place. I couldn't believe it. Our front door was battered and blackened as if an enraged bear had tried to bash it in.

Buzz sat on the sidewalk, whimpering. "They knocked on our d-door," he wailed. "Yelled at my ma. We were so scared we hid down behind the furnace."

"Listen, why don't you come stay with us?" I asked. "Neighbors helping neighbors, right?"

Buzz brightened and ran to tell his mother.

Clyde Oldham was inspecting the damage to the common. I marched out to see him. "Chief, we need that circuit judge, and the sooner the better. Why, you can see for yourself—"

Clyde nodded. "If we get on his schedule now, maybe when he gets here in a few weeks—"

"A few weeks! You're not serious? We can't wait a few weeks. We need him now."

"Well . . . well. Can't guarantee a thing, of course."

Then Tim and I went to see George. He was seeing patients, so we sat down to wait in his reception room. Tim picked up a magazine and began to read, but I perched at the edge of my chair, admiring the old high ceilings in this house and the intricate carving around the moldings, evidence of someone's fine old workmanship in a less hurried age. Across from me was a woman I recognized, a friend of Aunt Chloe's.

71

"I'm Bertha Parks," she said, suddenly recognizing me. "I'm picking up my prescriptions from Dr. George; then me and my husband's leaving town fast as we can. You see what those . . . thugs . . . did to the common last night? Fine goings-on!"

Just then George opened the door; he was wearing a white coat and looked so great that my heart skipped a beat. He ushered Mrs. Parks into his office, then pressed my arm. He smelled marvelously of disinfectant.

"Lisa," he said, his brows drawn together, "I've already called Boston, told them I can't get down this week or perhaps for a while. Even tried to call you last night to see how you were, but the phones were out. Clarissa was terrified."

I could feel the relief flood into me. "I'm so *glad* you'll stay," I breathed. "I can't tell you. . . ."

"Well, I figured we're going to need everyone," he said thoughtfully. "Just in case."

I told him about the damage to Aunt Chloe's house. "Everyone's frightened. You can almost feel it in the air." The prickles rose on the back of my neck when I just thought about last night.

George pressed my arm again. "I'll call you," he said, and I felt happy prickles this time.

When we returned to Uncle Simon's, the Sardoes had already moved in; I hadn't even had time to mention it to Aunt Chloe, but she was acting as if it had been *her* idea. We fell to work clearing out debris from her shattered living room; when we threw out the old draperies, the chemical reek began to improve. But that large burned spot on the wall where drapery goo had oozed all over it wasn't going to disappear until the room was repainted. Yet when she turned over the cushions on the couch and camouflaged the back with a blanket, the place at least looked habitable again.

It was Saturday, I suddenly realized, when Timmy had to work at Rampsie's store; usually he worked part of the morning both days of the weekend. I was just putting on my jacket when the chief called.

"Just got through to Judge Bream," he announced proudly. "He'd barely come in off the golf course. Sounded concerned-like when I told him what'd been happening. Be here Tuesday mornin'." Oldham's voice carried the inflections of triumph. "Just thought I'd tell you."

"Thanks, Chief Oldham. That's *wonderful* news." I circled the date on Aunt Chloe's calendar, even though I wasn't going to have a bit of trouble remembering. I felt pretty triumphant myself.

Then Buzz and I walked Tim to Rampsie's store. It was an old structure, appearing to have been a house at an earlier age; it was two stories, stark and austere because no other houses were immediately adjacent to it. No softening landscaping bordered it, only unkempt grass and stiff, tall weeds, setting it distinctly apart from the other carefully tended houses around the common. Its white paint was peeling badly across the front, and in some places the intact paint had yellowed, especially on the porch which wrapped itself around the front of the building. It was necessary to climb six or seven steps to gain entry to the store.

I hadn't gone inside the place for ages. It probably hadn't changed in ten years. Worn floorboards ran the entire length of the store, oiled with some kind of compound kept in a can near the door. Near the meat counter above our heads hung several lengths of flypaper, black with assorted fly carcasses. Rampsie was behind the counter slicing meat, an ancient relic with skin like yellow parchment, the thin veins blue across his skull. Part of one of his fingers was missing, a fleshy stump, and I wondered if someone had once inadvertently taken it home one day with his hot dogs.

Pops beckoned Tim to the cash register at the front counter without uttering a word, and Tim leaped forward. When I rounded the corner of a row of foodstuffs to pick up some supplies, I almost ran into Jaimie Rampsie; I'd never really spoken to the boy before—he was always hanging somewhere in the background whenever the Rampsie crowd gathered.

"Hi, Jaimie." The boy stood looking at me shyly and quizzically, his wrists hanging out of a jacket that must have fitted him three years ago. There was a wary, almost frightened look about his dark, intelligent eyes. He had a shock of unruly brown hair that tumbled over his forehead; he shoved it aside with quick, nervous gestures from time to time. He looked like Bob Rampsie, only forced through some kind of finer mold.

The boy seemed distinctly uncomfortable. He knotted his hand into fists at his sides. "Hello, Lisa." I figured he'd heard my name from Tim. For some reason, I felt uncomfortable, too, and cast about for something to say.

"You like working with your uncle, Jaimie?"

73

He thought a moment. "It's all right." There was a hint of a smile about his mouth.

"You worked for him long?"

He nodded again. "I live here." He pointed to the rear of the store, where I could see a door. It looked particularly gloomy and dark back there. When I turned around again, the boy had vanished.

Buzz and I walked slowly home, Buzz amusing himself by stepping on all the cracks in the worn sidewalk, so it took us a good half hour to get there. The common was ominously quiet. On an undamaged bench to one side, near the sidewalk, lay a somnambulant cat, soaking up the spring sunshine. The trees were shedding their pale green blossoms all over the cat and the bench. If one didn't look any farther, beyond the stout oaks toward last night's debacle, it could have appeared an utterly peaceful, romantic spot that painters might have loved in the Victorian era.

I helped Aunt Chloe cook dinner; like most New Englanders, they often ate their main meal at noon. I suggested pizza, to be made with the ingredients I'd purchased at Rampsie's store, and instructed Aunt Chloe and Mrs. Sardoe in its intricate manufacture. Mrs. Sardoe, her gray hair pulled back in a bun behind her round face, enveloped in a large apron, was a master at slicing mushrooms, I soon discovered, and I quickly put Aunt Chloe to work grating cheese. Aunt Chloe had never made pizza, so I demonstrated the intricacies of tossing the dough. I didn't want to tell her right off that it was the only thing I knew how to cook; she'd find that out soon enough anyway.

Then Buzz and I set out to meet Timmy again, strolling leisurely.

We were almost at the store when someone came shooting out the front door as if he'd been fired from a gun. Buzz and I threw ourselves off the narrow sidewalk to let the human projectile go by.

In a minute Pops Rampsie rushed through the door, yelling like a banshee. The first man almost crashed into us as we crowded off the sidewalk. He was a big man, and I knew he was one of the crowd out on the common, but I couldn't think which one. It wasn't Rampsie or Keaton. Then I recognized him: fat Hunk Hudman, churning down the road as fast as his stubby legs would take him.

Rampsie was still bellowing, shaking his fist and swearing, when suddenly I could see why; from Hudman's pockets hung lengths of sausage and packs of cold cuts, and something was falling out of his sleeves: cigarettes!

Rampsie was running after him, and despite his age, he almost caught Hudman, who by now had bogged down and almost tripped up on a length of sausage dangling about his ankles. Buzz and I stood there, bug-eyed; I almost felt like cheering, as if I were watching the race of the century, the fat cat and the old turtle. But no go, Rampsie was too old; he came back toward us, muttering and swearing and uttering strings of magnificent oaths. He didn't even see us as he stalked back into his store, where I could hear the front door slam with a clatter.

Buzz and I followed in Rampsie's wake and sidled up to Tim, who was unloading produce at the front of the store. He looked just a little stricken.

"What happened?" I asked him. I could still hear old Rampsie cursing at the back of the store, and there was a kind of pall over the place. The three or four customers were exiting fast, fearing bloodshed.

Tim shook his head. "Hudman again." He sounded pretty upset.

"You mean he swiped all that stuff?" I asked Tim. Buzz had begun to help Tim unpack, crouching on his haunches before the produce crate just like Tim.

"Sure. Does it all the time." His voice was subdued but emphatic. "It's about time Pops caught him."

"I thought Hudman was one of Bob Rampsie's best buddies."

"He is. But Pops can't stand the guy. Hudman's always swiping stuff from him. Pops knows it, too, but he never caught him until now."

I chuckled a little in spite of myself. That memory was going to stay with me for a long while: the blubbering, winded, fat Hudman puffing by us like a laboring penguin.

Then I had an idea. Pops was haranguing a reluctant customer in a strident voice about how he was victimized, how people robbed him blind, and how ungrateful some he knew could be, taking advantage of a poor old man.

Now there was nothing much to endear me to Pops; he was as hard as nails and looked a little like a thin rooster about to be put on the block, with his taut neck sinews, complaining, complaining. Jaimie Rampsie was behind the meat counter with him, trying to put things back in order, tidying up all the leftover meat scraps and scrubbing down with a sponge.

So I walked over to Pops, deciding it was now or never to make my pitch.

"Pops, I'm Lisa Sanderson, Tim's sister." I stuck out my hand. "Nice to see you again after so long."

He managed a kind of dry-lipped smile over his bad teeth and shook my hand. "Hello, Lisa," he said. "You back fer long?"

"A while." Then I looked around. "Sorry about what just happened. Can I help in any way?"

"You help?" He looked at me. "Don't I wish!" He swore under his breath again, returned to slicing meat, and began to mutter something about young pack rats. Time to make my pitch.

"Pops, did you know that the circuit judge was coming here next Tuesday? I mean, he's going to be at the town hall."

Pops held his carving knife suspended. "The circuit judge? What's he comin' fer?" By now the two or three customers left in the store were standing next to us, taking in what we were saying.

"He's going to hear some complaints from the citizens of Rowe. Disorderly conduct. All that noise on the common, those explosions of gunpowder. Some of those people broke windows in Uncle Simon's house and started a fire." I took a deep breath. "Would you be willing to enter a complaint for the theft here in your store? Against Hudman, I mean?"

All sound stopped in the store. Pops was looking at me incredulously, so that I could see his little eyes moving, searching inwardly. I realized very well the enormity of what I was asking him; both Bob and Jaimie lived with him, and Hunk was a good friend of theirs. It would be a risk for Pops, and we both knew it.

Pops was still standing there, as if in a trance. Tim was immobile next to me, staring up at the old man. Buzz hadn't the vaguest idea what was going on, he was bored to death by all this talk, and I could feel the gentle tug of his hand in mine.

I felt a little rotten standing there, tempting Pops Rampsie, but I stayed planted before him without moving.

Finally, Pops looked at me. "By gor, I'll do it!" he said vehemently. "By gor I will. Teach him something, that one." He contemplated me, his head turned slightly sideways. "When you say that judge is coming?"

"Tuesday. Can you remember, or would you like me to remind you? Tim can run over and tell you when he's here."

Pops began to slice meat again. "By gor, I won't forget," he repeated again, almost inaudibly, and soon he was taking orders as the customers crowded forward. Strike another mark in our column, I thought optimistically. First the judge, now Pops. Maybe we could persuade the judge there was something going on in Rowe after all.

We made a feast of the pizza, and Tim and Buzz pronounced it the gourmet event of their lives, even replacing the hot dog. I was on a temporary, very shaky pedestal, because soon I'd have to produce something else to demonstrate my epicurean acumen, and I didn't know anything else. All right, I'd read cookbooks all night if necessary, studiously and thoroughly like lawbooks, and dredge up something magnificently exotic.

All afternoon, the common remained blissfully quiet. Tim announced he was going to a Scout meeting over at the Callaghans'. Stu used to hold them on Sunday nights, I could remember, but now he'd rescheduled them for Saturday afternoons so that the boys wouldn't be out after dark.

"What are you doing in Scouts?" I asked Tim. He'd been a member of Stu Callaghan's troop for years.

"We're almost finished for the summer," he answered. "We're practicing in Mr. Callaghan's yard for the parade."

"What parade? Isn't the Fourth of July kind of far away?"

"Memorial Day. It's an even bigger parade than the Fourth."

I'd never been here on Memorial Day. "Where do you march?"

"We meet out there." Tim pointed toward the common. "We march around it; then we go down the road toward the mill. The Scouts always plant a tree in the common on Memorial Day." That explained the small grove of young saplings on the far side!

"Have you got a band?" I asked. I had difficulty imagining a parade in Rowe—there were so few people. But I could remember a parade on the Fourth, with everyone in town in it: the VFW in their old uniforms, firemen in a polished and waxed fire truck. All the wives were there as auxiliaries, and everyone carried some kind of flag advertising his affiliation. Perhaps I could think up one, like the Peripatetic Lawyers of America, and join the legions.

I stood on the front walk and, trying not to laugh, watched Buzz and Tim head around the common to the meeting; they proceeded in fits and starts, jogging a second, then stopping for a minute to discover something down a crack in the sidewalk, then spurting ahead once more. They passed the Macys', the Brittons', Rampsie's store, and finally opened the Callaghans' gate. I could just see them beyond the trees as they disappeared inside the Callaghans' front door. Two or three other boys arrived as I sat on the front steps watching. Aunt Chloe had handed Tim a note asking Minnie and Stu if they wanted to attempt their weekly bridge game or let it go for the first time in years. In this town, I'd noticed, although most people had telephones, they usually wrote notes; I'd concluded that it wasn't so much mistrust of the system as triumph of the personal approach, cutting out the middlewoman, who sat there plugging in the wires and who, incidentally, might be listening.

I was still sitting in the afternoon sun on the front steps, reading the paper, when a small truck drove up. It wasn't Bob Rampsie's flatbed truck, but a smaller one. Out jumped five guys, pretty young, say in their early twenties, who began to pull out a few lengths of precut wood from the truck. Soon they were hammering and shouting orders back and forth. One of them was already on the beer shuttle to Rampsie's store.

As I continued to watch, I could see that they were building some kind of platform, about four feet high. I figured maybe it was a reviewing stand, only I couldn't decide who was going to do the reviewing; everyone I knew was *in* the parade. Finally, they threw their stuff back in the truck, kicked the supports of the structure to make sure it was solid, then stood around admiring it for a while, drinking the beer. I thought maybe they should hand out raffle tickets; whoever guessed what this thing was could have it.

Soon one of the guys had brought out some big posters, hammered in a couple of nails, and hung the posters right on the ark. The letters were big enough; I could read them from here. STRIKE NOW, said the first; in a couple of minutes up went the other: ON STRIKE.

Uncle Simon, who'd heard the hammering, came out to join me.

"It's official, Uncle Simon. You really *are* on strike now. Do they still want you to go in for a while each day?"

We sat there, looking thoughtfully out into the common. "I'd hate not going to work," he said quietly. "Every day for almost forty years I've gone to work, even some Saturdays and, yes, an occasional Sunday. I'd hate not to work. If they need me, I'll go."

I pointed out into the common. "Do you know those men?" One of them was now standing on the platform, and some passersby had stopped to look.

Uncle Simon shaded his eyes with his good hand. "Never saw them before in my life. Union must have brought them in from outside."

"Then why don't they organize down by the mill? Wouldn't it serve

78

their purposes better to picket down there?" In all the strikes I'd had to do with, pickets marched around the place of employment, keeping people out who wanted to get in, and tried to make life so generally miserable for management that it upped the ante for wages or conditions or whatever.

"Oh, they're already picketing, but nobody hears the speeches down there, so they came up here. Here you can't miss 'em."

You certainly couldn't. One of those men had a megaphone, and he was bellowing at the gathering crowd. He was spouting a long string of abuses that mill workers had had to endure over the years; when the megaphone waved in my direction, I could hear him talking about vacation pay.

"Don't you have vacation pay and sick leave already?" I asked Uncle Simon.

He nodded. "But I think they're after something else."

I glanced quickly at Uncle Simon. "What could they be after?"

Uncle Simon still peered thoughtfully out across the common. "I think they're toughs just like Rampsie and his crew. I don't believe they really give a good goddamn about the mill."

As we stared out across the common toward the gathering crowd, I wasn't sure whether to believe Uncle Simon or not. There was genuine interest in what the men were saying because people had gathered before that makeshift platform and were listening attentively to what was being said.

I was still thinking about Uncle Simon's words, worrying subtly about the town, when swinging around the circle of the common, hell-bent, came the flatbed truck. To me that thing was a harbinger of evil, and arrayed on its back were the disciples; I could see five men on it, two in the cab and three in back, their legs dangling off the edge like dancing dolls. Once more it stopped in the middle of the street, the driver doused his engine, and the men piled out of the vehicle and walked abreast, loosely casual, surveying the scene.

Aunt Chloe'd also seen the truck; she slid quickly through the open front door like one magnetized by the action out there. "What are they going to do, Simon?" she asked anxiously, her hand on Uncle Simon's arm. "Should we lock the house?"

Uncle Simon shook his head, not answering. He touched Chloe's arm reassuringly with his hand.

I could make out Rampsie, Keaton in his cowboy hat, Hudman with his fat-boy walk. The other two, both with hands crammed into the pockets of their tight jeans, I'd noticed among the crowd before, but I didn't know them by name. Rampsie's head was above the others; he stood erect, shirt open at the neck, jacket fluttering in the breeze.

"I'm going," I told Uncle Simon. "I know it's crazy, but I want to see what's going on over there."

"No, no," Aunt Chloe began to protest, but Uncle Simon calmed her down. In a minute he was beside me, perhaps for my protection, but even more because he was as curious as I.

Another man stood on that platform now, and the first one leaned on it casually, talking earnestly to a couple of passersby. The fourth was handing out flyers about the strike, urging people to join the picket line. Uncle Simon and I reached the edge of the crowd, which numbered perhaps twenty people, not counting the strikers. It made me laugh at myself, thinking of twenty people as a crowd, but I'd begun to think in Rowe terms once again, reverting to my childhood.

"We can guarantee you a better shake," the man on the platform was saying with the megaphone to his lips like the barker in a circus. "Join the picket line tomorrow, tomorrow, tomorrow, and give yourself a break."

I peered up at this guy; he looked a little scholarly with those thick glasses, but a scar stretched across one cheek, and the glasses acted like mirrors so I couldn't see what was behind them.

Suddenly I took a look behind me and grabbed for Uncle Simon's arm with my hand, pulling him backward. I'd seen Rampsie bend down to pick up a rock. I watched him furtively, weighing it in his hand as if testing a rare diamond for its karat content, feeling it for the heft and thickness of that stone.

We'd begun to run before Rampsie decided what he was going to do with his rare gem. Uncle Simon and I stopped beneath one of the oak trees, panting, clutching the rough bark while we turned to look back. Those strikers didn't know Rampsie and his friends. The scholarly guy was talking some more, telling how much the union'd done for other mills just like this one and describing a bright kind of future for all of them, when we heard a sound like a cow mooing. I knew it was Hudman because I could see him do it, his hands to his mouth.

The speaker stopped a minute and listened, then gathered himself together and continued.

In a moment Rampsie'd put his fingers to his mouth and let loose a long, low whistle. For a minute the speaker almost stopped; he was as suspicious as hell and looking into the audience, trying to figure out who'd caused the noise.

In a second, another of the men was howling like a lovesick coyote. Now the crowd had fallen into silence, and a restive and uncertain mood overtook it—the dim suspicion of menace. Uncle Simon and I looked at each other and began to edge away again.

The man on the platform was walking back and forth distrustfully while his three friends began to patrol through the crowd like watchdogs trying to catch a scent.

In about ten seconds the first stone hit, right in the face of the scholarly man who was speaking. It missed his glasses by a fraction, but that was all we could see because Uncle Simon and I were beating it out of there as fast as we could go. So were the others; they looked as if they'd been caught in a thunderstorm, scattering like dry leaves.

Now the two groups were at each other. One of the strikers had found a wrench somewhere, and as I turned back momentarily, I could see him wielding it over his head. There was a din, with shouts and swearing.

By this time we'd reached the front steps of our house, and Aunt Chloe was yelling to us, holding the front door open. The minute we tore inside, she slammed it and leaned against its heavy frame with relief. The fight was still going on out there. Part of that platform had now been torn apart, and one of the strikers was battering Bingo Keaton with a length of wood from it—I could distinctly make out his bright red cowboy hat moving back and forth, crouching and weaving like a football player in the big game.

Then suddenly it was over. The strikers had run to their pickup truck, someone'd put it into violent motion, and the others dived onto it while it inched forward. One man was limping so badly I didn't think he'd make it, but the others reached over to haul him aboard.

Rampsie and his friends were left standing on the common alone; they looked like kings of the hill, an old childhood game I used to play right where they were standing now. They laughed and clapped one another on the shoulders, but they looked terrible. One was bleeding from his face, and their clothes hung off their backs. Keaton's hat had fallen to the ground; Hudman was almost carrying another man back to their big truck, which was still parked at the edge of the common grass.

"Are they going to leave?" asked Aunt Chloe hopefully, clutching

81

Uncle Simon's sleeve nervously with her fingers. "Do you think so, Simon?"

Rampsie and his cronies all were now gathered back inside the truck, moving it slowly, sedately, off the road. One of them, sitting on the back, stood up and gave a victory yell, which echoed around the houses of the common.

"Now maybe those boys won't come back," said Aunt Chloe. "Maybe that's enough, Simon. Ramspie's had his way, hasn't he, and the others?" She'd almost brightened a little. "Now perhaps they'll go."

Uncle Simon looked at me over Aunt Chloe's head and said nothing.

When the fracas was over, the Scouts came bursting from the Callaghans' house like confined floodwaters from a dam. Stu Callaghan moved among them, down the front walk, in the backwash.

"Can't say we got much marching practiced," Stu was grumbling. "With all that confusion, we just stood by the window and gaped." Callaghan touched Uncle Simon on the shoulder. "Are you going to work Monday, Simon? You really think it's safe?"

"I'm going, Stu. You?"

Callaghan nodded slowly. "I'll be there. You want me to come by for you?"

"Thank you, Stuart. I'd take it kindly."

"When is the parade you're practicing for?" I asked Stu. I couldn't seem to remember days of the week lately, much less holidays.

"Sunday, week from tomorrow. Always have it on Sunday, no matter when the holiday comes. Happens it *is* Sunday this year." My God, May 30 so soon?

Uncle Simon suddenly turned to Callaghan. "Stu, would you mind helping me board up the house today? Instead of our bridge game, I mean?"

It took Callaghan by surprise. "Why, where are you going, Simon?"

Uncle Simon had an angry glint in his eyes. Tim and Buzz had run into the house and left us standing on the sidewalk in the late-afternoon sunshine.

"I'm not going anywhere, Stu. Why?"

"Well, if you're planning to board up the house! That's what the

83

Parkses did before they left. So did the Maynards." He pointed across the common toward the empty Parkses' garrison colonial.

"I'm not taking any more chances," Uncle Simon said with finality. "Chloe's living room is already a shambles, and I'm not going to give 'em a chance on the rest of the house. But"—he tapped his left arm—"I'm not much good at nailing and sawing right now, so I'll need help."

"Count me in," I told Uncle Simon. "At least I can hold up the boards while you nail them."

Callaghan contemplated Uncle Simon for a minute. "All right, Simon. I'll go along with that. Give me a few minutes, and I'll be over." Stu headed back around the common toward his house.

"You're really worried?" I asked Uncle Simon. Somehow it was more a statement than a question. His face looked as pale as putty. I'd never seen that set to his jaw and that glitter of anger in his eyes.

"I'm taking no chances," he said grimly. "I don't like what I saw today, and I'm not going to leave myself open for any more. Lived here all my life, and I never thought I'd see what happened out there this afternoon." He pointed his hand vaguely in the direction of the common. "Used to be I'd sit by my window or on the front steps and look out there and think the world a good place. I'd take leftover bread from the table and feed the squirrels, even those fat pigeons, and feel them part of what I knew. Today"—he shook his head again—"I know what I saw, but it wasn't like what I ever knew before."

I wasn't as alarmed as Uncle Simon because I'd seen people like Rampsie and his kind coming in and out of our courtrooms every day down in Boston. I'd witnessed that same countenance on a hundred faces I'd run across, reflecting a kind of restive opportunism, waiting for the rip-off, the sly chance for gain. There are a million people like Rampsie and Keaton and Hudman, I thought. That look didn't surprise me one bit, but I never expected to see it so unabashed and intimidating, so close to my own face. I really didn't blame Uncle Simon for boarding up the front of his house.

Stu Callaghan drove up a short while later in his old clothes, with a long workbox and some lengths of lumber sticking out the back of his station wagon. Minnie Callaghan was balancing a big bag of rhubarb, a couple of boxes, and some utensils jutting from a pie basket. "If the men are going to hammer, Chloe and Mrs. Sardoe and me are going to make pies," she said. She was covering her tenseness with a flurry of words. "Was going to do it anyway, you understand—make pies, I mean. Might as well do something. Everyone else is. Here, give me a hand with this stuff. There's more in the car."

Within a half hour Uncle Simon was banging away on the house with his good right arm. I handed boards up to him while Stu sawed. The smell of fresh sawdust hit my nose like perfume; the fine brown dust clung to our clothes. I could smell the aroma of baking pies from inside the house mingling with the sawdust, and when I eased myself into the kitchen for a drink of water, pie dough and flour and crescents of sliced rhubarb covered everything. It looked as if we were planning a prolonged siege with all our preparations. By the time we finished boarding the windows it was long past dark.

"You going to bother with the back windows?" Stu asked Uncle Simon as we surveyed our work by the light from the bulbs on either side of the front door. Uncle Simon had fine wood dust clinging to his thick eyebrows, and my hair was frosted with it. I could even feel some down my back.

Uncle Simon nodded grimly. "If I can get to it."

"The barn, too?"

He shook his head. He stored tools and equipment in that barn, but it was almost thirty feet behind the house, halfway between us and the Sardoes.

"It'll have to go," said Uncle Simon. "You can't board up everything. Otherwise, what have you got left?"

He was right, I thought. What *did* you have left?

We were still working, hammering and sawing, when George drove up in front with Clarissa. He looked a little shocked when he saw the front of our house. "Don't blame Simon a bit," he said. "Would have come sooner to help, except I had to patch up a couple of people roughed up on the common. Ended by sending one to the hospital in Tremont." He took my arm. "Can I talk to you a minute—could you get away?"

I led Clarissa inside the house to meet Aunt Chloe, and in two minutes she was chattering with the little girl and introducing her to Mrs. Sardoe. Outside, Uncle Simon had already pressed George into holding the last few boards while he hammered them into place; then we all pitched in to clean up leftover boards and the tools. Never in my life had I seen a place with less inclination toward letting someone just stand idle for a while.

Finally, I fetched my sweater, and we walked down by the mill. It was a cool spring night with dampness hovering in the air. Happily,

I matched my strides to George's longer ones, feeling good standing close to him for a while and overjoyed to escape from Uncle Simon's hammering detail. George was wearing sneakers and jeans, now that he'd finished seeing patients, and my sandals made no sound on old and badly cracked macadam. The mill was down in a hollow, a little below the level of the common and the houses surrounding it. The place appeared as quiet as death; I was sure that the old, worn dark bricks hadn't changed in the hundred years since the mill had been built. High above us rode that tall smokestack with its tiny red light, but down here was another world. It made me shiver a little, and I snaked my arm into George's and held it close to me. To my surprise, his arm encircled my waist, and I held myself against it, wanting to purr and rub against him like a wanton cat.

We both examined the place, not speaking; it was almost as if we might be overheard down here. Around the building was a high chain-link fence, odd in its contrast with the old building. Strike posters had been fastened to the fence with lengths of twine and wire. The mill was a long building with tiny old windows, except for one section where Uncle Simon worked, which had been modernized with large panes of glass; other than that, nothing had touched these exterior walls in generations.

George dropped his arm and turned to me. "I called the school nurse, told her I'd like to do physicals on the sixth-grade classes Monday. She agreed all right, but she knows that something's been going on because it's an unusual request. I couldn't really convince her that this was routine." Then he looked away and began to pace back and forth before me. "Only trouble is, if anything's wrong with Buzz, I'll have to report it and tell that judge you said was coming here, despite the fact that you told me in confidence. I wanted to let you know. That's why I scheduled the examinations for Monday rather than later in the week. You see, I really couldn't suppress that information and square it with my conscience. I guess that's what I'm really trying to say."

"Thanks, George." But now I was torn; I couldn't betray Tim's confidence and release my information about Buzz to anyone, including the judge. I didn't know whether I wanted George to take that information out of my hands or not.

"I'd also like to know if you'd come up with me," George said. "It won't take me too long at the school, perhaps an hour or two. And then, of course, you could get a glimpse of the big city." He was laughing at me as he finished, his eyes crinkling.

I'd been meaning to go to Tremont to visit the police station and to see what legal services might be available up there. Trumbull had said there was a judge. What else would I find? And I'd spend the day with George. What other reasons did I need? I mean, what other reasons were there?

We turned our backs on the mill. I was glad to leave it; it was like a visitation from another century. I almost expected to see a ghost at one of those small windows, and I continually glanced over my shoulder nervously, as if someone might be following. The dark shadows of the trees moved about us as we climbed up the short hill to the streets. I could feel a chill down my back, and when George took my hand, I held his tightly and could feel the moisture in my palm.

"It'll be wonderful to get out of town for a day," I told him, speaking louder than necessary. "This place gets a little claustrophobic sometimes."

George nodded in tacit agreement.

We returned to Uncle Simon's, where the pies were cooling on racks all over the kitchen, and Aunt Chloe was cutting one for Tim and Buzz and Clarissa. When steam had stopped seeping from beneath the crust and he thought Aunt Chloe wasn't looking, Buzz stuck his fingers into the juice and licked the droplets.

George and I joined Simon and Stu Callaghan in the living room. They'd been talking about the town, gently reminiscing, but now Uncle Simon looked grim and worried. I felt a pall hanging over all of us, as if it were making up some of the air in the room.

Stu was leaning forward toward Uncle Simon, perched on Aunt Chloe's stiff parlor chair because nobody wanted to sit on the burned and smelly couch. "You think, Simon, that there's any hope of getting that strike settled early?" asked Stu. "I mean, it could only cause more trouble."

"Don't know," said Uncle Simon. At that moment we heard a loud rumbling outside, and Uncle Simon jumped up nervously from his chair to peer through the cracks in the boards on the window, thinking that maybe Rampsie's truck had returned, but it was just the bus from Tremont to Boston, its lights glowing in the dark. We'd been out in the common when it went by earlier, about the time the speechifying started.

Uncle Simon sat down again, running his fingers from the useful hand through his hair tensely. "If those strike organizers come back, we're going to have our hands full. You know it. I know it. All the people in this town know it. There'll be the strikers in addition to Rampsie and his ilk. Oil and water, have you stopped to think about it? This place will never be the same. You understand?" He was still looking at Callaghan. "Don't you agree, Stuart?"

Stu nodded slowly, his eyes on Uncle Simon's face.

"Maybe we should get together some of the people around here," Uncle Simon continued. "All the people about the common who are interested—the ones left in town, that is—sort of a nucleus, in case we're needed. Just to try to keep the lid on things."

Stu examined Uncle Simon's face in an interested way, nodding slowly. "Fine idea, Simon."

"You, George?" asked Uncle Simon.

I could see George weighing the possibilities, lacing his fingers together behind his head. "Sort of a standby committee, Simon? That's the idea?"

Something was tickling at me: I didn't like the idea. I felt very uneasy about citizens banding together for defense. Uncle Simon's groups would be a third force, opposing Rampsie, who opposed the strikers. "Let's wait until we hear what the judge has to say," I suggested to the men. "Maybe he'll get Rampsie's crowd off our backs for us. Then the mill business will take care of itself."

"All right," answered Uncle Simon. "I just meant, there's Stu there, and I'm here, and George. With four or five others, that's all we'd need for starters."

"How about Oldham?" asked Stu. "Will you include him, Simon?"

Uncle Simon nodded. "We need the man. Hell, we need everyone. We can't afford to overlook one soul!"

Suddenly George realized that it was getting late and that Clarissa was still here, playing checkers with Tim and Buzz. He gathered her up in his arms and carried her, giggling to the car. When I walked out with him, he called back that he'd be by at nine to go to Tremont.

It was a bright night with a waxing moon in a star-filled sky, but as I reentered Uncle Simon's house, it struck me that I could barely see the outdoor lights from inside the front hall; suddenly I realized it was because of all those boards nailed across the front windows.

Monday was terrible, as Sunday had been. Where had all those churlish clouds come from? It was a baleful spring storm, with the water lashing at the windows of George's car. His windshield wipers slapped frantically at the cascading flood.

"Thanks for doing this," I told George. I realized that he'd canceled afternoon office hours to check the school classes today, all so he could make sure Buzz was all right.

"Forget it," he answered. "I should examine those classes before summer anyway, so why not now?" Still, his face had a worried frown, and I knew he was thinking about the boy, as I was. I appreciated that concern and support, and I also recognized him to be my closest ally and friend. But I wasn't kidding myself: I was also a little in love with the guy, and how that mixed up in the formula I wasn't quite sure. I simply knew that this was a special day, and I intended to enjoy it.

Tremont was a big city by Rowe standards; it claimed twenty thousand people, at least six major businesses, and a host of little ones. Main Street was lined with shops, most of them prosperous-looking, and there was an air of affluence about the place. The town had put in a couple of shopping centers on the outskirts and was building a bypass. I couldn't believe it had grown so large it *needed* to be bypassed! Somehow I wasn't even sure if that constituted progress. There'd been a hassle about building a new courthouse, according to Uncle Simon, but the legal work of the city was still being conducted in the small, ancient but indestructible marble building across from the delicatessen.

We meandered around the main streets, then jutted off on one of them toward the school. I watched George maneuver the car through the new maze of traffic lights and one-way streets, marveling at what had happened to the old town.

"It's incredible," I said to George. "I wouldn't know how to find my way around—and I've been here a hundred times."

George nodded, then reached over and touched my shoulder. "Oh, you'd get used to it soon enough. The change has been just gradual enough so you don't notice it when you live here, but when you come back after awhile. . . ." Then he laughed when my eyes betrayed my surprise at the new pedestrian interval light at the beginning of Central Square.

When I looked at George, I smiled at him, and he smiled back. This was nice, I thought. I was excited being with him, watching him drive, moving the car about the new-old city. I almost felt as if this were stolen time, like playing hooky from something contained within the confines of Rowe. Up here, Rowe was only a wide spot in the road where you had to slow down to thirty-five miles per hour, and twenty around the common. I felt my temperature rise again, looking at George, and again I thought, this is nice, nice, nice. . . .

"You won't be bored while I'm in there?" asked George, pointing to the school, a long one-story building which extended a distance down the road and back into fields beyond. He tossed me the car keys.

"I think I'll go visit the long arm of the law."

"The cops?"

"The men in blue." I was laughing. "Gendarmes, the local militia. In other words, I'll call on the police. When would you like me to pick you up?"

"Two hours OK? Come inside if I'm late."

I watched him pull open the big school door. He was carrying his medical bag, and the nurse, who'd evidently been waiting for him, was treating him deferentially. I was envious; I wished lawyers got treated that way.

I cruised around the streets in George's car, getting my bearings. There were parking lots where stores used to be and stores where parking lots used to be. It took me awhile to find the police station, but finally, I located it right on upper Main Street near the park presided over by the statue of the Civil War general.

I asked the sergeant at the desk if I could talk to the police chief, and he told me the man had gone to a meeting for police officers in Atlanta, Georgia, and after that he was going fishing. But a middle-aged lieutenant came out from some inner recess of the building and motioned me to a conference room at the rear of the station, near the end of a long corridor.

The lieutenant was a serious, professional kind of man with a shock of thick brown hair and a heavy tan. He looked at me with eyes that didn't seem to blink, and I wondered if he closed them when he slept. I told him that I was from Rowe, visiting my aunt and uncle, and that I'd like to find out a few things about Bob Rampsie, his younger brother, Jaimie, Bingo Keaton, and Hunk Hudman. At first he didn't want to tell me a thing, but I said that I was a lawyer with a professional interest in the case. Then he began to open up ever so slightly, like a reluctant clam. For one thing, of course, he knew that I could subpoena the information, but he didn't know that I'd probably never bother. I told him that a circuit judge was coming through Rowe tomorrow, and it'd be mighty helpful to get up to date on those guys.

The lieutenant nodded. "Well, Rampsie's from Rowe; you probably know that," he said. I laughed and said that I was by now well aware of that fact.

"Hudman and Keaton are from Tremont. They were raised up here. Perhaps you've heard something about them in the last few years, too."

I shook my head. "Tell you the truth, I'd never heard about any of them until they started to act up on the common. But I practice down in Boston, you see."

"Well," he continued, "we had trouble with Hudman and Keaton as juvenile offenders. They were put away at the county farm on at least two occasions, once for car theft, another time for passing forged checks. They didn't serve long, but we kept such a good eye on them that they cleared out of town."

"Didn't they learn a trade at the county farm?" I was idiot enough to have the eternal and perhaps naïve hope that maybe something constructive got rubbed off on an occasional kid in a detention center, that he wasn't simply marking time until release.

"I think they taught Hudman welding. Seems to me the parole officer said he was really good at it, even exceptional. But I can't remember much about Keaton."

"You never had anything on Rampsie then?"

The lieutenant started to say something, then hesitated. "We've got a peck of suspicions. We know that a few stores around Tremont were burglarized. A couple of times shopkeepers got bashed over the head, violent acts. Everyone from little kids to old ladies. Hate to pin it to them, but we haven't had any more since they left town."

"Great! What can I do to get you to take 'em back?" I leaned forward, my elbows on that shiny table. "And what do you know about Clyde Oldham, the police chief? Does your chief know him?"

The lieutenant shrugged. "We all know him. Kind of, well, wishy-washy, right? But he's had some training, more than the chiefs in some of these little towns I could name."

"You know he hits the bottle on the sly?"

"Sure." He brushed some lint from the cuff of his uniform. "But then again, so do some others. Nothing to get excited about."

Suddenly I had an overwhelming urge to shake that lieutenant, to clutch hold of his neat uniform and tell him what was going on in Rowe, to hammer on him so he'd know how frightened we all felt. But that wasn't going to help one little bit, so I swallowed my frustration, looked him in the eye, and began quietly to relate to him what was

91

happening. I described to him carefully and graphically what Rampsie and his friends were doing. I didn't even swear. Then I explained about the strike at the mill and the clash with the strikers. I even described the way we'd boarded up the front of the house and that we weren't the only ones, but I couldn't tell him about Buzz Sardoe. I struggled to describe the fear in the town, but somehow in this modern office, in this bustling town, he didn't seem to comprehend what I was telling him, so that the words didn't carry sufficient import.

Yet he seemed concerned. "I tell you what," he said, twirling a pencil absently in his fingers, "if you've got any real problems, come back. I really mean it, always glad to help. But you won't need to worry now you've got the judge coming." He smiled and looked at his watch. "Wish we could help you more, but you see, Rowe's out of our jurisdiction."

"All right," I answered. "Whose jurisdiction are we in?"

"State police, but of course, they're pretty busy. And any help we give would be unofficial." A fleeting smile crossed his lips. "But I bet a million bucks you work things out; those guys'll just get bored hassling you and move on to other things."

"You're more optimistic than I am," I told him. "By the way, what did you say your name was?"

"Dowling. Just call up anytime."

I was out of the police station and into the street before I realized he'd never asked for my name. I even had a premonition that we'd meet again very soon, and I wished I'd told him.

I went to meet George. He dumped his medical bag in the back of the car, and we pulled away from the curb. "How's Buzz?" I asked.

"Goddamn idiots," he exploded. "Poor kid's had one hell of a laceration, but he's healing. Put him on antibiotics because there's been a little infection." His voice tightened. "I'd like to strangle those creeps. If it wouldn't mortify the kid and if he weren't doing all right, I'd report it. I may anyway."

"Please don't, unless you have to." Now I was consoling George, who was down with me in the pits.

"But he'd barely let me come near him," George said. "That kid's been through a hell of a lot of trauma. It's lucky he's a trusting kind of kid."

"Well, Buzz isn't that trusting anymore," I said. "He goes through agonies every time he sees those men." Before my eyes I could see the haunted look in his eyes, not even erased that day in the airplane. "It's going to be a long while. . . ."

"Poor kid," said George again. We were silent for a while as I drove through the center of town. "How about lunch?" he asked finally. The sympathy in his voice had stirred me, and I readily accepted.

George gave me directions. By now the rain had stopped. We wound our way through the city to the other side of town, and I pulled up before a new restaurant, small and secluded, in a grove of pines. George took my arm and led me to a table near the window; when we nursed our wine and he placed his arm against mine on the table, I began to feel better. What had happened to Buzz, my visit to Lieutenant Dowling, even the way I felt about George were doing a number on me. But when I told George how Dowling had reacted—while George pulled out his pipe and lit it, blowing contented smoke rings into the air as he listened—I stopped, and something caught in my throat so that I couldn't continue. Something was telling me that this wasn't my day. I could feel myself flushing from embarrassment, but I didn't even care.

When the waitress came over to take our order, George sent her away again. He'd put his arm around me; that felt so comforting I found my voice again, and I could tell him what the lieutenant had said about the men in Rowe, about their past criminal records. Then my throat filled again. I just couldn't get out of my head what all those people in Rowe were going through.

"Those men are really no good," I told George haltingly. "I really mean it. That's what the lieutenant was trying to tell me. They're born losers, every one of them; they've never done a good thing for *anyone*. Some of them stole from their own parents, turned on the people who tried to help them, violated those who loved them. And now they're in Rowe, George."

George ordered me another glass of wine and lent me his big white handkerchief. I knew that the waitress thought us a couple of lovers who'd had a tiff, and she left us alone to patch up the quarrel. I didn't even care *what* she thought; it was nice to have George beside me. His pipe emitted smoke rings above our heads, and now and then he made a little sucking noise on the stem when he drew in air. It sounded comforting in this quiet room, and I finally returned his handkerchief. "Thanks, George," I said.

George was looking gravely into the air past his smoke rings. "It was a bad day for all of us when those characters picked Rowe for their pranks. Unprincipled rabble—that's what Mrs. Parks called them that day she collected her prescriptions before leaving town. Rabble. Well, maybe that's what they are."

I looked at him. "A *curse*. That's what Aunt Chloe said." I shuddered involuntarily. "It gives me the creeps."

When we rose to leave, I could feel my reluctance. There was more to it than the good feeling I had with George: I feared going back. That was it. I had to admit it to myself. *I feared going back.*

We drove slowly home, the tires singing on still-wet roads. Something inside me protested every mile of the way, even every half mile. I'd been wondering: When was I going to see George again alone, when would he sit this close, when could I talk to him this way? I looked over at him, concentrating so intently on the road ahead, when I suddenly realized that he wasn't concentrating all that much, that he'd even slowed the car considerably.

Something inside me shifted, and for one moment I raised my hand, just wishing, and the next moment I'd placed it on his arm. From then on I couldn't help myself. I began to move it around. I couldn't stop.

There was a brief interval when I wasn't sure how it would be, what George would say, that maybe I'd overstepped myself—when he suddenly lifted his hand off the wheel and slid it behind my back. In a second I had my head on his shoulder, burrowing into his side.

"George . . ." I said, "George. . . ." I didn't know how or if he'd respond but I knew I wanted him terribly, that somehow I couldn't control what I said right then; I needed to feel his presence, to let him know I cared, to share my anguish. I'd known him such a short while. What difference did that matter? He was in my world, he loomed large in it, and I wanted him. That was it; I was aware of how much I wanted him.

"Hey, listen," he said, and I thought: He's going to push me aside or jolly me or patronize me. But his voice was soft, and he hadn't even withdrawn his arm while he wheeled the car onto one of those endless dirt roads in the middle of nowhere, in a tunnel of overhanging pines.

I'd already encircled his waist with my arms and closed my eyes, just feeling him close.

"Come here," he was saying as he jammed on the brakes and turned toward me. "Come. . . ." My arm had fallen from his waist, and I felt his erection; that was all I needed to know. He cared for me and wanted me, too.

"My God, George," I said. "I care about you. I can't help it. I care, please. . . ."

94

He'd reached for me, was holding me close. "George, I—" I couldn't say anything else because he'd placed his mouth on mine and was doing something marvelous with his lips, pressing them down and about mine.

I removed my clothes quickly, fumbling with the buttons; then I started to remove George's shirt; I didn't even know what I was doing. Wasn't first lovemaking with someone new supposed to be casual, controlled, exploratory, tentative? Not mine—I needed him, wanted him, couldn't wait to feel him inside me. I felt like one possessed. Perhaps he'd think me depraved and debauched, but I didn't care. Right then I didn't care one bit.

"It would be nice if you'd let me breathe," said George, chuckling, holding me with difficulty. "I mean, sometimes it's necessary. . . ."

"Later," I said. "I mean, breathing isn't everything. . . ."

"Boy, you can say that again," he said, pulling off his shirt. "It sure isn't. . . ."

Even in the confines of that car we made abandoned love. I thrust my tongue into the soft, moist opening in his penis, moving it around and around until we were both crazy. So if he thought I was brazen, so if he did, so what? I couldn't bother with such otherworldly concerns when George was right there, dark and exciting and smelling slightly of pipe tobacco.

Without even consulting him, I moved forward and on top of him—he had one of those cars with the seats that lie back—and almost claimed his penis for my own, taking it into my body with incredible relief. I didn't know how I was going to feel about this tomorrow, but for today I couldn't care less.

"Oh, George," I moaned slightly, then kissed him until I was drowning with abandon and relief.

George was writhing beneath me; his penis felt as if it were two feet long. "I can't control . . ." he muttered.

"Come," I was almost shouting. I'd had about five climaxes already, and he was doing divine things with my breasts and abdomen and the insides of my thighs, so that I was about to have a sixth—my back was arched and I could feel the ecstasy to my back teeth. Finally, we both came shuddering together, and I'd totally had it. It felt as if I'd just jogged thirty glorious miles and that I'd collapsed in complete debilitation—only George was still there, holding me.

"Lord," he said, coming up for air. "You really do come on."

I felt a wave of guilt. "Usually," I said, "I don't get that worked up, I'm rather reserved and. . . ."

He was still struggling for traction; he pulled out a shoe from beneath his elbow. "I'm terribly sorry to hear it. Can't think when I've been so thoroughly . . . and delightfully . . . used."

I rubbed my hand across the matted hair on his chest. "Next time I'll give you a warning, I'm sorry. . . ."

"Please don't. Can't tell you how much I like surprises. I mean, anytime the spirit moves you, just . . . whistle or something."

I started to laugh. He leaned over and kissed me, so tenderly for a minute it choked me up.

"I was afraid," I said, "that maybe you didn't care. I mean, I just went for you. You see, I've been caring for you for a while."

He leaned forward and kissed me again. "You never asked me how I felt about *you*. Been a little nuts myself since that night I saw you at Chloe's. Didn't think I should try to compromise you immediately, give you a little time. . . ."

I kissed him on the ear. "Seems I did go a little bonkers. Really."

"Let me arrange to be around the next time you do. No need to warn me ahead of time. I'll dress accordingly, no buttons, that kind of thing, unjammable zippers. Maybe I could just come nude. . . ."

I laughed again. It had been wonderful. It had even been super. I couldn't even wait to attack George again. He even had a little gleam in his eye when I told him.

gathered my clothing from where I'd scattered it in my depraved haste, George reversed to the main road, and we continued reluctantly down the main highway, which branched imperceptibly on its route to Rowe until we read the sign outside Rowe: TOWN OF ROWE, POPULATION 2127, PLEASE DRIVE CAREFULLY.

"Population *must* have gone up a couple since the sign was erected," said George.

"No, you're forgetting Mr. and Mrs. Parks," I answered. "When they left town, we regained the status quo."

It was a nice moment, with a feeling of contentment and peace and a chance to relax together.

But we didn't feel content for long. As we rounded the last turn into Rowe, there, in the middle of the common, was Rampsie's truck.

"Don't those guys ever work?" George asked me. "Where in blazes do they get their money?"

"Pops Rampsie, partly." I told him about Hudman's swiping the meat and beer. "They must be robbing the old guy blind. He's mad enough to testify about it before the judge tomorrow."

"You think he'll show?"

"He says so. I guess we'll have to wait and see." I reluctantly said good-bye to him at our house.

"What's been going on?" I asked Uncle Simon, who was sitting peacefully in the living room by himself reading; apparently he hadn't seen the truck, and I didn't have the heart to tell him. "Did they let you into the mill this morning? No pickets?"

"Not a soul." He folded the newspaper he'd been reading. "We walked in without any problems. Quiet. Don't know where they all went. But then there's no strike officially."

Aunt Chloe and Mrs. Sardoe were in the kitchen preparing dinner. Mrs. Sardoe was slicing carrots into thin orange wafers.

"Buzz says he saw Dr. George today," she said. "He says Dr. George give them all examin . . . how you say, examin. . . ?"

"Examinations," I helped her. "Physical examinations. I'm so glad. Then the kids will all be ready for summer, in the pink."

Mrs. Sardoe nodded. "My boy said he like Dr. George. He said he's a very nice man."

"Yes, Mrs. Sardoe, he *is* a very nice man."

Oldham was on my mind, and the judge tomorrow. I rang Oldham's number and held on until he finally answered. The man sounded tired.

"Chief Oldham, did you issue that subpoena to Hudman yet? As you know, Pops says he'll testify against him. And tomorrow morning the circuit judge will be here at ten. I'm sure you haven't forgotten." There was a silence. "Have you, Chief Oldham?"

"I haven't forgotten, Miss Sanderson. But I can't find Hudman. He hasn't been around."

"Well, I think he's here now. We just saw Rampsie's truck out on the common."

"All right." He sounded resigned. "I'll try to find him."

"You want me to come with you?" I wasn't sure he was going to make it without a chaperone. But I'd a million things in mind I'd rather do, practically anything in the whole world.

"All right. The more the merrier."

When I told Uncle Simon where I was going, he almost had a fit. "If those men are in that store, I don't want you there alone," he said, his voice rising. "I mean it, Lisa."

I tried to sound soothing. "It's all right, Uncle Simon. I'll be with the police chief, after all. What better protection. . . ?"

"Then I'm coming along." He clamped his free hand on the arm of the chair and pushed himself up. "Here, help me with this thing." He was wrestling with his sweater, trying to pull it over his cast. "And tell Chloe where I'm going."

He was pretty upset, muttering to himself. "I'd never face your father," he continued, "if I let you go over to that store alone." I knew it was useless to try to deter him, but I made an attempt at it.

"You're not going to have to face my father, Uncle Simon, and I'm perfectly old enough to manage for myself." But he turned an absolutely deaf ear toward my arguments.

Aunt Chloe was wringing her hands, watching us go out the door. But then we saw Clyde Oldham's police car cruising around the circle; he pulled up on the edge of the common nearest Rampsie's store. When he saw us, he stopped to wait, leaning against the car. When we came near, he crossed the road to us and tagged along behind.

"Lo, Simon, Miss Sanderson," he said.

"Lisa," I told him. By now I could see Keaton's red hat and the rest of him perched on a packing box upended on Rampsie's front porch.

The chief mounted the store steps slowly and deliberately, slightly ahead of Uncle Simon and me. He asked Keaton somewhat apologetically where he could find Hudman. I could see the envelope containing the subpoena in Oldham's pocket.

Keaton never opened his mouth. With great deliberation, he looked the chief up and down, then me up and down until I was shivering, naked, before him, finally Uncle Simon up and down. Then he flipped his thumb in the direction of Pops Rampsie's open door. But evidently he'd decided that something of interest might ensue, so he slowly removed himself from that packing box, wiggling his hips on it as if to break a vacuum, and followed.

Hudman was at the back of the store behind the meat counter, making himself a sandwich with some thick slabs of ham from the display case, dousing the whole with mustard. Next to him stood Bob Rampsie, a knife in his hand; neither man looked at us or acknowledged our presence, as if we'd suddenly turned invisible. Pops wasn't anywhere around that we could see, and the store appeared almost empty except for a couple of customers up front.

The chief cleared his throat, seeing Hudman watching him, the sandwich in his hand dripping mustard. "Hunk," he said, as if he were intoning in church, "I hereby. . . . " The chief fumbled in his pocket for the envelope with the subpoena, finally evidently grasping it. "I hereby . . . serve you with this . . . here . . . subpoenny."

Hunk, surprised, dropped the sandwich on Pops's counter, wiped his hand elaborately on the seat of his pants, and reached for the slim envelope. But he never got to it.

"I'll take that," said Rampsie, reaching quickly and flipping it from Hudman's fingers. "The fathead can't read anyway."

"I can, too," Hunk protested, reaching to snatch it back, but Rampsie was faster, and Hudman grasped empty air.

Rampsie opened the envelope slowly, his eyes all the while on Hudman's face, a thin smile playing on his lips. Uncle Simon stood right next to me; I could feel his hand on my arm; he was ready to get me out of there if anything should go wrong.

"Listen, Bob," said Oldham, protesting meekly, "this is something we can talk about, right?" But Rampsie was slowly pulling out that fancy sheet of paper with the seal on top. Then he began to read it aloud.

"To Harold Hudman," he read, "you are hereby ordered to appear in court on Tuesday, May twenty-fifth, to hear the charges against you, brought forward by one, Abraham Rampsie."

Bob looked over at Oldham. "*Pops*? *Pops* is bringing charges?" His voice was absolutely incredulous. "Aw, come on now, Clyde, old bastard. Hunk's not smart enough to do anything. You gotta be kidding!"

Oldham, somewhat taken aback, shook his head. "It's really serious, Bob. No kiddin'. Hunk, here, he's been stealin' from Pops—you oughta know it by now if you ain't blind—and Pops is gonna testify against him."

Bob turned slowly to Hudman. "You've been stealing from Pops?" His voice indicated that Hudman might be some form of insect life he hadn't met before. "You shit you. What the hell you been stealing from Pops, Hunk?"

"Nothin' much," Hudman answered, retreating against the counter. "Honest, Bob. You really think I'd steal from old Pops? Why, he's been keeping me in vittles, man. We both know it. You really think I'd steal from Pops?" Hudman was so scared that his body was trembling, and he looked up at Rampsie with a beseeching plea for forgiveness.

Suddenly Rampsie turned to glare at me. I hated his eyes; they did something creepy and miserable to me. Besides undress me, they implied that I was malformed and had a vicious soul. "Stop looking at me like that," I told him. "We've got our rights around this place, too."

"That right, lady?" He threw the subpoena back to Hudman, but it dropped on the floor, and as Hudman was ready to pick it up, Rampsie stepped on it.

Bingo Keaton was leaning on the counter behind me, a grin on his face. He was enjoying all this!

"Tomorrow morning at ten," Oldham said, watching the paper grind into the dirty floor. "Just don't forget it, Hunk."

"You really like to push people around, lady?" Rampsie was asking pointedly, looking at me, advancing a step.

"Come off it, Bob," I told him. "You know better than that. We haven't been giving you a hard time, it's the other way around, and you know—"

"Leave her alone," said Uncle Simon, stepping forward to meet him.

I thought for a moment that Rampsie might punch Uncle Simon, but the sight of Oldham standing there, openmouthed, seemed to deter him. But he'd cast those eyes back on me again, and I could feel that crawly sensation up and down my vertebrae once more.

Oldham stooped over to pick up the subpoena from the floor, but Hudman snatched it from his hand, squashing it to a pellet in his fist.

"Know what I like?" asked Hudman on a sudden inspiration. He reached forward for the knife on the counter, wiped the mustard off onto the paper, his dirty yellow hair falling into his face. "Ya see now," he said, "ya see now." The paper was soggy with mustard. Then he held it up, opened his big mouth, with dark crusty teeth, and swallowed it.

I looked at him, waiting for him to choke, but that paper slid down as smoothly as silk. There was a rim of mustard on his lips.

Rampsie was grinning, and Keaton had pushed his hat off the back of his head in admiration.

"Beats all," said Rampsie, shaking his head. "*Now* where's your subpoena, Chief?"

Oldham took a moment to recover. "It won't help, Hunk. You've seen it, that's all that counts. Tomorra. . . . "

Rampsie'd suddenly stopped smiling, and we turned to go. "You think you own this place, eh?" he asked, and I knew it was directed toward me. I didn't even look back.

That night Uncle Simon called together some town men to talk about the strike and the Rampsie crowd. Aside from George there were only four, and most of them I knew: Stu Callaghan, Ed Rhymer, who worked for Clyde Oldham sometimes, Paul White, a part-time fireman, and Oldham himself.

George was the first to arrive; we sat on the front steps and talked for a while until the others gathered. He was wearing that blue sweater again; it made me smile and lean toward him and

101

touch his arm. His leg rested against mine, and I swore I could feel the electric currents.

"Why the meeting?" George asked me quietly. "Any more trouble?"

I told him about Hudman and the subpoena. "It meant nothing to them, George, nothing. Uncle Simon's pretty upset."

George took my hand as we walked inside. "Can't say I blame him one bit, can you? Not after what we've already been through."

"I don't think we should do a thing except sit around and make sure we're prepared," Uncle Simon was saying. We once again occupied Aunt Chloe's blitzed living room. "Just in case they keep overflowing with their rowdying out there."

"Seems almost peaceful-like out there now," said Paul White. "Leastwise, when I just walked 'crost the common. Maybe everything's gonna pass by, and we won't have trouble."

"Maybe," said Uncle Simon. "Now, that'll be just dandy." By now I was beginning to think that if I heard that refrain once more, I could dance to it. George obviously felt the same way because he glanced over at me and shook his head almost imperceptibly.

"Has anyone heard any more about where the strike organizers have lit off to?" asked Stu Callaghan, glancing about the room. No one answered.

"Well, I wish to God," said Uncle Simon, "that they'd go away and not come back, at least for the present. We got enough going on out there without adding any more to the porridge."

"Fer sure," muttered Ed Rhymer. "Last couple of days been kinda quiet, considerin' what went on before."

"Don't worry," said Uncle Simon dryly, "they'll be back; I feel it. Like wolves and the croup, they'll be back."

I remembered Uncle Simon and the wolves. Once when I was a little girl, some wolves got into a flock of chickens he'd raised up in the old barn. Every night they'd nabbed a few more hens until Uncle Simon's flock became decimated. So Uncle Simon began to keep vigil, sitting inside the barn with his rifle while the wolves circled outside. One night they became too confident, giving up their natural wariness in their craving for Uncle Simon's chickens; they entered the barn, where he was waiting for them. I could remember that Uncle Simon strung up their carcasses on a wire before he cleaned them for their pelts. He knew a lot about wolves.

"You're not sure of that, Simon," answered Clyde Oldham. "That's just 'jecture. You and me—all of us—don't know a damn thing like that. This may be just a little social gathering."

"Sure hope so, Clyde," answered Uncle Simon. "And maybe I'm just an old lady. Excepting that we've got enough going to call the judge, and he hasn't been here in two years, and we're sitting here having this meeting. Seems like we're looking kind of glum for a social gathering."

George had been sitting quietly on Aunt Chloe's stiff parlor chair, his legs extended and crossed on the floor before him, hands laced behind the back of his head, squinting his eyes and listening to the men in the room. "Simon, why don't you think they'll just dry up and go away?" I could see he didn't think they'd leave either, but he was interested in Uncle Simon's corroborating opinion. "Don't you think the judge will be able to deal with them?"

"You're too damn suspicious, both of you," said Clyde Oldham impatiently.

Uncle Simon pulled himself erect on the chair and looked around, his eyes angry. "All right, I'll tell you why I think they won't go away. You want to know, Clyde?"

Oldham, who had been slouched on Aunt Chloe's maimed couch, leaned forward now and looked at Uncle Simon from beneath frowning eyebrows.

"It's because they *like* it here, Clyde, and because I don't think they've got anywhere else to go. And because we're confused and don't know what to do with them. We're disorganized and vulnerable. They know it. They've got too many people up in Tremont keeping an eye on them, so they've come down here where the pickings are better. And I'll tell you something else, Clyde: they're naturally cussed, born cussed, and they're never gonna change. That's why we can't deal with them. Now do you understand?"

George was nodding solemnly, and as I sat there, I thought of the lieutenant's similar words and of Rampsie's predatory eyes.

"'T any rate," said Uncle Simon, "for now let's call this a social meeting. And if we've got cause for another, I'll call it. At least we've met once. That's a precedent. Something's been established. That's the thing."

"Will you come to the hearing tomorrow?" I asked George after the others had gone. We were having a glass of beer, talking. Buzz and his mother were asleep, Tim was doing homework in his room, and I could hear Simon and Chloe getting ready for bed.

"Wouldn't miss it. Do you think Hudman will show?"

"He'd better. Contempt of court's a misdemeanor in this state."

I walked George down the front steps. It was overcast again, and a ghostly mist hung in the air, making the streetlights around the common glow unnaturally. I leaned against him a little in the mist, and his arms slipped about my waist comfortingly. Yet tonight I felt achingly tense despite George's presence.

"Your uncle Simon's frightened," he said, almost in a whisper, as if he couldn't quite believe his own words. "I never saw your uncle frightened before. It's kind of sobering."

"So are other folks," I answered, feeling the warmth from his body. "Across the way Mr. Macy began boarding his house today. I saw it when I went over to meet Tim." I hesitated a moment. "Do you feel frightened, too, George?"

He nodded slowly, his face was directly before mine. "We all are. It's hard to tell whether we're all just a little bit crazy or a little bit sane." He turned toward his house, and I walked him a little way. "Then again, perhaps we're seeing shadows when there really aren't shadows at all." He kissed me gently before he left. "But I guess we'll find out soon enough."

Somehow, right then, I discovered it didn't hurt so much with George there. I watched him slowly walk across the common in the mist toward his house and his daughter. His form disappeared in stages as if something were sucking him into a foggy vortex, and soon he'd completely vanished from sight.

Maybe we'd all get through this somehow, I was thinking. And perhaps it was true what everyone said, that all this would slide away as George's shape had just disappeared into that mist. Maybe we'd wake up one morning and wonder what we'd all been so worried about.

Suddenly I felt a little more optimistic when I reached Aunt Chloe's, and took the front steps two at a time.

11

J udge Bream arrived the next morning in a black Chevrolet convertible with a large, round state seal on the side. He was a middle-aged man, around fifty, with a head of gray hair and a dapper mustache. He looked hastily dressed, with his shirt sliding out of his pants in back and his jacket flapping open. When he emerged from his car, he picked up some records and tucked them under one arm, then grasped a briefcase in the other hand, except that the records cascaded to the ground, so that he had to put down the briefcase and begin again. He also carried a large shopping bag. I discovered later that he transported his black legal robes in it, rolled into a large cylinder so they wouldn't get mussed.

I was at the town office when he arrived, waiting with Sarah Wellington, the only town officer. She was almost seventy, alert, with swift, nervous movements like a small, sparse bird. She'd kept watch over the records—births, deaths, licenses—since long before I was born, but I seriously doubted she needed records. Her memory was voluminous, and like many legal librarians in my experience, she'd committed so much of the town's history to memory that if the place should burn down, she could probably recite the essential facts out of her head.

Sarah's office, where the judge was to preside, was small, but on state occasions such as this, the fire engine had been cleared from the adjoining room, chairs brought in, Sarah's desk carried into the new room for the judge to use. There was even a small green flag run up on the flagpole outside the building to indicate that the judge was in residence. Judges in Boston never had the deference of a flag, so in my opinion Bream should be highly flattered.

People were standing around the small building in the May sunshine; others arrived when they saw the flag. The two years since the judge's last visit were a long time in the life of this town. I could see faces pressed in curiosity to the windows at the far end of the building and people milling around outside, trying to decide whether to enter. Ed Rhymer lounged beside the door, dressed in his Sunday clothes, his recalcitrant blond hair standing straight up with brushing, admitting the principals first before he let anyone else in; Oldham must have asked him to do it because he seemed to have a certain proprietary air about his task.

Judge Bream changed into his robes in the anteroom off Sarah Wellington's office where the records were kept, stack upon stack. When the judge entered the room, we all rose respectfully just as in Superior Court in downtown Boston.

I spied Hunk Hudman at the rear of the room, and for the first time that I'd known him in our short but intense acquaintance, his hair was neatly combed, flattened to his scalp, and he was wearing a white shirt with a necktie. I understood why perfectly: directly behind him was Lawyer Trumbull, hands in his pockets confidently and unconcerned, leaning against the back wall. I was sitting next to Uncle Simon in the front row, but George hadn't appeared. I looked around for him expectantly, eager to catch sight of his tall form, but there was no sign of him, even across the common, which I could see through the wide window to the rear of the room. Directly behind us was Stu Callaghan, sitting with Paul White. Already the "courthouse" was full, and I could see townspeople standing outside. I'd assured Clyde Oldham that I'd appear as a witness if he wished.

"Boy, nobody's going to work today," said someone near me and the man opposite answered with a laugh, "Sure ain't. Been a long time since I seen so many folks in the same place at the same time." It was true. Even the people who commuted to Tremont to work had stayed home on some pretext.

Clyde Oldham, sitting across the small aisle, was wearing a uniform as clean as new, and I wondered if he had it stashed away for state occasions or if he'd spent the night in a Tremont dry-cleaning emporium because that uniform had seen some pretty heavy use lately.

Judge Bream was now sedately ensconced behind Sarah Wellington's desk, the worn surface of which had been polished into a high

106

patina. Clyde Oldham scanned the room somewhat apprehensively, then rose slowly to his feet. "Your Honor," he began with a quaver in his voice, and the judge moved somewhat uneasily in his seat. Suddenly he leaned forward toward Clyde with an apologetic cough behind his hand.

"Tell you what, Chief," said Judge Bream with a broad smile. "Let's make these proceedings informal. That way we'll all know what we're thinking. Doesn't that make sense? Now, you just tell me what's on your mind, and we'll speak off the cuff. OK with all of you?"

Great, I thought, a man with a light touch. Friend to us all. Gentle to local yokels. I smiled to myself. Maybe that's what we needed after all. All the legal formality in the world wasn't really worth two cents in the coinage of real justice.

"Well, Judge," said Clyde, his confidence renewed, "these fellows"—he pointed at Bob Rampsie, who'd just come into the room with Keaton, both barely recognizable with shaves and haircuts—"these fellows have been kind of rowdying up around here, disturbing some of the local folks. As you know, sir"—Oldham was even inclining his head deferentially—"the common out here is pretty central, and everyone can see what's going on anytime he fixes to stick his head out the door. Well, these fellows you see here, they've been rowdying some, Your Honor."

The judge leaned forward expectantly. "Just what do you call rowdying?" He'd donned tortoiseshell granny glasses, and his eyes peered at Clyde above the missing hemispheres.

Oldham pulled at his black uniform tie uncomfortably. "Well, some say they threw shotgun cartridges into a big fire they got going out on the common the other night. God-awful noise—heard it clean up to my place." That was the first time I'd even heard Oldham admit to knowledge of that episode; the information astonished me.

As I turned around slightly to see how Hudman was reacting, I saw that George had arrived; I'd been worried that something had happened to him in that fog last night and hated myself for not driving him home. I motioned him to the empty seat beside me that I'd been saving, and he began to edge his way slowly along the far wall. He appeared harassed and tired. "Minor surgery," said as he sat down. "Kid playing hooky stepped on a fishhook. God-awful time getting it out."

The judge was making notes on a little pad on his desk. "We've just begun," I told George quickly. "Clyde's the first witness."

107

George nodded, then quickly turned to contemplate Clyde, standing to one side before us.

"Go on," the judge said, looking up from his notes and waving his hand at Oldham.

"The noise goes on other nights, too, Your Honor—I mean Judge Bream. Sometimes radio playin', that kind of thing. People living around the common say they can't sleep nights, and some"—Clyde looked pointedly at Uncle Simon and me—"has been complainin' of it."

The judge took more notes, writing rapidly in a quick scrawl, then looked across at Oldham. "Enough, Chief Oldham, would you say, to constitute a public nuisance?"

The chief considered, then nodded his head slowly. "Maybe so, when you consider those men are obstructing the road sometimes with their truck."

At that moment I could hear Trumbull's voice, deep and cordial, from the rear of the room. "Your Honor, if I may, would it be possible to approach the bench?"

He sounded terribly correct and deferential in this small-town court of law, and I knew it was to flatter the judge and pay him due homage as well as to show his sophistication.

"I'm James Trumbull, sir, if you remember me, and these boys"—he indicated Rampsie, Keaton, and Hudman with a magnanimous sweep of his hand—"have asked me to say a word in their behalf."

The judge leaned back in his chair and nodded at Trumbull.

"Yes, Attorney Trumbull, I remember you. Please proceed."

Trumbull cleared his throat. "Your Honor, these boys have been enjoying themselves in the common, sir; they freely confessed it to me. They said, sir, that they didn't know what came over them, but all they could say was that perhaps it was the spring which made them act up. Also, they claim that on the two occasions when protests were made about their truck, both at times when they had unwittingly parked it too far into the road, there was another way around the common and that cars could easily have gone that way."

I'd rarely heard such an unctuous tone; Trumbull was instantly the soul of restraint and compassion, the voice of calm and forgiving authority. I turned to look around at the man and encountered the faintly smiling faces of Hudman and Rampsie, nodding at the judge.

"Your Honor!" I was suddenly on my feet, burning. I could feel a hot poker down my back and knew that I had to speak now or never. "May I address the court?"

Judge Bream looked at me questioningly.

"I'm Lisa Sanderson, sir, a practicing attorney in Boston, visiting relatives here. And I'd like to attest, Your Honor, to the noise in the common and also to the fact that my uncle's arm was broken in an encounter with those men—not boys—on the sidewalk. In addition, one night last week while intoxicated, they smashed a window in my uncle's house and set the interior on fire with a torch from that fire they'd started on the common. I'm sure that Dr. Almquist can describe to you the nature of the injury to my uncle's arm."

The judge looked at me hard, over the demarcation in his glasses, then asked George to describe the injuries to Uncle Simon. George slowly rose to stand next to me, arms crossed over his chest, and began to explain to the judge about the hairline crack, the chip from the bone, and the edema and discomfort that had occurred as a result. It was a clear, concise report; George made a good medical witness.

Trumbull was on his feet again. "Your Honor, another word, if it pleases you." He opened a pad in his hand, flipping back the page, and slipped on his glasses. "I have here a description of what happened from the boys—boys, Miss Sanderson—and they claim it was a dark night, and that there were no streetlights directly over the spot where the alleged encounter with Simon and Lisa Sanderson occurred."

Uncle Simon was muttering in my ear. "There are streetlights there. I know it for a fact. What's he trying to prove?"

I touched Uncle Simon's hand as reassuringly as I could and continued listening to Trumbull.

". . . there was no intention on my client's part to injure in any way, Your Honor. They simply happened to occupy the same sidewalk at the same time." Trumbull removed his wire-rimmed glasses and swung them back and forth. "In all fairness, sir, we will admit that there's been some ill feeling in this town partly because a mill strike is in progress, and you can imagine the effect of that on a town this size. But this certainly isn't attributable to my clients."

Judge Bream nodded understandingly toward Trumbull.

I was on my feet again. "The fire in my uncle's house, Your Honor. That can't be explained so easily. There was considerable damage to my uncle's living room as well as illegal entry. We've had to board up our house and so have some others on the street. Some have even left town."

"Did they come inside your house?" the judge was asking.

"No, sir. They reached inside with a burning stick. One of the men was partway through the window. They ruined much of the interior."

Trumbull was still standing; not once had he sat down or looked at me. He still held the center of the room like a captain at the helm of a ship. He fixed his eyes on the judge. "There were strike organizers out that night, Your Honor, and it might not have been my clients at all. Again, sir, it was night, as we have previously said, and—"

"We saw them," I insisted. "We could see those men from the upstairs window where we were looking down at them. They were definitely Attorney Trumbull's clients!"

Judge Bream nodded solemnly. "This sounds like a graver charge than the others. Private citizens ought not to be interfered with in this way. Will the boys please come forward?"

Rampsie and Hudman rose from their chairs and stood uneasily before the judge. Hudman twisted his hands behind his back, but Rampsie appeared relaxed, cool, casual. Were these the young men who'd been frightening Rowe? I wondered. They looked like thriving young mill hands, or salesmen, or gas station attendants trying to earn an honest buck. They stood together, erect, before the judge.

"Tell us what happened," the judge asked in a fatherly way. "Try to be brief but accurate."

I listened to Rampsie's even, controlled voice; when I looked away, angered, George touched my arm consolingly. We both knew that in this room it was almost impossible to convey what had occurred out on that common, even though we could see it through the window. Today it looked so green, so sunny, so placid. Rampsie's voice had even lost its edge of sarcasm, and I could hear almost a note of humbleness in it. I dug my nails into my palms in frustration. Trumbull had instilled a ring of sincerity into old Pops's favorite nephew almost overnight. I had to take my hat off to the alchemy. But I never did underestimate Rampsie's intelligence ever, not for one second.

"We went over to the Sanderson house, s-sir, and w-we'd been getting kind of a h-hard time from some of the people hereabouts, so's we w-wanted to a-pologize. Well, s-sir, they got so mad at us, this l-lady"—Rampsie pointed directly at me—"and the others, even threw stuff at us, that we just gave up and c-came back home."

"Then why were you carrying that burning torch?" asked the judge.

"B-because it was dark, like I said, Your Honor. And n-nobody'd replaced any of those lights burned out up there."

110

I leaped to my feet again. "That's not so, Your Honor. What's more, these men know it, and so does Lawyer Trumbull. And the streetlights are not burned out; it's bright as day beneath them." I realized that essentially the hearing had pitted Rampsie's word against ours, that the informality of the proceedings unfortunately had the effect of giving a sense of credence to his barbarity. It sounded like, but was totally dissimilar to, a court of law.

But the judge was nodding in a kindly way toward me. "We'll consider what you've said. I feel sympathetic to the rights of landowners, and in a town this size they're easily forgotten. I'll reserve judgment for a few minutes until I've heard all the complaints." He turned to Oldham. "What else have you got, Clyde?"

"One last item, sir." He consulted some jottings on a paper in his hand. "Petty theft against Hudman." He peered around the room. "Where's Mr. Rampsie?"

Pops was sitting toward the back of the room; he still wore the big white apron he used while cutting meat.

"Mr. Rampsie, will you please come forward?"

Pops raised himself partially from the chair, his face red, lips trembling slightly. "Mr. . . . your . . . Judge. . . ." His frustration was visible to all of us. Finally, as if the effort were too great, he fell back. "I—I ain't got nothin' to say."

"It's all right, Pops," said Oldham, his voice rising with authority. "Come on up now. Nobody's going to bite you."

I could see Bob Rampsie, half turned, looking toward his uncle at the back of the room. That look had crept back into his eyes again, like something half tamed.

"I tell ya, I ain't got nothin' to say," said Pops. "I'm not sayin' a damn thing."

Oldham glanced uncertainly at Pops, who was perched on the edge of his seat near the back door, looking as if he were going to bolt.

"Please, Mr. Rampsie," Judge Bream said. "If you've got anything you'd like to tell us, now is the time. I've got here"—he was holding a typed sheet before him, the replica of Oldham's—"that one of these boys stole something from your store. You'd like to press charges, am I right?"

"Nope," said Pops, standing awkwardly now in his place. "I changed my mind. It warn't nothin', and I don't want to say no more. Now I gotta get back to the store." He yanked the door open, and suddenly he was gone, as if he'd magically disappeared in a puff of smoke. Through the back window I could see his form, the white apron flapping, scuttling back across the common to his store.

Chief Oldham stood rooted at the front of the room, looking after Pops, astonished. "I'll be damned," he said, then turned apologetically toward the judge. "I don't know, Your Honor," he added a little plaintively. "Seems like we don't have a case anymore. Seems like we'll just have to let that one go."

The judge shifted uneasily in his chair, then looked at his watch and finally at his list. "That's all I've got, Chief. If there's anything else on the agenda, it isn't on my list."

"That's it then, Your Honor."

Judge Bream stood up, adjusting the voluminous black robes. "Then give me a few minutes to deliberate, and I'll pass sentence, particularly about the fire that was set at the Sandersons'." He left the room again for that tiny anteroom, his hands on the lapels of his robe, swaying slowly with each step as if in time to music. We sat down again to wait.

Uncle Simon was shaking his head sadly, peering down at the floor before him, where the fire engine had left a few drops of oil. "Nothing's going to come of it," he said quietly, almost fatalistically. "The man doesn't even understand."

George glanced quickly at Uncle Simon, appraisingly, then placed his hand on his shoulder. "Don't be so pessimistic, Simon. Maybe the judge *doesn't* live here, but he must get the picture. After all, it isn't as if he hasn't come to Rowe before."

But Uncle Simon was surprisingly adamant, continuing as if he hadn't heard George, almost as if he were talking to himself. "How can you tell that judge the mood of a place, tell him what's really been going on here so he'll understand?"

A pang of desperation overcame me, and I rallied to fight it. "I don't really think that Judge Bream is all that unobservant, Uncle Simon. Despite Trumbull and his model youth bit, all he has to do is ride around the common and see the houses boarded up."

"He won't, though," answered Uncle Simon. "Last time he came here, he was in and out of town in fifteen minutes. Don't think he saw any of it except the inside of this building."

George looked at me questioningly. I knew that he was wondering if Uncle Simon wasn't taking this pretty hard despite the fact that the judge hadn't yet rendered an opinion. I shook my head back at him, indicating that I didn't know where we stood, then turned back to Uncle Simon.

"Give him a chance," I said gently, trying to cheer him. "Bream wasn't born yesterday. A good judge has a third ear for just that kind of situation."

Trumbull had returned to the back of the room, where he was talking to Rampsie and Hudman. Hudman leaned against the rear wall, his foot flat on it—probably dirtying the taxpayer's paint, I was thinking—and Rampsie rocked on his heels a little as he conferred with the lawyer. I could see the judge through the tiny window in the anteroom door as he paced back and forth; the window was just about waist-high, so I could make out his hand holding a cigarette as he paced.

Finally, he was ready to come back; a puff of smoke wafted out the door as it opened. I was once again sitting on the edge of my seat, holding onto the side with my palms, when to my surprise I found them slippery with sweat. George was leaning tensely forward, too, his hands clasped before him. Uncle Simon glanced up hopefully, watching the judge arrange his robes once more.

"Will you boys please come forward?" the judge asked Rampsie and Hudman, moving his hand to indicate a position directly before him.

Bream waited a moment while the pair nervously moved forward to face him. This time Rampsie appeared distinctly tense, tearing savagely at a cuticle on one of his fingers. Bream looked searchingly at the men before him, then around the room, toward us, and finally at Trumbull, who was standing directly behind the "boys." The judge appeared to be about to reveal a divine truth, so serious were his face and manner. I turned away momentarily, despite the magnetic pull he exerted in that room at that moment.

"I'm going to fine you," the judge said finally, "on the basis that you've committed an offense rather than a misdemeanor. I'm not going to get severe or give any of you a hard time because I don't think you deserve it, and I'd like you to see the folly of disruptive behavior by yourselves. I'm not a disciplinarian. I'm a humanitarian, and always will be, I hope. But I want to caution you that you live in a small town, sensitive to upheavals and public disorders. I've seen it happen before that disruptions which ought not to have started suddenly got out of hand and had to be checked. But this time, as I said, I won't deal harshly."

I could see that Uncle Simon's good hand, on his knee next to me, had rolled into a tight fist.

"So," Judge Bream continued, "I'm going to fine you now, and caution you to behave like the good citizens I'm sure you are, and trust that a word to the wise will be sufficient. Chief Oldham, will you see the court collects the amount of thirty dollars from these defendants?"

I jumped from my chair. "Thirty dollars, Judge Bream? Did I hear you correctly? You said thirty dollars?" Why, I thought, that's what those men drink up in beer in one night! Couldn't the judge have slapped their wrists and let it go at that? "Don't you realize that thirty dollars is nothing, a pittance, a fraction—"

"Of course, Miss Sanderson. You didn't expect me to be vindictive, did you? I told you, I'm a humanitarian. You've got to understand—"

"How about *us*, what do you think about us, how are we to cope with this?" By now I was really furious. "Just how are we to manage what's happening here? What exactly do you suggest, Judge Bream?"

Again he was cool, unflappable. "You can call on me again, Miss Sanderson. I'll be glad to come another time. As for now, court is adjourned!" The man had even brought along a gavel; he rapped it soundly on the wooden table before him. It resounded throughout the quiet room like a gunshot.

I was in a daze, but George took my arm to get me out of the room. Someone said, "Miss Sanderson," and I thought it was the judge, but I simply couldn't talk to him. I strode from the room, but it felt like sleepwalking. I refused to look behind me because I knew that Rampsie and Hudman were there, and I couldn't bear to look at them.

George had to return to his office, where patients were waiting for him. Uncle Simon and I walked back to the house together across the common without talking. The sun was a blaze of fire overhead; as if in a cloud of fury I stalked across the wet ground, still sodden from last night's mist. We scattered a flock of pigeons in our path. Goddamn pigeons, I thought, always in the way. I kicked at one.

Uncle Simon walked with his head down. "Are all judges like that?" he asked me. "Aren't they interested in protecting people? Don't they really care?"

"Mostly they try to give everyone a fair shake, Uncle Simon."

"Do you call that a fair shake?" He was trembling slightly. "You think it's fair that those people"—Uncle Simon said the words with undisguised contempt—"got fined thirty dollars for what they did? That will keep them from acting up any more?" He kicked at a stone. "You know and I know that's small bait for big fish, and they'll be trying for bigger and better things."

I had to agree with him. I know that punishment could be a bad thing

114

sometimes, that the misuse of it caused more grief than good. In some of the courts where I've worked, I've seen terrible criminals walk away, free, followed by their fleets of lawyers, and I've seen people who really ought to get another chance caught up in the system. It was terrible, and to me, professionally offensive.

"They said we couldn't believe our own eyes," Uncle Simon was muttering. "What do they mean, that we can't believe what we see? Why won't they believe it when we say we saw who attacked us, in front of our house, in light almost as bright as the sun?"

Suddenly I looked up and stood still, speechless. Uncle Simon followed my gaze. The streetlight had been smashed. There were a million shattered pieces on the ground beneath it. I looked around the common as far as I could see: from where I was standing, there wasn't one single light remaining to illuminate the entire common of Rowe, Vermont!

PART

The fine of thirty dollars had outraged and unified the town. Uncle Simon was still inconsolable; I tried to reason with him to no avail. Wednesday, when George came over to breakfast, he couldn't calm Uncle Simon down either. I was worried about him.

"It won't help to become despondent, Simon," George said. "Everyone's upset. A couple of my patients called for appointments and couldn't talk about anything else."

Aunt Chloe wasn't to be appeased either. "Minott Swett says thirty dollars is a *reward*, a reward," she said. I knew that the mill's other bookkeeper had already called to talk to Uncle Simon this morning. "Why, thirty dollars isn't going to pay for the damage those hoodlums did to my couch, much less for the food they swiped from Rampsie's store, or for the wood to board up everyone's windows, or the damage to the common and to Clyde Oldham's car. Thirty dollars!" She'd thrown up her hands in outrage.

George and I walked somberly together with Tim and Buzz to the bus, in accordance with our rule that no one unaccompanied was to venture out on the common. "I can't get Uncle Simon to calm down, George," I said. "He's like one possessed. I'm sure he didn't sleep all last night. I heard him roaming around the house off and on until dawn."

George nodded. "He wasn't the only one. Put in a fair amount of pacing myself. Ended up by fixing the busted lock on my back door—hadn't locked it since I moved into the house. I guess we're all getting paranoid!"

119

We watched the kids climb onto the bus, really a large van partially funded by the school district, which transported the kids back and forth from school; then George returned to his house to see his patients. I'd promised Aunt Chloe I'd tackle making new living-room drapes with her—she'd found some old material up in the attic—and we set to the job, stretching out the cloth across the living-room floor and gathering it with, it seemed, pounds of pins. How Aunt Chloe could talk with a mouthful of pins I'd never figure out, but she never missed a syllable.

At four o'clock I walked out to meet the kids again. The cars that had been parked so sedately during that recent and estimable hearing had long since departed, and the fire engine was once again ensconced in its majesty in the firehouse-dubbed-hearing-room. All had been effaced, I thought, like a castle of sand. The good judge had come and gone, and we were back at the same old stand, trying to grapple with the realities of life in Rowe, trying to decide if we were still in one piece or if something vital had leaked. Our common was cursed, I'd been thinking, and I had no idea what kind of tribal ritual might be necessary to exorcise the demons.

Perhaps there was yet hope, I reasoned, standing at the edge of the road waiting for Tim and Buzz, and we'd look back at this time as the low point in some mercurial dip of fortune. After all, downswings always had their reciprocal upswings, I'd read somewhere, and perhaps we'd simply landed at ground zero yesterday. Or was I beginning to put too much stock in hope, like others around here? I rocked idly back on my heels, waiting for Tim, my hands pressed into the pockets of an old sweater, staring at the ground beneath my feet.

The school bus always came from the direction of Tremont, circled around the oval, discharging first the kids whose homes were on the common, then the others who lived down side streets. Perhaps from some ingrained sense of wariness in this place, I glanced up toward Rampsie's store. Behind the building, almost hidden by the old frame structure, was the flatbed truck, which suddenly came to life. As I watched, flooded with sudden apprehension, the truck slowly edged from behind the store, jouncing over the potholes in the vacant lot next to Rampsie's until it gained the blacktop of the road. I was standing on that sidewalk, watching as if that truck had become the polar center of my world, when I saw clearly that it was picking up speed. There were faces now vaguely visible through the front windshield, and someone was dangling a leg casually out the cab door.

120

I was hypnotized by the truck, like a moth before a flame; momentarily I became immobilized by my own inability to comprehend what was going on. I really expected it to continue circling the common, but suddenly I realized with a start that it wasn't about to. Someone in the truck had floored the accelerator, and I could see the ornament on the front of the hood, that shiny, voracious bulldog, leaping through the air at me.

Flooded with panic and sheer terror, I turned to flee toward Brittons' property directly behind me, where I knew there was a low stone wall. I dived for the opening.

I was through the opening and almost at the Brittons' front porch when I heard the crash of the wall. I turned around, terrified, clinging to a post on the porch; when I glanced back, there before me was the front of the truck, its nose thrust partway through the wall. Rocks from the structure caromed all over the Brittons' property like bowling balls; they flew with such force that one smashed through a side of the garage and another crashed into shingles of the house with a clap like thunder. But the truck had stopped. I was panting, still clinging to the post, looking back toward the truck, fully expecting to see it demolished from the impact. But there was some kind of plow attachment on the front, like a cowcatcher on old trains, very heavy and very shiny. For a panicky minute I wondered if that monster were going to charge into the Brittons' property after me, but then I heard a sudden guffaw from somewhere inside it, and out popped Bingo Keaton's head. Now that his red hat was back on his head again, he wasn't even recognizable as the man in the courtroom yesterday morning.

My legs felt wobbly, like rubber, and I couldn't seem to manage to move them, so I clung to the cool post of the porch as if it were all that remained in my insane universe. The truck suddenly reversed with a lurch, then began to extricate itself from the wall like an animal emerging from its burrow. The thick treads had ground the Brittons' yard to a quagmire. For one moment the door pushed open, and I could see Rampsie in the cab. He was sitting there by himself, silhouetted against the sky, giving me the finger. He didn't say a word, but there was a grin stamped on his face when he held that finger in the air, his eyes like slits. When I contemplated his face, I let go of the post and flattened myself against the house, but there was nowhere to go if that truck were to charge again.

The truck continued to back off through the opening in the shattered

121

wall; I could have cried with relief. I began to pound at the Brittons' door; luckily Mrs. Britton was inside, as terrified as I. She fumbled with the lock to let me in, then threw her arms about me, even though I scarcely knew her. She helped clean the mud off my clothes and gave me a facecloth rinsed in cold water. The icy cloth helped calm me down.

I couldn't bear to go outside to wait for the bus, so I watched for it beside the window with Mrs. Britton, who prepared a cup of tea for me. Both of us were silent, barely speaking above a whisper despite the fact that we were the only two in the house. Suddenly the bus arrived; I touched her hand and soundlessly opened the door. The kids spewed from the bus. Buzz waved at me and ran on ahead to see his mother. Tim yelled, "Hiya, Sis," then came tearing over, head down, as if he were charging the line at a football game; I grabbed him halfheartedly as he tore by.

He was full of pent-up energy from enforced sitting at school. "You look kinda glum," he said. "Things pretty dull around here, I bet." He was laughing. "Aren't you glad I came home to shake things up a bit?"

That night I couldn't tell Uncle Simon, but he knew something'd gone on. For one thing, he'd seen the Brittons' front wall—those boulders were still strewn all over the sidewalk, as if a giant had been playing jacks with them. I knew he was deferring questioning me about them until later. Why shake everyone up?

Mrs. Sardoe and Aunt Chloe were chattering in the kitchen, planning the booths on parade day; as usual, they'd sell cookies, relishes, cakes. Although now four or five additional families had left town, enough remained to contribute, in Aunt Chloe's opinion.

"We've got marching practice," said Tim. "Mr. Callaghan says we can practice out on the common, because we've got only four days left, and we'd better get cracking."

I began to protest about the common, but Uncle Simon caught my eye again. It was true, on parade day the common would be filled with people, and there was safety in numbers.

After everyone'd gone, he turned to me. "You'd better tell me," he said grimly. He hoisted his left arm to the wing of the chair, grunting slightly. The cast must weigh a ton. "I saw those tire marks on the Brittons' lawn, and they weren't put there by any car."

So I told him about the truck. "They're retaliating for my court appearance yesterday morning, Uncle Simon."

122

Uncle Simon nodded despondently. He looked as if he'd aged ten years since this whole thing began. "At least you weren't hurt. The Brittons' yard was a god-awful mess. Can't believe what I saw happened to that wall. What did you say they put on the front of that truck?"

I tried to describe it.

"Blades from a big plow," Uncle Simon said finally. "But how did they get them on?"

I recalled what the police lieutenant told me in Tremont. "Did you know that Hudman served time as a juvenile? And you know what else? They taught him welding in jail!"

Uncle Simon stared at me. "But plates from a plow like that must weigh two or three hundred pounds. Why, they'd have to be that heavy to demolish the Brittons' wall."

Aunt Chloe and Mrs. Sardoe had gone outside to watch the kids practicing; Uncle Simon and I perched on the steps to watch. I'd forgotten what fun kids have marching. There were only a dozen boys out there, but Stu Callaghan had them arranged according to height, with Tim in the last row and Buzz in the first. He was drilling them like a sergeant in the Marines and kept mopping his brow with a big handkerchief; when he gave his kids a breather, he came to stand next to us on the sidewalk, where we'd gone to meet him.

"Good thing we don't have to do this more'n once or twice a year," he said. "All I can stand, just makin' sure they're in step some of the time."

We watched the kids out on the common turning handstands and a couple shooting marbles in a spot devoid of grass beneath one of the big elms. "Is Jaimie Rampsie in your troop?" I asked.

"Usually. He stands in the same row as Tim; they're about the same height. He's gone someplace, I guess, because the boy hardly ever misses."

"Does he ever talk about his brother?" I asked Stu. "Somehow they don't seem cut from the same cloth. I mean, do they get along?"

Callaghan thought for a minute, shading his eyes to watch the kids cavorting. "I can't rightly tell you. You knew Jaimie lives with Pops? Well, Bob lives all over the place. Mostly with his father, I guess, in the old house couple of blocks back. But he's got a flock of girls, Oldham says, so he beds around. Sponges off them, too, Clyde says. Seems he hates his old man. Mostly I think Jaimie admires his brother sort of offhand, like he's the hero in a story."

Across the common, a small band of musicians was now gathering. I could see a couple of trumpets, someone with a drum, a few clarinets.

"Marching band," explained Uncle Simon. "They come out anytime anyone wants music, parade or whatever."

Stu Callaghan laughed. "Even when you *don't* want music, that band comes out. God-awful racket sometimes."

After another minute or so Stu glanced at his watch, then turned toward the Scouts on the common. "Time to get going," he said.

Uncle Simon and I had walked out a ways with Stu, and now we slowly returned toward our house. It was a lovely evening without a breath of air stirring, the sun gathering golden light in the common just before it sank behind some low hills to the west. Aunt Chloe and Mrs. Sardoe both were sitting on the front steps idly chatting, watching the musicians and the Scouts. Aunt Chloe had her hands to her eyes to ward off the low rays of that sun slanting across the large oval, through the trees. I could remember years in the past, when my family had come to visit, taking a walk around the common before we had drifted inside on a nice summer night; those walks were almost a way of life for the people of Rowe. Everyone knew he would see his neighbors on one of those summer night constitutionals around the oval sidewalk.

The sky behind Aunt Chloe's and Mrs. Sardoe's houses was now slowly darkening, so that I could just see the top of the barn behind the house, with the tall pines like growths protruding from the old roof. Behind the bushes between our house and the now-empty frame building of the Sardoes I could suddenly make out the movement of someone or something running between the two houses. It almost looked to me as if a deer had come from the woods. For a week a couple of summers ago a buck had appeared from those woods to graze on the common every night; Tim and the other boys had begun to leave salt and grain for the majestic animal, thinking that food in the woods might have been in short supply that year. But tonight it was dusky over there, and I couldn't make out the figure. I traced its progress behind the Sardoes', then the Macys', and finally, closer at hand. The figure disappeared behind the Brittons'. It wasn't a deer, it was a boy, and when I'd seen him a final time before he ultimately vanished behind Rampsie's store, I knew who it was: Jaimie Rampsie.

Before his final dash, I pointed silently, and Uncle Simon followed the direction of my finger. At the last moment Bob Rampsie emerged from the shadows of his uncle's store, grasped his brother's arm, and pushed him roughly inside the building.

124

I couldn't make any sense of it—Jaimie running furtively behind the houses that way. Why didn't he use the sidewalk? I also couldn't figure how Bob Rampsie had arrived at his uncle's store without anyone's seeing him; there'd been no car, no truck, no sign of any of those men. Why were they so furtive? Then I remembered that there was a small parking area to the rear of the store, where Pops had his groceries delivered; as I looked back toward it, I could see the hood of a low car just barely visible beyond the building.

But as I turned back toward Uncle Simon's house again, remarkably I could see the brilliance of the moon rising over the trees; the thought crossed my mind: I didn't know there was supposed to be a full moon tonight. And wasn't it a little early in the evening for the moon to be so brilliant? I placed my hand casually on Uncle Simon's arm to point it out to him, then tightened it, for the incandescent halo I had thought was the moon had become ragged against the darkening sky; the brilliance of the sky was actually brightening, so that what I'd mistaken for moonrise appeared in reality more like sunrise, with jets of orange shooting from it and streamers soaring in all directions. Suddenly I screamed, and Uncle Simon began to run frantically toward Aunt Chloe.

"Chloe! Chloe!" he was yelling. "Look behind you, Chloe." Now I could see black smoke curling into the air.

The roof of the old barn behind Uncle Simon's house was spouting flames like a geyser, and the light in the sky was so bright it looked as if day had returned to one side of the town while darkness lay upon the other. But all around the common I could see the orange reflection of the flames in the windows of the houses, as though the fire were burning inside each of them.

The Scouts were yelling at the top of their lungs, and Stu had momentarily stopped dead in the street. "The fire engine, Stu," Uncle Simon was shrieking. "Quickly, for God's sake, Stu. Get the engine!"

Callaghan had already turned on heel and was heading directly across the common, the whistle of his Scout uniform batting at his shoulder.

In a moment each of the Scouts had ceased their yelling and stood contemplating the mounting flames with something like awe.

The heat from that barn must have equaled the fires of hell because I could already feel it out in the street, and I began to speculate in a dazed way on whether the house could withstand it; there were only thirty feet or so between the barn and the house and perhaps fifty feet

125

to the Sardoes'. Uncle Simon's barn boasted a little cupola on the top, a small separate room all by itself, like a pimple on the pinnacle. Already I could see the flames in there, licking out under the roof.

By now Aunt Chloe had found her voice and was screaming in anguish. "What will happen to the house, Simon, to our house? Oh, Simon, oh, Simon." She'd begun to rock back and forth on her heels, wailing.

In a minute there was a hoot from the firehouse, more like the cry of an outraged owl than a fire engine, followed by frantic clangs from the metal bell stop the cylindrical engine.

Uncle Simon now had his arms about Aunt Chloe, and Tim stood next to me, bug-eyed, watching the flames; he kept trying to calm Buzz, who was crying into the sleeve of his Scout uniform.

I'd never seen anything like that fire engine before, and now I could understand why: There was no fire hydrant on the street, so the engine was a tanker, carrying its own water in a large reservoir on its back.

We all appeared to have sunburns with the red glare of the fire on our faces, as if we were burning with the barn. As I looked back across the common, the sky above us was as bright as high noon, except for dark fringes in the distance along the horizon. Overhead sparks shot into the intense sky; people must have been able to see the fire for miles.

Firemen were pulling out the hose from the engine and running it around the rear of our house. "Hurry it up, Charlie," one fireman was yelling to the other. "Christ, look at that thing burn! My God, did you ever see anything burn like *that*?" Those firemen, all volunteer, were buttoning into their clothes as they rushed from their homes throughout the town to answer the fire call.

Mrs. Sardoe and Buzz stood on the front lawn, staring up at the inferno of sparks above their heads. Aunt Chloe once tried to rush up the front walk to rescue something from the house, in case that should go, too. "But I've got to, Simon," she protested, "please let me go, I've got to go back. . . ." A fireman and Uncle Simon restrained her.

By now the flames had become too hot to approach the barn, and the firemen and apparatus filled the driveway, circling the house with their hoses. I was staring up into a sky filled with violent flames when I heard George talking to me.

"Jesus, when did it start?" he asked in a low voice, holding my arm. "Minute I saw those flames against the sky, I came running. Clarissa was asleep, so I left her with the housekeeper."

I was overjoyed to see him. His face was bright with the red flames in the night, and there was already a light sweat from the heat across his chin and drops of moisture on his sideburns and eyebrows. I reached up to touch the fine moisture on my own face. "It started just a few minutes ago, George. But look, already there's nothing left. The roof is almost burned through."

The firemen weren't even trying to put out the fire; instead, they were soaking down Uncle Simon's house. I could see the arc of the water shooting from the pathetically small hose, but at least there was pretty good force behind it. Water ran off the house, down the driveway and into the street, pooling onto the blacktop so that the road looked like a shining black moat, setting the common adrift from the houses surrounding it. That water was so warm you could wash in it; I could even see steam arising as it cascaded down Uncle Simon's driveway into the cooler water of the street. Uncle Simon was quietly talking to Aunt Chloe, his arm still about her, as she rocked disconsolately back and forth against him.

The night was filled with shouts, shrieks, and curses as the firemen attempted to control the blaze. "Shingles smolderin' over there," shouted one, and "Watch that roof, Jimmy," yelled another, "she's listing badly."

"What started it?" George was asking me. "Does your uncle keep any inflammable stuff up in the barn?"

"I don't know. Just tools, things like that." Then I told him about seeing Jaimie Rampsie running away.

George swore softly beneath his breath. "Do you think the boy would start it? Jesus!" He shook his head. "But he's just a kid."

"Maybe it's just coincidence, George. It could be, you know." But as I looked at his eyes, I knew he didn't think it was coincidence any more than I did.

By now half the town was awake; people stood across the common, away from the fire, watching the orange flames against the sky. As far as we could tell, our house hadn't caught fire, although Aunt Chloe had finally stopped rocking next to Uncle Simon, and both of them were standing, still as statues, watching for signs of flames in their house. Someone had taken it upon himself to direct through traffic around the other side of the common, to avoid the fire engine and the crowd of spectators, and we could hear his voice above the din: "Move it, mister, see the road, this way, this way!"

Soon the remainder of the barn collapsed in a huge shower of sparks, with a roar like a giant bellows fanning the flames, and the white glow of incandescent heat. Three firemen were operating the hose, maneuvering the long, sinuous length, with a fourth at the truck. For a few minutes their faces disappeared against the whiteness of the flames, and all we could see was their black rubberized clothing outlined against the raging fire.

Suddenly the firemen ran from behind the house, dodging the curled hose and apparatus strewn across the driveway and soaking lawn. The man in front shouted something to the driver, who'd already jumped into the oversized seat and gunned the engine.

"Where are they going?" I yelled to Uncle Simon. The fire engine at that moment pulled away from the curb, and dumbfounded, I looked after it as it raced down the street.

"More water," Uncle Simon shouted back. "They've just run out. Have to go get more."

George appeared as incredulous as I. "How far do they have to go get it?"

Uncle Simon gestured toward the west. "Dugby's Pond, only a quarter mile. They say ten minutes."

We watched silently while the fire rekindled itself in the absence of water, and the flames began to mount again from the fiery debris of the imploded barn. George and I began to pace nervously, glancing at Uncle Simon's house. Some of the shingles on the roof had begun to smoke. George tensely struck the fist of one hand against the palm of the other. "Can't they hurry?" he said impatiently. "What's keeping them so long?" Just then, from far away, we could hear the approaching clangs of the fire engine coming closer and closer from the Tremont road.

The truck and the men worked throughout the night, the truck receiving continual nourishment at Dugby's Pond. Eventually the flames slowly abated; at one time the firemen left our house to soak the side shingles of the Sardoes' house, which was beginning to smoke ominously from the continued heat. Afterward they quickly returned to ours, dousing the roof with water. Finally, Mrs. Callaghan took Tim and Buzz and Mrs. Sardoe to her house and put them to bed, but Aunt Chloe, George, and I watched until the barn was a smelly, wet mass of charred, twisted boards and smoke had ceased to erupt from the heat of the rubble.

There was a moment, in the heat and glare from the fire, when I had to look away for a minute; my eyes felt dazed and sore with the vigil, and the heated, reeking air made my nostrils and lungs ache with the smoke. George had gone home for a moment to check his daughter. I turned around, my hands in the pockets of my sweater, and slowly walked down the wet road, trying to accustom my eyes to the darkness. I wandered into the common, leaned against a tree, and touched the cool bark with my hand.

At that moment I heard the sound of laughter, incongruous to my ears in that flame-ravaged night. Coming from the ground on the other side of a tree was a voice I recognized, that of Bob Rampsie. And I also knew what he was doing before I even saw him: He was on the ground with a girl, and they both were laughing and enjoying themselves. Why, I'd almost fallen over them! Didn't he give a hoot, I wondered, if someone found him on top of some broad in the middle of the common, grunting like a wild boar in his labors? My eyes were becoming adjusted to the light. I had turned to leave when, not ten feet away, I saw Jaimie Rampsie! He was sitting on the ground, head bent forward on his knees, arms clasped about his legs. He must have been a lookout—but had fallen asleep at the switch. But then, I wondered again, would Rampsie really care if I saw him? Did it make any difference to him that I knew what he was doing behind the bushes?

I was halfway across the street when I turned around for some inexplicable reason to find Rampsie looking at me, his hair disheveled. He was pulling up his pants, staring at me with unmitigated malevolence. The woman was back in the shadows somewhere, I couldn't even see her, but out in the light from the fire I could see Rampsie clearly, and there was no mistaking his look. It certainly answered my question: He cared that I saw him!

In that brief moment his foot swung forward into the small of Jaimie Rampsie's back as the boy sat hunched forward, asleep. I could see the boy flop on the grass like a stuffed doll, all arms and legs. For a frightened moment I almost ran to him, but I wasn't strong enough to fight for him or persuasive enough to plead—I'd only make things worse.

When I returned, there was a man standing on the lawn talking to Uncle Simon. It was one of the firemen; his eyebrows and hair were almost burned off, and his face was blackened beyond recognition. George had returned and was talking to him.

"Didn't you have on your rubber coat?" George asked him.

"Had it on, Doc, until a timber tore it off." Despite his burns, he was loquacious and lively. "Didn't get hit, just plain lucky, but got that coat tore off gettin' out o' there. 'Magine some of it's back there in that fire somewheres.''

George had removed his bag from the car. "Sit down," he told the man. George began to slather ointment on strips from his bag, then tore up his own shirt. It was warm enough in the heat-parched air not to require a shirt anyway, but George had ripped the thin fabric to shreds and was placing it on the man's back. George's strongly muscled body was eerily lit by the red flames of the fire; he had a deep chest, more like a laborer's than a doctor's, and a narrow waist. I wanted to touch him all over again when I saw him like that, and to be with him like that day in the car; for a moment my throat felt full as I just thought about it.

George squatted on his haunches behind the man, slapping on the strips as fast as he could, as if he were applying fresh skin to the fireman's burned epidermis. There was a smell about the man like roasted meat. I stood next to George, trying to control my impulse to put my hand on his shoulder, to rub my hand over his biceps.

"He's got to go to the hospital in Tremont right away," George said, looking about at the spectators watching the fire.

"Sure," said a man nearby. "I'll go get my car." He was back in five minutes. The burned fireman seemed in no obvious discomfort; I couldn't understand it. I could see that in the sections of his back where the skin had burned away, moisture was beading in tiny droplets. George helped the fireman into the volunteer's car, and we watched them drive up the road to Tremont.

"Why can't he feel the pain, George?" I couldn't remember seeing the man so much as wince.

"The nerves are gone, burned away with the skin. Third degree. Poor devil's lucky he can't feel it."

The firemen continued to douse the fire with water during the night; just before daybreak smoke ceased to pour so heavily from the charred timbers and mangled debris which had once been Uncle Simon's barn. The volunteer who'd brought the fireman to the hospital returned near dawn, just as a faint gray appeared over the giant pines behind Uncle Simon's house.

"What happened?" George asked the man anxiously.

"They sent him down to Boston," the man reported, rubbing his jaw thoughtfully. "Said he'd need burn therapy. They didn't like the looks of him." He turned to George. "Said those strips of yours mighta saved his life."

130

Later, when George returned home once again to Clarissa, he looked as black as the firemen, as if he'd fought the fire just as intently. He'd continued the vigil with me, and with Aunt Chloe and Uncle Simon, all night. A fine char had covered all of us, and we were barely recognizable to each other, standing in that river of warm water, watching the flames consume our night.

Finally, hours later, the fireman said that we could go back to our house. Miraculously, nothing had been burned, but the smell was unbelievable. We threw open the windows and doors, but absolutely, in no way, were we going to kill that smell for a long time. Water from the hoses had leaked in beneath the back door and poured into the cellar, and Aunt Chloe, with moans of disgust, began to pull out rags and old newspapers to soak up the water. It would take days and weeks to put the house to rights; we all knew it, most of all Aunt Chloe. She began immediately the battle that had been enjoined against her territory, her fortress, with outrage and anguish.

Just before the last fireman left—it was Paul White, one of the men at the meeting in Aunt Chloe's living room so recently—he asked to speak to Uncle Simon. I'd never have recognized him; he stood outside the door, black with smoke and char from head to toe, exhausted, but with a serious, triumphant smile as if he'd won another contest. In his hand was part of a can of some kind without a lid over the opening. A strip of handle remained attached to the can by a length of blackened metal. The fireman held it up in the air.

"Is that anything you kep' in the barn, Simon?"

Uncle Simon took it from the fireman and turned it backward and forward critically in his good right hand.

"Never saw it before, Paul. What is it?"

"That's what I'm asking, Simon. Hopin' you could tell me. Container of some kind, probably held something flammable. Least, that's our guess. Besides that, there's a pile of rags back there behind the larches. Why they didn't burn, I dunno, but they didn't."

Uncle Simon shifted about uneasily. "You better tell me what you're thinking, Paul. I'm not much on the guessing game."

"Well, I'm thinking somebody set this here fire, that they left a pile o' evidence around, and it don't make sense because if somebody'd wanted to burn the old barn down, all they'd had to do was hold a match under the old floorboards." The fireman cocked his head at Uncle Simon. "You got any idea who'd want to burn your barn down?"

Uncle Simon nodded. "Sure do, Paul. Don't you?"

Paul looked at Uncle Simon for a minute, then dropped his eyes. "My wife said to me when she heard about the fire, 'Paul, don't you dare cross any of them scalawags out on the common, or else we'll get it, too.' Well, she was right, Simon. Ain't nobody gonna say boo to them after this. Hell, it coulda been any of us." He took the can from Uncle Simon. "Thought I'd ask anyway. Gotta turn in this can to Oldham for evidence."

I stood with Uncle Simon, smelling the putrid damp from the fire. I'd made us both a cup of boiling hot tea; we were falling asleep on our feet, and the scalding liquid brought us back to life momentarily. Aunt Chloe, exhausted, had thrown herself down for a minute on the burned couch in the living room and had promptly fallen asleep. Uncle Simon fetched a blanket from the upstairs bedroom to cover her. Morning light was beginning to mount higher and higher in the sky.

"You could leave," I told Uncle Simon. "There are lots of places you could go for a while. How about Boston? I'm sure that you could find something."

He shook his graying head, running the fingers through his thick hair in a motion of frustration I'd seen him use lately. "I'd be a fish out of water in Boston, Lisa. I'd never be able to live there. Most of my life I've lived in Rowe. Wouldn't know what to do anywhere else. Later on today I'll get up and go to work at the mill, and that's my life, all I know. Been doing it since I was a young man, and I can't see any point in changing now, 'spite of everything."

I looked longingly out the window toward the common and the road beyond, feeling the fatigue and ache on my eyelids. "Maybe I'm as tough as you are, Uncle Simon. Maybe not, but I'd like to think I am. Besides, I feel that this is my home, too." We looked into each other's faces in the wan morning light, and I could see his pale eyes in their heavy creases. There was more than despair and fatigue in them: I saw some kind of insane determination to survive. My God, I didn't even know that I had it, too, that uncanny urge to persevere.

When I climbed wearily into bed, I was still thinking about that great speech I made to Uncle Simon. I didn't even feel remotely tough; I was scared and perhaps crazy not to beat it back to my law practice down in Boston. As I stared at the ceiling, I could see the faces of some of the kids I'd represented, the blitzed courtrooms,

132

and my scarred desk cluttered with lawbooks; I realized instantly then that I'd never wanted to do anything so much as return to that life. I could feel it drawing me, compelling me, tugging at me, almost a physical constraint. But I also knew I couldn't leave Rowe now. I couldn't escape because there was no escape for me. It was that simple.

13

Later that morning, after a few hours' sleep, Uncle Simon began to pick sadly through the remains of his barn; there wasn't much left out there except a mound of sodden rubble, about shoulder height, still smoking slightly. The smell of smoke from our fire hung acridly throughout the entire town as if it were emanating from the very leaves of the trees and dew of the grass. The back wall of our house was as black as the few charred beams remaining from the barn, and what little paint was left on it had bubbled and browned like the brew in a witch's caldron. The Sardoes' house was almost as bad. In disbelief, Mrs. Sardoe walked over to it, touched the broiled clapboards gingerly, then returned to our kitchen as if she were in a daze.

Uncle Simon had found an old stick; he was pushing the rubble around with it like a dog rooting for lost bones. When he came across a blackened can of old nails he'd been saving, the twisted blade of a scythe, and the metal part to an old stove, he examined them fondly as if he'd discovered old treasure. But then he suddenly threw them back angrily, stood for a moment peering away into the trees behind where the barn had stood, finally into the field beyond that, and with an exclamation turned on his heel and returned to the house.

About noon I heard the sound of voices outside and glanced out the window; it looked as if half the town of Rowe had materialized on our lawn. I'd been helping Aunt Chloe clean up some of the mess inside. We'd been working with pails and even shovels, making channels for the slop to run out across the dirt floor of the cellar. When we took a break, there were all those people! Stu Callaghan had rounded up the

134

Scouts, and most of the people still left around the common had arrived with shovels, wheelbarrows, and brooms. Several kids were pulling wagons. I smiled, seeing those neighbors of ours, and felt a kind of relief come over me.

One neighbor even had a pickup truck, into which everyone began to shovel all that wet debris from the fire; he'd pulled up right behind the house, as close as he could without his wheels sinking into the soaking earth. When the truck was filled, he scooted to the dump over on the back road, then charged back for more.

Halfway through the afternoon some neighbors arrived to replace those who'd been working steadily for hours, and incredibly all that rubble from the barn had begun to disappear. Just then the phone rang, and Aunt Chloe called out the window that it was Clyde Oldham for Uncle Simon. Aunt Chloe and Mrs. Sardoe had been running ice water and lemonade out to the people working hard behind our house; the sun was high in the sky, and there was still heat coming from some of those old boards.

"Simon, do you see anything out on the common?" Oldham asked. "I'm down here in the Flats investigating an assault last night, doesn't amount to a hill of beans, but I been trying to raise someone up there. Seems like everyone in the whole town's up to your house. My wife got a call from somebody, didn't leave a name, and they told her I should take a look out on the common. You see anything out there?"

Uncle Simon and I peered out the front door. There wasn't a thing moving out there, nothing. It seemed quiet and full of peace, with just a light breeze stirring some of the trees. Compared to the burned-out scene behind Uncle Simon's house, this place looked like heaven compared to the ravages of hell. There was nothing but those fat pigeons, a length of hose that firemen either forgot or discarded, and someone asleep in the sun.

We were just about to turn back, to tell Oldham that it must be a prank, when I turned once again for another look. My eyes rested for a second time on the man sleeping so quietly in the sun; he hadn't stirred, but there was a strangeness about the position he'd taken, as if he'd become twisted in an odd, convoluted way. How could he possibly sleep that way? I was wondering. Then he moved slightly, ever so little, arching his back and shaking like a wet dog, but he never shifted from that odd position.

I started to run, and Uncle Simon was right behind me. "Get

135

George, get George," I gasped over my shoulder, racing headlong down the front walk.

I'd bounded across the street in two seconds; the man out there in the common was tied up in some way that I couldn't figure as I ran. His legs were fastened as if they'd grown together, and his hands were thrust behind his back so that most of his weight was on the twisted shoulder behind him. He was squirming and gagged, with his eyes wide open, as glassy and brilliant as two black buttons. With a start I realized the man was Pops Rampsie, trussed as neatly as a helpless carcass of meat from his own store.

"Pops!" I shrieked. He tried to crane his neck to see. In a moment I'd fallen to the ground beside him, peering into those black eyes which wouldn't focus. I could almost see my own image in the reflective, uncomprehending surfaces.

I tried to untie his legs, but black cord was wound around them, some kind of electrical wire, heavy and unyielding. Someone had looped and knotted it, then fixed it with a metal clamp so there was no way to untie, slide, or unhook it. Pops was moaning slightly through the gag of dirty rags stuffed into his mouth; I managed to remove them by inserting my fingers into his slack cheeks. He drew a breath of air, shuddering and tortured, and closed his eyes. I couldn't get his hands loose either; they were tied just as tightly as his feet, with lengths of raw leather like long shoelaces, which had been dampened so they'd contracted as they dried. They seemed to be cutting off the circulation in Pops's hands; there was a great puff of blue blood under the skin above those whitened wrists, and the ends of his fingers were blue-black, swollen to twice their normal size, the tips like small purple golf balls.

I had turned around, about to shriek for help, when I saw George running down the road—Uncle Simon was by now on his way to get Oldham. Just as I looked back at Pops, the man's chest started to contract with shuddering spasms, and a dry sound emitted from his throat; he began to vomit. The yellow, rancid mass filled his mouth and ran down his face; he began to choke on it, his entire body shuddering to free itself of the nauseous substance.

I pushed the man over, trying to get him on end so that vomit would run out of his mouth and not gag him, but at that moment George had reached my side: he flipped Pop's head back to clear out his windpipe. The minute George took charge, I started sprinting for Pops's store, up the steps to the wide front porch, through the door. I flung myself through the opening behind the meat counter and grasped the first implement I saw, a meat cleaver, which must have been used for cutting through bones because it bore a razor edge; I didn't give a damn what I grasped as long as it would sever rawhide and electrical wire.

I ran back toward the common and as I reached Pops, I could hear the sound of gagging, and I knew instinctively that the old man was strangling in his own vomitus. George immediately flipped Pops upside down, upending him as if the old man were a child, holding him so the vomit would run from his throat; by now people were running across the common to see what was going on. Just at that minute, the bus from Boston started circling the road, and as the people on it reached a point opposite us, they stared out, bug-eyed. I could see a couple of women pointing at us, and one of them was laughing, misunderstanding what was going on, as if we were staging a disastrous, ridiculous farce for her benefit.

I started to saw away at the electrical wire looped around Pops's feet, but it was tough and wiry as a snake, and the copper strands inside had some kind of incredible intensity and resilience. Pops's feet were still up in the air while George held him, letting him drain out like a damp fish.

Finally, the wire gave, and George helped Pops kneel over while I sawed away on the rawhide cutting through his bloated wrists. At last that separated, too, but when George let go of Pops momentarily, the old man flopped forward on his face like a rag doll.

George and I both looked at Pops at the same time and realized something: He was drunk. He was stone-cold blotto, and he didn't have a bone in his body, because his skeletal system had turned to jelly, at least until he sobered up.

"What'll we do with him?" I asked George. In answer, he lifted Pops onto his shoulder as if the old man were a bag of oats, head down in case there was something more which had to drain out, and lugged him across to Pops's store.

The store was almost empty because the few customers had now gone outside to see what was happening on the common. George carried Pops into the back and motioned Jaimie Rampsie, who stood shivering behind the meat counter, to open the door to Pops's living quarters at the rear of the store. Jaimie looked terrified; he flattened himself against the door he'd just opened as if he were hoping he'd disappear against it. George hauled Pops, still dangling like a trout from a pole, into the inner room and dumped him on a bed, face down with his head hanging over the end so he'd keep draining.

That room was a creepy, crowded, dismal hole with the window shades drawn. The only light came through some holes in the cloth shades. In one corner was a sink; on the floor were scattered bedding and shoes and clothing. I could also see a lighted cigarette on the edge of an old dressing table, which was mottled with a million burns gouged into its surface.

Jaimie was terrified, his eyes dilating, and I knew I had him at a disadvantage, but I grabbed his arm and shook it a little. "Did you help do this to your uncle, Jaimie Rampsie? And was it you who started our fire? Was it?" Before he could answer, Bob Rampsie and Bingo Keaton ambled through the door into the room.

"Get your hands off the kid," Rampsie said to me in a low voice. His eyes had narrowed, and for a moment I thought he might hit me. I was even steeled for it, but by then I'd become too infuriated to stop.

"You tossed that helpless old man out on the common?" I asked Bob, pointing. "How could you do that? Don't you care about him? Why, Pops could have died!"

Then Rampsie stopped, took a step backward, and wheeled about to see Pops sprawled, still retching, on the bed.

"*Who* threw Pops on the common?" he asked, his voice now unsteady. "You think I'd. . . ?" He turned to Jaimie. "Who?" he demanded. Jaimie was so tongue-tied he couldn't utter a word, so Bob hit him with a blow on the side of the head. "Who?" he demanded again.

George had been covering Pops with a seedy blanket when he looked over to see Bob hitting Jaimie. "Leave the boy out of it," he ordered Rampsie. "Christ's sake, Rampsie, can't you see it's none of his concern?" There was an exhaustion and a fury in George's face; he was a mess, covered with Pops's effluence, his hair hanging raggedly in his eyes.

"Who?" demanded Bob again.

"I don't know, Bob, honest," said Jaimie, cowering, his voice quavery. "I'd tell ya, Bob, honest, if I knew. Don't you know that?" His pleading with his brother had taken on a desperate note as he attempted to stave off another blow. Keaton suddenly laughed, a high-pitched rasp compounded of fear and contempt for Jaimie.

Bob, half-crazed, turned on Keaton. "*You* know who did it, don't you, you shit? You do, don't you?"

Keaton, dumbfounded, stared at Bob for one vulnerable moment. Then Bob made a dive for his throat but succeeded only in grasping his shirt, which he tore loose from the man's body until it was attached only at the neck. Then he began to twist.

"Get your hands off me," yelled Keaton, croaking as loudly as he could with his shirt collar cutting off his wind. "Get your dirty hands off me." He was fighting like a man possessed, clutching at his throat and trying to kick Rampsie at the same time.

"Leave him alone, I'm telling you," shouted George in a fury of exasperation. He dived for Rampsie, trying to pry his fingers from Keaton's neck. "I'm telling you, Rampsie, goddammit, let go!"

Suddenly Rampsie let loose with a shriek because George had his fingers on some nerve at the base of Rampsie's skull. George was pushing on that nerve with all he had, grinding his teeth, with an outraged look in his eye. Rampsie dropped to the floor, rubbing the sore spot on the back of his neck, while Keaton scuttled away like a frantic, uncoordinated crab.

Then Rampsie flipped over on the floor as if he thought George might kick him—and for a minute I thought he *might* kick him. His leg was back as if to try for a field goal, but then he stopped cold. It wasn't mercy he was feeling for Rampsie, I thought, as much as consideration of the time and effort he'd have to expend to set his broken bones; he didn't want anything more to do with Rampsie once we got out of there.

George nudged Rampsie tentatively with his toe, then addressed Keaton without looking at him. I knew he wasn't sure who'd trussed Pops, that he was just playing his luck. "Tell Bob who tied up Pops and threw him into the common, Keaton. And make it fast."

Keaton'd flattened himself against an old chair of Pops's in the corner and was clinging to it as if afraid it would walk away and leave him.

"Who?" Bob asked again, even more fiercely.

Keaton visibly gave it up. "Hunk," he said finally. "Who do ya think? You think I'd hurt Pops?"

I was flattened against the wall, breathing hard, feeling the oppressive dark in the room like a physical force. Sure you'd hurt Pops, I was thinking, you little bastard. Sure you would.

"Why?" demanded George. "Tell him why."

Keaton wiped some spittle from his lips, staring at Rampsie. "Hunk was just gonna teach him a lesson, Bob. You know that. Pops was

139

gonna tell that judge about him stealin', remember? Didn't mean nothin', really. Just rough him up a little, like."

Bob Rampsie stared at Keaton with narrow, hate-filled eyes. He reminded me of an animal, thin and vicious. I was so terrified I started to slide toward the door, as fast as I could get there. "You're a goddamn creep, Keat," said Rampsie. He looked furtively about to see that George was still poised above him. "I'm gonna deal with you, Keat. Jesus, Keat, you just wait. But first of all, I'm gonna get that little son of a bitch Hudman."

Jaimie Rampsie had been watching from the door like a frightened mouse, peering in timidly, yet ready to run at the least provocation. George reached around the door and caught him by the shirt. "Listen," said George, "you sit here next to your uncle, you hear? You're in charge, and he needs you. You understand? Anything happens to Pops, you come get me right off. I'll be at home, or leave a message."

Jaimie nodded dimly, his eyes on George's face.

"Now get Pops cleaned up," George ordered Rampsie, who was slowly standing up, his malignant eyes on George's face. Keaton had been surreptitiously sliding up the wall with his back like a cat's, and I could feel the mounting vibrations of renewed violence. George took my arm and pushed me out the door; I felt his steadying hand on my back.

As we left the store, Jaimie caught my arm timidly. He looked pale with terror. In a breathless moment he glanced from me to George and back again. "I did it . . . I did it . . . " he gasped. "The fire. I'm sorry, sorry. Honest to God." Then he fled, back into the shadowy room where Pops was lying on the creaking bed. I felt too exhausted and drained to react. I knew he'd told the truth. But, I thought, a lot of good it does. He should have saved his breath.

Yet I'd come to like the boy; he wasn't cut in the same pattern as his brother, an accomplishment in itself. I didn't know how he'd managed to escape. I knew he deserved a little extra consideration despite Uncle Simon's barn.

We both were a mess. George brought me back to his house to clean up. While I showered, we talked. When I glanced outside the shower curtain, there was George, naked as a jaybird. Not only that, but while the hot water poured over me, he was shivering. "Come," I said, "climb in with me. Aren't you supposed to shower with a friend to save water? I always believed in neighborly—"

140

So we soaped each other down. It was heavenly; but I knew he had something on is mind. "It's Clarissa," he said. "I've already called her mother down in Boston to take her for a while. This is no place for a child. A colleague of mine, who lives down in Fitchburg, is going to Boston tonight. He says he'll take her. Would you care to ride along?"

I was still zealously spreading soap over George's ribs, casting bubbles over the tiles far and wide. "I won't be in the way?"

He cradled my chin and gave me a watery kiss. "Of course not." He'd partly disappeared in the steam. "I'll make it up to you tonight, when I'm not such an old hen."

I watched the water cascade off his nose. "I'd feel just the same way, George. This is no place for a child." I began to rub myself dry with the towel he'd given me. "Come to think of it, it's no place for adults either."

Clarissa sat between us while we drove the long, straight highway to Fitchburg. She was a quiet child, and I liked her immediately.

"Do you like Boston?" I asked her. "That's where I live, too."

She nodded excitedly. "I like all the lights at night, when we drive through." She added wonderingly, "There are so many lights. But I like Rowe best. Until lately. Now I get scared."

George reached over and patted her knee. "You'll be better off with your mother," he said, "until all this blows over." He smiled at her, and she nestled her head against his side.

George's colleague was older than he, a quiet, distinguished-looking man. His wife listened incredulously while George described the disturbances in Rowe.

"You mean you have to put up with those men all the time?" she asked. "It doesn't seem possible."

"Oh, yes, it does," said George's colleague. "It happens all the time in a city. People just move into a neighborhood and won't leave. Never heard of it in a town like that, though. Nice little place. Been through it several times."

George held his daughter a moment, then kissed her good-bye. "In a few days I'll come get you," he told Clarissa. "Don't worry." But now her face had flushed with excitement, and she was obviously looking forward to her time in Boston; George turned away in relief.

On the way back we stopped for something to eat at a small restaurant by the side of the road; it seemed the only place open for miles around. The waiter brought us drinks, and I looked into mine and thought I could drown myself in it; I could suddenly smell the smoke from the fire in my clothes, and the reek of Pops's vomit, and the stale smell of his room at the back of the store. I wondered inanely if there was a smell to the fright all of us felt, if some of it covered our skins in some way, a growth like moss which came from prolonged association with pain and fear—which other people sensed and instinctively made them want to stay away.

I looked down into the bottom of my drink and couldn't swallow or even imagine having dinner. Neither could George. I felt in some kind of limbo. George retrieved my jacket and slipped it over my shoulders as we walked out to the car. He started the car and moved his free arm about me.

I was so comfortable cradled against George's arm that I'd fallen asleep by the time we reached Rowe. The common was empty. George continued around the oval, past Uncle Simon's directly to his house. When he stirred, I sat up.

He slipped his hand to the back of my neck, massaging gently beneath my hair. "I'm damnably poor company," he said, "but I'd love it if you'd stay with me for a while, like I said. I really need you."

I turned to kiss him softly on the lips. He felt warm, and I moved close to him. "If you hadn't asked me, I'd have been hurt."

George made coffee, and we both began to feel better. Afterward he turned on a string of lights throughout the house, holding my hand; he was leading me to his bedroom. He owned the biggest double Victorian bed I'd ever seen, a blockbuster, with a carved headboard and four tall posts—it must have weighed a ton since it appeared to be made of solid mahogany.

"My God," I exclaimed, "how did they even get that thing in here? It's huge!"

George laughed "Tell you the truth, I think they built the entire house around it. It was here when I bought this place."

When George kissed me at the door, I felt a momentary qualm, despite my great bravado on our last occasion and my desperate abandon. The fact was I hadn't experienced a lot of men in my life mostly because it'd been too hectic. I wasn't as worldly-practiced as perhaps I'd conveyed to George. I'd lived with that law student for a while and a couple of others off and on. But I hadn't let men that close while I was going through school, perhaps out of fear I might somehow lose my determination to continue. I started to explain that to George, but then some kind of alchemy took over, and when he kissed me

142

gently and understandingly, I ran my tongue between his lips and across his teeth as if they were candy, and I was off again, really caring for him. While I pressed my lips against his, he began to undress me. His hands were warm across my back as he unhooked my bra; I could feel my breasts loosen and fall against his chest. My panties joined my skirt and blouse, already in a pile on the floor; his hands moved across my buttocks, rounding the curves and spreading the crease behind. I opened my legs, all the while unzipping his pants and extricating him from the folds of his underwear—stiff and moist, and the softness of the tip, like velvet, drove me mad. I moved my hand over and over his penis, massaging it, drawing on it, pulling it out more. At that moment George lifted me onto himself. He was standing up, bending slightly backward; I'd spread the lips of my own body and found myself soaked and bubbling with expectant lubrication; George slithered into my body, filling me, it seemed, to my backbone. I crossed my legs about his back and began to move with his movements, entirely cradled, feeling his penis almost impaling me, dividing me, thrusting far inside.

But I couldn't move in that position, I was too restricted, so George, realizing it, carried me to the bed and laid me gently down on it, not once moving from me. I could feel my passion increasing with tidal force, exploding, begging for abatement.

"Wait, wait," I cried, but it was too late—George had come with a shuddering groan.

He caught his breath and moved his hand beneath my head. "God, Lisa, I'm sorry. I couldn't help it, I couldn't wait."

He still held me while he recovered. "Help me," I said, and he rolled me over, his fingers moving across my clitoris, now so sensitive that at the very moment I'd spread my legs I wanted to close them on his hand. I came so hard that my back arched and I gritted my teeth, consumed with my own transport. Afterward I lay next to him, fondling him.

"Listen," he said, smiling at me. "When you want me, all you gotta do is whistle."

"Across the common? Won't the neighbors think it a little strange? I mean, all that whistling?"

He laughed. "Forget it. They sure as hell aren't on my frequency."

14

George drove me home. I sat contentedly next to him, wishing that this warm, hazy feeling would last forever. If one could choose a state in which to be suspended for life, I'd opt for this one. Hanging above the common was a languid moon, bathed by a lazy mist which caught the moonlight in a soft, luminous way.

George kissed me good-night, on the lips and gently; it tasted good, and I was thinking how nice it felt as I eased myself in the back door, when I almost fell over Timmy. He was sound asleep in a desk chair propped up near the door. I knew right off he'd been waiting for me.

He'd be a great watchdog; I had to stumble around a bit, swear a little, sneeze a couple times before he came to. I knew that if he'd gone to all this trouble, he'd be disgraced forever if he couldn't get to tell me what was on his mind. Finally, I had to fall against his arm before he came to.

"Sis," he exclaimed sleepily, "I've been waiting for you."

"Have you *really*?" I replied very seriously. "I didn't know." And I breezed into the kitchen for a cup of tea, figuring I'd hear more when he was fully awake. I began boiling water in the teakettle; just before the little whistle blew, Tim had pulled himself together.

"It's Jaimie Rampsie," he said as if he were making some kind of great revelation.

"What's Jaimie Rampsie?"

"Who burned down our barn."

This was pretty old stuff to me, but if Tim had been sitting up half the night, I didn't want to flatten him with the news. "How'd you find out?"

"He told me."

I handed Tim a cup of instant chocolate. "You mean, just like that, he told you?"

"No. We all had a powwow up in the woods."

"Who's we all? Don't tell me the entire gang's coming clean?"

He shook his head. "He told me and Buzz. He's kind of frantic about it. I mean, his brother made him do it."

Tim looked a little frantic himself. I sat quietly waiting for him to get control.

"Jaimie says it was some kind of initiation like. I mean, he had to show he could do it. You understand?"

"No. He didn't have to do it, Tim."

"Well, he says to tell you he's sorry. He says it's a big mistake, and that's what he wanted me to say."

I nodded slowly over my cup of tea. "Great. Tell him to start rebuilding the barn then. He feels sorry, I feel sorry. Couldn't he have thought about it before he lit the match?"

Tim looked away sadly. "He's real scared, Sis. I tol' you. They slap him around sometimes."

I was tired of feeling sorry for Jaimie Rampsie or anyone else. "Do you think he'd go with me to the judge and tell *him* that?"

"They'd kill him, Sis. Look what happened to Buzz, just for kicks."

"Thanks. Tell Jaimie thanks. For what it's worth, I'm glad he's sorry."

Sunday morning when I awoke, there was a sweetish, sticky smell in the air. Somehow it had mingled with the odor of smoke from the fire, and the damp sog of the water-soaked house insulation, and the mildewy damp of the junk down in the cellar still dripping from its dousing. It took me a minute to sort out the variety of smells. When I finally realized that the new one was fudge, my mouth turned so sour I thought for a minute I was going to throw up. Then I recalled that the parade was today, and Aunt Chloe out in the kitchen had already begun to make her contribution to the food table; I could even remember in the past when those ladies out there did a land-office business of cookies, cakes, lemonade, and candied apples.

I lay in bed a few more furtive minutes, thinking of George and wishing he were here so I could roll over against him—a thought that began somehow to make me feel vaguely lonely. Next my thoughts revolved to Rampsie and his friends, so that I felt even more distressed and couldn't stay in bed any longer. When I opened the shades, it was a sunny day, and people were already gathered out in the common, working on the long tables which had been lent by the Congregational Church for the event. My loneliness vanished in all that activity, like an errant shadow, forced back into some recess of my mind, and I peered out onto the common again, feeling excitement and anticipation.

One of the men from the two-man part-time public works committee was arranging folding chairs in a small group at the edge of the common to seat senior citizens, of whom Rowe seemed to have an abundant share. Three or four other men were actually sweeping the street with big push brooms, collecting the junk in piles, then throwing it into a truck. Somehow, down in Boston, I'd contracted the misconceived notion that the entire world was mechanized, and I was delighted to find out just how wrong I'd been.

I opened the window, inhaled a breath of the fresh air out there to clear out the chocolate and smoky damp, and threw on my ancient bathrobe. Downstairs, the kitchen was aboiling with fudge and Tim and Buzz were sitting out on the back stoop, licking the pots.

I took my cereal out into the backyard, into the sun, and while I sat there, talking to Tim and Buzz, George showed up. It was the first really warm day, and he hadn't worn a sweater, just a light shirt, and the breeze was doing nice things to his hair, moving it around on his forehead. For a moment he smiled, the sun in his eyes; then he looked around the backyard, kind of stunned. I followed his eyes, and it came to me with a sudden shock what we must have looked like sitting out there behind the house, with the burned-out rectangle of the old barn behind us, those singed trees, and that stench.

I sent Timmy in for some coffee for George.

"You didn't sleep," I said, looking at him. He seemed a little haggard.

George shook his head. "Damn worried. You?"

"Not so good." Weird dreams of people dancing in some kind of flaming inferno had tormented me all night. "I wish I'd been with you. Maybe that would have helped."

He sat down beside me, balancing his coffee. "I wouldn't have been much comfort. I lay awake thinking about what's happened to this town in the last few days and couldn't sleep worrying about it. I think this place is going to hell. I've come over to talk to Simon about it."

I pointed toward the house with my spoon. "He's inside. Talk out here, OK? I want to hear. Besides, the smell in there will turn you green."

146

In a couple of minutes Uncle Simon and George were back again. Uncle Simon had been shaving; he'd forgotten a little patch of cream beneath his ear.

"We've got to do something," George said emphatically. "I've been thinking about it all night, Simon, and the time has come to make the effort if we're going to have anything left of our lives."

Uncle Simon perched on an old bench he kept outside. His face was as grim as George's. He rubbed his cheek thoughtfully, looking absently at the place where his barn used to stand. "I've been doing some thinking, too, George."

"Well, you suggested a standby committee that night, Simon, remember? Maybe this is the time to call it up. Might be just the deterrent we need. Too many people getting hurt. You know that as well as I do."

Uncle Simon nodded while George was speaking. "That's occurred to me too, George. Remember, that's what I really had in mind the other night. Leastwise, we'd know who to call and what to do in an emergency."

"Well," said George, continuing, "why couldn't Clyde Oldham appoint a few deputies? Starting today, with the parade. Simply leave them deputized afterward."

Uncle Simon rubbed his chin, deep in thought. "Good idea, George. I'll call Clyde. I'd volunteer right off, 'cept for this arm. Bet he could use me for directin' traffic, though."

Uncle Simon suddenly sounded more enthusiastic than I'd seen him in a long while. When he left to call Oldham, George fell to pacing on the singed grass with a rapt expression on his face.

"Are you worried about the parade, George?"

He nodded somberly. "There's been no sign of any of them or of their truck. Makes me damn uneasy, doesn't it you?"

I groaned; we worried when we saw them and when we didn't. Was it worse to witness what they were doing or to imagine what they were up to? But it had come as even more of a shock to me to realize I'd lost my cozy reasons why a town should or should not increase its legal authority by appointing vigilantes. I was downright frightened and, I thought, the more protection, the better, no matter where it came from. I'd lost my legal cool.

"Not only that," George was continuing, "but when I went over to Rampsie's store this morning to check on Pops, nobody over there'd seen hide nor hair of those creeps either. It's as if they've vanished!"

"How is Pops?" I could still see him, purple and bloated as a sausage, and for a minute I expected my coffee to come up.

The flicker of a smile lingered on George's lips. "Tough old coot. About four in the morning he got up to start carving meat. You know, he was so damn drunk he doesn't remember a thing that happened to him? They might have slipped him something."

"You're kidding!" I could hardly believe George's words. But that explained how a man who'd barely survived being murdered remembered nothing!

When Uncle Simon returned, he was still a little glum. "Finally convinced Oldham about the deputies, but I hadda browbeat him to do it. Even told him the town might be out after his scalp if he refused. Wants you to help out, George, if we get some fainty ladies. Pretty hot out there."

George left to get smelling salts and bandages for sprained ankles and salt pills for heat prostration because things were really beginning to blossom on the common. Women ran back and forth with plates covered with foil, and two men were unrolling a cylinder of clean paper to cover the food tables. I could hear Timmy tearing around in the house, looking for some part of his Scout uniform, and Buzz's screeches while his mother washed and polished his face with a towel.

Pretty quickly I was caught up in it, too, running that fudge in warm pans out to the ladies in the common. Groups were collecting like puddles here and there, and that god-awful band kept tooting away, practicing off-key trumpetry. This was obviously the social bash of the Rowe spring season; despite those conspicuous burned-out areas on the common's grass, everyone was carrying on as if nothing had ever happened out there except fun and games.

The enthusiasm was getting to me: I dug out from my duffel a skirt with daisies all over it, donned my yellow sandals, and borrowed a yellow ribbon for my hair from Aunt Chloe. I began to feel as if there should be a maypole out there somewhere, and if there were, I'd be the first maiden on the left until my wind gave out.

Soon I heard a terrific snorting as the manicured and polished fire truck arrived to assume its position in the parade.

Finally, Oldham arrived, sporting his fancy uniform with the epaulets and gold stripe down the pants.

George pulled up in his car again, then sat next to me, chuckling at that slightly daffy crowd on the common. "Haven't seen people enjoying themselves out there in a hell of a long time," he said. I laughed with him and moved closer to him on the steps.

At noon Oldham gave some kind of signal, which looked more as if he were giving the finger to everyone than starting a parade, but he twirled it around in the air a couple of times and then stepped regally into his car. Stationed around the common were those new deputies: Stu Callaghan, Harvey Allen, Paul White, Ed Rhymer. Uncle Simon was somewhere along the line of march, a canteen slung over his shoulder in case he got thirsty.

I sat there next to George, who was chuckling like crazy watching this adopted town of ours, half of which was out there in tight uniforms and moth-eaten plumed hats, playing slightly off key—and it looked absolutely terrific.

Someone blew a whistle—it seemed to be a plump man leading a group in motley blue uniforms. Flags waved as each phalanx marched by, the color-bearers holding flagpoles with the handle ends tucked into little pouches slung from belt straps.

Then all of a sudden they were gone. Phhhht, the parade was over, just like that! But it wasn't really over; it'd merely disappeared down the side street like a lake emptying into its tributary. I could hear them tooting in the distance from among those overhanging elms. All we had to do was wait fifteen minutes, and that hesitant, proud, badly tuned column would snake back again, but for the moment, that was it!

I laughed with George as we watched the parade disappear; we could scarcely believe it had come and gone so fast, except for a distant oompah receding from our hearing. Aunt Chloe and Minnie Callaghan were out there pulling in nickles and dimes hand over fist with their fudge and lemonade, and now that we could hear ourselves think until the band returned, we strolled out to get some.

George bought the lemonade. Then I fished out money for cookies and fed one to him while the crumbs slid down his open shirt by mistake; when I made as if I were going to dive down there to retrieve them, sure to make us a public spectacle, he laughed and told me to behave; but I was feeling pretty much like a little kid by then.

Suddenly we all realized that something was wrong. It was hard to tell how we knew, but every one of us knew it at the same time; all conversation stopped cold in the group around the common. In the middle of a chorus of "Stars and Stripes Forever," echoing from about two blocks away, the music went flat. It simply dissolved into shreds of sounds.

"Come on," said George, urgency in his voice. I was standing on tiptoe, straining to see what was going on through those trees, when he grabbed my hand. His long legs covered the road in three bounds.

I gave up, panting, halfway across the common but motioned him to go on because I was just holding him up. But then he stopped cold, standing there, staring; I was doing the same, as was everyone else about us.

Appearing from that side street was not the band or the marchers, but that goddamn truck of Rampsie's. Still in place on the front were those enormous battering-ram snowplow blades. But on the back, on that long flatbed surface, had been welded one, two, three, four—yes, five metal seats, of the kind fishermen use when playing a tuna! I'd seen them on a thousand boats out on the Charles River in Boston or down in the boat basin.

Not only that, but the seats were filled with those idiots: Bob Rampsie, Keaton, Hudman, and a couple of others I'd observed with them before. They were holding beer cans aloft, looking like some insane float in a Rose Bowl parade. At the back end of the float was the huge flag that usually flew on the tall flagpole right above our heads here in the common. The flag had been nailed to the tail of the truck, and it was dragging along on the ground, already frayed and muddy. But what caught our eyes first was not the men or the flag or the seats; it was a huge sign, with letters four feet tall, attached to uprights on the cab and at the tail of the truck, bearing the words ROWE BOYS in heavy black paint.

As I looked at that sign, something struck cold into my bone marrow. Before, they'd seemed like a scattered group out on the common, committing separate acts of individual violence without a collective identity. Now they'd coalesced into a bond, an entity: The Rowe Boys. I looked about us and saw this common in a new light: as some kind of battlefield, a common ground of vengeance, where warring factions clashed before our very eyes.

The marchers had scattered like a flock of frantic chickens. Some ran before the truck into the center of the common for safety, but there was none there. On the side street, cars of riders had been trapped and couldn't get by to the right or left, and now the drivers seemed to be panicking. One of them inadvertently drove over a culvert and crashed into a tree at the edge of someone's property.

George had already rushed over to help a hysterical old lady who was trying to get out of the car, which was tilted in the ditch at a crazy angle.

But the truck hadn't stopped. It was still coming. Rampsie was swinging his arm on its back like loony old Ahab after the whale. It didn't even brake at the edge of the common but plowed right on across the grass. Somewhere off to my right I could hear Uncle Simon's voice yelling, "Where's Oldham, where's Oldham?" grabbing each passerby desperately as if someone might be inadvertently concealing the police chief. The spectators were scattering in all directions before that truck and its insane crew, which was now bearing down on the food booths in the common.

I knew what that truck could do because I'd seen it demolish the Brittons' wall, so I started screaming, "Run, run!" Right in the path of the truck was Buzz; he stood there almost unaware, hypnotized, while everyone else was vanishing in all directions as if standing on a hot skillet. Not Buzz—he was fascinated. He couldn't take his eyes off that charging vehicle.

"Buzz, damn it, run, run." I was screeching so loudly that my voice had turned hoarse, but Buzz stood there still, stupefied by what he saw before him.

The truck never stopped, although it slowed for a moment. I couldn't tell if the driver hadn't seen the boy or if he'd really aimed at him deliberately, but I had a clear view of Buzz's face just before the impact—and I knew for a fact that Buzz never had any idea that truck would hit him. Until it connected, his attention was riveted on the engine before him, on that leaping bulldog—and not one line of worry crossed his face!

Perhaps, I thought afterward, that was what had saved his life: his relaxed limpness.

It was a glancing blow, knocking Buzz aloft as if he were a rag doll. Arms and legs flopped in a flurry; then the truck charged onward demolishing the food booths.

"You bastards," I shouted as I rushed over to Buzz. "You goddamn bastards."

There was nothing left of anything. Then I saw Clyde Oldham, still vibrant in his uniform, spotless in his boots, running down the street. Where's he going, I asked myself, where's he going?

The terrible realization slowly dawned on my fevered brain: Oh, no, Clyde Oldham, you fool, you fool. You're running away, you idiot, just when we need you. How could you do it? I watched him disappear into back lots, lost in the shadows.

We helped get Buzz inside. His head was a little bloody; even his

151

eyelids were a little bloody. I wondered idly how much more his poor mangled brain could stand. When he was on his bed in Uncle Simon's back room, George gently opened the boy's eyelids and peered into them with a flashlight from his black bag.

I glanced out Uncle Simon's window for a moment on a trip to Buzz's room with a washcloth and basin and noticed that the truck was still there. Although Oldham had vanished, his deputies were striving to cope with the scattered remains of the parade. The newly christened Rowe Boys on the truck sat in their fishing seats, yelling obscenities at the few people left on the common, now in the process of trying to salvage their broken chairs and overturned pie baskets.

A few minutes later, when I again glanced out the window, Bob Rampsie was standing up, making a drunken speech to the crowd. At the same moment I glanced over at Buzz, pale, with his mother crossing herself and muttering some kind of incantation next to his bed. Aunt Chloe was running back and forth with cold compresses for his head.

Uncle Simon stood like a statue, a cold gleam on his face, glaring out the same window. A moment later, when I ran upstairs to get something more for Aunt Chloe, I saw that Uncle Simon had climbed the stairs ahead of me, and I could see that he'd unlocked his rifle case and removed one of the long guns; he was rubbing the wood thoughtfully, his thumb moving up and down the smooth grain. When he saw me staring at him, he quickly replaced the gun, almost apologetically, then pretended to tie his shoe, as if that were all he'd really meant to do anyway. But he didn't bend over fast enough, and I could see the fury in his eyes.

I'd never seen that fury in Uncle Simon's face before, and it utterly shocked me. In my lifetime he'd always been the gentlest of men, full of compassion and truth. I'd never, ever, seen him make a hasty or uncharitable decision; he'd seemed a man of infinite mercy to me, and the shock of his face came upon me like a wound. I'd inadvertently looked into naked, stark rage; he'd become at that moment a man I'd not seen before. My face had flushed and tingled when I'd looked at him like that, at the top of the stairs, and I had felt the hair rising on my head.

As I looked out the upstairs window from where Uncle Simon was standing, I could see what Uncle Simon was glaring at: Bob Rampsie, lounging on that truck, laughing drunkenly. As I watched, he unbuttoned his fly with casual nonchalance and let fly a stream of yellow waste onto the common grass.

15

Monday morning I decided to drive Tim to school in Tremont and then to visit my old friend, the honorable circuit magistrate, Judge Bream. We needed help; perhaps talking to him personally would accomplish something that courtrooms couldn't. After all, I was a card-carrying member of the club. I dropped by the Tremont courthouse to locate him and was told he was over at his Montpelier office, two hours' distance. All right, I'll go to Montpelier, I thought. Desperation was beginning to eat at me like a corrosive poison, and activity and concerted determination were its antidotes. I called Judge Bream's office, and his secretary informed me he'd be in around noon. If I whipped Uncle Simon's old car into a frenzy, I might just lurch in about then.

I set out on the long ride to Montpelier. Usually I loved this countryside, with its stands of pine which unexpectedly thinned to scrub oak. The area was full of lakes, blueberries, even deer, although Uncle Simon told me that they'd been mostly hunted out by now. But today I concentrated on the road and the necessity of talking to Bream. That necessity felt like a cold stone in my solar plexus. It was there all the time now, and I couldn't seem to get rid of it. It was as if a private ghost were haunting me, keeping me perpetually unnerved and morbidly shaken. I hated that ghost, affixed somehow to my innards.

The road was narrow and wound through small, rather shabby towns. The trip took longer than I'd thought it would, but I pulled into that comparative metropolis, the capital city, shortly before one.

The judge inhabited a snazzy office where you lost sight of your ankles in his rug. He had a friendly, motherly secretary with white hair, who handed me a cup of coffee. I cooled my heels and noticed a comfortably upholstered chair with some kind of seal on the back; I looked a little closer, and there was "Ve Ri Tas." I remembered I'd seen the Harvard seal lately, and I realized with a start that it was on Trumbull's watch chain, right next to his Phi Beta Kappa key.

All right, old school, old ties, circles within circles within circles. It didn't mean all that. Bream had dozens of pictures displayed in neat black frames all over one wall of his office because, I thought, he needed deep roots, perhaps he wasn't so secure, so he had to display his origins and the places he belonged like college, law school, fraternity, and clubs. He was obviously a team player. One of these days I determined to get some kind of seal from the Brooklyn Law School, if it had one, cast it in gold, and wear a pair for earrings. I was going to impress the hell out of everyone. I felt sort of deprived, sitting in this chair.

Pretty soon the secretary announced that the judge would see me, and I marched into an office that was pretty palatial—it struck me that I was on the peanut-butter circuit while this man roved the caviar belt.

But I warmed to Judge Bream's manner. When he wasn't on the bench, he had a warm informality, seeming almost jovial. He forsook the plush chair behind his desk and showed me to a little alcove, where he offered me a glass of sherry. It was cozy as hell. Then he pulled his chair closer to mine and asked me what was happening in Rowe.

So I told him. I talked about the fire, the parade, what the men had done to Buzz twice (I was all through worrying about violated promises, I was more concerned about violated bodies and souls), and my seeing the chief run away. I got mad enough to tell him about the Brittons' stone wall and Rampsie's using the common as a public urinal. I strove to fill him in on what'd happened since his last visit to Rowe, struggling for some kind of dispassionate control like a good lawyer, but it all failed me; my fury seeped through every word I uttered.

"You must forgive me, Your Honor," I said. "These are all my friends and relatives, and I absolutely hate what's been happening to them."

He nodded sympathetically, shook his head, and rested his hands on his knees as he leaned toward me. "I understand what you're saying, Miss Sanderson, and I feel for you. I most assuredly do. I think you have a problem in that town, quite frankly, and I can really see the situation clearly. But it's happened in other places, too, so you're not alone by any means."

I looked over at the tan, healthy face above the paisley tie. "What makes *you* think we've got a problem in Rowe?"

He shook his head as if clearing the air. "I travel around a lot. I listen frequently to the same pattern. You're an isolated little town with a chief who's maybe, didn't you say, not aggressive?"

"That's the understatement of the year, Your Honor."

"Well, between you and me, I've heard that the previous chief was a strong-arm type, knocked too many heads. Especially down in that mill area, what do you call it?"

I'd heard all this before. "The Flats. But I don't see why that's important."

"Well, what happened is that people got upset. The chief threw his authority and his nightstick around, and Trumbull involved himself trying to defend them. It was a bad precedent. So what happened? Next thing they brought in Oldham. Believe it or not, everything calmed down for a couple of years."

I leaned forward toward Bream. "I already told you that a young boy got hit by that truck of theirs yesterday. I understand from Dr. Almquist, who attended him, that it was only a concussion and he'll be all right pretty soon. But he's still unconscious, and that boy could just as well have been killed."

"All right. Do you want to prepare a case against them?"

"Yes, sir. But I may have trouble with it."

He began ticking off on his fingers. "You've got a boy who's mentally retarded, unable to get out of the way when everyone else did. Besides that, you say he wasn't badly hurt."

"Just how bad is bad, Your Honor?" I could feel my fury. I knew he was right, and it was burning out every circuit in my body.

"And you'd have to try it before another judge if I discuss this with you. Of course, that's really no problem."

"I'd like to try for aggravated assault, Your Honor. That's a Class B felony in this state, isn't it?"

"Yes, but they may knock it down to simple assault, which is a misdemeanor. Then they'd be out on bail in ten minutes. You know that."

"All I'm looking for is some kind of deterrent, some weapon. . . ."

He sat back in his chair, slowly rubbing his palms together. "Miss Sanderson, I can tell you something which might help you, if you'll

155

keep it confidential. You must realize that the Tremont police are keeping a pretty good eye on those men because they've been in hot water for a long time."

"That's what Lieutenant Dowling told me."

He folded his fingers together. "Well, I've heard since I saw you last they're under suspicion for some robberies in the Tremont area and perhaps even farther away. I understand they come and go a good deal."

I informed him that for every two days in Rowe, they were gone six.

"Did you know," he continued, "that they're suspected of stealing cars, changing the registrations, then fencing them to Massachusetts and the Midwest? Lord knows what else they've been up to."

I sank my head onto my hand with a groan. What a pleasure it was to have such fine, upstanding men on our common, providing sterling examples for all the kids—like Jaimie Rampsie. I told Bream so. "Just how long are we supposed to entertain them?" I asked him. "How close are the police to them now?"

The judge shrugged. "I must also tell you that they might have committed a murder in Massachusetts last year, near Boston. You remember that family that was massacred last Christmas in Haverhill? The authorities are even beginning to think that some members of the crowd had something to do with it. Unfortunately it takes awhile to gather the facts together." He smiled ruefully. "Sometimes the wheels of justice grind exceedingly slow, as we both know."

So we were the bedroom community for mobsters. This room was beginning to seem unreal to me, and Judge Bream's face spun ever so slightly before my eyes. I could feel the sweat trickle down the back of my neck. It was a moment before I could answer. "Murder . . . Your Honor!" I'd seen murderers before, but always in confinement, flanked by guards, handcuffed to burly police officers. "Murder. . . ?" My stomach was becoming unglued.

Bream lit a cigar. "I suppose Dowling also told you about those rapes they suspected they might have committed. Can you imagine, as many as fifty? That's what the police say. For Christ's sake, they must have been knocking up women all over the—"

I drank Bream's sherry in one gulp.

He patted my arm in a fatherly way. "Don't mean to upset you, Miss Sanderson. Thought I ought to tell you this information because it might help. If you can hold on down there, the police might be able to remove those men from your vicinity pretty soon."

I swallowed hard. "I don't think we can wait much longer, to tell you the truth. We've had about as much as we can take. I think we're in some kind of limbo: beyond the jurisdiction of the Tremont police and too insignificant for the state police to worry about. I've begun to wonder if anyone cares at all."

"Oh, they all care. It's just that they're terribly busy, and they've got so much territory to cover."

"Don't we all, Judge Bream."

As I left Bream's office, I took a last look at a picture on the wall of the Vermont Bar Association at last year's annual confab in the Green Mountains. Smiling, confident faces. Good old Judge Bream was standing next to good old Trumbull, brothers in the bond. Circles, circles. . . .

The trip back filled me with horrors. I could see the faces of the Rowe Boys in the windshield before me. I could picture Keaton's cowboy hat, like the red plume of a rooster, and the scar on Rampsie's chin, and the fat encircling Hudman's waist like an arm.

When I arrived home, Buzz was still unconscious, but he'd stirred a few times. George, who'd been to see him before office hours, left word that he'd return later, and sooner if there were any change. Mrs. Sardoe sat beside Buzz's bed, rocking slightly back and forth, her hand on the bedclothes. There were a lot of things Mrs. Sardoe couldn't comprehend, but affection for her son wasn't one of them. Aunt Chloe was bustling around the kitchen, preparing meals for all of us; the place was beginning to look more like a hospital than a home. But then I glanced out across the common, and it didn't look the same out there either: demolished stone walls, beer cans, those huge tire marks on the soft grass, and the burned areas. The world had turned topsy-turvy!

Besides that, the workers had officially called the strike. Uncle Simon said he'd been attending an open meeting down by the mill all morning.

"They won by three votes," said Uncle Simon. He really seemed a little panicked. "Three votes, Chloe, did you hear that?"

"Stop shouting, Simon. Of course I hear you."

"Well, if it isn't one damn thing, it's another. I told them, I said, 'We've already got too much, what do you want to add more trouble for?' But not enough people down there even cared, Chloe. Can you understand that, they didn't care?"

"Please calm down, Simon," said Aunt Chloe. "When does it start anyway?"

"When does it start? Why, it's started already. What do you suppose I'm so upset about?" Uncle Simon had begun to pace like a stricken animal.

Aunt Chloe was starting to answer when she saw a group of workers out on the common, where they'd obviously come from the direction of the now-adjourned meeting down by the mill. They were talking together earnestly, gesturing. She watched them for a moment.

"This will come to no good," said Uncle Simon, continuing to pace. "No good at all. You mark my words, Chloe."

"Must you carry on so, Simon? Would you mind an extra dollar in your paycheck? Would it be so bad?" But she didn't sound entirely convinced herself.

Uncle Simon shook his head. "At what price, Chloe? None of us knows what the price will be, but you can bet that we'll pay dearly for it. You mark my words!"

Later, during a cancellation in his office hours, George returned to check on Buzz. He hadn't taken time to remove the white coat he wore in the office; tongue depressors, his stethoscope, some packaged bandages protruded from his pockets. Buzz had regained consciousness but was very pale, and his eyes roved a little disjointedly in his head. He tried to speak once, but no words came.

George patted him solicitously, then bent over the boy, to listen for his heartbeat and peer into the black pupils of his eyes with a light.

"Don't they ever pick on people their own size?" he asked. "It must give them some kind of special kicks to torment kids."

We walked out into the common afterward to talk; I was again waiting for Tim to arrive on the school bus. I told George about my visit with Bream, laying my hand on his arm. He smelled faintly of disinfectant, and despite the stiffness of that white coat, I could feel the muscles of his forearm beneath it.

"Good Lord," exclaimed George, "are we just supposed to sit around and wait until someone does something? I don't believe it!"

I nodded. "That's what the man said. Sure hope the cops pick 'em up soon."

George grimaced. "I'll go along with that all right." I could see the small yellow school bus lumbering along the road about two blocks from the common and turned to meet it.

"See you later?" asked George, smiling. After turning, he walked slowly and thoughtfully back toward his car.

I ambled toward the bus, watching the face of the bus driver through his big pane of glass. Suddenly his face froze, and he jammed on the brakes of his unwieldy yellow box, his facial muscles straining with the effort.

I turned immediately toward where the driver was staring, to see Rampsie's truck proceeding hell-bent toward the front of the school bus; the bucket seats, now empty of occupants, swung senselessly with the truck's motion. The truck was gathering speed and had veered onto the common in a collision course with the school bus.

Just as Rampsie's truck contacted the asphalt not ten feet before the school bus, he jammed on the brakes. There was a scream of tires, and black lines of hot rubber appeared on the road. Rampsie's truck skidded to a stop perhaps a foot from the front of the radiator of the school bus. The kids on the bus were shocked momentarily in place, too stunned to move. George and I stood rooted impotently, expecting one hell of a crash, looking dazedly at the steam arising from the tire tracks. I could just barely see Tim's face inside the bus.

"What in hell do they think they're doing?" I yelled to George. "They're all insane. . . ."

Tim had quickly piled off the bus. I was astonished when I looked at him. Gone was his fear; like Uncle Simon, his hesitation had turned to rage. He picked up a stone from the common grass and hurled it at Rampsie's truck; it hit the side, sliding harmlessly to the ground. Quickly he bent to pick up another and another.

But George had gone a little mad; before I'd even looked at him, he'd run to the far side of the truck, jerked the door handle open, and got hold of an arm, trying to wrestle someone from the cab to the road. "You could have killed someone," George was hollering. "You crazy goddamned idiot!" Now I could make out that it was Rampsie driving, and the man was fighting George for all he was worth.

"Get your shitty hands off me," Rampsie was yelling. He let fly a kick from the cab of the truck which caught George in the chest, sending him flying into the road. Then the truck began to back up—I could see that it had turned slightly and was heading for George.

I shouted frantically at him—but he could see it, too; he rolled aside as the truck was charging, barely clearing those big rutted tires. Then Rampsie gunned his machine and roared away, leaving George crouched in the road, staring after him.

George dusted himself off; by now the kids had all spewed from the bus behind Tim.

"Those creeps are going to kill someone before they're done," George gasped. "So far they've been damn lucky."

I ran up to the bus driver to take his name and address. "I may call you, Mr. Higgins," I said. "We're having a tough time with those men. Would you testify to what you saw?"

The man was obviously shaken; he stood outside his bus, holding to the side for support. "Of course, miss. Almost hit us, he did." He paused for breath. "Never had such a close call in all twenty years I been drivin'."

"I'm going to the state police tomorrow," I told George afterward. "We can't stand this any longer, I don't care what Bream says. Would you come along with me?"

He nodded grimly. "Just about given up the practice of medicine anyway. I think I'm becoming an expert in traumatic injuries. They ought to see me in the emergency unit of the General now!"

All the kids from the bus lit out for their homes at top speed. Now the truck had wandered back to Rampsie's store, where it was blocking the street. I looked over toward it with apprehension; it appeared like some hybrid form of fishing trawler with those odd seats, dumped on land by an uncanny and malevolent stroke of fate.

Tim ran to me. I hugged him as if he were precious flotsam retrieved from a stormy sea; then he, too, stood beside George and me, glaring at the truck.

But as we turned toward Uncle Simon's, I chanced to look up at the window, and there was Buzz standing in the frame of the glass. For a moment I was horrified, thinking that the boy shouldn't be up. But then I remembered that George had said he'd probably recover fast, in a few days. But what arrested me was the look on his face as he peered outward: not of pain, but of hatred and fear. There was a wealth of expression on that face, there for anyone to see. Recently I'd seen that same expression on Tim's and Uncle Simon's faces. My own frustration waned, seeing, besides the anger on Buzz's face, the set of fortitude and defiance in his glance and in the angle of his body, leaning forward against the glass.

Why, if *he* could stand it, I thought as I watched him up there, so could I, damn it!

The next night Uncle Simon called another meeting. It was the same group as before with one difference: He'd left out Oldham. There were Stu Callaghan, George, Paul White, Ed Rhymer from the mill, and me. We were a silent, grim group. George sat next to me, his arms crossed on his chest, listening to Uncle Simon.

"We've got to be ready if they pull anything more," said Uncle Simon. His eyes were slitlike in that once-placid face. "There's enough stuff going on out there to make the devil sick."

"You can bet there'll be more going on," said George. "Not much doubt about it. Just a question of when."

"What do you propose?" asked Ed Rhymer, twirling the brim of his hat in his hand. "We don't have any clout. Without Oldham, I mean."

Stu Callaghan guffawed. "Do you mean you thought we had clout with Clyde? Why, we all saw him runnin' away, tail a'tween his legs."

"Them guys have got away with just 'bout enough," said Paul White, the short, wiry fireman. "So what you proposin', Simon?"

"We need a lookout system," continued Uncle Simon. "Minute trouble starts, we'll have to let the rest know, either by phone or by messenger."

Stu Callaghan filled his pipe from a little oilskin pouch. "Those sound like good words, Simon, but we both know it takes awhile to cover everybody."

"Why not just alert the switchboard?" said George. "Tell Minnie to clear calls fast that have a priority. Someone could talk it over with her." He looked around. "Everyone here know her?"

161

"Sure," answered Ed. He was a plump man with a snow-white beard. "Hell, she's my first cousin. Lives upstairs right above the office." We all knew that night calls were handled from Tremont, but that our switchboard could be functional in an emergency.

"And citizen arrests are legal in Vermont," I suggested. "The average citizen can arrest just as surely as if he were a policeman."

Stu was scratching his head. "You mean you just walk up to a guy and tell him you're arresting him?"

"Sure. It's allowed under extreme conditions if a person suspects that someone is committing a felony. I think the statutes say something about being faced with deadly force. . . . "

"Yeah," said Ed, "but those guys wouldn't pay any heed. Lord, they don't pay attention to anything anyway."

"But it's legal and binding, Mr. Rhymer. They'd have to go to court to tell why if they resisted."

"Don't make no difference," Paul White broke in. "They'd be out in an hour, raising hell again."

I agreed silently. Half hour most likely. I looked about me, and a very eerie feeling flooded me: There was Uncle Simon with his broken arm. Upstairs was Buzz with a white bandage circling his head. Out the window was the space where our barn used to stand. I glanced out at the scarred common, then back at the men huddled in the living room, and finally into Uncle Simon's eyes. Involuntarily I shivered.

"Let them try it," Uncle Simon was saying, his voice darkly bristling. "There are other ways."

"No, Uncle Simon," I said firmly. "There aren't other ways. There are no other ways at all."

There was a hush in the room. I stared over at Uncle Simon with the certain knowledge that everyone knew exactly what we were talking about.

Uncle Simon's voice shook ever so slightly. "Do you really think I wouldn't consider . . . other ways . . . with all that's happened?"

George clapped a hand on Uncle Simon's shoulder. "It's all right, Simon. We can manage better than that."

There was a new tone in Uncle Simon's voice. "George," he said slowly and firmly, "look around you. You know what's happened to this town, I don't need to tell you. All right, you're new to Rowe, relatively speaking. I'm not. Neither you nor I ever met types like we've got here before, and we both know it." He pointed toward the common. "I hate it with everything I've got in me." His voice grew

162

vibrant. "Nobody's gonna touch anyone I know again, you hear that? I swear it, here and now. Bums like that, defiling our common out there, corrupting our town—why, they should have been shot long ago, like bobcats." His voice still shook. "To tell you the truth, there's a bounty on bobcats, just for getting rid of them. What about the human types?"

The room was silent except for Uncle Simon's words. I could feel the fabric of our lives tearing in some violent way and tried lamely to repair it. "Uncle Simon, there are legal ways, if you'll just wait awhile. . . . "

He backed off slightly, but I could see the persistent look on his face, the tight lips. "And what are those legal ways, Lisa? Do we look to Oldham perhaps, or to Judge Bream, or to the Tremont police? How about the state police? If I were to pick up the telephone now, who would I call? Better yet, who would come? And I agree with George a hundred percent that things are going to get worse, a whole lot worse, before they get any better!"

George took a deep breath. "Simon, you know the police are on their trail right now. They told Lisa so. It just may be that it won't take long now for them to catch up with Rampsie and his crew. We've got to give them the benefit. . . . "

"Sure, George. Do you believe all that hogwash? How long is long? I mean, how long is it really? Were they talking about days or weeks or months?"

Ed Rhymer pulled himself forward on his chair. "I'm with you, Simon. Who's to tell what'll happen? Now, with this mill thing, who's to tell?"

"Just the same," I broke in, "you can't take the law into your hands, Uncle Simon. You've got to act in a responsible manner. Do you know what could happen to us if you don't?"

"I know what could happen if we do."

"Simon," said George, persisting, "I'm for vigilantes, in the sense of keeping some kind of vigil, if you want to call us that here tonight—as long as we keep our heads."

"I intend to, George. Don't you worry yourself any about that. I wasn't born yesterday, you know."

"Neither was I, Simon."

Uncle Simon stood up in the middle of the room. "All right. We vote to stand together, or not, according to each man's conscience. Am I right?"

He turned to face each of us in turn. "Tell me," he demanded. He held his palm out to each of us. Paul White placed his palm down on

163

Uncle Simon's; then Ed Rhymer did the same. Stu Callaghan followed, then George, finally I. "A matter of conscience, then," said Uncle Simon firmly. "We act together. That seals it."

"For better or worse," I added. "I hope to God it's for the better."

After the meeting George signaled to me, and we met outside in the dark to talk.

"I'm worried about Simon," he said. "It's not like him to be so headstrong. I've never seen him like this."

"Me neither, George. But these are unusual circumstances." I was standing next to George, I wanted to touch him and have him make love to me, but there wasn't any time. A sense of foreboding hung over me even as we were talking. My God, not time to make love? All during the meeting I'd been thinking about being with George, lying next to him in his big bed, opening my legs to him. And here we were, without the time to make love, plagued by our necessity for self-preservation. It was one hell of a time.

"Uncle Simon's a really gentle man." I reassured George. "I don't know if he *could* become violent. You know, I've never even heard him raise his voice before, except under really rare circumstances."

"I know," said George. "That's what bothers me." He shifted so that our bodies touched. "What do you think about the others?"

I thought a moment. "Stu Callaghan's a lot like Uncle Simon; he's simply not a violent man. Paul White's a little headstrong. I don't know Ed Rhymer that well."

"How about you?"

I took a step away from him. "I d-don't know, George." The thought absolutely stunned me. I could barely think about it. "H-how about *you*?"

George nodded. "I'll tell you. I've considered it often enough lately. About what I'd do if I were pushed too hard. Well, I know damn well how I'd react." He paused a moment, then continued in a low voice. "I'd become violent as hell, an animal if need be. You can depend on it. I know it for an absolute fact."

We set on the next afternoon to visit the state police. George picked me up immediately after seeing his last patient. He had that same intense look on his face I'd seen the day before, which to my astonishment I'd discovered on my own this morning as I brushed my teeth: a tenseness about the eyes and a certain grim set to the jaw. I hated that look; I felt as if we'd all been starched too much in a laundry, and we might crack if we smiled. That was it: The smiling had become so difficult.

Tremont had a small contingent of state troopers. Most were located near the state capital and farther to the north, near the common border with Canada. I'd already made an appointment to speak with the commander, Colonel Sparrow.

The barracks were in a section of the armory, where the National Guard also had its quarters. There was a big drill room, with rows of guns all pointing toward the door, so that we stared into the black circles of their barrels as we proceeded. Around the edge was a walkway, the walls covered with governmental edicts.

"Colonel Sparrow is expecting you," said the secretary. George took my elbow and we went in.

When Sparrow stood up, I sucked in my breath. I was rarely confronted with spit-and-polish military types, except city policemen, and they were rarely as impeccable as this man. He was dressed in dove gray with stripes down the arms, lots of braid, and a big leather belt. He must have been over forty, but he was in pink of physical condition, not a hint of bulge over that belt, and those tight pants showed the flexing muscles in his thighs.

George and I introduced ourselves and then told him about the Rowe Boys, what they were doing there in case he hadn't already heard. I'd told it so much I was bored with my own recital, except that it made so much difference. I'd never pleaded a client's case harder than I pleaded our own.

Colonel Sparrow was taking everything down on a tape recorder, so I tried to speak clearly to facilitate its playback—all those deathless words—anything to help our cause. George began to describe Uncle Simon's arm and Buzz's head.

"There's a lot more violence going on in that town than you might realize," George said. "People down there are pretty shook up right now."

"I understand that, Doctor." Sparrow had a rumbling deep voice. "I've heard that you were experiencing some rough stuff, and I've sent cars through on patrol lately. But the Tremont police are inquiring into it right now, as you say Judge Bream mentioned to you. And you know that we're terribly short of manpower right now."

I understood full well what he was up against. There'd been a lot of drug traffic over the Vermont border from Canada, and a few nights before the police had staged a drug bust north of Berlin; there'd also been a kidnapping which the FBI had been called in to help solve. At the moment I couldn't have cared less.

"What are we to do then?" George asked. "Just sit around and wait?"

"My hands are tied," he said, somewhat apologetically. "I know it doesn't seem like much consolation."

I was getting fed up, absolutely. "It isn't," I said. "It really isn't. Don't you understand, we're really at the mercy of those guys? You're our last hope. How would you feel if you had a gang terrifying *your* neighborhood. . . ?"

He thought I was an edgy female. I could see it in his face. He thought I panicked easily. "Come now," he said. He was even a little miffed that I was a little miffed in his sancrosanct office. "Just sit tight down there," he said, brotherly-like. I thought maybe he was going to pat me on the head like a perverse dog or even give me an affectionate slap on the rump. "You'll get help soon, miss. . . . "

I looked down at his legs, incredibly tidy in those sleek, unblemished pressed pants. "What do you do in this big office?" I asked him. "Shoot craps on the floor? Stick pins in effigies of crooks? You get out of that chair, do you, to do something useful?" I knew I'd lost control, but I really didn't give a good goddamn.

George knew instantly that I'd ventured into distinctly rocky ground. I absentmindedly picked up the colonel's paperweight from his desk; it was some kind of medal citation. When I looked at it critically, wondering what dolt would give this man a citation, George obviously thought I was going to chuck it at him; he grabbed my arm and began to propel me out the door. The colonel started to follow, his brows knitted together.

We rushed through the secretary's office; she looked up at us, startled. I could already feel the back of my neck prickling with embarrassment. What must George think? I'd reacted like a goddamn idiot, a dolt, as bad as Sparrow.

"Incredible!" hissed George. "I don't believe it."

I deserved it. "I'm sorry, George. Really I am. I simply couldn't stand any more of that . . . crap. I just couldn't take one more word."

"*You're* sorry? Lisa, I was ready to hit the guy myself! One more word and I'd—" He took my arm. "What the hell do we pay some of our good old public servants for anyway?"

We were leaning against the armory building, dejected, looking at each other, when suddenly I was in George's arms, laughing while I cried.

166

I wiped my eyes. "We've blown it, George. He never even heard us. Where do we go from here?"

"I don't know. I'm fresh out of suggestions."

Behind us, through the window, were those cannons belonging to the National Guard. "How about one of those, park it on the common?" I even felt a little silly for a moment. "We'd never have trouble in Rowe again."

George leaned over and planted a kiss on my nose. "That's what I like, the quiet, feminine type."

"Sure. Winsome ways." I kissed him back. "Thanks for coming anyway."

"Anytime. I was an incredible help. Invite me again."

By the time we returned to town it was almost dark, and the common was thronged with strikers. It was becoming so darned popular, I thought, that soon they'd have to file claims. They'd erected a small platform similar to the one put up a couple of weeks ago; a large group had gathered about it. Here and there I recognized some of the workers from the mill.

"We'll hold out until fall if need be," a voice was saying through a megaphone. "Winter if we hafta." As we drove slowly about the common, we could hear scattered applause. I felt only alarm, premonitions of calamity, as I looked into that thronged common.

I'd heard labor leaders speak before, and most were a lot more persuasive than this man. I supposed that Rowe must be on one of the training routes for budding union organizers. The converted van they'd arrived in was parked on the edge of the common near that ersatz podium. It seemed to be where they ate and slept because curtains covered all the windows.

George whistled softly. "They've got a lot of courage to come back, after last time. Must be a lot of the those guys around with busted heads."

I peered into the darkening common. "They aren't the same ones. Maybe they don't know what happened to the others."

"Oh, they know all right," George answered. "I can guarantee it."

We were just about to drive into Aunt Chloe's driveway, across the common from the strikers, when we spotted Rampsie's truck easing forward from behind the store, lights out, the engine almost muffled. The common's lights were still broken, but the strikers were using some kinds of torches with long handles which they'd jammed into the ground for illumination.

There wasn't a noise coming from the truck, but I could now see shadows in the cab. Someone had lit a cigarette, a brief flare of a match, on the back flatbed, so I knew there were people sitting in those swivel seats. The truck stopped barely twenty feet from us, so that we could make out dark figures jumping lightly to the ground from the back and others emerging from the cab. Each man seemed to be carrying something in his hand.

"What the hell do you suppose is cooking?" asked George, peering into the gloom. "You can be damn sure they're up to no good."

We watched them separate and split into a wide ring around the speakers, disappearing into the darkness beyond. I could tell that one of them was Hudman—no mistaking that shape—when he was momentarily silhouetted before a lighted torch, but it had become too dark to recognize the others.

The speaker was still exhorting the crowd, rhapsodically describing the utopia about to descend on the lucky workers of the Rowe mill, when we could see Rampsie's crowd again, stealing up behind them from all directions. Suddenly there was the most god-awful broil. One of the Rowe Boys had brought a length of pipe down on a striker's head; his shrieks rang through the night.

But the speaker rolled off his impromptu podium as if he were an acrobat who'd been waiting for this all along. He jumped to the ground like a cat, making some kind of signal. At that moment, the doors of the converted van of the strikers flung open as if assailed by a high wind, and from the interior came a half dozen strikers, armed with bats and clubs. The crowd scattered like dry leaves, leaving the common once again to the grunting, straining fighters.

"Goddamn, I knew it," George groaned. He looked a little stricken. "Sure as death."

We retreated to Uncle Simon's front walk, where we watched the fracas in a kind of dull horror. In a moment Uncle Simon came out the door behind us. "I hope to God they kill each other," he growled. "Kill each other!" But as he watched, he was clenching his fists, and soon he was cheering for the strikers as if they were the old school. Earlier this morning he couldn't have cared less about either of them.

Suddenly someone was hurt out there, perhaps one of the Rowe Irregulars, because someone was hauling him laboriously off to the truck, throwing him unceremoniously up onto the platform as if he were a side of beef. In another minute, Rampsie was diving into the cab, followed by a tangle of other bodies, and we could hear the engine

168

grinding. Soon it had caught, and the truck started to roll. The other Rampsie men still on the common heard it, too, and took off after it like buffalo on the stampede, throwing themselves onto the giant platform by grasping the tailgate and wrenching themselves on board. Suddenly they seemed totally frantic that they might be left behind and began to fight for a place on that truck, pulling others off in their desperation.

In the center of the common, still lighted by the torches, the strikers claimed the field, like victors on the plain of Marathon. They'd flung their arms about each other, triumphant and laughing. Their faces were lit starkly by the yellow, fiery torchlights, so that they looked almost eerie, like a Walpurgis Night revel.

"Do you think I should send out coffee?" asked Aunt Chloe. "I've got some of those little plastic cups." I could scarcely believe my ears. A while ago the strikers were alien influences in Rowe to Aunt Chloe. Now, suddenly, they were the white team, being revived and resuscitated after their labors.

Uncle Simon shook his head. "Let's celebrate when the war's over, Chloe. This here's just a skirmish. We got a long piece to go, and what you just saw out there don't make things better. They make them a whole lot worse."

12

The next morning it seemed as if something inexorable and frightening and inevitable were happening to us now in Rowe and we had no way to stop it, or to turn it aside, or even to blunt it. We all were terrified—I knew it; we all knew it; we could see it in each other's faces—but no one wanted to say the words lest the entire fabric of our determination rend. Yet each of us was resolved to ward off the imminent danger, no matter how soon it came or in what form. But we were vulnerable—oh, how vulnerable we readily knew—but perhaps there was even a little of the heroic in us as a result of that devastating self-knowledge.

It was raining, but no one seemed to notice. The strikers were down by the mill picketing in force, and Uncle Simon and Stu Callaghan were let into the mill by union agreement; people Stu and Uncle Simon had known all their lives were yelling at them, thinking somehow they'd joined league with management. And Clint Eastman, the mill president, had come out to make a little speech.

Eastman lived not in Rowe, but in Tremont; I'd seen him only two or three times in my life. He must have been in his early sixties. He appeared thin and slight down there on the front steps of the mill, speaking in dignified tones almost too soft to hear. This was the third generation of his family which had owned the mill, he was saying, and he pleaded for the strike to get settled pretty damn fast so he could get back to making money. That wasn't exactly how he phrased it, but that was the way I translated it. In the town's interest, he said, he wanted to get the foolish thing over.

"We wanna eat, too, Eastman," called a young woman standing beside me. "We gotta new baby." She even held up the baby, a sleeping form wrapped in oilskin, for Eastman to see; if he'd heard her call, he never acknowledged it.

There were others going into that mill beside Uncle Simon: a skeleton force, they called it, to tend to certain machinery and to check some chemicals which had to be drained and replaced every day.

So Eastman was talking, standing there before his factory on the old stone steps. People walked around and around in the mill parking area and on the front grass in front of Eastman, carrying placards nailed to wooden strips. The mud was churning up with all that marching until it oozed over some of the marchers' shoes. The rain had now become a downpour.

Eastman kept talking, but his voice was so soft that hardly anyone could hear him. Soon the strikers began to chant, drowning him out entirely. Then some kid picked up a ball of mud and slung it at Eastman, but it missed and dropped into the rest of the slop at his feet. A few minutes later someone else lobbed another mud ball; this time it splatted on the front of his suit, leaving a wet, brown, dripping mess.

Eastman blanched. He'd never known this kind of treatment, and it was easy to see the outrage in his face. But he didn't retreat; he just backed off a step or two. Right next to him was another important-looking man, perhaps a vice-president in the company; I'd never seen him before either.

"This is no way . . ." Eastman began again, when SWAT, the next mud ball hit. This time it got the vice-president right in the face. He wiped off the junk, and both he and Eastman raced for the car parked to one side of the front building of the mill. Someone, probably a chauffeur, was waiting inside. For a minute the wheels of the big car spun in the mud; then they were gone.

I worried a little about Uncle Simon inside that building, but no one seemed to show much inclination for anything except picketing after Eastman departed so precipitously.

That afternoon I waited to meet Timmy after school as usual, standing at the bus stop area. Today, when Jaimie Rampsie got off with him, I barely recognized the boy because his face was black and blue. He boasted one hell of a magnificent shiner, and both cheekbones looked as if they'd been flayed purple.

"Whatever happened to Jaimie?" I asked Tim. "Good God!"

Tim shook his head. He was in a hurry because he was already late

171

for his job at Rampsie's store. "They beat up on him," Tim said. "Keaton and the others. I told you they did that sometimes."

"But why, Tim? Bob would do *that* to his own brother?"

"Not Bob. The others, for kicks. This time it was mostly Keaton. Keaton thinks Jaimie gets special treatment because he *is* Bob's brother, so sometimes he tries to even things up. Least that's what he told Jaimie before he beat up on him."

The rotten creep, I thought, the bastard. I bit my lip in anger. "Tell him to go see George, Timmy. He'll fix him up with something."

Tim shook his head. "He says he's OK. Besides, those guys lit out after they got roughed up by the strikers. Jaimie says they aren't ever comin' back."

Hallelujah, I thought. I'll believe it when I see it!

But days came and went, and still we saw nothing of the Rowe Boys. Except for the strikers, around the common things were quiet and even lazy, the way this town used to be. I'd walk Tim over to work at Pops's, then meet him and we'd stroll back again. Pops was up and around, working in his store as if nothing had happened. His mistreatment in the common hadn't improved his disposition either; he ordered Tim and Jaimie and the customers around as imperiously as ever. Uncle Simon had even begun to make some noises about taking the boards off the front windows when I contemplated them critically. I tried to remember the living room without that dark obstruction between us and the outdoors—and it seemed a long while ago. Buzz was slowly mending, but George had asked him not to go outside yet, fearing that the boy would become too active—so he was spending most of the day pestering Aunt Chloe and his mother. George had removed the big bandage around Buzz's head and substituted a large gauze pad, first shaving the head so the plaster would stick. The poor kid's head looked kind of grotesque, puffy and swollen beneath the bandage on one side as if someone had blown it up like a rubber tire. But it didn't seem to bother him any; he sat beside the upstairs window, looking out across the common, holding his head in his hand as if trying to support that extra weight.

Uncle Simon ventured out to work every morning for a couple of hours with Stu Callaghan, then returned home. Union representatives still made speeches on the common; George and I strolled out to hear them a couple of times. Once Uncle Simon and I chatted with the speaker, a man named Jerry Finnegan. I could vaguely remember him out on the common that night the Rampsie crowd was routed.

172

But Uncle Simon was apprehensive still. "The sooner it's over, the better," he told Finnegan. "Bad time for a mill strike. Rowe's having enough trouble. . . ."

He nodded his head slowly. "Way I heard it, Mr. Sanderson, is that Eastman won't budge. We can't help it. He's still pretty sore about that mud slinging down at the mill."

The strikers were still picketing, marching around and around, holding up placards. It was still raining interminably as spring seemed to hang suspended, unable to shift its gears into summer. The ground in front of the mill had become a quagmire. Planks and sheets of plywood had been extended over the mud, but they soon foundered like sinking ships and slowly sank into the ooze. Finally, some of the marchers dug little trenches which eventually drained away part of the surface water.

Toward nightfall of the second week of the strike, I again walked to meet Timmy, and Buzz once more accompanied me. George had just given him the green light to go outdoors once the rain had ceased, and that last drop fell not ten minutes before Tim was due home. The sky had just begun to clear in the west when Uncle Simon tore furiously across the common to the house from the road to the mill.

"Call White, Rhymer, George, Stu Callaghan," he gasped. "Tell 'em to get down to the mill pronto. I'll go get Oldham."

"Tell them *what*, Uncle Simon? What's going. . . ?"

He pointed behind him, as if I could see. "The mill," he gasped. "Down at the mill. They've brought in strikebreakers."

By now Aunt Chloe had come outside, hearing Uncle Simon's shouts. "Strikebreakers?" She seemed to be practicing the word's pronunciation, as if she'd never said it before. "Who?"

Uncle Simon rushed away again. "Who do you think? The Rowe Boys, that's who. Eastman must've brought 'em in to bust up the strikers. At least a dozen down there."

I dispatched Tim and Buzz to fetch Ed Rhymer, then Paul White at the firehouse, while Minnie on the switchboard told Stu Callaghan, and I informed George.

"You're kidding," George said, incredulous. "Jesus. I'll be right over."

I met Tim, then hurried back to the house. "Did you see Rampsie or the others at Pops's?" I asked him. "I simply can't figure out where they came from."

Tim shrugged. "Not even Jaimie knew they were around. Musta come in from the other side of town."

Uncle Simon had returned to the mill; when I arrived down there, a battle was going on. Uncle Simon, Stu Callaghan, and a handful of employees had somehow managed to get back inside the building behind those massive doors, which they'd bolted. Rampsie, Hudman, and a couple of others were trying to bash in the heavy oak with their shoulders, but the doors were holding. Next, they used a heavy metal pole they'd found somewhere, employing it as a battering ram. Keaton had swiped a woman's placard and was clobbering her with it. Other marchers had been pushed into the wet ground and a couple of strikebreakers leveled kicks at them as they lay defenseless in the ooze. Near me a man was stretched out, face down in the mud.

I ran toward him, attempting to extricate his nose from the water; I'd barely managed to turn his face and was trying to unplug his nostrils when someone kicked me in the side. In a kind of agonizingly horrendous slow motion I felt his shoe sink into my ribs and breast as if I were soft jelly; with a gulp which felt as if I were swallowing the universe, I heard the snap inside my rib cage followed by a twang like a violin string breaking and then a lacerating pain. "Oh, my God," I said aloud, and knew I was crying—how could I be crying so fast? It felt as if a hot lance had been shoved clean through my chest. I realized that someone was trying to move me, and I moaned and came up protesting, "Don't take it out, don't take it out," because I'd gotten it into my delirious head that if they removed that lance, I was going to bleed to death.

I was dimly aware that George was carrying me somewhere. I regained consciousness just long enough to realize that we were in his car just beyond the mill and that, back in the trees, the Rowe Boys had stashed their truck so nobody could see it.

"Can you hold on?" George asked me gently—he was puffing from lugging me up the incline away from the field of battle. "There are a couple of other people hurt pretty badly down there. I've got to help. . . ."

I nodded feebly. He laid me on the back seat of the car as carefully as if I were a cracked egg. I tried to breathe evenly because every minute my ribs burned.

While I was reclining in George's car, the door open beside me, Clyde Oldham pulled up next to me. He didn't see me because I was lying there flat on my back, a casualty in the war, but I could see his face as he looked down toward the people fighting below us in the mill yard. I could witness plainly the expression of loathing and disgust and apprehension on it. I didn't really blame him.

"Stop, stop, stop," Oldham suddenly shouted. He was blowing a whistle, but nobody paid him any attention at all.

"Clyde," I gasped through the open door. Lord, how it hurt to talk. "Beep your horn, Clyde. Someone's going to get killed out there." After that I couldn't talk anymore; I just didn't give a damn if anyone got killed or not. I passed out again right on the back seat of George's car, my feet stuck out the door.

I didn't know how long it was before George returned. When I opened my eyes, he was filthy with clinging mud, and blood streamed down his face from a cut above his eye.

"Someone pulled a knife," he muttered, almost offhand. "I never even felt it."

"Where's . . . Oldham?" I asked feebly.

George climbed into the car. "He's arrested a couple of them. Believe it or not. And he's helping get the injured ones out."

George drove me home as carefully as he could. It was only two blocks, but it felt like two miles over potholes. He helped me out of the car, but the pain was almost unbearable. His own face was bleeding so badly that before he could get me to my bed, with Aunt Chloe's assistance, we both were smeared with his blood.

"I'm almost sure she has broken ribs," I heard George tell Aunt Chloe. "But I won't know until we get all this junk cleaned off."

Aunt Chloe sponged off the mud while George applied pressure to the wound over his eye because he was slowly going blind with the blood draining into it. When he began to examine my ribs, the pain made me gasp.

"It'll have to be X-rayed," he said. "And I've got to set it. Can you stand it?"

When I looked at that gash on his face, I knew I could stand my ribs.

"I'm going to give you something for the pain," he said. He snapped open his medical bag and removed a colorless vial with a screw top. Blood was running down his face again, rimming his eye. He brushed it away, then filled a glass with water in the bathroom next door, watching like a mother hen while I downed the orange pellets he held out to me. "That'll make it easier," he said. "In a few minutes. I guarantee you'll feel better."

Lord, I hoped so. I lay back on the bed, waiting for a miracle to

175

happen. George had removed a syringe and some other things from his bag and was looking into the bathroom mirror, examining the gash. "What are you doing now?" I asked, watching his critical appraisal of himself in the glass.

"Stitching up this cut, or it'll never stop bleeding." He sounded as if he were pronouncing a detached medical opinion to a colleague.

"You're going to do it to yourself?"

"Sure. Pretty simply, really."

He never blinked an eye; he might have been sewing up someone else's skin. When he finished, he examined himself critically.

"Not bad hemstitching," he said, peering at the wound closely in the mirror. The gash was crossed with neat strands of black thread like fine teeth. "If I do say so myself."

"You're making me sick," I said. "Can't you please stop it?"

"Sorry." He grinned at me. "Sewed up so many of these things, hardly matters whose it is."

George mostly carried me out to the car. I was feeling better with those pills, but it was no picnic. I could barely manage the jar when I walked, but it was better than before.

"Pack her something," George told Aunt Chloe. "I'm not bringing her back tonight unless she feels up to it."

"There you go," I said, grimacing. "First you drug me; then you transport me to your house like a common hussy."

"You bragging or complaining?" he asked, easing me into the car.

"Well, I'm sure not complaining." I gritted my teeth as the car hit a bump at the end of the driveway. "But I think you're getting damaged merchandise for all your trouble."

George showed me the lines of my ribs on the X-ray plate, mixed with the white nebulous mass of the rest of my innards. He pointed to the darkened areas where the bones were cracked. There were three of them, neatly busted.

"Got any idea who kicked you?" George asked.

I shook my head. Had I known, George would have done him in by nightfall, judging by the look on his face. I told him about the man lying face down in the mud. "Do you know if he's all right?"

"Never saw him, unless he's one of the guys Oldham picked up. Maybe he'd crawled out. Things were pretty wild down there."

"What are we going to do now?" I'd never felt as defeated as at that moment. I was a flop. Here I lay, crusader for law and order, defender

176

of the Rowe common, misguidedly trying to help Aunt Chloe and Uncle Simon—with broken ribs, moaning.

"Oldham just called," George answered. "Sounded a little panicked about the mayhem. More scared than I've ever heard him. So we're going to meet over here tonight." George was applying great lengths of adhesive tape to my naked flesh. This was the depths of my misery: stripped before my lover, who was trying to hold my collapsing body together with pieces of adhesive plaster.

"Why here? Why not his house?"

"Because this is neutral territory. I even volunteered. Besides, you're here, and if you feel well enough, I knew you'd want to sit in."

"Wouldn't miss it. But who's 'everyone'?"

"Your uncle Simon and Oldham. Jerry Finnegan, representing the union people. Oldham thinks it may cool everyone off. He's called Trumbull to contact Rampsie."

I could hardly believe my ears. "They're all going to get together in *one* place at the same time? *This house?*"

"That makes you uneasy?"

"Hell, yes, It makes me frantic."

18

George fussed over me while I tried to get comfortable enough to nap; he brought me soup and tea and cocoa and all manner of things that even Aunt Chloe might have had difficulty dreaming up. Finally, when he kissed me, I told him that was best yet, that *now* I felt better, but for God's sake to go away so I could drift off for a while. Just before the meeting was to convene, George woke me up.

It was nice waking up in George's bed, but even nicer having him dress me: slowly, his hands warm over my body, lingering enchantingly here and there.

Trumbull was the first to arrive; he was in an affable, expansive mood, even expressing regret over my broken ribs. To my astonishment, he handed me a bottle of wine. "Oldham told me about it when he called," Trumbull said. "I thought this might ease the pain."

Now I knew very well that Trumbull wasn't all that altruistic. Maybe he was getting a little worried about the activities of his "boys." At any rate, it was a great vintage.

George looked a little like a pirate, with that swollen wound above his eye. Come to think of it, none of us looked too good except Trumbull, who seemed pink and plump. I thought he seemed remotely uncomfortable about it, too, associating with us disaster victims; maybe he was afraid we'd bleed on him.

"Oldham's worried," George told Trumbull. "Even he thinks it's time we got a handle on this situation."

Trumbull chuckled. "'Bout time, I'd say. Hear people're getting pretty upset."

178

I held my tongue because I wanted to tell him it was a whole lot his fault, encouraging Rampsie's little mobsters. I almost choked instead.

In a few minutes Uncle Simon arrived with Oldham. Uncle Simon still looked pretty peaked to me, as if he weren't sleeping well. His face was a little pale, and his eyes seemed somehow sunk deeply into his head. "You're sure Rampsie's coming?" he asked Trumbull.

"Yep." Trumbull waved one of his soft white hands confidently. I took to wondering if there was a special place they put lawyers who assaulted other lawyers, like one of the inner circles of hell.

Jerry Finnegan, the union organizer, slid in the door a little uncertainly, as if not sure he was in the right place; George pulled up another chair for him. His face was a mass of scratches; he had a huge welt behind one ear, and he walked with a slight stoop. He was still swearing about the mill battles. "Goddamn sons of bitches," he said to no one in particular. "You know what I'd like to do to those sons of—"

"Arrest 'em, that's what," said Clyde Oldham. "You're all invited to the arraignment. Regular picnic. You comin', James?"

Trumbull was obviously amused by Oldham. "Don't need to, Clyde, old buddy. Since you got things so well under control."

I wasn't surprised at Trumbull's confidence; we all knew those bloody little bashers of his would get another slap on the wrist.

"How come those guys just happened to be visiting when the strikers got assaulted?" I asked Oldham, with one eye on Trumbull. "Bit of a coincidence, wouldn't you say?"

Oldham shrugged. "Looks to me like they might have been recruited somewheres."

I believed Clyde. There were always toughs for sale. Cross some crooks' palms with enough silver, and they'd do in their grandmothers. There were men in prison right now who'd committed murder for ten bucks.

"And I suppose," said Uncle Simon, leaning forward toward Clyde, "that none of those men would tell if they'd been paid or not, or who'd paid them, just assuming. . . . "

Oldham nodded warily at Uncle Simon, glancing furtively at Trumbull. We all knew that the only person with any interest in busting heads down at the mill was Eastman, and standing right there before us was his mill lawyer, who wasn't about to let out a peep, even supposing he knew what Eastman had been up to.

Jerry Finnegan was glaring at the lot of us. "Oh, you'll never get that out of anyone, I can guarantee you." He rubbed the back of his neck gingerly. "That's the kind of money gets passed in little bills in manila envelopes, don't you know—"

At that moment Bob Rampsie burst into the room. He didn't bother to knock, just yanked open George's front door and stalked in on us. His jaw was thrust forward, his face glowering. He wore a pair of old jeans, a ripped shirt, and a filthy sweater with part of the sleeve missing. His sneakers had knotted laces, the canvas torn, and his encrusted socks drooped about his ankles. He smelled something fierce. He couldn't have changed his clothes or even combed his hair since the fight down by the mill. I even felt sorry for Trumbull—the man looked a little apoplectic—because his client was rebelling against him, and he didn't like it one little bit.

"My God, Bob," he said, "couldn't you at least have. . . ?"

"Sit down," said George, offering him his chair. "It's all right, Bob."

Bob's feet left a muddy trail on George's rug. "I don't want to sit down." Then he caught sight of Jerry Finnegan. "You expect me to stay when that . . . turd is here?" Rampsie's fists curled by his side.

Finnegan had arisen slowly from his chair. "I won't be insulted . . ." he said menacingly.

"Insult, ha!" Rampsie was shrieking now, out of control.

Trumbull had Rampsie's arm. "Bob, you're making a damn mistake. . . ."

Suddenly Bob flung himself at Finnegan, his head low, aiming at the man's chest. Finnegan slammed against the wall, falling over a table. The table leaf snapped off its hinges, crashing to the floor; then a thin leg buckled. Now George was trying to wrestle Rampsie off Finnegan, who was on his back, kicking upward as hard as he could in close quarters.

At that moment Trumbull grasped Rampsie by the back of his sweater, shirt, and perhaps backbone for all I knew and lifted him off Finnegan with one hand. Then, with his free hand, he slapped him across the face. "When-I-tell-you-to-stop, I-mean-it, damn-you," he said. "Now I don't want to see any more of that shit around here!"

There was absolute dead silence in the room. Finnegan picked himself off the floor, clinging to the wall; Rampsie stared at Trumbull, his jaw open. Trumbull was still clutching the clothing from Rampsie's back in his big fist—odds and ends of rags without Rampsie attached. But Rampsie had sagged slightly, and his eyes wavered. Trumbull pointed to the empty place on the couch beside me. "Sit down," he ordered. "Over there!"

Great, I thought. Why doesn't your reeking child sit next to you, O Mighty Commander? I looked up at Rampsie, the shock of streaky muddy hair hanging onto his forehead, that voracious look in his eye.

Now Oldham leaned tentatively forward, pointing at Rampsie. "You gotta stay away from the common," he said, " and you"—he pointed at Finnegan—"gotta stay away from Rampsie. You hear? That's the reason for this meeting."

Oldham had been drinking, and we all knew it. A cold gleam came into Rampsie's eyes.

Uncle Simon stared at the rug before him. "You know we're still deputized, Clyde. From the other day, at the parade, and—"

Trumbull jumped from his seat as if he'd been stung. "Now *that's* illegal, for one goddamn thing, and you know it damn well, and besides—"

Uncle Simon stood up. He looked furious. He was tapping on his cast, the sound echoing hollowly as he made his points. "All right, James, then what would *you* suggest? We've been to the Tremont police, to Judge Bream, even the state police. We've got a whole lot of satisfaction from the pack of 'em. Everyone tells us it isn't their problem. Well, you know whose problem it is? I can tell you easy: It's mine! I live right here. Only at the minute it isn't much like living. Tell you the truth, I'd call it dying." Now Uncle Simon was shouting, even louder than Rampsie. "That's what we're doing, James, you hear. We're dying in this town, you understand me?"

"But if you deputize those men . . . " Trumbull was protesting.

Suddenly I realized that Rampsie was talking to me, pushing against my arm with his elbow. "You gonna be a deputy, girlee, arrest people just like your uncle says?" His voice sounded so low and theatrical I almost laughed. Except for the glint in those hard eyes.

"What the hell difference does it make to you *what* I do?" I asked. I sure wasn't ready for this: Uncle Simon going to pot before my eyes, then this creep making nasty noises at me.

"Because," he said, shifting ever so slightly, "if you do, I'll break every goddamn bone in your body."

I couldn't have heard right, so I leaned forward, taking a second look at Rampsie's face. But it had altered suddenly. When I looked to see if anyone'd heard, they all were talking together or looking at

Trumbull; Rampsie's face was once again devoid of expression, as if it had become a mask wiped clean of human response.

Trumbull was standing to leave; clearly he'd had enough. I didn't blame him. "Well, Clyde," Trumbull was saying, rubbing his hands together, "I don't know if we've accomplished anything. Hope to hell—"

At that moment someone started beating on George's front door, yelling and pummeling at it as if to break it in.

"What in blazes?" said George, wrenching the door open.

In rushed Jaimie Rampsie, agitated and filthy beyond belief. He looked wildly about at us, then spotted his brother. Jaimie's face was streaked with tears. "Pa!" he blurted out in a long wail that ran my blood cold. "Pa, Bob. Somebody's killed him. He's dead, Bob, dead."

Bob had already closed the gap to his brother, grabbed the boy by the shoulder, and was shaking him until his teeth seemed to chatter in his head. "Where's Pa, Jaimie? Christ's sake, don't just stand there blubberin'. Tell me!"

The boy's eyes were wide with terror, "D-down by the mill, Bob. Covered with m-mud. You oughta see!" The boy let out another wail, full of fright and terror. "They say you come, Doc. 'cause they need you bad."

I struggled to my feet, my ribs aching like fire. "I saw a man with his face in the mud, but I'd never seen him before. And he wasn't dead then. Then someone kicked me. . . ." Even the thought made my ribs burn with the pain all over again.

George streaked out the door right behind Clyde Oldham. Uncle Simon waited with me for George to return. "Do you want to try for home?" he asked me. "We could make it if we go slow."

I could barely manage to suck breaths of air into my sore chest. "Tomorrow, Uncle Simon. I'll make it then." I tapped his arm and smiled. "The halt and the lame, Uncle Simon, that's us. We should form a comedy act."

He'd calmed down now and looked pretty depressed. "Not exactly a picnic, Lisa."

Within minutes Oldham and George had brought old Rampsie, Pops's brother, in through the rear door of George's office. They placed the body on an examining table and began to clean the dirt off his features.

I recognized him immediately. Despite the mud and confusion down by the mill when I first saw this face, I recognized the wasted features,

182

sunken cheeks, and prominent nose. It was the same ascetic face as Bob Rampsie's and Pops's, with the same hint of cruelty about the mouth.

"Rampsie's father?" I was amazed. "Aunt Chloe's told me about him."

George pushed back the damp, muddy hair of the dead man, which was dripping murky water all over the examining table and down onto the floor. George contemplated the man's face for a moment. "Eccentric as an old coot, they say. I haven't laid eyes on him in a long time either."

Oldham nodded, peering over George's shoulder at the corpse between us. "Queer as a three-dollar bill, if you ask me. Used to beat up on Bob fairly regular, till Bob got too big." He shook his head. "Hadrian was a hard man to savvy, for sure."

George touched a spot on the old man's skull. "There's a hell of a good contusion right here," he said, gently probing it. "Looks like someone cracked him a good blow with something pretty heavy."

Oldham bent over it suspiciously, touching the purplish welt glistening beneath the dark hair. Then George slid back the sheet, exposing a craggy, knobby body with a sunken chest and protuberant stomach. He began to sponge off the skin to remove the grime and stopped. Right in the middle of the man's abdomen was a small purplish slit. Somehow the skin didn't quite cover it; it looked like a fish's mouth, soft and gaping.

"By God," said Oldham, wonderingly. "A knife wound, look at that! Would you believe it?"

George bent over, probing the neat incision. He shook his head. "I'll believe anything, Clyde, when it comes to the Rampsies. Anything at all."

"Wonder who did it," said Oldham, gingerly touching the wound. "Saw lots of head busting down there, but nobody with knives. Just you and this guy"—he looked up at George—"got slashed."

"I wouldn't quite call it a slash," George answered, his fingers probing the wound. "It damn near went through him." He measured the wound with a long stainless instrument. "Whoever did this meant business. The blade must have been at least eleven inches long."

"Eleven inches!" Oldham held up his fingers the approximate length of the wound. "Been a long time since I saw a knife that long with such a thin blade."

I remembered very well a knife that length and that fine, but for a moment I couldn't recall where. Then it occurred to me. "Pops Rampsie, that's where. Pops uses one for slicing meat. I've seen it on his counter several times."

George was still examining the body, bending over the dead man. "Must have severed his ventral artery. Couldn't have picked a better spot if he'd been a surgeon."

Why would someone have used Pops's carving knife? And why would old man Rampsie's body lie in the mud down at the mill all during the day, undiscovered until so late?

"Could the man have been stabbed up at Rampsie's store?" I asked George. "If so, he might have wandered down toward the mill, where he knew there was a lot going on, just to get help." I tried to picture Rampsie, wounded, staggering across the common to find someone who'd help him stanch his wound.

"I doubt it," answered George. "This man probably fell near where he was wounded. He wouldn't have enough blood left after thirty seconds to stagger anywhere."

We stood next to the body, looking sadly down at it, holding the steel rim around the examining table with our hands. The dead man, naked and innocent in his death, was stiffening before us.

"Then it musta happened at the mill, if that's what you're sayin'," said Oldham. "Why kill the bastard down there?" He may have been tipsy before, but he was making pretty good sense now. He answered his own questions. "Maybe with all the fighting down there, somebody figured nobody'd notice a stiff. Good way to get rid of one. Then again, maybe the guy who did it didn't mean to do the old man in. Sure wish this old beggar could talk."

George and Oldham replaced the sheet over Rampsie's body. Then George signed some forms that Oldham gave him and released the corpse to Oldham's custody. Together they placed the body in Clyde's car, and the police chief left with his grisly burden for the Tremont coroner.

Later George lifted me into his bed as gently as if I were a child. "I'll sleep in the spare bedroom, so as not to jar you," he said. Then he gave me a dose of something to ease my ribs, which were aching so badly that I couldn't get comfortable in any position; soon I began to feel groggy all over. The walls began to move in slowly in a comforting way, as though they were right there to touch, not across the room.

"I think one of the Rowe Boys did it," I told George a little thickly. "Killed the old man, I mean. Don't you think so? Wouldn't it be nice if

184

those idiots killed each other off, one by one? Then we wouldn't have to worry anymore."

George was somewhere up in the haze next to my bed. "I wouldn't count on it, but it's a great idea."

"George?" I could barely see him now. "I'm sorry for conking out on you. Thanks for letting me stay. Don't you think I'm a rotten guest?"

But then I could see his face close to mine, and he was smiling at me. Somehow I felt like a little girl, and George was tucking me in just as my father used to do. I felt an incredibly warm, drowsy, and cozy feeling. Things were falling away rapidly.

"George," I said, about to leave the world behind, "just this minute you reminded me of my father. Isn't that funny? You're so much like him, it's ridiculous."

Vaguely I realized he'd kissed my lips gently. Dad never used to do that.

19

The next day the police flooded Rowe. Early in the morning I could see Colonel Sparrow's state police car circling the common. It gave me smug satisfaction finally to observe his squads of gray-clad troopers running about the town, questioning strikers, swarming over the porch at Rampsie's store, chasing down the side street where Old Man Rampsie had lived in his down-at-the-heels house. It took a murder to get the cops here, but we'd finally succeeded. Once again the firehouse was appropriated, Sarah Wellington retreated into her inner office, and Sparrow claimed the old desk that Judge Bream had used during the last memorable trip through town.

My ribs felt 100 percent better, and I could breathe again, albeit not very deeply. This I attributed to the fact that when I awoke this morning, George brought me coffee, toast, and eggs in bed, with a chaser of aspirin.

"This is a great hotel," I said. "Do you always give such good service? I may never leave." The improved state of my rib cage even allowed me to laugh a little, especially when I saw George's concerned face looking at me.

"Maybe I'll keep you, provided you can cook."

"Damn. I knew there was a hitch." Then I listened while George sat on the bed and told me about Sparrow.

"He's questioning people all over town—Finnegan, Rampsie, Pops, Keaton, Hudman. Even your uncle Simon. Nobody can figure who put the shiv in Bob's old man."

I propped myself up on one elbow. "Why Uncle Simon?"

186

"Because he was down there when the fight was going on. Granted he was in the mill building, but Sparrow's wondering what he saw. Wants to see you and me, too. Can you be ready in a half hour? Doesn't want me until this afternoon. Obvious favoritism. I tried to get you out of it, but he wouldn't listen." He smiled grimly. "Been up since dawn, talking to the Tremont coroner about the knife wound. They still find it hard to believe we've really had a murder."

I climbed out of bed without assistance; the thick tape that George had wrapped around my ribs was as stiff as a board, but it provided reinforcement. Without it, I'd have collapsed like an unsound building. I could even slide on my clothes if I took a deep breath between layers. But my skirt zipper did me in, as did my shoelaces. George came to my rescue.

Sparrow had brought along his secretary. Before her was a stenograph. It seemed as though everything anyone said to Sparrow got set down for posterity; he must have had a storage vault the size of Grant's Tomb.

Colonel Sparrow was across the room, interviewing one of the strikers. I could hear him ask the man if he'd seen the deceased Rampsie at any time during the fracas.

The striker, obviously ill at ease, answered in monosyllables, pointing to a map on Sparrow's desk showing the mill and its environs. When the striker shuffled away, Sparrow motioned to me.

He watched me while I sat down on the chair opposite his desk; my ribs still hurt, and I sat slowly to keep from clanking them together. I looked into his unblinking gray eyes.

He shuffled around some papers on his desk, arranging several into piles. "Good morning, Miss Sanderson. I understand you were down by the mill during that . . . altercation. May I ask why?"

I could feel my ribs transmitting electric jolts as I sat in that stiff chair. "Because I'd walked to work with Uncle Simon. I was very worried about him."

Sparrow's neck bulged slightly above the tight collar of his uniform. I could see the prominent cords of his neck muscles. This morning there was a slight stubble on his chin; he'd had a bad night. "You saw the dead man, I understand. He was lying in the mud?"

"Yes. I turned him over and cleaned the mud from his nose. It was all I could do at the moment. I never saw him again—until last night, of course."

187

"Do you think he'd been knifed then? Did you see blood?"

"I can't remember any. It was so muddy down there. But he might have been a bystander, hanging around. Many people down there weren't part of the strikers or of Rampsie's crowd. He, for instance."

I could hear the fingers of Sparrow's secretary moving on the keys of the stenograph.

"Well, I guess we've been wrong about them," Sparrow said thoughtfully. "Seems where there was smoke there was fire after all, like you said, Miss Sanderson. Course, one expects a certain amount of roughing up during a mill strike, but we sure never expected to have a murder on our hands." He studied the papers before him. "The chief's gonna be mighty upset when he hears about it."

"Heaven forbid you'd have any difficulty over our little . . . altercation," I said.

"Well, it's all the inquiries, the red tape, that sort of thing. Chief had another training clinic set for San Francisco next week. He's going to be pretty upset." Sparrow glanced at me from beneath faintly arching eyebrows. "And I suppose you hold us partly responsible, Miss Sanderson. Like maybe we could have done something. . . ."

I couldn't answer.

"Well, we've got our problems, too," he said. He whirled around to his secretary. "Turn that goddamn thing off, will you?" Then he turned back to me. "Like I told you, we don't have enough officers to patrol Tremont, much less Rowe. I mean, you aren't—"

"Even in your jurisdiction," I finished. "I know, Colonel, you've already impressed that on me."

"Well, you can go now." By the look on his face, I knew that I or Rowe or both had ruined his whole morning. I wasn't feeling particularly hospitable, with my ribs making violent music and Sparrow sulking at me about what we were doing to his goddamn chief's schedule.

"For what it's worth," he added suddenly, "we're all sorry for what you've gone through. I want you to know that we're assigning everyone we can to help you." He indicated the policemen on the common through the window with a magnanimous sweep of his hand.

I nodded wearily. "It's not really today I'm worried about, Colonel Sparrow. It's tomorrow when they're gone, and it's just us again."

During the afternoon I moved my things back to Uncle Simon's house.

"You don't have to leave, you know," said George. "You add a certain class to the place."

"I'd only be in the way. You're busy with patients, and I don't want to leave Aunt Chloe and Uncle Simon right now. Besides, I'm feeling better."

Sparrow was now interrogating the Rampsie crowd. From Uncle Simon's house I could see Hudman and Keaton crossing the common from Rampsie's store to the fire station. The fire engine was still parked outside the building, to make room for those interrogations going on inside. I could even see Pops Rampsie on the front porch of his store shaking his fist after Hudman.

Tim and Buzz were playing marbles in the backyard, in the blackened strip between the house and where the barn used to stand. Once it had been grass, but the roots had been fried away by the fire.

"Hey, Sis," yelled Tim. He didn't even bother to look up because he was cleaning up on Buzz's marbles.

" 'Lo, Lize." A chamois cloth marble bag hung from Buzz's belt, the tassel swinging against his leg. "You come home, see us again?"

"I've only been gone one day, for heaven's sake. Besides, the old ribs are doing better, can't you tell?" I rapped against my rib cage with my knuckles; the adhesive plaster echoed smartly. Buzz looked at me appraisingly, his head still bandaged.

"You don't look so good," said Buzz. "You look . . . kinda . . . bad."

I laughed at him. "Thanks a lot. Listen, you don't look so good yourself. By the way, have you seen Jaimie Rampsie? I've been worried about him since his father got killed."

Buzz pulled marbles from the chamois bag and began absently winding the cord about his fingers. "Scared," he said. "Jaimie scared."

Tim looked up. "What's he scared about?"

Buzz rewound the cord about his fingers in the opposite direction. "Why's he scared, Buzz?" I asked the boy.

Buzz sucked in his cheeks. "Because he know who killed his pa, that why." Buzz was looking around surreptitiously as if someone might be listening. "Why you s'pose?"

At that moment, my chest felt worse than it had down by the mill. "Why?" I could barely say the words. "Who killed him?"

"Won't say," answered Buzz. "Just he know, that's all."

I grasped the boy's arm. "Buzz, could you find out? I mean, could you ask Jaimie?"

Buzz shook his head. He seemed suddenly frightened. "I not ask Jaimie. He scared! I already tell you. He scared of *them*."

I looked at Buzz, feeling helpless. "It's important, Buzz. Important. Do you understand?"

"I try, Lize." his voice was simple and ingenuous, as if now he'd turned to other thoughts. "I tell you if Jaimie say."

That night George came over after seeing his last patient. It was almost ten. He'd spent so much time with Sparrow and on the phone to the county coroner that he'd had to reschedule some of the patients to evening. I related to him what Buzz had told me.

"Do you really think Jaimie knows anything?" George asked. "Couldn't he have been pretending or even bragging?"

We were perched on the front steps in the dark. Inside, Aunt Chloe and Mrs. Sardoe were already in bed, but Uncle Simon was sitting over the kitchen table oiling all his rusty tools from the cellar which had been soaked in the water, and he'd even pulled down his guns from the rack for a cleaning.

"I don't know. I think it's entirely possible he's heard something. Jaimie knows what's going on over there; he's always hanging around in the background, taking everything in. I don't think they realize he's there half the time."

George's long legs skimmed the edges of the steps below us. The night was warm, hazy, with no stars visible. A soft mist, rising from the damp of the common grass, hung in the air like a low cloud. Fireflies flashed by us, winking their cold, pinpoint lights.

"Sparrow's about given up," George said. "At least, that's what he told me. He said they don't have a damn clue to what happened to Old Man Rampsie. He told me whoever did it's keeping it an awfully tight secret."

"Did he expect him to confess?"

"Could be." I could hear his low chuckle.

"You know that three-quarters of the crimes in this country are never solved at all? And do you realize who usually is the victim of the unsolved crime? Someone like Rampsie. Sure, he was a kind of miserable man. He beat on his kids, and I hear he scrounged money off Pops. He was considered the dregs of the social order by the people of this town. If no one solves his murder, he's just another statistic, and Sparrow's not going to spend a whole lot of time trying to dredge up the facts on an isolated crime in a mill town. Now, if someone had put the carving knife into *Eastman,* we'd have police all over this place for the next three weeks."

190

George turned to me in the dark. "You're beginning to sound like a cop hater."

"No, I'm not. Never. It's just the inequities of the system. Good police are absolutely vital to a community. But they've got their priorities. Old Man Rampsie, in Rowe, Vermont, just doesn't happen to be one of them."

I could see the planes of George's face, his open collar, the shadow of his eyebrows in the light from the house. "Then what do you think is left to us that we haven't done before? What do other people do, faced with the same unsolvable situation? Which way do they turn?"

"I can tell you what some people do. The process is already beginning. Have you seen what Uncle Simon's been up to the last hour? He's meticulously oiling his guns. It's giving me the creeps, I can tell you."

"He won't really use them, will he? For God's sake, wasn't that all bluff the other night?"

"I hope so. But he hasn't had those things out in a couple of years. And it isn't exactly the hunting season."

We both turned and squinted across the common; there was some kind of noise coming from Rampsie's store. It was now almost eleven. The night had become slowly hazier, and the fog over the common looked like steam over a boiling pot. I could picture this from the air: giant pillows of white, cushioning a low-lying area like a shroud. From our perspective down below, it was just plain eerie.

We could hear voices, low rumbles of sound coming to us as if through a tunnel. "Can you make out what it is?" I asked George. My senses were muffled by the fog.

"It sounds like someone's moving something," answered George, cocking an ear toward the strange sound. Every now and then we could hear cursing from somewhere in that white formless mass.

"One's Hudman," I told him. "I'd know his voice anywhere." It was low and rumbling, halting in its delivery.

There was no sound of any vehicle. George had now stood up, leaning forward toward the sound, straining to hear. "They're lugging something across the common. What in blazes do you suppose it is? They're having an ungodly struggle with it."

The sounds continued for another five minutes. Finally we heard someone laugh, a low, guttural sound. The thought crossed my mind that maybe they were drinking out there, but this somehow didn't have the sound of a carefree debauch.

191

Then suddenly the sounds ceased. The front door of Rampsie's store slammed, and we heard more laughter. Within a minute in the distance a car started, drove off, and once again we were left alone in our mist-enshrouded world.

"I don't like it, George." Now I was standing, too, trying to see something, anything, through the fog. "What do you suppose they're up to?"

George had already started down the front steps. His sneakers were as quiet as cats' feet. "I'm going to take a look. Will you be all right here?"

"Of course." Besides, I thought, Uncle Simon's just inside the door with what amounts to a small arsenal for protection.

George disappeared onto the common, losing substance slowly as he vanished into the mist, like a ghost in a play. First he'd become featureless, then formless.

In five minutes, which seemed like a solid hour, George raced back again, panting, trailing shreds of moisture as if it were a diaphanous garment. He looked as if he'd seen a ghost himself.

"There's a man out there!" He was gasping for breath. "Hanging from something, must be a light pole. I can see only his feet in the fog."

I jumped up from the steps. "How'll we get him down, George?"

"Car. Turn it around. I'll get Simon." He raced up the steps past me while I dived into his car, parked in our driveway.

I'd barely turned the engine over when George ran from the house holding a hacksaw. Uncle Simon was hot on his heels. Uncle Simon was still grasping the rifle he'd been cleaning.

"Jump in, Simon," yelled George. "Hope to God I can find the place again."

I spun the wheel, whipping the car about in the street, and took off across the common, cutting rivers of green through the water-laden grass. Ahead of us was nothing but flocks of white down, wet and suffocating. The windshield beaded with the saturated air.

George was standing on the front bumper of the car, directing me, like an overgrown hood statue. Even though he was so close, his forward hand had disappeared in the fog.

"Had to be hanging from a streetlight," George yelled back to us. "Tried to catch his foot to hold him up, but he was too high."

We circled the edge of the common on the inside of the light poles, noting each one as we passed; no light emanated from any of them to help us.

"Over there, over there." George gestured while Uncle Simon and I hunched forward, trying to make our way in the fog.

At that moment we saw a man dangling from nowhere, and I slammed on the brakes. He was high above us, trussed in some kind of sack, a cord about his neck. He was staring at us, his eyes bulging. His mouth hung open. It would be a miracle if he were still alive.

"This way," yelled George. I tried to maneuver the car directly beneath the hanging figure. Now I could see the thick cord about the man's neck and the whites of his eyes, brilliant in the headlights from the car.

"Can you reach him?" yelled Uncle Simon to George. His voice had a note of desperation.

George was standing on top of the car now. From that height he couldn't quite reach the rope from which the man was swinging. "Simon, give me a hand," George called.

I steadied Uncle Simon as best I could with my sore ribs as he climbed first to the hood of the car, then to the roof. After a moment's discussion he bent forward, and George, steadying himself as best he could, climbed on Uncle Simon's back; this gave him more than a foot of extra height.

Those two looked like a bad acrobatic team, George on top of Uncle Simon, shakily trying to reach the cord about the hanging man's neck. It was a frantic team; they seemed perilously close to tumbling off the car. George, now standing his full height on Uncle Simon's back, just barely managed to grasp the cord.

"Someone's got to catch him . . ." called George feverishly. "He's going to fall when I cut the rope." I held George as best I could about the waist, trying to give him as much stability as possible while he sawed through that heavy hemp rope. As I peered up, I could see why the man hadn't strangled: The rope was so thick that it not only didn't choke off his windpipe but actually seemed to have given some support to his neck. But if George hadn't found him when he did, I was sure the man wouldn't have survived.

A steady sound emanated from the man, a combination moan, gag, and gurgle way down in his throat like an animal rumbling in fear. The goose bumps rose on my arms, and a chill encircled my neck like a ring of ice. I couldn't hold the man fully, and neither could George, so our burden hit the top of the car with a thump when he fell. George and Uncle Simon, using his good arm, slid him down the car, from the roof to the hood to the ground. Then they unlaced the cord from his neck, peeling back the hemp bag which covered him. The man's face was bloated, but the eyes had ceased to bulge; instead, they'd contracted into small, fine holes in his face as I stood there, watching it happen. The rope had left burns, ugly and red, about his neck like the high collar of a priest. Suddenly the features assumed a familiar form. The man was Keaton, limp, without his red cowboy hat for once, almost strangled.

Keaton couldn't talk; instead, he continued to utter that long, eerie, low wail. George reached back inside his throat, trying to clear away his tongue, which had swollen to cover his esophagus. George wiped the bloody mucus from about the man's mouth with his handkerchief.

"What happened?" George asked Keaton gently, leaning over him. "Can you tell us?" This was a different Keaton from the man George had had to deal with in the back of Rampsie's store when Bob Rampsie had tried to attack him.

The man's eyes began to roll again uselessly in his florid face. "We damn near didn't make it," said George, feeling the man's pulse. "He may have brain damage as it is, deprived of oxygen that way. . . ."

"Do you want me to go get Oldham?" asked Uncle Simon. "Maybe we need him."

George nodded. "Lisa, help me. We'll get air in fast. Hold his head back." George straddled Keaton, then forced the man's jaw open, placing his own mouth over it in an effort to induce the man's own reflexes to take over. Uncle Simon backed up George's car and spun the wheels before he disappeared again into the fog.

For ten minutes there wasn't a sound on the common except Keaton's shallow, rasping gasps, George's deep breaths as he drew into his lungs enough air for two, and the slow friction of my hands over the man's throat in an effort to evoke deeper breathing. Not a noise arose from Rampsie's store or from any of the other houses about the common, but perhaps not enough people remained around the common to make a noise. Most of the houses were deserted now; only Stu and Minnie Callaghan remained on the far side. Over here, Uncle Simon had boarded his house; the Sardoes were living with us, so their house was dark. And the Brittons had retreated to the back of the house, so no one ever saw them anymore; they'd become hermits as surely as if they lived in the woods by themselves.

"Is he breathing?" I asked George during a momentary pause. Keaton's throat still vibrated like that of a man with a bad cold.

"Barely. Just about enough to sustain life, I'd say." From his pocket, George produced a small, thin pocket flashlight; lifting the lid of Keaton's eye, George peered into it, then flicked off the light doubtfully. Soon Uncle Simon's car rolled back onto the common. Inside was Oldham. But this time we'd run out of luck because the man was looped.

"Clyde," began George, "we've got another one for you." Then he looked at Oldham. The police chief had sunk to the ground, kneeling over Keaton, talking to him in a thick voice. George glanced over at me, then at Uncle Simon.

"Didn't think he was so bad when I picked him up," said Uncle Simon apologetially. "I was in too much of a hurry to notice."

"Maybe you'd better go home, Clyde," said George quietly. I shared his frustration because Oldham could have provided invaluable aid to us tonight.

Uncle Simon was the most upset of all. "Go home and sober up, will you, Clyde? For God's sake, can't you leave the damn booze alone?"

Oldham was almost too drunk to protest. "No need to get huffy, Simon," he began, but Uncle Simon was struggling to haul him to his feet with his useful arm, even swinging his cast as leverage.

"Time to go, Clyde. We've got our hands full enough without nursing you along, too." He pointed Oldham in the direction of his home and gave him a little shove. "Sleep it off, Clyde. Beat it now."

Oldham was unsteady on his feet but sober enough to get home, in my opinion. After all, where could one get lost in Rowe? But he stopped cantankerously and glared at all of us.

"Let's get him to the hospital," said George, lifting Keaton's shoulders. "I've done all I can for him here. Simon, help with the legs. Lisa, hold his head, will you? Let's go now."

"Who done it?" asked Oldham thickly. His intoxication seemed to be wearing off somewhat with the shock of seeing the injured Keaton. "Who attacked Keaton?"

Uncle Simon was struggling with Keaton's limp, gasping form. "That's your job, Clyde, remember? You find out who did it." Uncle Simon succeeded in immobilizing one of Keaton's limp legs, while George and I grasped him about the shoulders. "They came from Rampsie's, Clyde, if that's anything to you."

We hoisted Keaton into George's car, lowering the seat so he could lie flat. The road was dark from Rowe, and we didn't see any lights until the outskirts of Tremont, where gas stations and a couple of all-night establishments cast colored lights into the fog.

The two short wings of the little Tremont hospital were brightly lit. George, with Uncle Simon helping him as much as he was able, carried the man while I ran ahead for an attendant. In minutes an accident room orderly and nurse were propelling Keaton's stretcher down the hall. George supervised his admission; then we three drove slowly back through the dark night to Rowe.

No one said a word until the outskirts of Rowe. Then I was startled to hear Uncle Simon's laugh.

"For a little town nobody ever heard of, we're getting a little hard to forget, eh?" Then he laughed again.

The sound of that laugh, high and shrill, made me shrink back again against the cushions of the car. I caught George's concerned glance as he turned partially toward me.

Perhaps we *were* getting hard to forget, and Uncle Simon was right. At any rate, by six o'clock the next morning three state police cars were parked, bumper to bumper, at the edge of the common. I'd never expected that much action so fast, and the earliness of the hour filled me with misgivings. I called George to tell him what I was seeing. "Did you call the state police last night?" I asked him.

"No, but I informed the hospital personnel what had happened. They must have passed the word along."

I dressed quickly and strolled out onto the common. George was just swinging around the other side in his car. He parked it quickly and jumped out. He seemed pretty tired. I think we'd all given up sleeping on a more or less permanent basis.

A state trooper stood near one of the three official cars. His face was glum, no-nonsense, creased with efficiency.

"What's the trouble, Officer?" I asked the man. "We live here. My name's Lisa Sanderson."

The man hardly looked in my direction. "There's been a murder, miss. Will you"—he pointed to George—"please get that car of yours off the street immediately?"

I glanced at George. "Keaton must have died in the hospital. Did they tell you about it?"

George turned toward me, a stunned expression on his face. "It can't be Keaton. I called up just a few minutes ago, and there'd been no change in his condition. They had him in intensive care."

George approached the officer. "I'm Dr. Almquist. Last night I brought a man named Keaton to the hospital. He was still alive then. Can you tell me what's happened to him?''

The officer turned to look at George. "Don't know a thing about any Keaton, Doctor. But we'd like everyone off the common for the time being. Please go home. We'll call you if we need you.''

George shrugged and appeared even more puzzled. Inside the house everyone was awake except Tim and Buzz.

Aunt Chloe was wrapped in a formless cotton brocade bathrobe with worn tassels. Her hair was askew. She and Uncle Simon were peering intently through the cracks in the boards over the front windows.

"Who. . . ?'' I started to ask when Aunt Chloe pointed silently toward the street. A police car had just moved away, leaving our view unobstructed.

Aunt Chloe's finger trembled. "Whoever . . . it . . . was . . . died,'' she stammered, "is out in the c-common right now, w-wrapped in an old blanket.''

Uncle Simon was straining to see. It was simply impossible to tell; the blanket covered almost all of the figure on the grass, except for the feet and some hair on top of the head.

We didn't have long to wait; two uniformed state policemen, having separated themselves from the six or eight standing before the police cars, began walking toward our house. One of the men carried what appeared to be a gun wrapped in a cloth. A police car had turned on its revolving blue-white light; the flashes streaked around the houses in the early-morning light.

One of the policemen knocked at Uncle Simon's front door. He was a short, burly man with large hands and wrists and an abrupt manner. "Does this belong to anyone here? It's registered to a Simon Sanderson.'' He removed the cloth and wadded it into his pocket.

I looked at Uncle Simon, then down at the gun; it was Uncle Simon's rifle.

Uncle Simon flushed a deep red. "Where did you find it?'' he asked the officer. "That's mine.''

"We found it out in the common. Are you Simon Sanderson? If you are, we want to know what you were doing with it last night.''

"Wasn't doing anything with it, except carry it along. I'd been cleaning it. In case you didn't hear, there was a man hanging from that streetlight, and Dr. Almquist, my niece, and I cut him down. Brought him up to the Tremont hospital.''

"You might as well know,'' said the trooper, "that this is the weapon,

198

near as we can tell right now, that killed Clyde Oldham. We found it beside the body."

I reached out instinctively for Uncle Simon's arm. "Killed Clyde Oldham!" My arm felt paralyzed to the fingertips. "Killed Clyde Oldham!" The words simply wouldn't penetrate my brain. "When did Clyde Oldham die?"

"A few hours ago, the medical examiner said. Perhaps around midnight. Apparently he ran into Rampsie's store accusing a man named Bob Rampsie and someone else called Henry Hudman of stringing someone to a lamppost in the common. Same man you found, no doubt. This morning Chief Oldham was found out on your common, shot to death, with this gun beside him." The police trooper looked intently at Uncle Simon. "What we'd like to know is: What were you doing with the gun, and did you shoot Clyde Oldham?"

We all were transfixed; I could barely talk. My God, what had we done to Clyde, leaving him alone last night? What had possessed his poor befuddled brain? How had we failed him? But now Uncle Simon's head was on the block; I'd ache about Clyde later.

George touched the trooper's arm. "Mr. Sanderson was with me a good part of the night, Officer, as was Miss Sanderson. Took most of the night just getting Keaton up to the hospital, waiting around for him to get settled. We both can vouch for him."

"I was with him at home afterward," I told the officer. "Someone was with him all night."

The trooper shook his head. "But no one was with Mr. Sanderson *all* the time, right? He could have come back out here when all of you had gone to sleep."

"It's extremely unlikely. Besides, we would have heard a gunshot." I looked into the steady eyes of that trooper.

"Not necessarily," he answered coolly. "*Someone* fired a gun. How would you know if it was or wasn't your uncle?"

I instinctively knew better than to argue, but I couldn't help it. "He's not guilty of a damn thing, Officer, can't you understand? He simply dropped his gun out there. That's the exact fact."

"Maybe, lady. But we're going to take him to the office for questioning. Colonel Sparrow wants to talk to him. We're supposed to be up there right now."

"You can't hold him long. Only four hours in this state. . . . " I felt like a terrier, holding the man's leg with my teeth. If only I could detain him long enough, make my point. . . .

199

"Don't worry, lady, we know all the rules. Come on now, Mr. Sanderson. All this stuff isn't going to help your case one bit."

"Case!" Now I was shouting. "Since when is it a case? He hasn't even been arraigned. You touch one hair of his head, and we'll charge you with defamation of character, false arrest, conduct unbecoming." In my fury I felt everything going to pot again, and George grasped my arm steadyingly. "It won't help, Lisa." He was right. I looked into the cool, careful eyes of the troopers and realized they'd heard all these protests a hundred times before from a hundred different people, for endless good or bad reasons.

"Don't you worry none, Miss," said the second officer, who'd been standing by idly listening to our exchange. "We'll take good care of your uncle. Please come now, Mr. Sanderson."

Uncle Simon rubbed his head in confusion. He was walking down the front steps between the two officers when Aunt Chloe remembered his jacket still in the closet and tried to run after him with it.

I took it from her and put my arm about her. "He doesn't need it, Aunt Chloe. It's a warm morning."

"But he catches cold so easily." She was almost frantic, clutching that jacket in her hand. "Please give it to him."

"Don't worry. I'll take it along. I'm going with him."

"So am I," she gasped. I could see that she'd begun to shiver inside that bathrobe, even though it was heavy enough for a winter's night. She was halfway out the door before I could stop her.

"Stay here, Aunt Chloe. Tim and Buzz need you to get ready for school; they've got to leave in an hour."

"I'll go," said George. "Don't worry, I won't let him from my sight.". . ."

I shook my head. "You've even got morning office hours today. Besides, you've had to cancel so many lately that people will be upset. No, I'll go."

I got ready while keeping an eye on the troopers and Uncle Simon on the common. They were still intently asking Uncle Simon questions and seemed put for a few minutes. When I glanced up, Tim and Buzz were clinging to the railing on the stairs; Buzz had thrust his legs between the rails so that they dangled into the downstairs hall. Tim bounded down the stairs and motioned me into the kitchen like a conspirator.

"I asked Jaimie," he said, "what you asked me, about who stabbed his pa."

"Go on. What'd he say?"

200

Tim's bony ankles thrust out of his too-short pajama legs. "He said Keaton did it."

"Keaton!" I was facing Timmy over the kitchen table. Today there was no tablecloth on it, and I leaned over its pitted surface. "But why would Keaton kill Jaimie's father?"

Tim shrugged. "Jaimie wasn't all that sure, Sis. He says there was a fight about money one night when Keaton was drunk. Keaton tried to rob Old Man Rampsie. Jaimie heard his pa and Keaton yelling about it at the old house. Keaton had a knife. Jaimie ran away."

Of course, that was the answer. Bob had taken retribution swiftly for what Keaton had done to his father.

"Don't let on to Jaimie I told you, or anyone," Tim said. "He wouldn't have told me if he'd thought I was gonna pass it on."

I shook my head. "Not this time, Tim. It's not going to help much anyway because Jaimie has no proof. But I'll use anything I can dig up to help Uncle Simon. You understand?"

Tim thought about it a minute. "I understand," he said finally, quietly.

When Aunt Chloe shouted that Uncle Simon was getting into the troopers' car, I dashed for Uncle Simon's old Buick; it could make the trip to Tremont without me by now.

The troopers questioned Uncle Simon at the barracks about his gun for more than three hours. For a while they appeared suspicious of anything we said, especially when we kept asserting that we'd been together inside the Tremont hospital when his gun had been supposedly killing Oldham. Finally, in desperation I remembered Police Lieutenant Dowling, whom I'd spoken with that day so long ago. He'd volunteered to help out if I needed him sometime. Well, this was that sometime! I called him from the barracks.

The officer at the desk hesitated. "I'm afraid he's still at home in bed, ma'am. You say you're the lawyer lady who talked to him awhile ago? I remember you. He was up real late last night talking to people about some guy strung up on a tree or something down your way."

"I know all about it. Perhaps I can help if you'll only get him up."

The sergeant still sounded doubtful. "Well, I'll give it a whirl."

A half hour later, Dowling arrived at the barracks. Uncle Simon had been sitting before an officer at a long table, looking lost, like a child. He seemed older than I'd ever seen him. He rubbed his hands together aimlessly before him, until the chafing began to drive me crazy. When Dowling arrived, much to my relief he took over for the man questioning Uncle Simon.

"I had to clear it with Colonel Sparrow," Dowling said. "But the colonel says he can stand the help. Any time a police chief gets killed, the priorities on solving the crime rise considerably, as you can imagine."

I could imagine very well. That's what I was counting on. The lieutenant appeared pretty sleepy; he was wearing his off-duty clothes: dungarees, hiking boots, and an old plaid shirt. He began to interrogate Uncle Simon himself, while the first officer took notes on a large yellow pad.

"Uncle Simon didn't have anything to do with that crime," I told Dowling. "He really didn't, Lieutenant."

"Then who do you think killed Oldham, Miss Sanderson, if your uncle didn't? You must know practically everyone in the entire town."

"Well, I can guarantee you one thing. You can bet the Rowe Boys are at the bottom of it, Lieutenant, and not Uncle Simon. Somehow I think you've got your villains terribly confused." My head was beginning to ache, and I could feel my anger as I looked over at Uncle Simon sitting so despondently at the table.

"The . . . Rowe Boys?"

He didn't even know what they called themselves; to us those words were part of every conversation. "The men I told you about—that's how they refer to themselves now. Rampsie and the others."

He wrote something down on a paper, then looked up. "What happened the last time you saw Oldham alive, Miss Sanderson?"

As I looked about this interrogation room with its polished table, then at the wall behind me, which boasted a new coat of paint, the feeling came to me that there was no reality to the world outside. A hundred people filed through here a month, the innocent, guilty, the onetime offenders, DWIs, hit-and-runs, felonious assaults, a motley crew. But as I looked over at the lieutenant, I thought to myself, maybe the man cared. I was sure I could see it in the way he looked at Uncle Simon. He wasn't a head buster, like some I'd met.

"All we know," I told Dowling, "is that Oldham had been drinking when we saw him. We told him to go home. We—Uncle Simon, Dr. Almquist, and I—were not apart for the next two hours but tended to Keaton, who took all our time and attention. I have no idea where the police chief went after that. Why don't you try Rampsie's store? It seems to be at the hub of our community!" I added the last with undisguised venom and contempt, then sat with my head down, ready for whatever Dowling had to dish out.

But he nodded sympathetically, contemplating me with his pencil suspended between his two fingers like a miniature bridge. "We'll try the store, Miss Sanderson, both ourselves and the state police. We'll want to join in forces on this. But it may be that Sparrow will want me to take charge of the Rowe situation. I understand he tried to call me early this morning."

I'd rather work with Dowling than Sparrow any day. "Where's your chief, Lieutenant? Last time we called, he was at a meeting out of town."

"He is now, too. Attending a seminar in detection methods out in San Francisco. Probably wouldn't have gone if this had come up before he left. Even took a couple of men with him."

"How about letting me take Uncle Simon now?" They were still asking questions, and he'd pushed himself to the back of his chair like an animal at bay. I knew right then that if Dowling said they were going to keep him longer, they'd have to arrest both of us to keep him there because I felt a very disagreeable mood coming on, centering on Uncle Simon's inviolable rights.

But Dowling rose and snapped shut the book he'd been filling. "Please don't go anywhere, Mr. Sanderson. We'd appreciate it if you'd stay in touch for the next few days."

Uncle Simon turned to the lieutenant as if the man might be joking. "Where do you think I'd go, Lieutenant Dowling? My home is in Rowe. I haven't been away in eighteen years except to go to Boston to visit Lisa."

Dowling nodded slowly. I hurried Uncle Simon to the car before the police could change their minds.

On the way home Uncle Simon turned to me once. "Did you ever know anyone who went to jail who was innocent, Lisa? I mean firsthand, not like you read in the papers?" He slouched down in the seat next to me, staring ahead.

Well, I'd never forget the incident. "The woman wasn't my client, but a friend told me about her. Happened in Boston last year. The victim was a nice, law-abiding lady who got attacked by a neighborhood crazy one night." I snapped my fingers, taking one hand from the wheel. "Right out of the blue, just like that. He actually cut her throat, this monster, and she was on the operating table for four hours. Then she was in critical condition for days and out of work for weeks.

"Her attacker, whom she actually recognized, was finally arrested and released in five hundred dollars' bail for a later appearance in court. But my friend's client, the lady who got slashed, got tired of showing up all the time in court and then going home. So when the case was set for trial once again, five years, I'm not kidding, after the original attack, the lady decided it wasn't worth the trouble, and now she was living in another state besides. So she just didn't show.

"Well, the accused didn't either. So the judge issued bench warrants for *both* of them. The police found the victim, who wasn't hiding, but not the accused, who apparently was. And so the *victim*, the woman, landed in jail for contempt of court. She was photographed, finger-printed, and handcuffed, then taken away to jail, where she stayed for two days. The man who'd slit her throat never spent five minutes in the jug. So when my friend found out about it, she was so mad that she represented the woman free of charge and got her out of jail. But to tell you the truth, I don't know how long they might have kept her if my friend hadn't come to her aid."

Uncle Simon continued to stare at the road. His face was so immobile that I couldn't tell what was going through his head. "I'm ashamed to say, Uncle Simon, that people *can* go to jail for crimes they don't commit. But that's the only one I know about, and it was for only two days."

Uncle Simon continued to stare before him, his face so rigid that I couldn't tell if he'd heard me or not. But then he began to rub those dry hands together again, and the prickles mounted up and down my neck once more, and I knew he'd heard.

The sun was high in the sky as we entered Rowe. Somehow its brightness left the common drained of its color, as if it had been bleached. The pale spring colors had disappeared. I wondered: Was the common once really green, or had the stamping, marauding crowds who'd scampered across the grass, violating young roots during the past weeks squeezed the last chlorophyll from quivering stems? But no, I could see a jubilant green fringe to the grass near the street, which must have been a triumph of healing nature over the forces of desecration.

Aunt Chloe was sitting beside the front door, watching for us through the frosted windows. I almost knew for a fact that she hadn't moved from that spot throughout the hours we'd been gone.

Tim and Buzz tore down the stairs from the landing where they'd been apparently playing a nonstop game of checkers, watching for us. Aunt Chloe took Uncle Simon's hand as he entered the door and hugged him. She didn't even ask what had happened; it was enough that he'd come home.

204

21

With the disappearance of the police back down the road to Tremont, and the death of Oldham, and the obvious intent of the Rowe Boys to stay put in Rampsie's store, something frighteningly final began to take over the town. We all knew instantaneously and without doubt that we were terribly exposed and that we didn't have recourse. There was a danger outside we could no longer manage by barricading ourselves because there was no way to isolate ourselves effectively from the world. Indeed, our isolation, which had brought us in Rowe our peculiar sense of peace and even unity for so long, now was our threat. Nevertheless, it seemed impossible to believe that in this day and age, in this so-called civilized country, we could have failed to find sustenance from others.

First thing in the morning, George had woken me up. I hadn't the vaguest idea of time when I'd come to. Instead, I'd been staring at a flashing light on the ceiling. It shimmered and flitted about my bedroom like an errant butterfly. I'd discovered what it was by tracing it meticulously to its source with a wrenching intensity that lifted my eyelids: the face of George's wristwatch, reflecting the daylight like a mirror! He was sitting near the foot of my bed, almost within reach, a small frown on his forehead, absorbed in the text of a medical journal.

Without further ado, he began to talk. "When you didn't wake up, I decided to sit down to wait. Nothing better to do." He was flipping the pages as if he'd found something utterly fascinating within the confines of that journal. The light from his wristwatch face flashed once again across the ceiling, down the wall, and vanished as his hand turned over. "Hope you don't mind."

Before he'd given me a chance to answer, he was off again. "Of course, I had to bribe your Aunt Chloe to let me up here. Told her I needed to check your ribs, and she thought that sounded perfectly plausible. We doctors get away with murder. By the way, would you care to let me check your ribs?"

I let fly with my pillow. I missed, and the pillow squished innocuously against the wall; George pretended he hadn't even seen it. My ribs *did* ache, but I wasn't about to tell him so right then.

He looked up from his reading. "You want me to leave? Hated to disturb you, but this seemed like such a nice, quiet place to catch up on my reading."

I turned over in bed, determined to make do without my pillow. "Must be fascinating reading, for God's sake."

"Enlightening. All about myocardial infarctions. I could give you a learned discussion, if you've got a couple of spare hours, on the origin, treatment, and prognosis."

I groaned, pulled the covers over my head.

George laughed. "Don't worry. But you were really out. Must have been in the third zone of sleep the entire time I was sitting here. By the way, I brought you some coffee. Maybe it's still warm."

I reached out an arm from the covers. The coffee was lukewarm, just the way I liked it. "How's Uncle Simon? Is he up yet?"

"Last couple of hours. Both Sparrow and the Tremont police have been out there, asking a million questions. And the strikers are assembling down by the mill, first time in a week. Listen, you can just hear them."

I grasped my robe at the foot of the bed, swinging my legs out. Across the room, my window was open. I listened beside it, straining to hear. Far away, almost like the sound of the wind, I could hear the distant sound of chanting voices. I looked questioningly at George.

He nodded.

"How long has it been going on?"

"Since dawn."

"They haven't been molested by Rampsie's crowd?"

"Too many cops in town. Take a look." I peered out the window. A string of police cars once again lined the common.

"And they've arrested Pops Rampsie for the murder of his

brother." I almost laughed. "Pops! You've got to be kidding, George."

In answer, George pointed out the window to where the men surrounded Pops, talking to him.

"On what grounds did they arrest Pops?" I asked.

"Because he'd threatened his brother so often they finally came to the conclusion he'd done it. And it was his knife, and—"

"But Pops threatens everyone, and he works with that knife. . . ."

George laughed a little. "Sure. Sooner or later they'll probably find out it wasn't the old man, that most likely Bob did it to keep Oldham quiet. Undoubtedly Oldham *had* found out that Bob strung Keaton up that night—after all, Jaimie told Tim. Bob must have been desperate to protect his own skin—and he saw Uncle Simon's gun and managed to get it away from Oldham." George shook his head. "But for now. . ." He seemed discouraged when he left again for his office; I dressed quickly and came downstairs.

I watched as the caravan of police cars departed with Pops, their gold shields shining on the car doors. As the prime suspect Pops had been loaded into the middle car. They had to handcuff him to the burly officer sitting in back with him; he was so scared that he'd wet his pants as they pushed him inside; even from here we could see the spreading stain and could hear Pops's protests in his shrill voice. That car even had a grille between the back seat and the driver; they weren't taking any chances with Pops.

Before they left, Sparrow made a final visit to our house. Aunt Chloe had let him in, and I could hear her voice shaking with fright.

Sparrow appeared out of sorts, roughing up his short hair angrily. "You knew, of course, that Oldham came into Rampsie's store after you left carrying your uncle's gun. Dead drunk. Started screeching at the top of his lungs that he knew who'd strung up Keaton and stabbed Rampsie's father. Waving your uncle's gun around like a damned lunatic."

Poor Clyde. I felt incredibly sad for him.

"Just the same," persisted Sparrow, "I don't want your uncle leaving town, even though he's free to go for the time being. You never can tell. . . ."

Somehow I had a terrible time being civil to this man. I looked down at those tight gray pants and his marvelously muscled thighs and felt my solar plexus tighten. "Colonel Sparrow, the only way you'll get my uncle back into your custody is with a warrant for his arrest, which we both know is ridiculous. Now I'm really terribly busy." I accompanied him to the door. "And please don't frighten my aunt with any more conjectures about arresting Uncle Simon. She's an old lady and isn't used to being pushed around. The last time she talked to a police officer was twenty years ago, when she got a ticket for overparking, and she still hasn't recovered!"

When Sparrow left, I turned around, and there was Uncle Simon facing me. He'd heard our entire conversation. "I'm going to call the committee," he said in a resigned voice. "With the police gone, and Clyde, we've got nobody. You looked out the window? The Rowe Boys are gathering, and the strikers, too. . . ."

Aunt Chloe, frightened, stood behind him. "You'll only make things worse, Simon. Maybe there won't be any need, wait and. . . ." But her voice didn't sound too steady.

Uncle Simon shook his head. The cords in his neck were prominent, and I was startled to realize how much weight he'd lost. "I know, Chloe," he said, almost in a whisper. "I know, don't you?"

I would have thought him melodramatic, if I hadn't just seen for myself that neat line of police cars departing and Bob Rampsie with his crowd of thugs on the front porch of Rampsie's and heard the chants of the strikers distantly, down by the mill. We lay exposed, vulnerable— and the thought drove me frantic. I got on the phone, and Tim and Buzz were dispatched once more around the common.

George was the first to arrive. He was breathless. "Saw the strikers marching up from the mill as I came by," he said. "Pretty slowly, but they're coming all right."

"What're they up to?" I asked Timmy and Buzz, peering out the two windows. "Tell me!"

"No good! No good!" said Buzz, dancing up and down. George had just removed the boy's bandage, and he looked a little better except for a dent above the ear and a large purple discoloration covering the entire side of his head, even extending into the skin beneath his hair. "They up to no good, Lize. Mama say they up to no good."

"Stop that nonsense," snapped Aunt Chloe. Her nerves seemed about to snap, too. Then she regretted what she'd said and added more gently, "Go talk to your mother, Buzz. Comfort her."

Buzz nodded, watching Aunt Chloe's face with his liquid black eyes. Then he ran off to his mother's room in his halting dogtrot.

I heard Uncle Simon once again at that old black telephone in the hall. He was still calling. "Get them together, Stu. I'll get White; you get Rhymer." That's all he said, but Callaghan knew immediately what it was all about.

George paced back and forth up and down the room. "Good God, it's gang war, dog eat dog," he said. "Half the police force of southern Vermont was out there today, and it's jungle law the minute they leave. Wonder what the hell it's going to be like tomorrow."

A minute later Uncle Simon shuffled back into the room, a lifeless expression on his face. "White won't come," he said, slightly choked.

George halted in his pacing. "You mean he's not even worried?"

Uncle Simon's voice sounded a little strangled. "He says he's going to lock the door of his house, and he's not going out for anything. Says he's gonna sit by the front door with a shotgun, and if anyone tries to get in. . . ."

"Well, good riddance," said Aunt Chloe, "if he's not going along with everyone else."

Uncle Simon stalked stiffly from the room. I could hear Aunt Chloe running after him. "What are you up to, Simon?" she was asking. Her voice had risen in intensity. "Tell me."

"What *is* there to do?" I could hear him answer. "There's nothing, Chloe. It's every man for himself." She returned, looking stricken.

"What's he doing?" asked George, looking after the door where Uncle Simon had vanished.

I suddenly realized. I could hear his footsteps on the floor upstairs above our heads. "He's getting out his guns again. I think everyone's gone a little crazy."

"Crazy," said Buzz, like a small echo. I hadn't even seen him return. He held my skirt, twisting back and forth beside me. "Crazy. Uncle Simon crazy."

"Shut up, Buzz," I snapped at the startled boy. "You cut it out or I'll spank you!"

I never would, and he knew it, but he turned from me and hid behind the door like a frightened mouse.

George was still pacing. "Do you know, I'd even arranged for Clarissa to come back for a visit today? It doesn't seem possible." He shook his head, stopping momentarily in mid-stride.

Aunt Chloe suddenly burst into tears. "What did we ever do in Rowe to deserve this?" she asked a little plaintively. "What did we ever *do*?"

I put my arms about her. "It's all right, Aunt Chloe." Once she'd comforted me the same way when I was a child. "Things will change,

209

you'll see. One of these days Rowe will be the same again." I knew it didn't sound like much solace, and I only half believed it myself.

George suddenly pointed south of the town. "Big crowd gathering down there. Just saw Finnegan's red sports car, the one he had that night at my house."

"How many are down there?" I asked.

"Couple of dozen. Things have picked up at Rampsie's store, too."

I ran to the window and apprehensively peered out. A knot of men was standing around, sitting on the front steps and milling around on the common. Above the others I could see Bob Rampsie's head, and I was struck again by what might have been nobility in those features: ascetic, virile, and proud if cast in another mold. But to me he was cold, detached, almost imperious—contemptuous. Dumpy Hunk Hudman slouched beside him, throwing something into the air, a ball or rock. They all had begun to advance toward the common, at first casually, then with more determination, several of the men fanning out behind Hudman and Rampsie. As they came closer, I could see they had something dangling from their wrists; they seemed like balls with metal spikes protruding from them, large nails or railroad spikes. They looked like porcupines, lethal and deadly. They appeared homemade, and I thought: My God, Hudman's been busy with his welding torch again.

I quickly picked up the phone in the hall. "Minnie, get me the police, Lieutenant Dowling. Fast! Fast! This is an emergency."

The phone clicked at the other end. "Hello, Tremont police. Sergeant Bonner speaking."

"Sergeant Bonner, this is Lisa Sanderson in Rowe. May I speak with Lieutenant Dowling immediately?"

The sergeant was very professional; his name was new to me. "He's not in, miss. What did you say your name was?"

"Sanderson. Sanderson." I was almost shouting. "Where is he, Sergeant? We've got an emergency down here in Rowe. We need him right away!"

Bonner didn't say anything for a minute. I knew he'd handled a million crank calls, and he was trying to figure out if I fell into this category. There was simply no time to convince him otherwise now; there was just no time for anything. "Sergeant," I said, "we're going to have real trouble down here in Rowe in the next few minutes. Where can I reach him, for God's sake?"

The man came alert. "Search me, Miss . . . er . . . Sanderson.

Colonel Sparrow said he'd already spent half the day down there—I heard him talking to Dowling awhile ago—and his kid's having a birthday party. What shall I tell him?"

"Tell him the strikers from the mill and the Rowe Boys are about to murder each other again. If he doesn't get down here fast, we're going to have one hell of a brawl."

"All right, I'll try to reach him. Doesn't mean I can. . . ."

"Try! Try! Please." I slammed down the phone, confident that he'd come. Right out there beyond our front steps were those insane gorillas about to let loose more havoc on our little town, and not a goddamn soul cared. I'd tried all I knew, used up all the store of knowledge I thought I could employ to get help. Uncle Simon was right: It was every man for himself. But let the devil come, we'd manage somehow!

George took me by the arm, pointing out the window. Behind me stood Aunt Chloe, grim-faced, her chin thrust out. Gone now was her indecisiveness; she stood at the door of her kitchen belligerently as if defying the very gods to act against her. On the small pine table near the door Uncle Simon was aligning his two rifles and an old shotgun. Tim and Buzz, chattering in fright and excitement, watched him.

I followed the line of George's finger. On the common, both groups were approaching each other from opposite sides like some kind of insane stage play, cast by a mad producer for an impossible and demented audience. Then I could see that all the Rowe Boys carried that same weapon, a ball with sharp nails protruding. Hadn't I seen one before in a museum showing artifacts from the Middle Ages or perhaps from some period even earlier: in Roman times during gladiatorial combat? My God, who thought up that one—Rampsie with his sadistic intelligence or predatory Hunk Hudman? Perhaps it was another of the wolf pack. So they were all out to get retribution for the assaults of Jerry Finnegan's strikers, for the night they had been jumped on the common. There was about as much sanity out there as one found in most wars; it could fit roughly in a peapod.

I could hear Mrs. Sardoe upstairs, the beat of her rocker moving back and forth on the bare floor and her open crying; it grated on me—what right had she to cry?

"Can't someone shut her up?" I asked. "For God's sake, Buzz, stay with her."

George started to say something, but I couldn't comprehend what it was. Outside, the two groups had come together and were doing mortal battle. As I looked out the window, I saw the home-fashioned spike ball of one of the Rowe Boys land on the head of a striker I recognized, and immediately the blood welled on his head, soaking his hair and pouring down his face. The man's scalp was laid entirely bare with that one swat!

"Make them stop," I found myself shouting to no one in particular. "Can't anyone make them stop?"

One of the strikers had a club. He must have held it behind his back or stashed it behind a tree. He began to bash in all directions, hitting at the faces about him rather than at the bodies. I thought as I watched him: The way to annihilate bodies is to bash at heads, and this monster knew all about it, because he came prepared. There were a couple of people on the ground already, lying underfoot, being stumbled over and bled on.

You insane fools, I was thinking. Can't someone do something? All of you are going to die out there. Does this have to go on? Doesn't anyone have a shred of sanity left?

When I looked back outside again, some poor guy was staggering across the road from the common to our front walk, dripping little spurts of blood like a sack with a slight leak, and the man was holding his hand over the hole somewhere about his abdomen as if that'd keep all the red gush in. George had already spun out the door to catch the staggering man in his arms as if he were a wandering, lost child, holding him while he gentled him to the ground. In a second George had stripped off his clothes, probing frantically for the wound.

Behind him, Uncle Simon ran out of the house to help George with the clothes. Uncle Simon's eyes were absolutely wild; he was yelling at the man on the ground as if he'd lost his senses, telling him to hold on, to stop bleeding, not to give up; Uncle Simon knew that man on the ground as well as I did. It was Harvey Allen, who worked with Uncle Simon down at the mill—and he was bleeding his life's blood all over our lawn. On one side of his head was the mark of that insidious instrument Hunk Hudman and those others were wielding like gladiators before the carnal emperors of Rome. "I hate you, Bob Rampsie," I found myself shouting, "and I defy you to touch us, you scum of scum, look what you've done to us."

The strikers were falling away. They looked almost valiant, like soldiers retreating before the volleys of their foe. But suddenly I lost sympathy for even the strikers because I'd caught sight of the switchblades in their pockets, long and thin like silver wands,

212

rapier-sharp, and I knew very well what was going on out there in the heat of that fight. There were more men on the ground now; both George and Uncle Simon were pulling them onto our lawn, grasping an arm or a leg and tugging them to safety. Already George had flipped a tourniquet made from his own sock about a man's arm, and Uncle Simon was pressing against Harvey Allen's wound with his hand, trying to keep his guts in. I tried to help, attempting to free those wounded men of their bloody clothing; our front walk was beginning to look like the scene of a slaughter. We'll never get rid of this blood, I was thinking in dazed horror. Every time we looked out the door from now on, all we'd see would be this blood, running and pooling like a red tributary on its way to a sea.

The struggle on the common was silent of human voices. I could hear muffled grunts, scuffles, groans. How was it possible to fight so quietly? I wondered. How could this man before me sustain a knife wound in the belly and not shriek? Then I realized the man before me was dead. The hole in his abdomen, the loose-edged flopping hole, had ceased to bleed because there was nothing left to drain from it.

"What can I do?" I asked George, gasping, my breath stopping in my throat. "Tell me, please, how to help."

"Hold this," he said, turning over the tourniquet to me. His voice was almost coldly detached, highly efficient. I relaxed some and did what I was told; I knew George had handled emergencies before and was coping. He'd already pulled his medical bag from his car and dumped the contents on the ground. He was spattered with the blood of the men before him. He went from one to the other, methodically examining, probing, patching. Beside the dead man were three others. One was a striker with the wound on his head; another, a Rowe Boy with the side of his head smashed by a club. His ear had been partially torn off and dangled as if it had become unglued from that red strip on one side of his head.

"Towels!" George yelled, peering around at me. "Quickly, the bleeding." When I looked at George's face, I saw the desperation in his eyes—he was working on some inner programming, as frantic as I. I rushed for the door of the house. Inside, crouched beside the window, were Buzz and Tim.

"Towels!" I yelled at them. Buzz was white with fear; he was actually trembling. I started fishing towels from Aunt Chloe's closet. Upstairs I could hear Mrs. Sardoe wailing and Aunt Chloe trying to comfort her. I ran outside to George with an armful of towels.

"Have Chloe call the ambulance, Tremont hospital," George yelled to Tim, who was trailing along behind me now. "Quickly. Tell them we need plasma. Now!"

I heard another moan, and there was Jaimie Rampsie crawling across the street on all fours like a dog, blood dripping from his mouth. He looked terrified, his eyes awash with horror and reproach.

I rushed to him, half lifting him from the ground despite my sore ribs. He couldn't talk. "Jaimie?" I asked. "Good Lord, what happened to you?" He seemed to be suffocating, unable to breathe. I looked at his blue face, the bulging eyes. He was gurgling something I couldn't understand. "George, help him. Help him!"

George forsook the man on the ground, whirled around to take a look at Jaimie, then pulled the boy's shirt open. Already his chest was discolored, and the ribs appeared misshapen and deformed. The skin was curdled and blotchy over his bony frame. George's fingers moved quickly. "They've hit him with a club," George said, now prodding around the boy's back. "Ribs mostly broken. Lung may collapse."

He put me to work breathing into the boy's mouth, to puff up the faltering lung. I was learning fast, after Pops, Keaton, now Jaimie. "Lungs collapse without a rib cage," George explained, gasping, trying to clear the boy's mouth. He leaned over Jaimie's form, holding him for me, head back and mouth open, while I tried to force my breath into his mouth. With his other hand, George was holding the tourniquet on the first man's bleeding arm.

Jaimie's eyes were almost closed. He looked at me sadly, mournfully, almost in apology. I pressed my mouth to his and breathed, counting rhythmically. Once he groaned, and I found myself crying, dropping my tears into his eyes.

Behind me, the fighting had ceased; there was no one left to carry on. I looked around quickly and saw only battered remnants of the men who'd gone into that battle so casually swinging those grim little metallic porcupines from their wrists. The strikers were helping each other, carrying those who couldn't walk between them, supported on bloodied shoulders. Who the hell thought up this game? I was thinking. Who in hell thought this one up?

I could hear the siren of the ambulance far down the road from Tremont, wailing like a desolate wolf in the distance, the shrillness mounting into the dead calm of this impeccable day in May. For once someone had answered a call for help with alacrity. I could feel my face perspiring, the beads of sweat replacing the tears I'd rained on Jaimie's face. My chest ached, overburdened by breathing for both Jaimie and me. George was on his hands and knees, applying tourniquets and bandages from one to the other of those mangled men. Before me was a small mountain of Aunt Chloe's towels, saturated, and the ridiculous thought crossed my mind: She'll never get them clean, never, because bloodstains are almost impossible to remove. . . .

Suddenly I looked up, and Bob Rampsie was above me, staring at his brother. "What-are-you-doing-to-him?" he asked, enraged, spitting each word like an oath. His face was smeared with dirt; his shirt, ripped from his body. He reeked with the smell of sweat and drying blood.

I didn't have time to talk; every intake of breath was becoming an agony. "What do you think. . . ?" I asked him, gasping. Time to breathe again, one, two. . . .

"What did they *do* to him?" he asked again, almost hysterical. "Poor little Jaimie, what did they *do*?"

My temples were pounding. "Not what *they* did—what did *you* do? Can't you see. . . ?" Time to breathe, one, two . . . .

"Go away," he said, pushing me to the ground roughly. "I'll do it, not you."

I tried to get back to the boy, clawing my way past Bob to Jaimie again. I could hear the beat in my head still. But no one was there, breathing for Jaimie. "Do it, Bob," I shrieked. "He won't make it unless you do."

"Don't touch him," Bob warned again. His arms encircled the boy. He staggered to his feet carrying his brother.

"Leave him here," I was beseeching him. "The ambulance. . . ." I pointed toward the sedate white vehicle just emerging from the Tremont road, its siren echoing against the ringed houses.

"I'll take him," Bob demanded in a low voice, almost a growl. He began to move down the front walk haltingly with Jaimie in his arms, cradling him like a child.

At that moment George, occupied a distance away with those injured men on the ground, realized what was going on and looked up. "Put that boy down, Rampsie. Where the hell do you think you're going with him?" George's hair was in his face. There was a layer of blood and sweat smeared across one cheek.

For a moment Bob hesitated. His face was contorted with a mixture of contempt, arrogance, and even fear. With a desperate lunge, George threw himself at the man's legs and succeeded in grasping an ankle. The ambulance driver had already stopped before our house, and an attendant rushed from it.

"Help me," George shouted, panting as he tried to hold Rampsie. "Stop this man, for Christ's sake, stop him!"

Bob whirled, rage in his face. "You do, and I'll kill every damn one of you." It sounded full of bluff, like a child, until I glanced over toward the common: Hudman and two or three other men were staring at us. They appeared filthy, barely recognizable, but they'd survived the battering and were biding their time, waiting for Rampsie to stagger across the street with his brother.

I was on my knees in the grass. "Let them go, George. We can't stop them now." I knelt on Uncle Simon's lawn, feeling as if all that was vital in my soul had drained away into the ground before me. At that second I remembered a conversation I'd had with Uncle Simon a short while ago, when I told him I thought the world was ultimately composed of law and order, and I also had in my mind that meeting in his parlor short days ago. As that memory flashed into my befogged mind, I jumped to my feet. "I arrest you," I yelled at Rampsie, now partway across the street. "I arrest you, Bob Rampsie, *for endangering the life of that child.* Do you hear me?"

It sounded so melodramatic that I was ashamed. I could hear the pathetic sound of my own voice in its outraged, anguished cry against Bob Rampsie. It was ludicrous, laughable, and I never expected him to stop. I'd blown my last hope, the final shred of my integrity as a person, lawyer, citizen, woman. But he mustn't take Jaimie Rampsie.

He never turned back. George and the ambulance driver and his assistant were transferring the men on our sidewalk into the ambulance. The assistant, a deft, red-haired man in an immaculate white uniform, had already forced a small oxygen mask over the nose of one of those eviscerated men. Then he caught sight of the second man; George had covered him with a towel. The attendant looked at George, a harrowing question on his face. George nodded dejectedly. "Better forget him," he said, "and get on to the others."

The driver shook his head wonderingly. "My God, man, what the hell's been going on down here anyway?"

George was too preoccupied to answer. "You'd never believe it if I told you." They quickly transferred the men on the ground into the ambulance, and George jumped inside to assist the driver, who was struggling to start the intravenous flow of blood into an injured man's veins. I could see him, working in the back, straddling the man who'd

216

been knifed. Then the attendant took George's place, the driver slammed the door, and the ambulance drove slowly away.

I watched after it with apprehension and something close to panic. "George, help me. We've got to get Jaimie Rampsie back." I pointed to Rampsie's store, where they'd taken him. "He's going to die over there if we don't help him."

The door to the house opened, and I looked up at Uncle Simon. He glanced dumbly about the front lawn at the blood, which was also daubed over the sidewalk as if an errant painter had tripped. "Where'd they go?" he whispered hoarsely. He was clutching in his hand the rifle he'd been cleaning so assiduously the last few days, the mate to the one he'd lost on the common the night Oldham was murdered.

I pointed to Rampsie's. "They've taken Jaimie away. Over there, at the store."

Uncle Simon's hands were shaking; in fact, his entire body trembled.

"Go back inside," I told him, as gently as I could. "Please, Uncle Simon. And for God's sake, get rid of that gun."

He turned around, dazed. I could see Aunt Chloe inside the door and Mrs. Sardoe's face at the upstairs window.

Tim and Buzz, when they saw that the ambulance as well as the strikers and the Rowe Boys had gone, let themselves out the door behind Uncle Simon and stood bewildered on the front lawn, looking about at the havoc. Towels, bandages, parts of clothing were scattered all over the place. Buzz sat fingering one of the little metal weapons the Rowe Boys had used, pushing his stubby fingers against the sharp little points projecting from it. He held his finger up to me, questioning; there was a drop of blood on the tip.

"Wipe it off," I told him, "and help Uncle Simon into the house. Then throw that thing away into the trash where I'll never see it again."

George and I set off for Rampsie's store. The place was as quiet as a tomb. I could feel my heart thumping painfully, turning over and over as if a small bomb were exploding among the debris of my sore ribs. But I knew we didn't have much time left if we were to help Jaimie Rampsie. And although Dowling hadn't arrived yet, I was sure it was a matter of minutes before he did, racing down the Tremont road with his contingent of police.

I stared at the ground, then at George's sneakers, splotched with blood. He walked on his heels with deliberation, treading heavily, yet walking swiftly. He was determined and very angry. I could hear his breathing, smell the heat from the tarred road, hear my heart in its distraught thumping. Maybe, I thought, we're too late, too late, too late. . . .

A couple of Rampsie's cronies were standing outside the store on the porch like statues, watching our approach.

"Where's the boy?" George demanded of one of the men. The man jerked his thumb toward the store behind him. I looked hesitantly; the place was empty, there wasn't a soul there, but the door to the back room was open. We could hear sounds from it, hushed and intermittent. George strode to the door, flinging it open with his foot.

Inside, I could make out about five people; Bob Rampsie, Hunk Hudman, a couple of Rampsie's friends who'd been out on the common, and, on the crumpled bed where Pops had recovered from his assault, Jaimie Rampsie.

"We're taking the boy," said George firmly. "You can't hold him, Rampsie. For God's sake, don't you know you'll kill him?"

Rampsie was sitting beside the bed on a rickety chair in the semidarkness, his head in his hands. He didn't even look at us or acknowledge our presence.

George grasped his arm. "Jesus, Rampsie, what's wrong with you? He's your brother, isn't he? Don't you care what happens to him?"

I looked anxiously over at the boy on the bed; his eyes were listless, staring above him toward the ceiling. I wanted to touch him, to reassure him.

I began to plead with Rampsie, "Bob, don't you know it's a crime to keep someone from medical help? It's irresponsible, heartless. . . . "

Rampsie didn't move a muscle. He was rigid, detached. It was eerie, unreal.

George was beside himself. I knew his thoughts were mine: that the boy was right across the room and that Bob was standing in his way. Suddenly George moved forward and pushed Bob Rampsie to one side. "*You* may be a goddamn bastard, but *I'm* not," he began.

Rampsie jumped to his feet like a cat, lashing out and hitting George as hard as he could with the side of his hand. "You touch my brother just once, you goddamn motherfucker," he said, "and you're dead. I told you once—how many times I gotta tell you?" His voice was a shriek of fury.

George stopped, partially stunned by the blow, but even more by Rampsie's voice. He had turned tentatively toward Jaimie on the bed; with the force of the blow, he fell forward onto it. George reached toward the boy, stretching out a hand toward Jaimie Rampsie's face, touching the skin. Suddenly George pulled back the bedclothes. Jaimie was naked, cold, dead.

"How could you, Bob?" George moaned, still touching the dead boy. He moved his hand over the thick curls, then withdrew it. George took hold of himself almost visibly and backed off the bed. Finally, he turned to Rampsie quietly. "I hope you can live with this, Rampsie, and die with it. I hope you roast in hell for all you've done to us and to your own brother. Even more, I hope you never forget this moment, never."

George stood a moment without moving, his head down, fists clenched. Then I saw Bob Rampsie's outraged face. I'd never seen a man so angry. His eyes had become red coals, and his teeth were bared, like a dog snarling.

"You-think-you-can-talk-to-me-like-that?" Rampsie asked through clenched teeth, his lips barely moving. "Why, you shitty asshole. . . . " Then he turned on George and hit him again.

"Stop that! Stop!" I screamed. My stomach turned with outrage and horror. "Isn't it enough that you ruined our town, hurt my Uncle Simon, started a mill war? Now your brother's dead." I gulped, feeling sick, about to vomit. "Jaimie was more decent than you—he even told Tim you'd strung up Bingo Keaton, your best friend, to that lamppost." Then I fell to sobbing in a corner behind me.

In a minute, Rampsie had my arm in a vise. "He didn't tell you any such thing, you bitch!"

I shook my head, terrified. I couldn't answer. "Leave us alone, Bob," I moaned over and over. I was convulsed with sobbing, I could hear myself, and I was ashamed. I couldn't seem to stop or regain control or think what to do next.

I looked to George for help, but the men had him; they had wrung back his arms, knotting them behind him. "Leave us alone," I shrieked at Rampsie, fighting, "What have we ever done to you? What have we done?"

Rampsie threw me on the bed next to his dead brother. I could see the whites of Jaimie's eyes, the motionless lashes, feel his cold skin. "No, no, no!" I yelled, fighting to get up.

"Leave her alone, damn you," George was shouting, his voice guttural with the effort. "Get your goddamn hands off her!" He was struggling furiously with the men, trying to dig his elbows into them as they twisted his hands. When he tried to kick at one of them, Rampsie lifted his chair and brought it down on George's sneakered foot with all his strength. George barely winced but kept twisting against those men until a couple of them tied his hands with something while the third wound his feet in a sheet from Jaimie's bed. Finally, he was completely immobilized, vanquished, unable to move, roaring in outrage and anger. He tried to shake himself loose, to twist himself free, but he finally collapsed, exhausted.

"Get away from me," I was screaming at Rampsie. I looked toward the door, hoping that someone would come into the store. But who, I wondered, was left out there? I knew the answer. The door was closed tightly. Rampsie'd even bolted it.

"Take her clothes off," Rampsie commanded. I looked at him, unbelieving, not comprehending what he'd said.

"No, Bob," I said. I began to pant. "Come on, Bob, stop it. Don't you dare touch me."

"Him, too," said Rampsie, pointing to George. "And make it snappy. I'm sure as hell not going to spend forever in this hole."

The men tried to pull George's pants off without removing his belt; they began to swear until one of them flipped open the buckle and slid out the belt. He wielded it like a whip, flexing and looping it in his hand. A grin came to his face as he maneuvered it back and forth like a snake. Then the second man ripped off George's khaki pants, demolishing the thin fabric of his shorts with his fist, grasping it at George's fly.

The sight of George naked before those people churned my brain into a fury. I felt an overwhelming tenderness for him at that moment, a pity—and my fingers curled into fists at the indignity he was suffering. I swore beneath my breath and tried to turn away, but the men had me wrenched into position, unable to move.

My light blouse ripped off when Rampsie tore at it with his hand. He stood holding the soft fabric, looking at it as if it weren't really there. Then he dropped it contemptuously to the floor and reached for my bra, trying to snatch it off as easily, but the straps held. Swearing, he flung me backward onto the bed, where he made a second try, wrenching the straps from my shoulders. The two cups of the bra slid down to my waist, still fastened stubbornly by the back catch, which was too intricately interlocked to let go. Only the adhesive strip over my ribs remained.

I could feel the room as if it had turned to ice, as if I were freezing, as if my breasts and nipples had become numbed and no longer belonged to me. I wish they didn't, I thought in anguish—I wish they weren't part of me for these men to see. Bob Rampsie had suddenly reached forward to touch my breast; I could feel his fingers on my nipple. His hands were rough, calloused, and I shivered and tried to turn over on the bed, but the men who'd tied George were holding me down. I could hear George trying to get to me, grunting and swearing with the agony, but the men had tied him to something, perhaps the doorknob, and the others had him immobilized about the chest, but through it all I could still hear him trying to wrench free.

I was ashamed, mortified to look into Bob Rampsie's face while he fondled me, but he was leering into mine, and as much as I loathed and detested him at that moment, I found myself unable to ignore him, as if I were magnetized by those hunted eyes. "Look at that," he said to his friends. "Will you just look at that, Sammy? Come up and take a feel, Sammy. Now you just don't feel something like that every day."

Sammy spat on the floor. "Get on with it, Rampsie, for Christ's sake. You gonna take all day? What you wanna keep us waiting for?" He started removing his pants. The other man behind him laughed, a low sound. He kept his eyes on my breasts as if there were nothing else in the room. "Get on with it," he said again, but his lips were thick, and he staggered slightly, trying to pull off his pants, balancing on one leg.

"*Leave her alone!*" George was yelling. His voice sounded frantic, desperate, crazy; for a second I didn't realize it was his. He began shouting for help, but the man nearest stuffed a piece of cloth into his

221

mouth, cramming it home with stiff fingers, then he used George's belt to keep the rag in place.

I was frantic with fear for George—I knew they could close off his breathing that way. Now I could feel myself losing control, slipping into confusion, realizing there was no way to turn.

"Don't let them do it," I beseeched George, but I knew he'd done all he could. At intervals I could hear a high-pitched scream from him, as if he were communicating on another wavelength.

"Leave us alone," I beseeched Rampsie. "Please, Bob. For God's sake, have mercy. Can't you have mercy?" I was an animal, groveling, beseeching. I'd have sold my soul for ten minutes of freedom, to help George, even for a breath of fresh air.

"Call Hunk," Rampsie commanded the man at the door. "Tell him we got a great big surprise."

I looked up at Rampsie's eyes; they were without humanity or remorse. But he's got a human brain, I was thinking. He took off his pants in front of me, slowly. He was enjoying every moment, deliberately taking his time. When he took off his shorts, he was having an erection. I could see it even before he'd removed them, the bulge of material over the crotch.

"Get the doc over here," said Rampsie. He had a low laugh in his throat, almost a gurgle. He reached out and grabbed George by the arm. "You like this broad?" Rampsie was asking George. I could see George's eyes, above the material they'd stuffed into his mouth; they were almost closed with anger and shock.

"Then you're gonna show us you like her, asshole. You hear me? You're first one in, you unnerstand? I'm next." Rampsie's voice was jubilant, excited. "How do you like that? You like her, you do it good. We'll make sure." Then Rampsie hit him playfully in the chest. "You do it good, Doc, or we'll cut the goddamn thing off, you hear?"

Rampsie had George by the back of the neck. "She's all yours, Doc. Now let's see how you do it. You so good at fixing things, let's see you fix this one." Then he laughed raucously and hit George again, this time in the abdomen. I could see George cringe in pain.

"Now, Doc," said Rampsie, his voice in a kind of tortured rage, "you get it up, you bastard, or I cut it off, just like I told you." Hunk Hudman stood next to Rampsie now, a grin on his overstuffed face, fat and lewd. "Gimme that knife of yours, Hunk, and let's see what the doc can do."

I looked at George's eyes again; they were almost pleading, too,

222

sunk far back into his head. I tried to roll off the bed, but another man helped the first at the head of the bed to hold my hands, while the second tied my feet to the springs. The bed was old-fashioned, with a high metal headboard and a missing footboard. Rampsie pushed George onto the bed. He grasped George's hand, placing it on my bare thigh. I could see George's eyes, pleading again, apologizing, grasping the edge of that soiled mattress in anguish. I cared for him terribly at that moment—I felt his plight as my own.

"*Get it up,*" Rampsie was demanding, screaming at George, the veins bulging at the side of his head.

George's anguished eyes were searching mine, and he shook his head, removing his hand from my thigh.

"*Get it up!*" screamed Rampsie again. Only this time he reached over and stabbed George on the hip with his knife. "That's the last time, Doc. You know what I'm gonna do to you if you don't do like I tell ya, right? You don't screw her, Doc, and you're never gonna screw anyone again, you goddamn son of a bitch!"

Perhaps I passed out for a minute or two, but when I came back, I could hear Rampsie's exultant voice; "That-a-boy now, Doc—isn't that fun? Regular stud, the old doc is. Now stick it in, you bastard." He must have hit George again because I heard a grunt, and suddenly I could feel George penetrating me. It was agonizing, I wasn't ready, and I could feel a torturous pain like a hot poker between my legs, despite the fact that I knew he was trying to enter carefully.

"For Christ's sake, get some grease," Rampsie yelled. "Go get some goddamn grease, Sonny." Someone went somewhere and returned with something terribly cold. The man placed a gob between my legs and began to push it inside. I tried to pull away.

"Feel good?" he asked, caressing with his fingers. "Don't you worry none. I'll have my turn soon."

I'd clamped my eyes closed, but I could feel that George was above me by the way the mattress heaved. This time I could feel his penis sliding into my body. I was outraged, revolted, sick despite my caring for him, feeling his persistence in the recesses of my body where he'd come before because I'd loved him. Yet at the very moment when I was revolted, I felt terror for his vulnerable body, for the exposure of himself to the mockery and cruelty of these filthy men. I wanted to force my legs together to thrust him out, hurt him despite myself. I knew then how much I'd loved him, and his touch to me at this moment was a torture unlike anything I'd ever felt before—and it filled me with

223

unspeakable loathing toward the dark shapes I saw moving above me in that execrable room.

"You gotta squeeze it out, Doc," said Rampsie. "That's the last part, remember? Just lay it in there, leaving your calling card, nice and easy. Let her know she's been laid." This time there was a lot of laughter.

I knew that George was having trouble climaxing. He was stiff and full, but he couldn't ejaculate. It was as though he'd gone as far as he could with the energy he had, but the natural process had become so arrested that it had malfunctioned. I was suddenly frightened for him, terrified. Do it, I was saying. Please, God, get it over with.

"You gonna take all night?" Rampsie snapped at George. The menace was back in his voice. "Christ, man, can't you see there are four others of us waitin'?"

Hunk Hudman was standing beside me now. I could see his face clearly and hear him breathing. I'd never heard a man breathe like that before, a rasping sound as if something had stuck in his throat. Rampsie suddenly blew up. "Pull the goddamn thing out and make her suck it, asshole. I just about had it with you, you know that, you goddamn turd?"

I could feel George's penis leave my body. "Open your mouth," demanded Rampsie. "He's gonna cram it down your goddamn throat, you bitch."

I clamped my teeth together and turned my face into my arm, which the man at the head of the bed was pulling on with all his strength. By now I was so frantic that he slipped a cord, tied like a noose, about my hands and twisted the cord about the bedpost. I couldn't move at all, no matter how hard I tried. Hudman leaned forward, trying to pull my face off the bed in order to force me to open my mouth, but I'd made my neck as rigid as iron.

"Hell, forget it!" said Rampsie. "I'm not gonna wait around all day." I could feel another jounce of the bed, the mattress heaving once again. I'd almost forgotten that Jaimie Rampsie's body was next to me still; someone had pushed him over against the wall. I opened my eyes, damp with the strain of fighting against the men holding me, and there was Rampsie above me. I could see his engorged penis for a minute; it was long and angry red, with lengths of red hair growing from the base, around the testicles. I could see the blue veins on the side, slightly raised, and the opening at the tip, dripping moisture. I wanted to scream. My body buckled and twisted, recoiling from the sight. I tried

224

with all my strength to close my legs, but the rope from the springs was cutting into my ankles like a sharp knife. Rampsie was over me, thrusting. He pushed as hard as he could, not quite in the right place, invading some of my soft tissue. I could feel his penis slither, burning, as he sank himself into me. He wriggled his bony chest on my breasts, twisting them, grunting and sweating.

I was so rigid that my backbone felt as if it had fused, and I was trying to pretend that this really wasn't happening to me, that this revolting organ of his wasn't in my body; he wasn't using me this way; it was nothing, nothing to do with me.

I could feel Rampsie's thick chest hairs, like wires against my breasts. He was jerking savagely with his penis, in and out, painfully. I suddenly realized he was angry, and I opened my clenched eyes for a second.

"Start pumping, damn you," he was growling into my ear. He dropped a little lower on my body, so that I could barely breathe. "Pump," he whispered into my ear, "and I'll make it really swell for you."

I thought I was going to be sick. "I won't." I said into his ear, my teeth clenched. "You pig!"

He laughed deep in his throat. "That's what I really like," he said, "a hard woman. I like that." He was still moving. I could feel his pubic hair on my legs, rough and irritating. Suddenly he ejaculated. There was a shudder, and he clamped his legs together. I groaned with the spasm he'd had, the violent jerking.

"You *like* it," he said, his lips back exposing his teeth. I could feel the warm, sticky sperm on my legs. "I'll be back," he said. "You're pretty good, you know that, you slut. You could learn."

His ear was still next to my face. I clenched my teeth. "I hope you roast in hell, Bob Rampsie, you perverted prick." I could feel a terrible tension like electricity moving up and down my body, as if some vital nerve had been touched. "You're insane, and I hate your guts."

Rampsie moved off me, laughing. With his free hand he reached forward and slapped my face. I tried to bite his hand, but he was too fast for me. Then I bent forward and tried to bite the other hand before he could remove it from the bed; perhaps I could sever a finger. But he jumped away, still laughing, and Hunk Hudman was in his place, fat and lathered with sweat. He was violent and rough; when he clung to me, his fat layers stuck to my breasts like a vacuum.

225

By then I knew that I was hurt, that something'd torn in my vagina; the pain was searing, and I began to groan again.

"You take it pretty good," said fat Hudman, thrusting harder into my body. I could feel his blubber against my body—heavy, stinking, gross. "Now I'll really give it to you," he said, laughing in a high, excited voice. He arched his back, sinking his penis as far as he could. "You really like to take it, you stupid broad, you!" He pumped and discharged.

I couldn't stand it. "Please, I'm torn. Can't you stop for a while, just a little while?"

The next man was over me when someone grabbed him by the arm. I could hear Rampsie's voice. "She's hurt," Rampsie said. "She's bleeding, look at the goddamn bed."

"Gimme my turn," said the man on top of me. "Come on, Bobby, you had your fuck." He was almost pleading, like a tearful child.

"Sure," said Rampsie, his voice hard and commanding. "You'll get yours, Tiny." He reached over the bed, cupped my breast with his hand. "Then Lisa's gonna stay around for a while, isn't she?" he asked, bending over my face. "We're gonna be able to find Lisa when we want her, aren't we?"

The room was swimming around me so I couldn't see anything. Suddenly there was a crash at the door that reverberated in that small room like an explosion. In a moment I heard another, followed after a short pause by still another. All I cared about was that the men were off me and I could breathe again. That was all that mattered, that breath of air and the weight off my body. I'd never experienced a moment so sweet, so full. It was enough for then.

Vaguely I heard Uncle Simon's voice: frantic, high-pitched.

"Apes, apes, apes," he was screaming. "What are you doing to my niece, you filthy apes?" Then I heard the crash again: my ears felt compressed as if my eardrums had burst inside my head, and I was temporarily deafened. There was something clean and purifying about the smell of that gunpowder: the acrid tinge of the smell and the terrible and violent thud which somehow stabbed my brain into functioning, like electroshock to a dying man.

Then momentarily all was quiet. I opened my eyes, trying to see into the dark over my head. There was a hand on my cheek, like the brush of a feather, and Buzz was looking into my eyes. "Poor, poor Lize," he was saying over and over, "Poor, poor Lize," stroking my face. In a moment Uncle Simon had untied the ropes; resting across his broken arm was his rifle. He was talking to himself, unable to stop. "Serves you all right, you bastards," he said again and again, "serves you all right." I looked up into his glittering, feverish eyes.

Suddenly I was hysterical. I sat up and couldn't get my legs together; something had given way inside my body. Tim was freeing George; he was almost smothered by the gag and was lying, semiconscious, on the floor. Buzz was still patting my arm. The smell of the gunpowder had replaced that of blood, vomit, sweat, semen, putrefaction.

I managed to stand upright, sobbing, clinging to Buzz. Around my feet were the bodies of those men who'd pressed on top of me. I enjoyed the sight. I loved it. They're dead, dead, joyously dead, I thought. I felt as if that were the ultimate gift: seeing those men dead about my feet. Rampsie was crumpled next to my ankles, shot through the chest, still moaning. I reached over and touched the blood on his chest, wetting my hand in it. It was still warm, lovely. I came out of the room, staggering, staring at the blood on my hand. I spread a little on my face, across my cheeks. I sobbed to myself, feeling the ache inside me like a knife pricking some bursting bubble of pain. The tears were atoning, healing. I loved the blood; I wished at that moment I could bathe in it, absorbing it through my pores.

Buzz had his arm about me still, crying. I had no clothes left on my body. One of George's sneakers had been ripped off. A shred of his shirt hung from his neck, with the pocket left on it. It must have been late afternoon, not quite dark. Some people had gathered on the street outside the store; they stared at us. Tim had tried to wrap my nakedness in a sheet from the bed, but I could see the blood on a corner, and I shoved it off; the air felt good, good, and I was proud of my body: It had survived.

A woman came forward. "Don't cry, don't cry," she said to me. "Don't cry, darling, it's all right. Don't cry, love."

I didn't even know I was crying, but then I realized I couldn't see her through my tears. I thought it was Mrs. Britton.

Then I saw others of my neighbors. They stood with their heads bowed, and a couple of women and even a man wept. They knew what had happened in that store. "Dear, dear, dear," a woman was muttering as I passed by. She was wringing her hands. "Dear, dear, dear," I could hear her still behind me.

The townspeople stood back as we passed by. We walked slowly, so slowly, across the common, as if we were barely moving at all, as in a dream. At first I thought I might fall, but my legs seemed to become stronger.

I'd survived; the fresh air told me so. I walked with hesitant pride, barely staggering. I left my body to the breeze, to the cool night, drinking in that coolness as if it were water in which I was bathing. Those men were gone, gone, gone. We'd never see them again; we were free. I could feel the smile on my face and almost touch the triumph in my soul.

George was having trouble walking; Uncle Simon and Tim were steadying him. I touched his arm, but we didn't speak. Buzz walked next to me, still holding my arm. "Nice Lize," he said, stroking gently still. I turned to him and pressed his hand.

"We did it," I told him, my voice a sob. "We did it, Buzz. You and I, all of us. Oh, dear God, we did it!"

Buzz stumbled next to me as we walked across the common. I could just see the light in Uncle Simon's house through the boarded-up windows. "They won't bother us anymore, Buzz, isn't that great? No more, no more, Buzz." And I began to sing quietly, startled by the sound of my own voice, as if I'd never heard it before. I didn't know the words I sang; I made them up as I went along. I wasn't even sure they *were* words. And it wasn't a song I'd ever heard before—but it sounded as natural and sure as if I'd known it since my birth. All I remembered afterward was that it had to do with salvation and joy and liberation and love.

When I turned my back on the store, I entered Aunt Chloe's house as if I were past a threshold. I didn't want to remember; I wanted it behind me. I couldn't remember; I'd have to start again and not think of the past. Something had wiped it away, even though I knew it still lurked. With all the strength of my body and mind, I'd forget and try to begin anew. There was will in that, yes, there was salvation, because that's all there was left.

Aunt Chloe looked at my face, dried her tears, and led me to my room as if I were a cripple or an infant, put out fresh clothes on the bed, drew me into the shower. I stood beneath a jet streaming the hottest water I ever felt; it corroded my skin, seared my face. I tried to reach inside myself, to open my womb to the hot, cleansing water, to free myself of all traces of that other world. There was pain inside my vagina when I tried to clean there, and I had to stop.

"How is George?" I asked Aunt Chloe when I discovered he'd gone home. "Is he all right?" My heart skipped a beat, fearing for him.

Aunt Chloe nodded. "Said he wanted to be alone. Didn't want to be driven, even talk to anyone. When I asked him, wasn't he afraid to walk home after dark, he said, 'What's to be afraid of anymore, Chloe?' "

I lay on the downstairs couch, blitzed as it was, because I didn't want to be away from my family. I wanted to see them, to hear them talking, to watch, to touch them. They'd survived, too. Uncle Simon had showered, even shaved. He was very pale. "Make some tea, Chloe," he said. "Just like always. Just give me a cup of your tea."

Aunt Chloe looked at him, a worried frown on her face. She made the tea, going through the ritual; the teakettle sang; she stirred the tea leaves, strained them into his cup.

"Simon, don't you think we'd better . . ." Aunt Chloe began.

"Sit down, Chloe," Uncle Simon said. "There's nothing more needs doing now." He looked ill.

Buzz and Tim, very subdued from the events of the last hours, were sitting cross-legged on the floor, cleaning the guns. Tim pushed a long cotton swab on a wire through the barrel of one of the rifles; Buzz polished with a soft cloth.

"Do it again," commanded Uncle Simon without looking.

"But it's slicker'n a whistle," protested Tim, lifting the gun carefully by the trigger. "You wanna see?"

"Do it again!"

Tim nodded, reaching for another wad of cotton.

"Then lock 'em up in the rack good, you hear, polish the case, and burn the rags. Then we won't mention it again."

Tim squinted up at Uncle Simon, then over at me. "Don't worry, nobody'll ever know. . . ."

But Uncle Simon'd already turned back to us. "Tomorrow I'm gonna put in a garden, Chloe. Been thinking on it. Almost too late already. But first I'm gonna pull those boards off the windows and touch up with some paint."

Aunt Chloe glanced at Uncle Simon, astonished; then she looked intently into his face. She pushed back a wisp of hair. "Well then, Simon, I hope you won't forget zucchini this year. Remember last year. You clean forgot. . . ."

"I won't forget zucchini," said Uncle Simon with annoyance. "You don't have to keep reminding me, Chloe."

"I don't mean to harp on it, Simon, but last year we didn't have it all summer, and—"

"All right, for heaven's sake, woman!" Then he reached over and patted her hand.

George returned later, walking through the dark night like a silent ghost, until he came into the light from the bulb Uncle Simon had just replaced in the fixture outside our front door. Long-starved moths were desperately fluttering about it, eager to immolate themselves against the hot glass. Even though Aunt Chloe had expressly forbidden me to move, I couldn't stay in bed, I was like one possessed. I found I was able to stand and somehow move without disabling pain.

230

When I saw George approach, I was able to walk to meet him on the common, taking one slow step at a time. I wanted to touch him, to hold him, but instead found myself staring mutely at the silent stars. So much had happened between us, such terrible things, unbearable violations, and I was frightened lest our flesh never touch again. About us was absolute quiet—but now lights shone at the Callaghans', the Brittons', even at the Macys'. I could see the shape of George's head against those lights, just enough to make out the planes of his face, the dark of his hair. I felt his hand reaching for mine, touching my arm. I held it between both of mine, rubbing my fingers between his, touching his fingertips to mine. I turned his palm over, pressing it against my face. My tears wet his fingers. I held myself momentarily against him, until I felt the pain again.

"I need some help, George," I finally whispered. "Medically . . . I'm torn. . ."

His face was creased in concern. "Do you want to go to the hospital in Tremont?"

"No, only you."

"Then come."

He took my hand, leading me across the dark common to his house. He examined me in his quiet office. "You need some stitches. Do you mind?"

I shook my head, feeling my hair flick across my cold cheeks.

He applied a needle to my lower back. While he stitched, he told me that he'd already called Clarissa's mother, that his daughter would be back soon. We talked distantly and somewhat formally, like old friends at tea. "I'm going back to Boston soon," he said, threading the curved needle again. "Been away too long. I need to get in touch again." His voice was low and almost without resonance.

When he bent over me, his head was next to mine. I reached over for him instinctively, touching his arm, bringing him closer, clutching him.

"Oh, George," I said then, sobbing. "Oh, my God, George, where are we? Oh, my darling, what are we going to do?"

I'd never called him darling before, or flooded that way, or felt such despair, even in that terrible room across the common. Had our flesh turned cold for each other? Were we to be forever distant?

"My darling, what terrible things have happened . . ." I began again, then choked.

His arms were about me instantly. His head was on mine, pressing, his arms cradling me. "Oh, Lord, if you care," he said, "if it hasn't

231

been too much, if you don't hate me. . . ." He was sobbing with me, his head against my breast.

"I love you," I said. "Don't you know? Can't we just try to pretend it never hap—?"

He held me tighter. "I love you, too," he said. "But sometime we'll have to talk. Not now, sometime. Just hold me. We'll manage. But knowing you care makes all the difference. . . ."

We held each other, ignoring the oddness of the place, the peculiarities of the hour, the idiocy of the situation, the despair which had possessed us. Finally, he released me, and sat beside the examining table, waiting for the anesthetic to wear off. He held my hand quietly in that room, where the silence felt golden, like velvet, and the only sound was the purr of some machine or other and our slow breathing. His chair beside me was so close that once I laid my head on his shoulder, rubbing my hand over his thick, curling hair, pulling my fingers through the ringlets, fingering the sideburns. I buried my face in those dark locks and found myself crying again, but then I borrowed his handkerchief, blew my nose, and felt better. I felt I'd be all right. It would be all right. George would be all right. We'd be all right together.

When the numbness had ceased, he helped me from the table. "You'll need codeine tonight," he said. "And sleeping medicine." He sounded a little professional, and I could feel a smile on my lips.

"I'm all right," I said. "Please don't worry, I *am* all right now." I squeezed his hand. "And I'm not going to pay your bill."

He drove me home. As we rode around that common which had been so full of terrors, I wondered if we could ever walk across the place without flinching.

The night was clear and George drove with one hand, the fingers of the other intertwined with mine. But I couldn't look toward the store, and neither could George. At that moment it didn't exist for us; I'd forgotten it momentarily. If someone had asked me exactly where it was situated on the common that night, I couldn't have said. I stood on Uncle Simon's porch and watched George drive back home. Just before he disappeared, he waved in the distance, and I waved back. I even made a wish on one of the bright stars above us, and I realized I hadn't dared entertain a hope or a wish in a long time now.

Two days later Lieutenant Dowling called from police headquarters in Tremont. I could feel my throat tighten and fury constrict my chest.

"Heard that you had a ruckus on your common, Miss Sanderson.

We're trying to get to the bottom of it. Couple of men in the hospital. I've already been over to see them."

I took a deep breath. "Lieutenant, you have no idea how badly we needed you. We were desperate, at the mercy of—"

"I don't blame you at all, Miss Sanderson. Why, the third man died. We really regret—"

"I'm delighted you do, Lieutenant. I'll spread the word around, that you regret—*regret,* wasn't that the word you used?—our, er, ruckus. That'll make everyone feel so much better, I'm sure."

"Well, like I said, we're trying to get to the bottom of it. Got the entire force working on it. But those guys in the hospital never got a good look at whoever hit 'em, so we're working a little in the dark, but I'm sure we'll find out something sooner or later."

Despite the alarm cascading down my spine, I hunched the receiver against my shoulder casually. "What a shame you're having so much trouble, Lieutenant. After all, this is such a small town, and we're not even in your jurisdiction."

"Well, I can assure you we'll find out something. Already we're making progress. We've heard from the Michigan police that they suspect Rampsie and Hudman of fencing hot cars out that way a few weeks back. By the way, you haven't seen them around since their bash with the strikers, have you?"

I looked out into the sunshine. Uncle Simon had now removed the boards from the big window, and light flooded into the hall. "Things have been pretty quiet around here, Lieutenant."

". . . Michigan police are really hot after them, so I knew you'd be pleased to hear that pretty soon we'll probably get them for something besides simple assault."

"How delightful. I'll certainly pass that good news along. That ought to cheer everyone." My head was beginning to ache; I rubbed my neck to ease the muscles.

There was a sudden silence on Dowling's side. "Miss Sanderson, everything's all right down there, isn't it? You don't sound like yourself somehow."

"Is that so, Lieutenant? I'm sorry. It's just that I'm very busy this morning. I've been planting a garden and had to run all the way into the house for your call. . . ."

"Oh, well. . . ."

"So thank you for your good news. Now if you don't mind, I've got to run. Uncle Simon needs me to help plant the zucchini."

The afternoon was warm, and the sun, high. Uncle Simon plowed the strip behind the house where he'd always kept his garden. Aunt Chloe inserted the seeds while I hoed dirt over the rows. Inadvertently I thought of the sun shining down on Rampsie's store.

"Is the doors locked?" I asked Uncle Simon quietly. "No one will walk in there?"

He tilted his head slightly under the green-shaded fisherman's hat which he always wore in the sun. "Went back and nailed it solid, then took the sign down." He looked up, and his face grew dark. "Now watch out, you're standing on my row of seeds."

I watered the rows from a long hose attached to Uncle Simon's outside faucet. The hose extended across the blackened area where the barn had stood; already grass and strawberry vine had begun to cover the rocks that had once been the barn's supports.

Buzz and Tim ran cold drinks from the house and fetched tools for Uncle Simon. George was holding office hours for the first time in days; later he'd planned to meet Clarissa in Fitchburg and bring her over afterward.

At noon Uncle Simon received a call from Eastman. "Simon, we want you to know that we've just about settled the mill strike. Attorney Trumbull's been negotiating for some days, and he's finally made some of those people see the light. We'll have a final meeting tonight, inside the mill. Thought you might like to be present. Afterward we'll have a small ceremony in front of the mill. I thought, as one of the core group, perhaps you'd like to say a few words, about how grateful. . . ."

Uncle Simon wiped the garden dirt from his face. "I'm sorry, Mr. Eastman. The fact is, I haven't time. If I feel like it, I'll look in. Right now, I'm much too busy."

Eastman's voice was incredulous. "Simon, need I *remind* you that we all act together in this thing. A show of solidarity. . . ." I could hear his voice across the room, where I was scrubbing the dirt from beneath my nails into the sink.

Uncle Simon let the receiver drop onto the cradle.

That night George and I sat on the front steps, watching the moon over the trees on the common, our shoulders touching as we leaned together. Buzz, Tim, and Clarissa were playing among the big oaks; we could see them darting among the thick trunks. We'd been watching them idly, seeing their forms flitting back and forth, when we noticed Stu and Minnie Callaghan circling the common, chatting idly. When they saw us, they quickened their steps. "Are Simon and Chloe in? Thought we'd rechallenge them to a rubber of bridge. About time, don't you think?" I could smell the acrid fumes from Stu's cigar. He laughed. "Wouldn't want them to get too good for us, practicing by themselves."

They were still playing bridge after midnight; when Tim and I returned from walking George and Clarissa partway home. I could still smell Stu's cigar as I lay in bed and found the old aroma, which used to gag me, reassuring in an indefinable way.

Uncle Simon and Aunt Chloe had been talking about going to church the next morning when a Tremont police car drove up, circled the common once, and came to a sudden halt before our house. Inside was Lieutenant Dowling. I was barefoot, wearing dungarees, preparing to work in the garden again. He knocked at the front door.

"Come in, Lieutenant. Will it take very long?"

The lieutenant stepped inside the door. He carried his visored hat in his hand and smoothed his hair several times, as if wind had mussed it. "This really is an official call, Miss Sanderson. I know it's going to please you. I've got warrants here"—he extracted two envelopes from his pocket—"for the arrests of Rampsie and Hudman." He held them for me to see: long, white pristine sheafs. "Knew you'd be pleased, being a lawyer and all. And I know how concerned you've been, so I thought I'd come by myself. Seen either of them around yet?"

I felt that day suddenly turn cold, and icy slivers cascade up and down my vertebrae. Even the ground seemed to shift precipitously, and my voice didn't sound like my own.

"No. Come to think of it, I haven't."

He stared at me a minute. "Well, you'd certainly know, wouldn't you, if you had?"

I tried to smile. "Indeed, we all would, Lieutenant. That's a fact."

"Then there's been no sign of them? I mean, this is the last place they were seen after the fight with the mill people."

"Well, you know how they are; they come and go a lot. I think you even said the same thing once." I swallowed hard. "Isn't it a lovely day?"

"Very nice. Say, you've unboarded your house. *That's* what looks so different. Lot lighter in here than last time."

"Isn't it? Uncle Simon thought it about time. . . ."

"And there are kids playing out on the common. Funny. Never saw kids out there before."

I pointed out the door. "My brother's the one with the red hair. Timmy. I've been watching them."

He was scratching his head. "Odd, isn't it? Not having seen kids before, I mean. Come to think of it, there are several young couples living in this town."

I picked up my trowel where I'd left it on the front step. "Please excuse me, Lieutenant. If you've finished. . . ."

"Sure." He turned to leave. "Getting hot." He wiped his forehead with a sleeve. "Looks like we're going to have one hell of a hot summer." He started down the steps. "If you see those men, let us know, Miss Sanderson. We're trying to find them every place we can think of. First time we've had anything to pin on them. Not much—car theft—there'll undoubtedly be some other indictments soon, but this one'll put 'em out of commission for a while."

At the curb, Dowling turned once again. "Beats all. I mean, how a town can look so different from one day to the next. Right pretty little town, Rowe."

"Always has been. Have a good day, Lieutenant."

He was just pulling away from the curb when he stopped one last time and called through his open window, "By the way, Miss Sanderson, has Rampsie's store been closed for long? Tried the door awhile ago and found it shut up tight. Has the old man gone away? We didn't hold him long, you know."

My voice had turned thick, and I coughed trying to clear it. "I don't know, Lieutenant. Lots of people come and go, if you'll notice." Pops seemed to have just disappeared, frightened to death, Aunt Chloe had said. "He's got relatives up north," she'd added. "Bet he'll never come back."

Dowling hung an elbow out the window of his car and slowly cruised around the common, peering intently to left and right, ducking down to see each house, then disappeared along the road to Tremont.

I quickly searched out Uncle Simon—he was repairing the motor to his saw. "Uncle Simon, you've got to do something. The store. . . ."

Uncle Simon was studying the metal chain of his saw. He was very casual and barely looked up. "Been thinkin' on it a little myself, Lisa. Right now, this saw's taking all my time." I watched him muttering to himself, inserting a drop of oil into the workings of the old machine. I grasped his arm.

"Uncle Simon, don't you realize there's danger? For God's sake, please. . . ."

236

He stood up to his full height. "Everything in its time, Lisa. I'm a very patient man myself and don't like to be flustered. Flustering never helped anyone. Now if you'll just relax on it, I'll give it some more thought. Here, now, doesn't this saw look just first-rate?"

He was even whistling a little tune.

When I felt the skin on my neck prickle with panic, I knew we couldn't wait much longer.

The next day Trumbull strolled casually across the common; he knocked at the door and asked to see Uncle Simon. Although the mill was back in almost full operation, I'd succeeded in persuading Uncle Simon to take a few days off. At least Trumbull looked tan and fit, as if he'd found time for golf at last. Tim and Buzz were playing marbles on the front lawn; school had at last let out for the summer. I was helping Aunt Chloe set out pots of geraniums along the porch.

"Got a call from Dowling," said Trumbull. Worried because he can't find Rampsie. Asked me to keep my eyes open. I told him I hadn't seen any of 'em for a week."

Uncle Simon listened to Trumbull, barely blinking.

"You heard about the indictments?" Trumbull asked. "Police in Michigan waiting to hear."

Uncle Simon rubbed his ear. "Maybe they've vanished for good this time, James."

"I don't know. Seems like they always return sooner or later." He stretched in the bright sunshine. "Well, I'll tell Dowling we haven't seen 'em. Funny, though. Saw their truck a couple of days ago parked behind that old house Rampsie owns. Even went in there to take a look around. Regular flea trap!"

I picked up the phone and called George. "I'll be right over," he said, alarm in his voice. "We just can't let things slide this way." George arrived at our house in ten minutes.

"Listen, Simon." he said, confronting Uncle Simon as he cleaned his

238

tools in the kitchen, "whether you want to or not, we've all got to do something. Together. Make plans. You with me?"

"I know, George. Of course, I'm with you. It's just that for the first time in weeks—"

"You don't need to tell *me*."

Fifteen minutes later, while we were still talking, Dowling drove up. We'd been standing beside the front door and saw his car and the way he looked around before he came up the front walk to our house. "Let him in," Uncle Simon said to me.

Dowling was standing outside in the warm sunshine, holding his visored hat in his hand. "Listen, Miss Sanderson, I hate to bother you again, but those men are still missing."

I fought for control and time. "What men, Lieutenant? Do you mean Rampsie and his crowd?"

"Of course, I mean Rampsie. Who did you think I meant?"

"That's really too bad. Mr. Trumbull told us you were particularly concerned."

"Well, it's more'n concern, for your information. We've even got bulletins out on 'em. Can't understand where the hell they've gone. Keep thinking they'll show up here, but they don't."

Uncle Simon shook his head. "Guess you'll have to ask whoever saw them last," he said. "Can't rightly remember who that was."

"Why, you *all* did," exclaimed Dowling. "Leastwise, that's what I understand. After the fight in the common. We asked those men in the hospital the same question, and that's what they said."

Uncle Simon appeared to be going to say something, then abruptly changed his mind. "Well, I *do* seem to remember that's when I last saw 'em," he muttered.

Dowling leaned forward toward Uncle Simon, his eyes blazing. "Seems to me you've got an awfully short memory, Mr. Sanderson. Why can't you remember that damned fight all of a sudden? What the hell's the trouble with all of you anyway?"

George thrust his hands into his pockets. "It isn't that we can't remember, Lieutenant; it's that we're trying to forget. I guess you can't understand that. We've been through a hell of a lot, in case you don't realize it, and I think you'd do the same thing."

Dowling nodded, rubbing his head solemnly. "I suppose. Maybe. Don't mind telling you that this thing's getting on my nerves. Nobody can figure where they've gone—there's been no sign of 'em for a week. We've been combing all their old haunts."

"Shame," said George, his hands still in his pockets.

"Two-bit punks," said Dowling. "Can't even find what rock they're under. Damn strange."

"Not really," answered Uncle Simon. "Remember, they used to be gone for a week or two sometimes, and nobody really cared. Except us, I mean. Now suddenly they're popular."

We walked down to the police cruiser with Dowling. He stepped into his car, seeming uncertain and restless. Then he stopped in his tracks and smelled the air. "God-awful stink," he said. "Smelled it when we came in. Is the mill operating again?" He peered toward the smokestack.

"Part-time," answered Uncle Simon. "Probably something stuck in the chimney. Always takes a few days to burn it out."

Dowling reached into his pocket for his handkerchief, holding it to his nose. "Jesus, I hope for your sake they clean it out pretty damn fast."

Uncle Simon was staring across the common, a fixed expression on his face. "Next time you come, that stink'll be gone, Lieutenant. I can absolutely guarantee it."

We stood by the curb watching until Dowling had vanished up the road to Tremont.

"Get the others," said Uncle Simon to George.

I started for the house. "I'll begin calling."

"No!" Uncle Simon was shaking his head. "Don't call, go directly. We'll go fetch everyone directly. Rhymer, White, the others; tell White if he doesn't come this time, I'll break his goddamn neck. Tell him he knows what to bring and we need him 'specially. I'll go get the others in the car."

Uncle Simon never even questioned driving his car with that cast on his arm, and neither did the rest of us; we never thought of it. The way he was employing it, that cast was a part of him. His sudden resolve heartened me.

Aunt Chloe had slammed the windows of the house, so nauseating had the smell become. Some trick of air circulation on the common had made the stench appear to derive from the mill's tall chimney rather than from the store at the far opposite end.

"Stinky, stinky, winky, pinky," Buzz was chanting, jumping up and down the front steps. holding his nose.

"Buzz, go home to your mother if you're going to make that racket," snapped Aunt Chloe. Mrs. Sardoe and Buzz had already moved back

240

to their own house. Aunt Chloe finally slammed the back windows of the house, then lugged down the attic fan to move some of the odorous air from the house.

That night after sundown Paul White, Uncle Simon, George, and several other men from town casually circled the common, then disappeared into the dark behind Rampsie's store. Clarissa had come to play with Buzz and Tim. Within a half hour, the smell of smoke drifted across the night air, a relief from the stench that had been permeating it. Within ten minutes the roof of Rampsie's store was burning, vivid against the night sky. Buzz, Clarissa, and Tim forsook their game of checkers to watch.

"Fire! Fire!" said Buzz, pointing. "Store no more?" We all were peering through the front windows again.

"I know all about it," said Clarissa, pressing her face to the glass.

"You don't know anything," Tim responded. "Not a thing, Clarissa. And don't you dare let on that you do."

Clarissa stopped, chastened.

"Sorry," said Tim. "Let's get back to the game. That's nothing but an old fire. We've seen better ones than that."

The store burned fiercely for more than an hour. Uncle Simon returned home once; beneath his coat was an empty plastic bottle, which he buried carefully at the bottom of the trash container in the backyard. "Now it's time to call the fire engine," he said. "Paul says to do it now."

Within minutes after I put in the call to the firehouse, the fire engine stampeded around the common, clanging the ancient blackened bell on its hood.

"Where'd they ever dig up that old thing?" asked Aunt Chloe, her voice rising in disbelief. "Why, it couldn't even put out a bonfire!"

"Behind the firehouse," Tim answered. "They keep it for the firemen to practice on. Never even saw it work before." To me it looked like some kind of tinker toy from a past age.

After midnight Aunt Chloe put Clarissa to bed at our house; neither George nor Uncle Simon had returned from the store. Aunt Chloe and I maintained a vigil beside the front door, watching the flames subside.

Suddenly Aunt Chloe let out a shriek. Driving down the street was Rampsie's flatbed truck, the gleaming sheet metal of the bulldozer blades shining beneath the streetlights. Aunt Chloe screamed again. I was transfixed, terrified, watching the metal monster invade our common once again.

Uncle Simon ran out of the night from the direction of the store toward it, as if ready to do battle single-handed, David against a peculiar Goliath—when George's head popped out of the cab. Uncle Simon was already yelling up to him, giving instructions.

Aunt Chloe collapsed against me in relief. "I thought it was Rampsie," she said, gasping. "Dear God, I thought he'd returned." I held her trembling body for a moment until she'd recovered.

Tim was out of bed again, hearing the excitement. "What are they going to *do* with it?" he asked me, peering from the window. "I don't get it."

Uncle Simon began to run down the street beside the huge vehicle, appearing diminished in size. He was yelling and gesturing toward George, directing him toward the smoking remains of the fire. We could see Ed Rhymer's bald head in the cab with George, helping him with the controls.

Before the spot where the old store had stood, the giant machine came to a stop, lowering the blades ominously with a wrenched grinding of the gears; then it began to move jerkily forward. Before George and Ed could get it under control, that machine had wiped out a substantial pine tree and demolished a length of curbing; finally, they straightened it and inched it forward again. Before the blades of the truck, the first pile of debris from the fire cascaded into the blackened cellar hole in a shower of sparks.

Men on the ground were urging and cajoling the huge machine backward and forward, yelling up to it words of encouragement.

"Thataway, George, " shouted a florid man. "Now, two feet more, keep it comin' now." Rhymer peered out the side window, mopping his face with a large rag.

Other men on the ground pushed charred debris into the hole: blackened beams, hunks of cement, smoldering timbers—even the large metal receptacles where Pops had kept garbage, lures for clouds of summer flies. Then the blades of the machine filled the void with still another volume of dirt, all the while directed by Paul White, who flailed his arms as though conducting a symphony orchestra.

We'd long ago forgotten about sleep; Tim, Aunt Chloe, and I sat on the front steps watching the machine work backward and forward through the night, wielding those giant blades with increasing precision. Toward dawn the foundation hole of the old store was filled, and George and Ed Rhymer, taking turns with the machine, began to scrape dirt from the area behind the store to cover the charred surface.

The men of the town were still gathered there—none appeared to have gone home—and stood about, cursing and shouting encouragement. I looked about at the ring of houses; they were dark no longer. Front lights were lit brightly, to provide illumination for this midnight revel, and someone had replaced all the streetlights on this side of the oval.

When the sun came up, George and the others had finished. He and Ed stood together in the cab, surveying their handiwork. Then they turned and circled the common in an almost triumphal way, waving to the neighbors as they departed toward the side street, Old Man Rampsie's house, and the resting ground for the Rowe Boys' infernal machine. However, at just that certain moment of victory, it coughed repeatedly as if it'd contracted a sudden cold and, with a prolonged, percussive burst, stopped dead.

Paul White and Uncle Simon immediately took off after it, cutting obliquely across the common. Tim and Buzz were right behind them, pajamas and all—and Aunt Chloe and I followed. George and Ed were frantically throwing switches and pulling levers while other townspeople hung from the vehicle, offering suggestions.

"What's the trouble?" I yelled up to George. He looked disheveled, grimy, a little like a desperado.

"Damned if we can figure it. Just stopped dead. Simon's going for his tools."

Then men began to pound and prod at the mechanism of the vehicle. Almost everyone in town had come from the houses about the common; I glimpsed the Brittons, the Ritchies, even the Parkses, whom I'd last seen in George's office weeks ago. I hadn't even realized that some of those people were back in town. Mrs. Ritchie and Mrs. White were serving hot coffee to keep the men awake and the kids had been put to work running tools to their elders.

Why, I thought with astonishment as I looked around, the entire town's here, gathered together, and everyone seemed to be contributing in some way: skill, tools, coffee, encouragement, advice. We'd all rallied together, each bolstering the other. As I'd looked at Uncle Simon's face and into the countenances of those townspeople, I could see reflected there a kind of determination and spirit I'd not seen there earlier. We'd all survived a hell of a lot, that look seemed to say, and we're closing our ranks. And just as we'd survived as individuals, we were trying to come together as another entity, a town once again.

Rampsie's truck, against the lightening sky, appeared like some great beast that had died out there at the fringe of our common, grotesque in the shadows from the streetlights and the flickers from flashlights held aloft by a group of men examining the machine's innards. Soon Uncle Simon and George, treading heavily, returned to the house. Tim and Buzz trailed after, each holding up one side of Uncle Simon's heavy toolbox.

"Won't go!" Uncle Simon was muttering. He was smeared with grease, his shirt in tatters—I think he'd been using pieces of it to clean the machinery. "Damn thing won't budge," he said again, then swore softly. Aunt Chloe and I followed the men into the kitchen, where Uncle Simon soaked a towel in cold water and rubbed his face wearily with it.

"Tough luck," I said to George, touching his arm sympathetically. He was trying to scrub the heavy oil from his hands. I handed him a towel. Both he and Uncle Simon looked a little gray with fatigue.

George shook his head wearily. "Tried every damn thing we could think of. Hudman was some kind of incredible mechanic!" He pondered it a moment wonderingly. "We'll have to wait a couple of hours before we can find someone to help us out, who knows what to do."

Uncle Simon glanced over at him, "Don't worry, George, we'll get somebody. Frank Connors just took off for Tremont—won't take Frank long, I can guarantee it!"

I understood one thing as I looked at Uncle Simon at that minute: He wasn't dejected anymore, he hadn't rubbed his hands together in days, and he was full of fight. Uncle Simon was a sleeping tiger aroused.

George nodded, drying his hands. "Not a damn thing to do now except wait. . . ."

Aunt Chloe and I had just finished making breakfast when a car circled the common, stopping opposite the machine. Tim, who'd been out front with Buzz and Clarissa, tore in.

"Mr. Trumbull," he whispered. "Comin' here. He's been snoopin' around."

"Then why don't you ask him in?" said Uncle Simon. "Where are your manners, boy?"

Uncle Simon handed Trumbull a cup of coffee. For some reason Trumbull had lost his pink glow of health.

"Jesus Christ, whatever happened to the store?" he asked "Did the damn thing just disappear?"

"Burned down in the night, James," answered Uncle Simon. I stood listening to the exchange, holding my breath.

244

Trumbull was scratching his head. "Why, you'd never know it was there. My God, it was there one minute and gone the next!"

George was standing beside me, casually leaning against the doorjamb. "Old store, James. Went up like tinder. I'm really surprised you didn't see it."

Trumbull sipped his coffee absently. "I'm just returning to town now—spent last night in Tremont. All-night stand, getting that mill contract out of the way." He looked over at the stalled truck of Rampsie's. "So they've returned at last."

Uncle Simon was still cleaning his oily fingers. "Nope. *We* used it. Came in right handy, too, till it busted."

"*You* used it?"

"Had to bury those burning timbers, James," said Uncle Simon. "Like to set the whole town on fire, in the wind."

"There wasn't any wind," answered Trumbull. "Least not in Tremont. And when are you going to get that thing out of here? It's blocking the whole street."

"Soon as we're able, James. Can't help it for now."

Trumbull finished his coffee, then peered out into the street and across the common again. "Pretty damn strange, if you ask me. Whole town's awake. Forgot so many people lived in this burg." He rubbed his head again. "You tryin' to convince me that store just disappeared off the face of the earth, just like that?" He snapped his fingers. "Why, I never heard of such a strange, goddamn. . . . Just wait until Dowling hears this one!"

"Oh, come on, now, James," said George. But I could hear the alarm in his voice. "We already told you. . . ."

Trumbull turned and walked slowly to his car; George and Uncle Simon followed right behind. "Frankly," said Trumbull. "I don't give a good goddamn what happened to those little bastards, but . . . Lordy, just wait until Dowling hears this one!" Then he waved a plump hand, climbed back into his car, circled the common, and disappeared among the pillars of his home across the way.

Within an hour Dowling had returned; I figured that Trumbull must have given him a fast update on the turn of events in Rowe. Mechanics from a Tremont garage were now working on Rampsie's truck, leaning against the engine cowling, trying to figure how Hudman had rigged the controls. Most of the men who'd been working on it earlier, like George and Uncle Simon, had never gone home but were still embroiled in the repair of Rampsie's creation, watching, offering suggestions and encouragement to the mechanics. Even the women stayed, speaking together in knots and looking on with curiosity.

A young sergeant named Pillson had accompanied the lieutenant this time. Pillson whistled when he saw the beleaguered truck. "That's what I been hearin' about?" he asked Dowling. "How'd anybody dream up a thing like that?"

Dowling had removed his visored hat in the warm air. He stalked around the stalled vehicle, examining it criticially from all directions. "I hope to hell you get it out of there fast," he informed the men. "Don't you know it's illegal. . . ?" Then he squinted past the machine through the trees of the common, tilting his head a little. "And the bloody store *did* burn down, just like Trumbull said. Christ's sake? It was right there yesterday!"

Several of the men had stopped work to listen to Dowling. "Couldn't stop the fire once it got to going," explained Paul White. "Old place went up like tinder."

"And just who are you?" asked Dowling. "I suppose you live around here, too."

"Yes, Sir. Paul White. I'm a fireman. Up most of the night with that fire."

Dowling grunted. "What's so special about the fire that you've got to bulldoze it? Look over there. You'd never know anything was there if you hadn't seen it before."

"Burning embers," began Paul. "Flying all over the place. . . ."

"Embers? What in hell are you trying to tell me? It was a damn calm night. You expect me to believe rubbish like that? Thought you said you put out that fire."

When Paul started to protest, Dowling turned away. "Come with me," he barked to Pillson.

The two tramped over the common toward the freshly turned earth where the store had stood. Uncle Simon, George, and I followed with the other villagers. The policeman paced up and down, leaving footprints in the soft earth. I could hear Pillson's voice, breathless as he trailed along behind the frowning Dowling: "You don't mean that you're really gonna go to all the trouble of digging it up, Lieutenant?"

"Damn right I am. Gonna have a crew over here this afternoon, before anything else around here disappears or gets burned down."

George crammed his hands into his pockets. "Exactly what is it you're looking for, Lieutenant?"

Dowling's jaw was set. "Dunno exactly. But it won't be the first time

246

I've gone on a wild-goose chase, and probably not the last. You stay here, Pillson, while I go call the station."

He returned to the police cruiser, where we could see him through the window talking on the police radio. When he returned, he sat down on the common grass beneath a shading maple. "'Dozer's gonna take awhile, Pillson, so you better get comfortable."

The men ceased work on Rampsie's truck; instead, they conversed in low tones among themselves, glancing frequently toward the two policeman.

For two hours Dowling and Pillson waited, not exchanging a word. At one time Pillson, who'd been leaning against a tree, fell asleep, and we could hear him snoring, a persistent rhythmic sound like a bubbling teakettle. Later on George approached the men.

"Too bad, going to all this trouble, Lieutenant. We just buried the thing. You really mean to dig it up?"

"Yes, Dr. Almquist. That bother you any?"

"No, Lieutenant. I'm just inquiring. Seems like an awful lot of effort. . . ."

Later Aunt Chloe arrived with lemonade. The day, one of the first of summer, shimmered with a diffuse sun shining through waves of moisture. When she offered some to the policemen, Dowling scowled and refused, but Pillson eagerly grasped the glass and gulped its contents down.

"There's lots more," Aunt Chloe said.

"Thank you, ma'am," began Pillson. "I'd sure like—"

"You've had enough," Dowling snapped.

The two began to argue. "They're nice," we could hear Pillson saying. "I don't know what's eating you, Lieutenant. What're they gonna do to us anyway?"

Dowling leaned back against the tree. "I don't know yet, Pillson. But I'm sure as hell going to find out damn quick!"

I took Pillson's empty lemonade glass. "You're heartless." I could hear the bantering ring in my voice. "Treating Sergeant Pillson that way."

"Well, I can be a hell of a lot more heartless than that, Miss Sanderson."

I stood over him, looking at the top of his head, at the flecks of gray beginning in his hair. "It's really flattering, all this attention, Lieutenant Dowling. Awhile ago we couldn't get anyone to pay us heed at all. I came to see you for help, remember? I went to Sparrow, then to Judge Bream. I practically came on my knees, trying to impress you that we were having trouble in Rowe. I think you thought I was becoming a pest, a nuisance. You never even answered my call for help before the fight on the common that killed a man." The lump in my throat was threatening to close it over. "And now we can't get rid of you—you sit here to defy us all. *We're* the enemy, aren't we, Lieutenant? You're going to make us suffer for any inconvenience we might have caused you or for any injustice you feel we might have caused those men."

Dowling never answered. I walked back to the house slowly, my legs feeling stiff, my body aching. George slipped an arm about me.

The men Uncle Simon had called together slowly arrived at our house. Most had been on the common all night or quickly arrived from their homes, where they were catching up on needed sleep. Half stood, half sat around Aunt Chloe's kitchen table; all appeared worried but alert despite their all-night vigils. I glanced around at familiar faces, by now almost as close as family: Paul White, Stu Callaghan, Ed Rhymer, George. There were also several men I didn't know but had seen frequently these last days.

"One thing," said Uncle Simon. "You all gotta know it now, I gotta tell you before we go on. I'm the one went into Rampsie's store . . . after Lisa and George. This is my . . . fight, and I want you to know it right off. It isn't like the rest of you need to stay mixed up in it anymore, and I want you to know it." He stopped and looked at them intently.

Paul White, who'd been sitting quietly, staring at the marred finish of Aunt Chloe's kitchen table, looked up quickly at Uncle Simon. His voice was quiet and very firm. "You're forgettin', Simon. I burned down the store. Even supplied the . . . savvy, and some of the equipment. That counts me in, too. You understand?"

Ed Rhymer coughed and hooked one finger under his thin suspenders. "You figure, Simon, the whole town isn't in on this? Hell, I just took the boards off *my* windows yesterday myself. Isn't a soul doesn't know what was in that there store. Why, you think you're the only one?"

Another man I'd never met before laughed softly. "I helped with the bulldozin', Simon, and Mike here helped Paul torch the place. Hell, we figure we been in it all along."

Stu Callaghan nodded. "Come on, Simon, we been friends since kids. You don't need to ask any of us. Why, you know that. We been going through hell in this town for months now. It got to where it was

248

them or us. What choice did we have, any of us? I mean, what choice did we *really* have? None, Simon, we all know it, each one of us. We're in this thing together, for better or worse. I'm not kiddin'."

George and I looked at each other; we both knew that Uncle Simon could spend years in prison, the last years of his life. But the town *was* involved, irrevocably and deeply, as George and I were, all of us; the ripples from those dead men encompassed us all. We conferred for more than an hour, mindful of Dowling and Pillson on the common—trying to improvise our tactics. When we left the house, we had the glimmerings of how we'd proceed.

The bulldozer arrived at last on a large truck from the Tremont road. Dowling impatiently watched it drive down the ramp from the truck, exchanging a few words with the driver. Finally, he pointed to the site of the store, gestured emphatically, even kicked at some of the loose fill over the old site. Soon the machine began to work, throwing up bucketfuls of soft dirt from the area of the original cellar while Dowling ran about, shouting orders. Slowly, one after the other, the people about the common who'd returned to their homes again came to the site of the old store to watch.

"Get back," Dowling promptly yelled at them. "Move away. Give the 'dozer room." He turned to Pillson. "Get those people out of here. Can't you see they're in the way."

Pillson was obviously tired and bored, but he dutifully turned to shout at the crowd. "You heard the lieutenant," he bellowed. "Get back there." Only a few people in front budged.

"I'm telling you, back up," he repeated. His face was red with frustration and the heat. "You back up, or someone's gonna get hurt. I mean it. Now you had your warning." A group of townspeople were now standing at the edge of the excavation site, and some kids played about the hole.

The bulldozer operator swung his machine, edging back the layers of rubble closer and closer to the crowd. Dowling motioned him impatiently forward; pointing to the next spot he wanted overturned. Suddenly, without warning, a section of foundation hole crumbled, and someone fell in, flipping to the bottom in a tangle of arms and legs.

"Buzz, Buzz," shrieked one of the kids who'd been playing next to the hole. I could hear Timmy screaming, right on schedule.

I rushed to the edge of the hole, catching Uncle Simon's eye and brief nod.

"You beast," Mrs. Britton was shouting at Dowling. "How could you be so cruel? The poor, poor child. . . ."

"Oh, Buzz, are you all right, Buzz?" I called.

Dowling rushed to the hole peering down at the boy. "I *told* everyone," he protested. "I *warned* you. Don't say I didn't because I did." He started to climb down into the hole, but Stu Callaghan stopped him. *"We'll* do it, Lieutenant. Get the doc." Then Stu himself began to laboriously climb down the steep banks of the pit.

"Which one of you's Dr. Almquist?" yelled Pillson. "For God's sake. . . ."

George was immediately behind me. He snatched his medical bag, now almost disreputable in its battered condition, from behind one of the bushes where he'd stashed it not twenty minutes before.

"Step aside," said George loudly. He elbowed through the crowd and clambered into the foundation hole where Buzz was lying helpless.

"Is he all right?" someone in the crowd called. "A little kid, a poor child!"

Dowling stared about himself defensively. "For God's sake, you'da thought I killed him." Then he peered down into the hole again. An edge of concern had crept into his voice. "Can you get him out?" Finally, he himself slid down into the small crater after the boy and the men. "Let me help. Here, I'll take his head.

"You take his feet," said Stu Callaghan curtly. Panting, they managed to carry Buzz to the grass beside the crater dug by the bulldozer.

I rushed forward, standing beside the boy, who lay carefully unmoving on the grass. "Oh, Buzz, Buzz—you poor child!"

"Give him air," George was pleading. "Please move back. That means everyone!"

While Pillson crouched beside Buzz, George pointed toward the police cruiser. "Call for the ambulance on your radio. It'll save time. Hurry!" Then he removed lengths of adhesive gauze from his bag and began to wind them about the boy's head.

"Are you all right?" asked Uncle Simon, bending over Buzz. "Speak up, boy, Can you hear me?"

Buzz shook his head, moaning slightly.

Pillson was still crouched beside the boy. "What do you think is wrong with him, Doc? Is he gonna be all right?"

George shook his head sadly. "Don't know, Officer. Head's awfully swollen on that side. And his speech is fuzzy. Possibly there's even brain damage." I held my breath because Buzz hadn't said a word, but Pillson didn't seem to notice the slip.

Dowling rushed back from the cruiser. "They're already on their way. Said to just sit tight."

We all stood beside Buzz, waiting, watching his limp form on the grass. Aunt Chloe leaned over him, and Mrs. Sardoe wrung her hands over Buzz's inert form. Suddenly the ambulance screamed down the road from Tremont, siren blaring. George looked at his watch. "Twelve minutes! My God!"

The ambulance swooped around the common toward Dowling, jerking to a stop before him. The group around Buzz opened up to let the attendants through. George conversed with the men briefly, supervising Buzz's transfer to the stretcher, then into the ambulance.

The driver scratched his head for a minute; it was the same man as before. "What the hell's going on down here anyway?" he asked. "Last time it was that stabbing."

"Take good care of this boy," said George. "I'll be along to see him. No telling how serious those injuries might be."

The driver nodded gravely. Then he slammed the door and proceeded up the road to Tremont.

A woman in the crowd became hysterical. "I hope you're satisfied," she said to Dowling. "You see what happens when police become callous. . . ." It was Minnie Callaghan.

Dowling was now obviously flustered. He stamped around the spot where Buzz had sprawled, looking angry and perplexed. Then he motioned to Pillson. "Tell the damn 'dozer to stop. Now! Now! Do you hear me?" He and Pillson supervised the reloading of the bulldozer onto the truck. Paul White and Uncle Simon even assisted, cajoling and directing the operator. At last Dowling and Pillson climbed back into the police cruiser. Dowling, red-faced, looked around the common one last time; then his car raced up the Tremont road.

"By God!" yelled Ed Rhymer. "I've got a whole case o' beer in the back of my pickup. Let's break 'er open."

George turned to me, grinning, and took my hand. "We'll go get Buzz in a half hour," he said. "I'll sign him out of the accident room, give them some damn cock-and-bull story." He looked positively triumphant. As I glanced around at our neighbors, they all were whooping it up, slapping their thighs in delight as if we were about to stage a block party.

251

We'd almost forgotten about Rampsie's truck in the excitement—it sat there still, blocking the road, a hunk of fouled machinery.

Paul White walked over to it and impetuously gave it a kick with his foot. "Let's get this goddamn thing outta here, one way or the other, if we have to dismantle it a piece at a time. I'm sick of looking at it."

The men had barely fallen to work again on the insides of the truck when we heard sirens in the distance; within seconds Dowling had returned, slamming his brakes in front of us.

He slowly stepped from his car, bristling in his fury. "Just what do you think I am?" he asked, strutting up and down before us. "What do you take me for? A greenhorn? A ninny?"

We watched him in astonishment as he paced before us.

"Whatever are you talkin' about?" a woman in the crowd asked.

"You mean I have to tell you? That kid you sent to Tremont, the one looked so sick? Well, I called on ahead. They *know* him at the hospital. Kid used to come in regular for speech therapy. And he was *born* with a big head like that!"

I quickly glanced over at Uncle Simon; he was looking straight ahead of him at Dowling, with Aunt Chloe beside him, a look of defiance in his eyes.

"What are you going to do now, Lieutenant?" he asked quietly.

"I'll tell you, Mr. Sanderson, since you ask. That damn 'dozer's gonna dig up every timber of that store until I'm satisfied what's down there. You hear me?"

The operator'd been drinking beer with us; now he guiltily threw his can away and stood beside the store site, awaiting Dowling's orders. A crowd of kids, Tim among them, crowded about the bulldozer, examining the machine and touching its metal skin.

A man who'd been working on Rampsie's truck faced the lieutenant. He appeared almost apologetic standing before Dowling, tensely clasping and unclasping his hands. "Leave us be," the man said. "We been through a heap o' trouble down here, Lieutenant. Can't you please just leave us be?"

Dowling turned fiercely on him. "You haven't seen trouble yet if we find something under all that dirt. I can absolutely guarantee it, you hear me?" Then he turned to the bulldozer operator. "Now, Tom, I want that thing going immediately!"

The operator sprang into his machine, adjusting the controls and pushing the starter. There was a grinding, wrenching noise for a few seconds, a cough, and finally the sound of scraping metal. Then the machine stopped abruptly.

The operator thrust his head out the window. "Something's wrong, Lieutenant. It was goin' fine before."

"Try it again," shouted Dowling. "Probably just cold."

"Don't seem hardly likely," the operator yelled back. "Damn thing's hotter'n a firecracker."

The operator grinded the starter again, and once more the machine belched ominously. "Overheated," the operator said. "I told you so. Knew it wasn't cold."

"Well, get out of it!" Dowling yelled. "Now! Now! This minute, you hear?"

The operator descended from the cab, peering uncertainly at the lieutenant. "What are you going to do?" he asked.

"Start the damn thing myself, what do you *think* I'm gonna do?" He turned toward the crowd in the common. "You're all so damn smart with machines, see if *you* can fix it."

The men stared up at Dowling, sitting in the cab, then at each other, and finally moved reluctantly toward the machine.

"We're not 'xactly experts, Lieutenant," said an old man, shifting his pipe in his teeth. "Can't even get Rampsie's rig moving over there."

Ed Rhymer, who'd been inspecting the rear of the bulldozer, walked slowly toward Dowling, holding something in his hand. "Don't know how, Lieutenant, but somehow you got sand mixed up with the works of your machine."

Dowling examined the gas cap for a second, turning it over in his hand; then he threw it vehemently to the ground. He wheeled toward Pillson, who'd been trailing behind him. "Pillson, godammit, call up and get another 'dozer down here fast—fast, you hear? And when you call the station, tell 'em I'm sitting down here until I find what's under all that dirt if it takes all night. You hear me?"

Pillson sprinted for the police cruiser. Dowling turned toward the crowd. "Now go home, all of you. I mean it. In five minutes I don't want to see anyone out here. If I do, I'll run you all in for loitering." Surprisingly, his words had the sound of a plea.

Most of the townspeople began to move slowly toward the edge of the common, where they regrouped again, silently waiting. We returned to our house; Aunt Chloe and Uncle Simon disappeared inside, but George and I stood tensely on the front steps, watching. A few of the younger people had remained sitting in a group on the common; they even began to sing. The sound of those voices was almost eerie.

"How much luck are they going to need to trace those bodies to Simon?" George asked.

I thought about it a minute. "Plenty, I'd say. I don't see how they could do it."

Within an hour another bulldozer had arrived from Tremont, along with two more officers and a second police car for escort. While Pillson and Dowling directed the bulldozer into place, the police made a small cordon with their bodies so that no one could pass near the old store site. They even drove spikes into the ground and ran rope from one to the other.

Within minutes of the first incision by the bulldozer into that soft earth, everyone from the town had gathered once more, drawn together by the unspeakable horror of what was befalling them, behind the ropes which Dowling and the other officers had erected. George clenched his fists, flexing and unflexing them as the bulldozer dug deeper and deeper. A neighbor returning from his work in Tremont had brought Buzz home; the boy, subdued, held my hand, watching as if hypnotized while that bulldozer worked the ground methodically, back and forth. Tim absently threw a stone up and down into the air, also watching.

Within fifteen minutes, the bulldozer had plucked a charred body from the earth. The officers gathered about the singed corpse as the bulldozer nudged it gingerly from the hole.

I could stand no more. I turned and left the common, almost running. George touched my arm to tell me that he was right behind me. When I looked about, our neighbors all were scurrying away, too. There seemed an almost desperate insistence for all of us to escape that place again, to find air we could breathe, to flee that grisly reminder of recent terrors.

I turned on Uncle Simon's front porch to look back once. Dowling was reaching for a bullhorn one of the policemen had placed on the grass before him. He turned, expecting to see us still gathered there waiting for him. But when he wheeled angrily, the bullhorn raised expectantly to his lips, no one was before him. We'd all gone, vanished, fled—to our homes.

The store foundation remained uprooted and open, a silent rebuke to the town, for three days after the police had dug up and removed the bodies for analysis. On the third day some of the townspeople began to cover it over again, gathering together with shovels and wheelbarrows.

Lieutenant Dowling arrived in Rowe on the morning of the third day after the bulldozers had dug up the bodies. He marched to the center of the common with his bullhorn. Buzz and Tim, who'd been playing marbles in the shade of an old oak, looked up, startled. So did a couple of old women sitting on a common bench, visiting. At the first sounds Uncle Simon and I peered out the window onto the common, then wandered slowly out there. Other policemen lounged beside the police car, looking nonchalant, but Dowling seemed an almost solitary figure standing in that place by himself, almost like a statue, mouthing those words which echoed back and forth among our houses. I looked about him as he talked; areas of grass scorched by fires a month ago were now almost green and virtually impossible to find.

"I want every gun in this town, every one," he was bellowing through the bullhorn. "You might as well pile 'em up right here where I'm standing. We'll search your houses if we think you've got any hidden." He motioned toward three other policemen now slowly coming forward from the police cruiser.

In a few minutes Trumbull arrived, driving slowly about the common and coming to rest beside the police cruiser. "Heard the commotion, Lieutenant. What in blazes is going on?" He wore blue slacks and an open shirt; behind him in his car were slung his golf clubs. I'd even forgotten it was Saturday.

"Trying to find the gun that killed Bob Rampsie and the others," replied Dowling. "I know damn well it's right here under our noses somewhere."

Trumbull sounded incredulous. "So what are you going to do? Confiscate every gun in town? You must be kidding!"

"Trumbull, I thought of every other way. You got any better idea, I'd like to hear about it."

"Lieutenant," I protested, "I hope you've got search warrants before you invade any of our homes."

Dowling pointed to the cruiser. "Don't you worry none, Miss Sanderson. The ink on 'em's nice and fresh."

Trumbull thought a minute, his large head in profile. "If it'll help any, Lieutenant, I can give you a list of everyone I know who's got guns. Do a little shooting myself when I get time."

"Appreciate it." Dowling sounded almost deferential.

"Hell of a lot of guns, though," said Trumbull. "This is hunting country."

People were beginning to emerge from their houses in response to Dowling's command; some carried their guns with them. "Throw 'em there," Dowling said, indicating the ground before him. "And hurry it up. Gonna take most of the day as it is!" It was beginning to get warm again, and Dowling mopped his face and pulled down hard on the visor of his hat to shade his eyes.

More and more of the townspeople were moving across the common. "Go and beat on doors," Dowling directed the other policemen. One was Pillson. "And let's get a move on."

The first of the villagers now stood before Dowling expectantly and placed their weapons before him. "When we gonna git 'em back?" a boy asked. He was about Timmy's age.

"When I feel like it," Dowling answered, then relented when he saw the rebuke in the boy's eyes. "In an hour or two. Come back then."

"I'll wait," said the boy, sprawling on the grass, his eyes fixed on his weapon.

Two hours later more than a hundred guns had accumulated in the pile. Pillson and another officer took the police cruiser and the bullhorn and cruised down the side streets, demanding more weapons, directing their voices at the houses as they cruised by. The sound of that bullhorn echoed throughout the town. People had come from their houses to

256

watch, perching on their front porches and steps. George and several of his patients emerged to watch the proceedings; when he saw me in the distance, he waved, then crammed his hands into the pockets of his white coat as he watched the policemen pass in front of his house.

Finally, Uncle Simon strolled slowly across the common grass, carrying his two rifles and a small pistol. When he held them out to Dowling, his face was inscrutable; it was impossible to know what thoughts were passing through his head. He peered levelly at Dowling and waited.

"Throw 'em onto the pile," Dowling commanded. "I'll get to them soon."

"I'll hold them," said Uncle Simon.

Dowling had been bending over a young boy's shotgun, holding it cocked and sniffing into it. "You fired those guns recently?" he asked Uncle Simon.

"Yes. One of them."

Dowling looked up. "Why?"

"Just firing at varmints, Lieutenant. Had to clean 'em out, if it makes any difference to you." The listless look had returned to Uncle Simon's eyes.

"Let me see it." Dowling grasped Uncle Simon's rifle, peering down the barrel. "You cleaned it?" he asked accusingly. "What did you do that for?"

"Always do. Never forget to clean my guns after I use 'em."

"What kind of bullets did you use?"

Uncle Simon shrugged. "I don't remember. Why?"

"Well, what kind have you got at home?" Dowling's voice snapped with impatience.

"All kinds, Lieutenant."

"You got lead hollow points?"

Uncle Simon thought a minute. "Yes."

"You know that's what killed Rampsie and his crew?" Dowling pointed to the nonexistent store.

Uncle Simon barely blinked at Dowling.

Dowling pulled at the collar of his uniform. "You know we can trace that kind of bullet now?" he said. "We've got ways. . . ."

I leaned forward toward Dowling. "Not very often, Lieutenant, and I'm sure you know it. Hardly ever, in fact." Dowling thrust his face into mine. "You're so goddamn cocksure, Miss Sanderson, you know all the answers. Damn you. . . ."

I felt miserably sad and depressed again. "It didn't have to be this way,

Lieutenant." I motioned toward the pile of guns. "I didn't want it so. None of us did."

Before us a mountain of firearms was growing on the grass; it was almost waist-high. Around the pile stood those who'd contributed to the steady accretion of those guns: both kids and adults. When Dowling looked back at the pile, he saw water pistols, toy plastic machine guns, pop guns. On top lay a cap pistol. Nearby one of the policemen had returned triumphantly from a foray down a side street with more guns gleaned from the people who lived there, as triumphant as a miner with his cache of gold.

"Take your guns," screamed Dowling in a fury of frustration. "Take the goddamn things." He kicked at the nearest. Then he turned to the sergeant. "Now let's get the hell out of here, Pillson. And I hope to God I never see this shitty town again!"

A week later Uncle Simon and I walked around the common. The sky was overcast, and the weatherman on the Boston station said we'd have rain by sundown. Uncle Simon and I were oblivious of the weather; we walked slowly. He studied the sidewalk before us, while I nervously broke into bits a small stick I'd found in the grass.

"I don't know what you'd do it for, Uncle Simon. Why on earth would you? You want to throw away everything—your entire life? You know, Dowling hasn't a clue!"

He kept his dogged pace, not looking to right or left. He waved his hand carelessly. "You don't have to tell me all that, Lisa."

"Then what *do* I have to tell you, Uncle Simon? For God's sake, can't you listen to reason? You're free, scot-free, can't you comprehend. . . ?" For the last half hour I'd been as eloquent as I'd ever been in my life, as impassioned as if I were pleading for the life of a condemned man before his peers.

"I would never feel right about it, Lisa. It would haunt me to my grave. I might as well die here, this minute. Perhaps I'm too old. You see, I believe in a just God. . . ."

"Come on, Uncle Simon. Think of Aunt Chloe. . . ."

"That's all I *do* think of, Lisa. Can't you see there's no other way for me, no other way? I've been over it, then over it again, and I always end up at the same place."

"Does Aunt Chloe know?"

"Of course. I haven't told her, but she knows."

He was infuriating, obstinate, incredible. But I loved him and understood him; I wished to God I didn't! I took a deep breath and began to talk to him as if he were a client, the most important client I'd ever had. I fought to be dispassionate, and couldn't; nevertheless, I told him about the specific laws involved, what chances I thought he risked with the local authorities, what the police would say, what Judge Bream would say. Before, I'd always indicated to a client what he could and couldn't do if he became involved with the law, what bail was an option, but Uncle Simon had no money, had nowhere to go, and wasn't about to skip town.

Still hoping to dissuade Uncle Simon, I nevertheless pulled out all the stops. "If you persist in implicating yourself this way, I'm going to take the damn thing to the Supreme Court. I won't allow it, Uncle Simon. I mean it. If you persist in this idiocy, which I hope to God you won't, I'll get you the best lawyer, and we'll fight it. . . ."

Uncle Simon stopped dead. "Why do I need a defense? I freely confessed, I said. . . ."

Uncle Simon and his insufferable conscience! "Don't you see, Uncle Simon, that *you* have rights, that this town as an entity has rights, that we'll have to argue that you were justified. . . ."

"All right, Lisa. But I want *you* to defend me, I won't take anyone else because you were involved. . . ."

I shook my head. "It wouldn't be ethical, Uncle Simon. It's because of my involvement that I couldn't be dispassionate a long time ago. And it requires someone with infinitely more experience than I've got. But I hope to God you'll reconsider, because in my opinion what you're doing is suicidal."

We stood for a moment opposite the site of Rampsie's old store; someone had planted pink and white petunias in the soft dirt over the area.

We turned back. "And I've got to return to my work in Boston, Uncle Simon. Besides, George will be there— and that's important to me."

It was becoming more than important, I thought—I wanted to be close to him, now that he'd returned to his hospital affiliation. I missed him on the days he was gone. Last night we'd slept together for the first time since . . . that last time in the store . . . and there'd still been pain and trauma and fright, which both of us knew would take time to resolve. He'd held me in his arms, in that enormous bed of his, and caressed me so gently, and I'd fondled him back, so that the terror had almost subsided but not entirely. There was a moment when I felt him move inside me that I almost screamed again, and at that second I didn't want to receive him any longer—but then we spoke loving words to each other. "I love you," we said, and those words helped, as they'd sustained lovers since time began.

George and I planned to meet over the weekend in Boston to walk the Freedom Trail and visit the Aquarium with Clarissa and Tim and Buzz.

"Will you have to testify, Lisa?" Uncle Simon persisted. "If it came to trial, I mean? In court, about what happened to you?"

"Of course. I can manage. But, Uncle Simon, don't you see how foolhardy . . . we may not be able to free you, because the court may not think you had any right to do what you did. You may go to prison. . . ."

He nodded. "I know. I couldn't live with what I've done, don't you see? Don't you really see?"

"No. Please don't talk about it anymore. Wait until things have gone by, until—"

He was shaking his head. "They'll never go by, Lisa. What's done is done. There's no going back, only forward. We each have to do what we must do, and there's no other way. . . ."

Uncle Simon held open the front door. Outside a light rain had already begun, and our clothes were lightly sprinkled with the soft misting, like dew. The rain was welcome; the grass on the common was becoming parched in the summer sun, and there were dried patches on Uncle Simon's lawn.

Uncle Simon hung up his coat, then lifted the receiver of the telephone. I grasped his arm. "Please reconsider, Uncle Simon. Give it more time. Think about it longer. Discuss it with Aunt Chloe."

He shook his head. "Time for thinking's past, Lisa. I already done the thinking. There's no use for any more."

In the kitchen Buzz and Tim were eating doughnuts Aunt Chloe had just baked. I reached for one, then put it down again because I couldn't eat.

Aunt Chloe stood beside the kitchen table, listening to Uncle Simon clicking the telephone receiver to summon the operator. For a moment there was no other sound in the room. I stood next to her, then took her arm.

Aunt Chloe stirred herself. "Never knew boys to do nothing but sit around all day, and eat, eat, eat. . . ." She sounded a little testy.

She began to clear the table. We could hear Uncle Simon in the hall, speaking into the telephone. "Hello," he said in a firm voice. "This is Simon Sanderson. Would you please connect me with Lieutenant Dowling in Tremont? I've got something I'd like to tell him."

ACKNOWLEDGMENTS

The author wishes to acknowledge with special gratitude the help of the following people: Professor Donald F. Hendrie, Jr., Professor Emeritus Elizabeth A. Green, Alice Jeghelian, Ph.D, Daniel P. Schwartz, M.D., and Professor George Cuomo.